PRESENTED BY
WILLIAM ATWOOD

with illustrations by

Kathryn Schaar Burke

EASTON AREA PUBLIC LIBRARY
515 CHURCH STREET
EASTON, PA 18042-3587

MULE BOY

This story is set against an authentic geographical, historical
and operational backdrop. As the coal boat *Onoko Princess* journeys
back and forth along Pennsylvania's Lehigh and Delaware canals during
the months of March, April, May and the first three days of June
1862, vignettes and anecdotes taken from the oral histories
of canalers have been woven into the tapestry.

Copyright © Canal History and Technology Press, 2004
Story © Joan Gilbert 2003

ISBN: 0-930973-30-5 (paperback)
       0-930973-31-3 (library edition)
Library of Congress Control Number: 2004102613

**Canal History and
Technology Press**

National Canal Museum
30 Centre Square, Easton, PA 18042-7743

~❧ To my family ❧~

With special thanks to
Richard Arner, former canal worker and Lehigh Canal historian,
for being so generous with information and anecdotes

and

John Drury, President of the Mauch Chunk Museum in Jim Thorpe,
for interesting me in researching local history

Soon shall thy arm, unconquer'd steam! afar
Drag the slow barge, or drive the rapid car;
Or on wide-waving wings expanded bear
The flying chariot through the field of air.

Erasmus Darwin, 1731–1802

Max and Lucy were calling to him, their heads over the split-rail fence.

CHAPTER I

Dawn was breaking as ten-year-old Wilhelm Oberfeldt crossed the village green at Weissport with his father, Manfred. They were on their way to the boat yard. It was the beginning of March 1862. The Lehigh Canal had been filled after being drained for repairs during the winter. It would open for boating next morning.

Oil lamps appeared in the windows as the village awakened. Most of the men in the area worked on the canal. Some were carpenters, building and caulking boats. Others hitched rides on carpenter boats to repair locks, gates and dams. Some dredged the canal and filled breaches in the towpath. Others drove mules. A few, like Manfred, were boat captains. Three of the villagers were locktenders. They opened and closed the gates to let boats pass through Weissport's three locks.

Wilhelm skipped along excitedly at his father's side. He could not wait for morning when his father would start hauling coal along the canals. Although he was only ten, he was an expert on the canal. He knew all the coal boats by their numbers and who captained them, and could tell you the depth of each lock and the name of the locktender. This was hardly surprising. He had listened to canal talk all his life. His great-grandfather had helped to build the canal, his grandfather had built boats, and his father had risen from walking the towpath as a mule driver to captaining the finest Lehigh Coal & Navigation coal boat on the Lehigh Canal. Tomorrow, he would carry on the family tradition. When he, his mother, and thirteen-year-old sister Annie set off in the morning, he would drive the mules that towed his father's boat, Lehigh Coal & Navigation Company Coal Boat Number 322, affectionately known to the family as "The Onoko Princess."

In other boating seasons and other years, Manfred had hired mule drivers from the Weissport stables where young men and boys hung out, hoping to find work on the canal. But this year was different. His son had reached the age when he himself had first walked the towpath with his own father's mules. Now the time had come for Wilhelm to earn a living. This was no hardship to Wilhelm. All winter, he had waited for the day the *Onoko Princess* would cast off.

"Pa, has Joe Maginley finished caulking and painting the boat?" Wilhelm asked eagerly as he and his father walked down Canal Street.

"Ja," replied Manfred, his German accent still strong after two generations. Although Pennsylvania Dutch was spoken up and down the canal and Manfred could speak it as well as any Dutchman, his ancestors did not come from the German Palatinate, where most of the settlers along the river had come from. His family were Rhinelanders. Unable to get the Old Country out of his speech, he always substituted a 'v' for a 'w' in a word. "She's back in the vater. Joe has finished caulking and painting her and his mules have pulled her down to the canal."

"Then we can start out in the morning?"

"Ja! Ve vill take on coal at Mauch Chunk and head to Bristol vith the load."

"How far is Bristol?"

"All told, it is about a hunert and six miles."

Wilhelm's mouth dropped wide open. "A hundred and six miles," he echoed. "Gosh, Pa, that's a long way!" For the first time, he was facing the reality of walking hundreds of miles, back and forth, along the Lehigh and Delaware Canal towpaths. "I hope I can walk that far."

"If Lucy and Max can, you can!" his father retorted.

Lucy and Maximilian, Max for short, were the Oberfeldts' mules. Even though the *Onoko Princess* belonged to the Lehigh Coal & Navigation Company, the company that built and operated the canal, the mules that towed her were Manfred's. Lucy was the lead mule and Max, the shaft mule. He pulled the boat behind Lucy. When there was a female mule, or "molly," in the team, she was assigned the position of lead mule so that her male counterpart, or "john," would be sure to follow her. Lucy was a jigsaw of white and gray patches, and Max was a rich chestnut color. Both mules were strong and tall at the flanks with shiny coats and bright eyes, but they had different personalities. Lucy was gentle and obedient, but Max, when he felt like it, could be downright stubborn. Like most canal mules, Max and Lucy were well taken care of. Without two healthy mules to tow a hundred-ton boatload of coal, there would be no pay check for a boatman.

Manfred patted the top of Wilhelm's head reassuringly. He did not want his son to be disillusioned before they set out. "Don't vorry, Vil, if you get tired, your ma or sister vill spell you."

The first faint streaks of daylight were creeping up from the eastern horizon as father and son — captain and mule driver — passed through the gates to the boatyard. Although it was early, the yard buzzed with activity and noise. Workers, on a deadline to get as many boats as possible in the water by morning, sawed, hammered, caulked and painted as fast as they could. In the stables and inside the three-bar fence enclosing the stable yard, mules of all colors and sizes stomped and snorted as stable hands cleaned up their muck. It was as if neither man nor beast could wait for the canal to open three hours before the next dawn.

" 'Morning, Joe," called Manfred to Joe Maginley, supervisor of the boatyard. "Did you finish vorking on my boat?"

Just like Manfred's accent revealed his origins, so did Joe's Irish brogue. "She's ready t' go, Capt'n. Oi toied her up abuve Fisher Lock so y' can git t' Shiraar Lock before ol' man Shiraar opens the gaates." Shirar Lock was Lock 7. Like most boatmen, Joe called the locks by the name of their locktender rather than by the number given to them by the Lehigh Coal & Navigation Company.

Weissport boatyard was three and a half miles down the canal from the coal-loading chutes at Mauch Chunk. Besides the Company boatyard, there were three private boatyards where boats were built and repaired. Although most coal boats that plied the Lehigh Canal belonged to the Company, some were owned by the men who captained them. These privately owned boats carried a variety of goods up and down the canals. Some hauled coal for the Company; others transported lumber, grain, farm produce, and whatever else was needed to sustain life in the towns and villages along the canal. Unlike Company boats, they had to pay tolls for using the canal.

Impatient to get going, Wilhelm tugged at his father's sleeve, doing his best not to let Joe see him. But little escaped Joe Maginley. A man of the old school, Joe believed that children should be seen and not heard. "Oi can see, yer oop an' raaarin' to go, yoong feller," he said bitingly. "Oi oonderstand, yer'll be earnin' yer keep this yerr."

Wilhelm drew himself up proudly. "Yes, sir, I'll be drivin' my pa's mules."

"That's a pretty responsible job fer a yoong lad, the loikes o' you. Them mules can be ornery critters!"

"Lucy and Max ain't!" answered Wilhelm, darting off in the direction of the canal. He wanted to be first to spot the Company's rust, blue and white bullseye trademark on the bow of the boat and the carved head of Princess Onoko, the beautiful Indian maiden, that graced her stern. Unlike others on the canal, the Oberfeldts had given their boat a name. In beautiful lettering beneath the carving was the name "Onoko Princess."

The *Onoko Princess* was a section boat. Instead of being one continuous length, she had two hinged sections, each containing a large coal hold. The sections could be uncoupled to facilitate turning in the sixty foot wide canal, and loading and unloading. Although the *Onoko Princess* was Boat Number 322 in the Lehigh Coal & Navigation Company's fleet, Wilhelm felt she belonged to his family. With her neat, ten-by-eight-foot cabin partitioned off from the coal hold in the rear section, two bunks — each big enough to sleep two people — a stowaway table, bench, storage chest and stove, this sleek eighty-seven and a half foot-long, ten and a half foot-wide beauty would be the Oberfeldts' home until the canal iced over in November. When the boating season ended, the family would spend the winter in Weissport with Wilhelm's maternal grandparents, Reuben and Emily Kintz. To make ends meet during the off-season, Wilhelm's father would do odd jobs at the saw mill, or work for the Ice House, cutting blocks of ice from the canal and storing them to sell during the hot summer months to keep food from spoiling.

Manfred bridged the gap between the *Onoko Princess* and the canal bank with a makeshift gangplank. Wilhelm could just as easily have climbed over the side but, knowing his father would be displeased if he left an unsightly mark on her hull, he scampered across the plank. The *Onoko Princess* stood proud and ready in the water, shipshape from bow to stern. Her rust-colored deck gleamed with fresh paint, her gear was stowed where it was supposed to be, and her coal hatches were battened down. In the cabin, the stove for heating and cooking shone like ebony and not a thing was out of place. Wilhelm's mother and sister had seen to that. All yesterday, Mary and Annie had been hard at work ridding the cabin of cobwebs, dusting the furnishings, and making the bunks. As soon as the village store opened, they would stock the cupboard with staples to last for most of the trip.

The Oberfeldts were one of many families who lived and worked on the canal. Although most Company boats were operated by a two-man crew of captain and mule driver, Manfred preferred to take his family along when he sailed the canals. Boating as a family meant that each person had to be able to take over the duties of another. Annie helped her mother with domestic chores and relieved the mule driver when needed. After being a canal wife for fifteen years, there was nothing Mary could not do. She could drive the mules as well as any mule driver, handle the tiller, and take the *Onoko Princess* through a lock better than most boatmen. This suited Manfred. Besides liking to have his family for company, he was thrifty. With his wife and children on board, he did not have to hire a mule driver, cook his own meal, or pay a locktender's wife to wash his clothes.

Wilhelm followed his father around the deck as Manfred inspected the *Onoko Princess* from bow to stern until he was satisfied that everything was in order.

"Now all ve need, Vil, are the mules. Seeing you are my new driver, you vill come vith me to Jake Gilbert's to get them."

Jake Gilbert operated a flour mill in New Mahoning. During the winter, he cared for Lucy and Max in return for using the mules around his mill. Most boatmen made this kind of arrangement. They found a farmer, or a miller like Jake, who would not mistreat their animals and let him work them during the off-season in return for food and shelter.

Mahoning Valley was a fertile stretch of farmland that ran beneath the Blue Mountains to the west of Weissport. Surrounded by hilly terrain, it was the bread basket of the area. Livestock, produce farming, and milling had gone on there for more than a century.

The dirt road through the greening countryside seemed never-ending. Manfred was in a hurry and Wilhelm had to walk briskly to keep up. By the time they reached the mill, his calf muscles were aching. Maybe — just maybe — his father would let him ride Max or Lucy on the way back.

They could hear the creaking and groaning of the wooden water wheel before they turned down the lane. Water, diverted from the Mahoning Creek, was flowing through a swiftly moving sluice, turning the big wooden wheel that ran the machinery to grind grain into flour. The mill had been in the Gilbert family for more than a century. Jake was the proud descendant of Benjamin Gilbert, whose family was taken hostage by a band of eleven Indians on April 25, 1780. Sixty-nine-year-old Benjamin Gilbert died en route to Montreal, Canada. The rest of the family, their neighbors the Pearts, a hired hand, and a young girl who happened to be picking up flour at the mill were held captive for two and a half years before they were released. As the tale of the Gilberts' harrowing experience spread throughout the valley, the family — and their descendants — carried with them an aura of heroism.

When Manfred and Wilhelm walked into the mill yard, Jake Gilbert was expecting them. There was not a soul in the valley who did not know that the canal was opening in the morning. Wishing to take advantage of the mass transportation route, Jake was hard at work bagging flour and oats and loading them onto a wagon. As soon as the Oberfeldts left, he and his trusty old mare would take the bags to Weissport where they would be loaded onto Gunther Meyer's boat for shipment to the industrial towns in the lower Lehigh Valley.

Jake stopped what he was doing, and greeted Manfred with a handshake. "Your mules are over there," he said, pointing to a small field behind the mill. "I'll be right sorry to lose 'em. Them's two good, strong beasts you have, Manfred." All winter, he had worked Max and Lucy, delivering flour to customers in Mauch Chunk and Lehighton, up and down the Mahoning Valley and as far as Lansford and Tamaqua.

"Take these, Vil," said Manfred, handing his son the two halters he had brought with him. "If you are going to be my driver, you vill have to learn how to halter the mules."

There was pride in Wilhelm's step as he strode across the yard to fulfill the first of his new responsibilities. As he went behind the granary and opened the paddock gate, he shuddered. It crossed his mind that this was where the Indians had whisked away the Gilberts. He would have turned back, but a sound that was a cross between the hee-haw of a donkey and the neigh of a horse greeted him. Max and Lucy were calling to him, their heads over the split-rail fence. He made a clucking noise with his tongue like his father. The mules responded and followed him to the barred gate. Standing on one of the bars, he pushed their heads down and slipped the rope halters over their long ears. When he was done, he climbed down and patted them. Pleased with the attention they were getting, Max and Lucy nuzzled him with their wet noses. Proud of accomplishing the task his father had set him, he walked back across the mill yard, hidden by the mules on either side of him. Haltering Max and Lucy was easy; harnessing them to the boat was much harder. There were collars to put on and dozens of straps to buckle, and he wondered if he would be able do it when it came time.

"Are the mules haltered?" asked his father, not quite knowing what to expect. To make sure, he checked. "You did right vell, son," he complimented, throwing Wilhelm a lead rein. "Clip this to Lucy's halter. You take her and I'll take Max."

This was not exactly what Wilhelm was expecting. He was hoping his father would say he could ride one of the mules.

Manfred sensed his son's frustration. "Vhat's the matter, Vil?"

"I thought you might let me ride Lucy." Then, looking a little shamefaced, Wilhelm added, "I'm tired."

"Voe is me! Ve've only valked five miles and you are tired already! Vhat's goin' to happen vhen you have to valk the towpath eighteen hours every day? Ve had better get this straight before ve set out: there vill be no ridin' the mules vhen the boat is loaded."

"I …" Wilhelm stopped himself from continuing. With times so hard, it would be easy for his father to get someone else to drive his mules.

"No matter!" said Manfred, as he hoisted Wilhelm onto Lucy's back. "You might as vell ride."

Lucy was not in agreement. She shook her head and stomped her feet. Having pulled the mill wagon all winter, she was not used to carrying anyone on her back. Besides, for four months she had gorged on Jake Gilbert's plentiful supply of oats and had put on weight.

"Whoa, girl!" shouted Manfred, patting her neck as she showed her objection. "You've been spoiled all vinter. *Bestimmt*, Lucy, you're as fat as butter! You vill have to haul more than Vilhelm tomorrow."

Lucy settled down under Manfred's firm touch. With Wilhelm straddling her back, and Manfred walking between her and Max, they set out for the boat yard.

If Wilhelm thought his work was finished when they got back to Weissport, it wasn't. It was six months since Max and Lucy had been shod. After trekking along country roads all winter, hauling flour for Jake Gilbert, their shoes were wearing thin. The square nails barely held what was left to their hooves.

Lifting their hooves one by one, Manfred inspected them. "Both beasts need shoeing. You vill have to take them to Jim Leiby, the blacksmith. If Leiby is too busy, Charlie Fisher, the locktender, vill shoe them for you. I vill be over after I see Joe Maginley."

Wilhelm was tired and hungry, and more than ready to return to the boat. But, attending to the mules was his job, so he did not complain. Dwarfed by the giant half-horse, half-donkeys on either side of him, he walked them to the Company blacksmith shop. He hoped no one would be waiting, but he was wrong. Pairs of mules were standing outside the forge with their drivers, and he took his place at the end of the line. He had no need to go to the lock house for Charlie Fisher. Charlie was busy at the anvil, working as hard as the blacksmith.

The line moved slowly. At last, it was the turn of Wilhelm's fidgety charges to go inside. The heat from the forge was overpowering. And as Wilhelm led Lucy and Max inside, he felt like throwing up. There was no escape. Each time the fire died down, either the blacksmith or the locktender flared it up with the bellows. Taking ready-made shoes from the rack, they held them with tongs at arm's length over the blazing coals until they were malleable enough to be hammered into the correct size and shape. Satisfied that the shoes would fit, they immersed them, hissing and sizzling, into a barrel of coal water. One after the other, the two men sized mule shoe after mule shoe, each custom-fitted to a particular animal's hoof. The hissing and sizzling and hammering did not phase Lucy and Max. They were used to the noise. When their old shoes were removed, they did not so much as flinch when the new ones were nailed in place. So that the job would be finished quickly, the blacksmith shod Lucy and the locktender shod Max. By the time Manfred showed up, Max was getting his last shoe.

"Doesn't it hurt, Pa?" asked Wilhelm, shuddering with each sharp tap of the hammer as the locktender nailed on the shoe.

"Nein. Mules have thick horn covering their feet. They don't feel a thing. That is, unless ve valk them on hard ground vithout shoes. Then their hooves get vore down and they start to falter."

When the last nail had been driven, father and son each took charge of an animal. Max and Lucy trod lightly on the cobble stones to test out their new shoes as they crossed the yard to the stable. As Wilhelm filled the manger with hay and put feed in the bin, he prayed that the last chore of the day had been done.

Manfred and Wilhelm were not the only ones who had a busy day. On board the *Onoko Princess*, the cupboard was stocked, the stove lit and a pot of beef stew bubbling on top of the burner. Everything Mary and Annie Oberfeldt had to do for the early-morning departure had been done.

"Mmmm … smells good!" said Manfred, sniffing appreciatively as he came through the cabin hatch with Wilhelm.

"Supper's ready," said Mary, ladling the stew into bowls as they hung up their coats.

Manfred moved the bench over from its place near the wall and settled his large frame between Wilhelm and Annie. Mary pulled up the spare stool. Before anyone could sneak so much as a spoonful, he said, "Let us not forget to say Grace."

When Mary had seen to it that the children had said their amens, she asked, "Are we ready to go?" Only part Pennsylvania German, and having spent her early years in Philadelphia, she did not have a Dutch accent. And she tried to make sure her children didn't acquire an accent.

"Ja, ve are ready," he answered. "It is a good job I asked Maginley to save a stall for the mules. The stable and yard are overflowing. It beats me vhere all them beasts come from."

"What time are we leaving, Manny?" After the luxury of rising at seven during the winter, there was nothing Mary dreaded more than the first wake-up call of the season. It came about three-thirty in the morning. She hated getting up at such an ungodly hour. But all things considered, rising early was better than staying home without her husband. When Manfred became a boat captain she had tried staying in Weissport. But life was lonely without him. And, when a boatman's wages depended on the number of trips he made along the canal during the boating season, Manfred's visits home had been brief.

"Early!" answered Manfred. "Ve're tied up above Lock 8 so ve can leave as soon after three as possible. I vant to get to Shirar Lock before George opens the lock gates so ve vill be vone of the first boats to load at Mauch Chunk."

Time was money. Paid by the load, boatmen had to make as much headway as possible during boating hours. The gates were chained shut at ten o'clock at night and did not open until four the next morning.

Manfred could tell Mary was worn out. "Get some vater from the barrel, Annie, and vash the dishes for your mother," he said when they finished eating. "She's done enough vork today."

Annie did not feel like going out into the cold to get water. Nor did she feel like washing dishes.

"Wil can get it," she answered huffily. "I helped Ma all day."

"I walked to Mahoning with Pa to get the mules," countered Wilhelm.

"Yeah!" retorted Annie. "You rode Lucy on the way back. I saw you, so don't think I didn't."

Manfred frowned at his squabbling children. "You heard vhat I said, Annie. Get the vater, and vash the dishes. And, you, Vil, let down the bunks and fix yourself a place to sleep. Ve're turnin' in for the night."

The argument ended. On board the *Onoko Princess*, and anywhere else for that matter, Manfred's word was Law. Annie went on deck and filled the enamel dishpan with water from the barrel, then came into the cabin to wash the dishes. Wilhelm was also quick to respond. He unlatched the bunks from the wall for the others, and made a bed for himself. His father and mother would share the bottom bunk and Annie would sleep above them on the top. His bed was a mattress of ticking filled with straw which he laid on the cabin floor; his covers, thick woolen blankets.

When the dishes were done and beds ready, Manfred banked the stove for the night and extinguished the oil lamp. As the wick flickered and died, a plaintive voice came from the floor. It was Wilhelm. "You didn't tell us the story of Princess Onoko, Pa."

"Yes, Pa, tell us about the princess," chimed in Annie, snuggled up in a comforter on the top bunk. "Remember … she is our good luck charm."

"Vith so many things to think of, I forgot. But you are right, *mein kinder*. Stay still and listen."

Telling the legend of Princess Onoko the first night on board was a family tradition. Six years before, when Manfred was given command of Company Boat 322, they decided to give her a name. The night before her maiden trip, they all sat around the cabin table racking their brains, trying to think what to call her. When Mary suggested "Onoko Princess" and Manfred told them the ancient legend, they all knew they had found the perfect name. From that day on, Company Boat Number 322 was known as the *Onoko Princess* to the Oberfeldts.

That spring, when traffic was slow and the weather good, Mary had taken over the helm so that Manfred could spend time carving the head of the beautiful Indian maiden out of a piece of oak. When he was done, he etched the princess's name beneath it in fancy German lettering. Next came a coat of varnish to protect her likeness from the elements, and he nailed the carving on the stern. Annie won the toss-up to christen the boat. As if Lehigh Coal & Navigation Coal Boat 322 were the newest and most important frigate in the U.S. Navy, she smashed a bottle of canal water against her hull, and proclaimed her the *Onoko Princess*. From that day forward, on the evening of the first journey of each new season, telling the tragic story of the Indian princess was regarded as a good luck ritual by her crew.

The only sound heard in the cabin was the music of water lapping against the hull as Manfred began the familiar tale.

"Onoko was a beautiful princess of one of the Lenape tribes that roamed the mountains surrounding the magnificent gorge of the Lehigh River. She lived in a glen above Mauch Chunk vhere vild game vas plentiful, and fruits and berries grew everyvhere for the picking. Vone day, vile gathering blackberries along the river, she met Opachee, a handsome brave from a rival tribe. Over the summer, they met in secret, afraid to tell the varring chiefs of their tribes that they had fallen in love.

"Unlike Princess Onoko, Opachee had no royal connections. His father vas not a tribal chief. He vas a fine young brave and a skilled hunter who, under ordinary circumstances, vould have made a good suitor for Onoko. But circumstances between the two tribes vere not ordinary. Their enmity vas bitter and it had gone on for many moons. Opachee knew that asking Onoko's father for her hand vould take more courage than facing an enemy tribe single-handedly in battle.

"To impress the Lenape chief, Opachee journeyed into the remote forest and took aim with his bow and arrow at the finest game he could find. Trembling, he laid magnificent specimens of elk, bear, and deer at the feet of Onoko's father, and asked for the princess's hand in marriage. Filled with venomous hatred at the loss of his eldest son in battle, bitter at past skirmishes over territory and game, the chief raged and threatened Opachee. Under penalty of death, he banished the young brave from the glen and forbade him from ever seeing Princess Onoko again.

"Onoko's heart shattered into a million pieces vhen she heard vat her father had done. Blinded by the tears streaming down her cheeks, she sped up Broad Mountain, neither knowing nor caring vhere she vas going. Scratched and bleeding from the rocks and prickly underbrush, she scrambled up the steep chasm, drawn ever upvard by the sound of cascading vater. The next thing she knew, she vas standing at the foot of the highest vaterfall in the glen. Nestled amid vild rhododrendron and mountain laurel, canopied by the tallest fir trees she had ever seen, a stream of vhite vater tumbled over a cliff in a long glistening veil. She climbed up the side trail, used by her father's hunters, and stood at the top of the streaming vater, mourning the loss of her lover. Unable to live vithout him, she threw herself off the top of the falls and landed in the vater churning among the rocks seventy-five feet below."

Manfred paused, moved by the sadness of the tale. Gathering himself together, he said quietly, "And that is how Glen Onoko got its name, and how the falls vhere the Indian princess met her death became known as the Onoko Falls."

As Manfred ended the tragic story, the only thing that broke the silence was Annie's sobs. "You didn't finish, Papa," she whispered, her voice breaking. "You forgot to tell us about the ghost."

"Oh ja ... the ghost!" exclaimed Manfred. "Vell ... if you climb up to the falls on a bright sunny morning vhen a rainbow arches the crest, you vill see the Spirit of the Mist, the tragic ghost of Onoko, gliding across the shimmering vhite vater."

Rocked by the gentle motion of the water, the crew of the *Onoko Princess* thought their own thoughts and drifted off to sleep.

CHAPTER II

It was black as pitch when Manfred blew into the small hole he had drilled near the top of a large conch shell. *Wooooo-wooooo*. Its rich, velvety tone filled the cabin. In Manfred's world, the conch shell had two uses. He blew into it long and loud to warn boatmen and locktenders that the *Onoko Princess* was passing along the canal, and, in the blackness three hours before dawn, he blew into it softly to let his crew know it was time to get up. This morning, Wilhelm did not need the conch shell to awaken him. He had walked the towpath all night in his imagination. As the velvety sound filled the cabin, he sprang up and had his bed rolled up before it faded away. He had waited for this day all his young life.

His father smiled as he lit the oil lamp. "Oh, I see you're rarin' to go. Hurry up and dress. It's the driver's job to fetch the mules. The sooner ve get them beasts harnessed to the boat, the sooner ve vill be on our vay."

There was no time to wash. Wilhelm pulled his trousers over his underwear and bundled himself up to ward off the March chill. "I'll be back real quick, Pa," he said, scrambling up the steps, letting the hatch cover fall open with a bang.

"You'd better not be in such a hurry, you forget to feed the mules," reminded his father, amused at his son's haste.

"I won't, Pa!"

"And remember to shovel the stable. Joe Maginley vill never give us a stall agin if you don't clean up the muck. The manure goes on the heap at the back of the stable yard. The farmers around here are right glad to get the muck for their fields."

Although it was always Manfred's habit to go through a list of reminders, he had no need. This was the first time Wilhelm had ever been in charge of anything, and he was determined not to forget a thing.

It had been more than three months since Max and Lucy towed the *Onoko Princess*, but when he came into their stall, they knew exactly what to expect. As he curried their coats, they stood by patiently, and whinnied with pleasure at the feel of the comb. When the grooming was done, they lowered their heads for their halters. Wilhelm shoveled the stable and wheeled the barrow of muck to the heap. Then, looking ever so small, he led his charges over the mule bridge that crossed the canal to the towpath. Next came the task he dreaded. He had to harness the mules to the boat. His father showed him how to put on a harness last season, but just in case he had forgotten, Manfred was there to supervise.

The mule harness had been stored on board the *Onoko Princess* all winter, and Manfred laid it on the ground exactly as it would go on the mules. Faced with the daunting array of straps and buckles, Wilhelm wondered if he could remember which strap went where. Lucy was the lead mule, and Wilhelm harnessed her first. Pushing her head low, he put the bit in her mouth and buckled the thick leather collar around her neck to protect her from the straps as she strained to pull the boat. The complicated body harness came next. Helped by his father, he threw it over Lucy's back and buckled the straps under her belly. It was Max's turn next. He went in the shaft behind Lucy. When he was similarly outfitted, he harnessed the mules one behind the other and moved them into towing position ahead of the boat.

Manfred checked the straps to see that they were buckled properly. Satisfied that everything was in order, he got back on board the *Onoko Princess*. Slipping the extra-large knot at one end of the rope into a notch on the towing post, he threw the other end to Wilhelm. Wilhelm hooked it to the back of Max's harness, then, tethering the team to a tree and putting on their feed baskets, he joined his family in the cabin for a quick breakfast.

Before casting off, Manfred walked around the deck, lighting the nighthawker warning lanterns. Unlike most boatmen, who preferred to stand up and steer, Manfred liked to sit down between locks. When he first got command of the *Onoko Princess*, he built a tall seat like a bos'n's chair atop the cabin. Seated there now, hand on the tiller, his view along the canal obscured only by the lingering darkness, he shouted, "Forvard, Vil! Ve are ready to go."

Wilhelm inched the mules forward until the tow line was stretched to its full one hundred and fifty-foot length. One step, then another, and another. Lucy and Max had to strain hard to get going. Then, suddenly, the *Onoko Princess* gained momentum. Light as a feather, she was moving gracefully through the water, her wake parting the surface in a gentle V. The first of Wilhelm's many long treks along the towpath had begun. Annie sneaked back to her bunk after breakfast, but Mary stood on deck watching her son's initiation. Wilhelm had done everything perfectly, and she could not have been more proud of him.

The *Onoko Princess* was the first Company boat to leave Weissport. With three and a half miles to go, she should reach the loading dock at Mauch Chunk shortly after daylight. The towpath curved around a bend beneath the dark mountains as it followed its course between the canal and the Lehigh River. The Lehigh was the mother of the canal. Both were linked by the water they shared.

Like a Viking of old, Manfred sat at the tiller keeping watch. Several lanterns ahead silhouetted the terrain. They were nearing Lock 7. It was time to alert the locktender. He blew into his conch shell. *WOOOOOOOOOOOOOOOO!* This time, the sound was not gentle and velvety; it was assertive and long. Trumpeting off the rock faces to the east, it swept along the canal and river, echoing off the mountains to the west. And George Shirar heard it. Having tended the gates at Lock 7 for many years, George could distinguish the boat horns of those who had traveled his way before. There was no mistaking the sonorous boom of Manfred Oberfeldt's conch shell. By the time the *Onoko Princess* reached the lock, he had let out the water and opened the large wooden miter gates at the lower end. With no boats coming down the canal out of Mauch Chunk, the lock was ready for her to pass right through.

Getting the *Onoko Princess* through Shirar Lock was the first test of Wilhelm's navigational skills. Before the season ended, "locking through" would be an operation he and the mules would perform a thousand times and, in the years following, thousands of times after that. But, this morning, it was a new experience, and he led Lucy and Max forward tentatively, afraid to go too fast or too slow. Too fast and the *Onoko Princess* would crash into the pilings; too slow and she would founder outside the gates.

Ahead of the lock, a mule bridge crossed the canal and Lucy and Max slowed down as they approached it. Their action was instinctive. Although they had worked at different tasks all winter, they did not need a novice mule driver to tell them what to do. "Whoa," called Wilhelm, more out of ego than necessity, for the mules had already come to a halt. When he unhitched them, his father hauled in the tow line and steered the Onoko Princess under the mule bridge into the empty lock under her own momentum.

Like every lock on the Lehigh Canal except Lock 1, near Mauch Chunk, Lock 7 was a hundred feet long and twenty-two feet wide, wide enough to hold two boats side by side that were traveling in the same direction. In the dim light of lanterns, it looked short and narrow to Wilhelm. And, for a moment, he wondered if the *Onoko Princess* would fit inside it. But he need not have worried. Empty of coal and riding high in the water, she glided majestically under the mule bridge, through the miter gates and into the chamber without even touching the walls.

"Here, catch this!" shouted Manfred, throwing the tow line back to Wilhelm as he steered the *Onoko Princess* toward the towpath side of the lock. "It is time to snub the boat." 'Snubbing the boat' was a rite of passage for a new mule driver, and, although Wilhelm knew that snubbing meant tying a boat up, he did not know how it was done. But before he could ask, his father began to bark out orders. "Take the line to the top end of the lock — qvick, son, qvick," he shouted as Wilhelm hesitated, not knowing where to go with it. "See that niggerhead over there on the side of the lock — the round black thing on top of the concrete platform at the upper end? — vind the tow line around it — again! — vonce more! Ve don't vant the *Onoko Princess* to break free vhen the vater starts coming into the lock."

Snubbing a boat, or securing it to a bollard inside a lock, was one of the more critical tasks on the canal. A boat that broke loose in a lock or one that coasted too quickly over an open drop gate could ram into the miter gates and unhinge them, draining an entire upstream level of the canal. Manfred puffed hard on his pipe, eagle-eyed as he watched his young son double-loop the line around the small, round cast-iron bollard. "Is that all right, Pa?" Wilhelm asked when he was done. His father's answer was to nod and signal the lock tender to change the level.

Shirar Lock was a standard lock. It was filled through the drop gate at the upper end, and emptied through miter gates at the lower end. With the *Onoko Princess* secured inside the lock chamber, George Shirar turned the crank to operate the rack-and-pinion gear. Groaning, the toothed gears meshed together and the miter gates closed behind her. She was afloat in very low water. To raise her to the next higher level, he walked to the wicket shanty at the upper end of the lock and opened the wickets above the drop gate. The iron plates rotated and water flowed through them, filling the lock through valves near the floor of the chamber. Wilhelm watched anxiously as the water gushed into the lock. But he need not have worried. The *Onoko Princess* stayed secure as she rose gracefully to the next level on a nine-foot tide. When the water level in the lock was the same as that in the upper level of the canal, Wilhelm unwound the tow line from the bollard and hitched the mules to the boat. Leading them forward, the *Onoko Princess* passed over the open drop gate into the next higher level of the canal. The Indian maiden had taken her first step up the forty-six-mile water staircase. It took forty-nine standard locks to overcome the three hundred and fifty-foot drop in elevation between Mauch Chunk and Easton, and she would pass through each one of them, and the eight guard locks, every time she ascended and descended the Lehigh Canal.

"Great job, son!" exclaimed Manfred jubilantly. "You snubbed her real good! I cannot say that about some of my past mule drivers!"

Praise from his father was rare, and Wilhelm beamed. "I guess I'm just lucky." Feeling that the mules were partly responsible for his success, he rewarded them with a pat. "Max and Lucy knew just when to stop outside the lock gates and just where to wait."

"You could say," joked his father, "elephants — and mules — never forget!"

Beyond the lock, the Mountain of the Sleeping Bear crouched to the east, its flanks sweeping down to the canal. Known to the Lenape Indians as "Mauch Chunk," it was the mountain from which the town got its name. To the west, the sheer cliffs of South Mountain cradled the river. A March wind swirled through The Narrows, between the two mountains. With six locks to go before they arrived at the coal chutes, Wilhelm was freezing.

Shivering, he plodded on as darkness began to disperse. The whistle of a steam engine disturbed the silence. It blew and blew, echoing off the flanks of the sleeping bear, gaining force as it sounded along the river valley. The first Lehigh

Valley Railroad coal train of the day was on its way to Easton along tracks paralleling the canal. The whistle was shrill and disturbing. Lucy and Max jerked in their traces and quickened their gait. And Wilhelm had to run to keep up.

"Whoa!" shouted Manfred as the *Onoko Princess* began to heave precariously. "Hold 'em beasts back, son!"

Exerting all the strength his young body could muster, Wilhelm pulled hard on Lucy's harness. Whether it was Wilhelm's tug on the harness or Manfred's yell, the dappled mule responded and the team slowed down. It was a while before the *Onoko Princess* regained her equilibrium. The train crew watched in amusement as Manfred righted her. Spooking a mule team was a game played against canalers by the drivers of the "iron horse."

"*Gott im Himmel!*" roared Manfred, shaking his fist at the retreating train, "vhat pleasure do you railroaders get from scaring the living daylight out of our mules?"

"Why do they do it, Pa?" asked Wilhelm as he stood outside Lock 2 with the mules, waiting for the gates to open.

"Ve're their competition. That's vhy! They're in the business of hauling coal like us. Vone of them train vhistles spooked Helmut Ritter's mules so bad last year, his boat beached itself on the towpath. That's all ve need on our first trip!"

Shaken from the experience, Wilhelm vowed that the next time a train roared down the tracks he would take Max and Lucy as far as he could across the towpath and turn their heads away.

Lock 2, the Weigh Lock, was a mile south of Mauch Chunk. It was the only lock on the Lehigh Canal where coal cargoes were weighed. To prevent boat traffic from backing up, the Lehigh Coal & Navigation Company constructed two locks side by side. Standard Lock 2 was on the towpath side of the canal. Parallel to it, on the berm side, was the Weigh Lock. The dual construction enabled empty boats to pass up the canal while loaded boats, traveling south, were being weighed.

"Vil," shouted Manfred, "Ve have to get the boat veighed before ve take on a load. At the beginning of the boating season, the veighmaster needs to know the tare weight of the coal boats — that is the veight vhen they are empty — so that he can figure out the veight of the load vhen they come back down the canal."

Wilhelm looked perplexed. "Do we go into the Weigh Lock the wrong way, Pa?"

"Ja, son. Ve have to enter from the lower end. This means that ve need enough momentum to carry the *Onoko Princess* to the berm side."

With his father bellowing out instructions, Wilhelm increased the pace of the mules as they approached the lock. Then, on signal, he detached them from the boat. The *Onoko Princess* was adrift. Manfred pulled sharply on the steering post and she moved into the open Weigh Lock on the far side of the canal. Her tare weight was duly recorded and, attached once again to her tow rope, she was ready to pass on up the canal to the next lock.

The Weigh Lock was the seventh lock Wilhelm had helped his father navigate that morning. He was getting used to the procedure. But it was too soon to be complacent. Another half mile and he would face a different kind of challenge. The *Onoko Princess* would enter slackwater in the Lehigh River for the first time.

Lock 1 guarded the entrance between the Lower Division of the Lehigh Canal and the boat basin at Mauch Chunk. It consisted of two locks in tandem, one behind the other, and was the longest lock on the Lehigh Canal, with the smallest lift. Depending on the water level in the river, it lifted or lowered boats only one and a half feet. But its low lift did not lessen its importance. Not only was it the main source of water for the first five and a half miles of the Lehigh Canal between Mauch Chunk and Parryville, it was the gateway to Mauch Chunk basin, the principal hub for the shipment of anthracite coal on the Lehigh Canal.

As the *Onoko Princess* approached the miter gates, Wilhelm unhitched the mules from the tow rope, and followed the same procedure he had for all the locks he had gone through that morning. Without so much as a bump, she slid gently into the middle of the double lock chamber. He snubbed her like a pro, and waited for the miter gates at the upper end to open. Unlike a standard lock, a guard lock had miter gates at both ends. With only a foot and a half of water needed to level the lock with the river, the Indian maiden quickly passed through the upper gate and into the bustling boat basin.

Not only was Mauch Chunk the center of operations for the Lehigh Coal & Navigation Company, it was the junction between the Lehigh Canal's Upper and Lower Divisions. The forty-six mile Lower Division, from Mauch Chunk south to Easton, was finished in 1829; the twenty-six mile Upper Division was started north from Mauch Chunk to White Haven in 1835 and completed three years later. Between the two divisions was the boat basin, a slackwater pool formed by a dam across the Lehigh River. Boatmen called it "catfish pond." The basin's southern boundary was Mauch Chunk Dam, located near the entrance to the Lower Division. Its northern boundary was Packer Dam. Named after railroad magnate Asa Packer, builder and chief shareholder of the Lehigh Valley Railroad, Packer Dam crossed the Lehigh River at the start of the Upper Division.

As the *Onoko Princess* entered the basin, the waterfront on both sides of the river was bustling. Coal was coming into Mauch Chunk from everywhere. It came into the west bank from Summit Hill by the Switchback Gravity Railroad, and from the Panther Valley mines by the Room Run Gravity Railroad. It came in to the east bank from the Beaver Meadow mines, and down the Upper Grand Section of the canal from mines in Beaver Meadow, and from mines in the Wyoming and Susquehanna valleys through White Haven at the head of the navigation. Until 1855, when Asa Packer opened the Lehigh Valley Railroad, the Lehigh Canal was the only mass transportation route for coal in the area. That year, coal shipments on the canal peaked. In the railroad's first year of operation, competition had already begun to erode the importance of the canal.

With the *Onoko Princess* safely in the basin, Wilhelm stood onshore awaiting orders from his father. "Take the mules to the stables, vhile ve load," shouted Manfred. "Ve're taking on coal from the chutes at the Svitchback so ve'll have to hitch onto the cable ferry to cross the river."

The towpath was on the east bank of the Lehigh. The coal chutes and the Switchback, the gravity railroad connecting the mines to the canal, were on the west. A cable ferry that looked like a giant clothes pulley hauled boats from one side of the river to the other. With the precision of someone who had done it many times before, Manfred threw the tow line to the cable-ferry operator. It landed right at his feet. The man hooked the *Onoko Princess* to the pulley and started the machinery. Hitched to the thick wire rope like a fish that had just been caught, she was towed across the river to the coal chutes. When she was nudged into a berth, Manfred tied her up; then he helped Mary and Annie ashore to escape the dirty business of loading.

As she and her mother set off along busy Susquehanna Street, Annie could hardly contain her excitement. Passengers from the Philadelphia train were making their way from the Lehigh Valley station across the wooden footbridge to the prosperous west side of town. Some used the railroad to visit family and friends. Some came to find work in the booming industrial town. But most were rail excursionists, sophisticated Philadelphians who, for $5.25, could take a train to the scenic mountain town, spend ten days at a fine hotel and enjoy an eighteen-mile round-trip thrill ride on the Switchback Gravity Railroad. The same railroad that brought coal from the Summit Hill mine to Mauch Chunk was fast becoming a tourist attraction.

As the procession of passengers crossed the bridge, shabbily dressed women and men mingled with elegant ladies in ermine-trimmed capes escorted by gentlemen in bespoke tailored three-piece suits. Bell boys in red uniforms, looking like toy soldiers, pushed carts piled high with luggage to the Mansion House Hotel on Susquehanna Street and the American Hotel on Broadway. Horses, pulling carriages, stomped the muddy streets, or neighed impatiently as they waited near the footbridge for passengers. With a crack of the whip and a coin or two to the driver, excursionists could ride in style to their hotel or visit one of the town's sights. With its magnificent scenery, exhilarating mountain air, and thrilling Gravity Railroad, Mauch Chunk was no longer just a grimy coal-shipping outpost. It was a thriving Mecca for tourists. Posters decorating the Lehigh Valley station proudly proclaimed Mauch Chunk "the Switzerland of America," second only to Niagara Falls as the most popular destination for rail excursionists.

Away from the coal-shipping operations along the waterfront, the town took on a prosperous air. Along with the fine hotels, imposing churches, and large brick and stone buildings — architectural masterpieces even in major metropolises — the homes of Mauch Chunk's new millionaires lined Broadway. Ironically, this was an extremely narrow street wending its way upward through the cleft between South Mountain and Mount Pisgah. Overlooking the river, on the lower slopes of Mount Pisgah — grandly named after one of the mountains that overlooked the Promised Land — the mansions of the richest of the *nouveaux riches* vied for position and lavishness. Standing imposingly behind ornate iron railings and entered through elegant *portes cochères*, they were the ultimate in Victorian splendor. Everything, from exotic woods and imported wallpapers to furnishings and works of art, was the best money could buy. And why not? As

America industrialized and the demand for "black diamonds" grew, enterprising men rose from rags to riches in the booming coal-shipping town. By 1850, out of a population of 3,000, Mauch Chunk could boast of having thirteen resident millionaires. Unseen by those who crossed the Lehigh River from the train station were the shanties of those whose hard labor was bringing prosperity to Mauch Chunk. Following the dusty coal road out of town, straddling the hill tops, they were out of sight and mind of the grand houses and their occupants.

On the sidewalks of the thriving town, tourists mingled with millionaires and those who toiled to make their bosses rich. It was market day and everybody who was anybody was to be seen in Market Square and strolling along Broadway. Excited by the hustle, bustle and sophistication, Annie was wide-eyed.

"Oh, look, Ma, isn't she pretty?" she exclaimed, turning to gawk at a young woman in a dark green velvet dress and matching bonnet. "What a gorgeous dress! I want to be just like her when I get married."

"Married!" exclaimed her mother. "Aren't you a bit young for that?"

But Annie was not deterred. "I wanna wear fine things and be so rich I can buy anything in the whole wide world. Maybe … just maybe … I'll be an actress."

Mary smiled, and thought of her own girlish dreams. Certainly, they did not include living on a coal boat. Not wishing to tread too hard on her daughter's fancies, she remarked thoughtfully, "Darling Annie, we never know what life brings."

"Where do you think that lady came from?" asked Annie, her gaze following the young woman between the Romanesque pillars of the Broadway Hotel.

"Probably Philadelphia!"

"Are we going to Philadelphia on this trip?"

"Most likely we'll be towed along the tidewater to the waterfront."

The waterfront was not exactly what Annie had in mind. "Can we go into town and see the State House? Teacher told us that the Declaration of Independence was signed there and the Liberty Bell is in the Declaration Chamber."

"Now, Annie, you already know the answer to that!"

Mary was a no-nonsense person. With its uncertainties, life on the canal had made her that way. Even though they would stay on board the *Onoko Princess* when she was towed down the Delaware River, they had no money to fritter away in town. Manfred would not get paid until they got back to the Weigh Lock. Even then, they had to save what they could. Winter in canal towns was

"Let's go and look in the windows of the Continental Clothing Store, Ma."

hard. Canalers were not paid for the three or four months the canal shut down, and they could not depend on finding extra work.

Disappointed with her mother's no-nonsense answer, Annie turned to more immediate avenues of enjoyment. "Let's go and look in the windows of the Continental Clothing Store, Ma. We have lots of time. Pa will take ages to load."

With Annie, one thing had a way of leading to another. And Mary hesitated. If she let Annie get near the shops, she would be lucky to escape without spending the few pennies in her purse.

"Please, Ma," begged Annie, "I promise, I won't ask for anything."

"Promise?"

Annie nodded, and, before her mother knew what was happening, she was being ushered across Susquehanna Street to Harlan's Building in Market Square.

The Continental Clothing Store was well named. It was the finest store in all of Mauch Chunk. Although it catered to the average Mauch Chunker from racks in the basement, it was the mannequins in the windows, displaying ready-made copies of the latest European fashions, that took Annie's eye. Each time she visited Mauch Chunk, they grew more fancy. With tightly corseted waist lines and protruding bosoms, elaborate coiffures, and painted Chinese faces, they were dressed in the finest gowns of satin and silk, velvet and brocade of every hue. Hand-painted, gold-fringed silk scarves, as big as tablecloths, draped their bare shoulders. Pearls from the Orient, and multicolored beads, hand-crafted from finest Austrian crystal, adorned their swan-like necks. With elegant bangled arms raised in greeting, they beckoned well-to-do tourists and rich Mauch Chunkers inside the emporium to purchase the treasures it held.

Annie gazed from mannequin to mannequin, mentally trying on everything they wore. Satin or velvet, maroon or green, embossed or embroidered, pearls or beads, whatever they had on did not matter. She pictured herself in every fine dress and piece of jewelry they wore.

They must have stood there for a half hour. This time, it was Mary's turn to hustle. "Come on, girl," she said taking Annie's arm, "we can't stay here all day. Your father will not be pleased if we are not there when he's ready to leave."

That was true. Anything that held the *Onoko Princess* back made her father furious. Reluctantly, Annie tore herself away ... at least, from the Continental Clothing Store! Two doors away was another attraction.

Volner's was the first ice cream parlor and confectionery store in Mauch

Chunk, and in towns for miles around for that matter. Hearing that ice cream parlors were all the rage in Philadelphia and New York, the enterprising Volners decided to open one in Mauch Chunk. Like the Continental Clothing Store, Volner's was patronized mostly by tourists and well-to-do Mauch Chunkers. Those who labored for low wages could not afford to spend hard-earned money indulging their sweet tooth. Well, almost never! Manfred's last end-of-season treat for his family was ice cream at Volner's. And Annie had not forgotten. Sitting at one of the small round marble-topped tables, savoring one of Heidi Volner's homemade wafers piled high with her hand-churned ice cream, bottled strawberries and whipped cream, she felt like a princess. How she would have liked to relive the experience! But with money short, she would compromise and settle for a brightly colored stick of Dutch candy.

"Can we buy a candy stick, Ma?"

"Annie, love," protested Mary, "I told you. Papa has not been paid."

Annie looked crestfallen, but did not give up. "Then, after he gets paid, can we buy one?"

"We'll see!" answered her mother, with the usual noncommittal answer she gave when she did not want to make a promise she could not keep.

Wilhelm could not cross the river aboard the *Onoko Princess* with the rest of the family. He had to turn the mules loose in the stable yard where they would stay until the boat was loaded and back on the east side of the river. With Max and Lucy relishing their break and several hours to kill, he decided to walk over the footbridge and watch the *Onoko Princess* load. Halfway across, he met a platoon of army recruits marching in formation. He moved aside to let them pass. Led by Captain Chapman, a Union Army hero and recruiter for Mauch Chunk, the young men were on their way to catch the next train to Philadelphia. Having proclaimed their loyalty to the Union cause by unfurling a flag from a hemlock tree on South Mountain, a thousand feet above town, they would join Lincoln's Army to fight the good fight in the Civil War. Following them tearfully, reluctant to bid good-bye, were their mothers, sweethearts, and wives. The train roared into the station and, amid the tears and waves of the women, the recruits climbed on board.

Smoke from the engine rose above the bridge, and Wilhelm scampered to the other end to escape it. The *Onoko Princess* was moored near the coal docks, her fresh rust-colored paint glistening in the morning sunlight. Six Company boats and the private boat *Black Diamonds* were ahead of her. Having wintered in Mauch Chunk, their captains had made sure they would be first in line to load.

On the bluffs above the waiting boats, the coal wagons of the Switchback Gravity Railroad trundled eternally along the outside perimeter of the cemetery to deposit their loads. It was not yet noon. The Switchback was built as a coal carrier but, as more and more rail excursionists descended on the small mountain town, it divided its time between hauling coal and passengers. Passenger cars were relegated to special times. They departed from the foot of the Mount Pisgah Plane for Summit Hill at 7:30 and 11:30 a.m. and 3:00 p.m. daily and returned to Mauch Chunk at 9:00 a.m., and 1:00 and 5:00 p.m.

It was still not time for passenger cars, and Wilhelm watched a long train of empty coal wagons groan up the six hundred and forty foot-high Mount Pisgah Plane. Pushed up the incline by a barney car, powered by a stationary steam engine on the summit, they crawled to the top, whizzed down the backside of the mountain, and ascended the four hundred and fifty-foot Mount Jefferson inclined plane the same way. The ride up the planes was slow; the ride on the downhill slopes was a hair-raising thrill. With only a brakeman in control, the empty wagons hurtled by gravity to Summit Hill. Loaded wagons returned to Mauch Chunk along the original single-track line at speeds reaching sixty miles an hour.

When the loaded wagons reached the bluffs above the river, they were un-coupled. One by one they descended to the waterfront down a short plane, provid-ing the motive power to pull the empties back up the incline. A chain mechanism tipped each wagon, and its load pitched toward the back end and opened the tailgate, adding another load of coal to the reservoir. Waiting in the river were the coal boats. When the gate at the top of the coal chute opened, shimmering, glimmering, blue-black nuggets of anthracite tumbled end over end into the coal holds. As each boat finished loading, it was hooked to the cable for the trip back across the river.

At last, it was time for the *Onoko Princess* and the private boat *Black Diamonds* to take their places beneath the coal chutes. With a wave of his hand, Manfred signaled that everything was in order. The gate on the chute opened and an ava-lanche of coal roared first into the rear, then into the front section of the boat. The noise was deafening; the dust, asphyxiating. Rising in clouds, much to Manfred's disgust, it covered the newly painted deck with a dusting of black snow. Working dockside to make sure coal flowed uninterrupted, laborers coughed and spat, and did whatever they could to rid their mouths and nostrils of the black grit.

The minute the clock struck eleven, tourists started to walk up the hill to the Switchback terminal to board the 11:30 train. Wilhelm was envious. Engulfed in a symphony of sound, he took in the scene from the top of a pile of timbers on the wharf. Cog wheels turned, machinery clanked, steam engines hissed, train whistles blew, and coal wagons clanged against one another as they were shunted onto sidings. Punctuating the industrial medley were the horns of boatmen. Blowing and honking in a dozen different keys, they bounced off the mountains surrounding the basin, echoing off one another in a grand symphony. So great was the volume, it took three sharp blasts of the conch shell to get Wilhelm's attention.

"You've been sitting there vatching that Svitchback for over two hours vhile the *Onoko Princess* vas being loaded!" shouted his father, cupping his hands to make the sound carry. "Run over the bridge and get the mules vhile I call for your Ma and Annie on the boat horn. Ve vill pick you up on the other side of the river." Then came his usual warning. "And, Vil … feed the mules or they von't be fit enough to pull the load."

With her hold full of coal, the *Onoko Princess* was five feet three inches lower in the water than she was when she was empty. To compensate for the displacement and improve the steering, Manfred tightened the chain that heightened the rudder, and switched tillers. He would not lower the rudder again until the *Onoko Princess* got rid of her load.

Three blasts on the conch shell announced he was ready to leave. This time, they were loud and long. And Mary and Annie heard them outside Volner's. They ran down Broadway and were soon on board. But haste was unnecessary. Boats of all kinds were lined up along both banks of the river and plying the waters in between. It seemed as if every boat that ever sailed up and down both divisions of the canal wanted to cross from one side of the boat basin to the other that morning. It was another two hours before the *Onoko Princess* was hooked onto the cable ferry to get back to the towpath side of the river. By then, it was late afternoon.

Wilhelm returned to the east side by the footbridge and was waiting with the mules when the *Onoko Princess* finally arrived. He caught the tow line his father threw to him on the first try and hitched Lucy and Max. The venerable Indian maiden was starting out on her first trip of the new season down the canal. She would travel along the Lower Division to Easton, then on down the Delaware Canal to its terminus at Bristol. On board, she had ninety tons of coal, plus the Oberfeldts' two-hundred-pound allotment. They would use part of the allotment for cooking and heating the cabin, and trade the rest for goods and services along the way.

Getting back into the Lower Division through Guard Lock 1 was slow. Manfred was impatient. Eight boats were ahead of them and more were coming up the canal to load. Before the *Onoko Princess* and her companions, the private boat *Black Diamonds* and two Company boats, could enter the double lock, they had to wait for the level to change five times.

Journeying down the canal meant reversing the locking procedure. When it was the *Onoko Princess*'s turn to enter the double guard lock, she passed through the miter gates and joined the three-boat formation inside. Snubbing the boat at Lock 1 was not a problem. When the water was let out through three small wickets, or doors, in the miter gates at the lower end, the level dropped only a foot and a half. It did not take long before the water level in the lock was the same as that in the canal. The *Onoko Princess* and her companions were hitched to their mules and passed, one by one, through the open gates on their way down the water staircase.

WOOO WOOO woo woo. They were halfway to the Weigh Lock when a boat horn answered itself off the cliff faces of Bear and South mountains. "A boat's comin' up the canal, Vil," yelled Manfred. "Ve have to pull over and drop the line."

Dropping the line to let another boat pass was a new operation for Wilhelm. He knew that an empty boat had the right of way and a loaded boat had to yield, but this was the first time he had ever performed the maneuver.

"Listen carefully to vhat I say," shouted his father. "Take the mules over to the far side of the towpath and stop."

Wilhelm did as he was told, and led his charges onto the grass verge. "Whoa," he shouted, tugging at the harness when Max and Lucy moved too far. "Is this all right, Pa?" he asked anxiously when they stopped where he wanted.

"Ja, *sehr gut!*"

"But … the boat's still moving."

"Ve can't stop her completely. You vill have to adjust. Go forvard a little, but don't pull on the line. Make sure there is enough slack for it to sink beneath the surface so that the other boat can pass over it."

Wilhelm led the mules forward to catch up with the drift, then stopped for a second time. He was ahead of the *Onoko Princess*'s bow. The line had enough slack in it to submerge. On board, Manfred was doing his part. He steered the *Onoko Princess* away from the towpath toward the berm side of the canal. To slow her momentum, he turned the tiller at right angles across the stern. With the boat and mules positioned correctly, he motioned to the other captain to pass. A wave of thanks from its captain, and the empty boat sailed over the *Onoko Princess*'s tow line on its way to Mauch Chunk to load. With a jubilant "giddyup" to get the mules going, Wilhelm had passed another navigation hurdle.

But there were more hurdles to come. The empty boat had barely gone by when there was another challenge, and another delay. They had reached the Weigh Lock. On the way up the canal, the *Onoko Princess* had been weighed to determine her tare weight so the procedure was not exactly new to Wilhelm. The only thing new was that, this time, she was loaded and, like every loaded coal boat passing down the canal, she had to be weighed to make sure that her cargo did not exceed one hundred tons.

Four coal boats were in front of the *Onoko Princess*, and she had to stand in line again to wait for them to be weighed. A signal to enter from the locktender, and Wilhelm led the mules forward. Their pace was perfect. With just the right momentum, the *Onoko Princess* drifted into the weigh lock and Manfred maneuvered her over the scale. Barney McBride, the weigh master, made sure she was positioned correctly, then he closed the gates and drained the lock chamber until the *Onoko Princess*'s hull rested on the scale. He figured out the tonnage by subtracting the tare weight of the empty boat, listed on the manifest, from the weight of the loaded boat, indicated on the scale. Satisfied that his calculation was correct, he exclaimed, "Yer in the munny, Cap'n. The load's as near nointy tons as ye can git. Of course, that's not countin' yer own two hundred pounds."

"You had better not count that!" joked Manfred. "That von't last long! Ve vill have to trade most of it for goods along the vay."

Like all canalers, Manfred was a good bargainer. Even when he had money in his pocket, he did his best not to pay cash for anything. Most farmers along the canal were willing to exchange a chicken, or a bushel of vegetables or fruit for a sack of coal. And most store keepers were also obliging. But in places like Mauch Chunk where coal was cheap, and in popular waterfront hangouts where proprietors accumulated more coal than they could use, coal was not always a commodity that could be traded and Manfred had to pay for what he wanted with cash.

It was not time to feed Max and Lucy so Wilhelm walked them to the lower end of the lock and waited for the miter gates to open.

"Here, son," said Barney, signing the bill of lading, "everything's in orderrr. Hold on t' this fer yer pa. His wages'll be waitin' fer him on the waaay back."

To compensate for the double width of the side-by-side locks, Manfred threw out extra line and Wilhelm hitched Lucy and Max to the tow.

"Ye look like yer handling them mules roight well fer a lad yer age," remarked Barney as he gave the nod to Manfred to proceed. "Yer pa'd better watch oot! If ye keep this oop, Oi bet, ye'll be handlin' the tiller yerself real soon."

Wilhelm smiled proudly as he took the *Onoko Princess* back into the canal. As he walked along the towpath by the side of the mules, he took out the bill of lading and looked at it. Before the water dropped eight and a half feet to the next level at Lock 3, he handed the paper to his father. "Pa," he said, looking concerned, "I think Mr. McBride made a mistake."

"A mistake!" echoed Manfred, unfolding the bill of lading. "That's not like McBride."

"It says, Boat 322 weighs just over a hundred and ten tons. But you only took on ninety tons of coal!"

"Son," said Manfred laughing, "you forgot to take into account the veight of the boat. Vithout her load, she's just shy of twenty tons."

Wilhelm busied himself with the mathematics. "Then she's a hundred and ten tons with the load."

"She's a little more than that! You have to figure in our coal. She's a hunert and ten tons, plus our two hunert pounds of coal."

"Oh," said Wilhelm, upset at his stupidity. He would never make the same mistake again.

The next lock would be another test of Wilhelm's snubbing skills. This time, he had to snub the *Onoko Princess* before the lock level was lowered. Snubbing a boat was easier in a rising lock, and he was apprehensive. Lock 3 had a drop of 8.3 feet. This was about average for a Lower Division lock, but to Wilhelm, it seemed enormous. He had gotten away easy at Lock 1 and the Weigh Lock. With its low lift, Lock 1 had not required much skill on his part and, whether it was Barney McBride's custom or that he did not trust the novice mule driver, he had taken care of everything at the Weigh Lock.

Wilhelm approached Lock 3 tentatively and untethered the mules so that his father could take the *Onoko Princess* into the lock. This time, she did not have to pass under a mule bridge. Mule bridges were almost always at the lower end of locks. The snubbing procedure was the same as it had been coming up the canal, with one important exception: on the way down the canal, the line had to be double-roped loosely around the bollard to allow enough slack for the boat to drop as the water level in the lock went down. With some help from his father, Wilhelm figured out the length of the line perfectly. As the lock emptied through the miter-gate wickets, the *Onoko Princess* dropped without a hitch to the next level. Unwinding the line from the bollard, Wilhelm tethered the mules and towed her back into the canal. He had accomplished another operation successfully.

The going was rough on the towpath. He was walking into the wind. It lifted up his jacket and blew down his neck, making him shiver. His father was not faring any better at the helm. Since leaving the Weigh Lock, they had passed through six locks. One more, and they would be at Weissport. Manfred's goal had been to reach Parryville by nightfall, but delays at the coal chutes, cable ferry and Weigh Lock had been longer than he expected. Beat after a long day of standing in line, much to the delight of his family — most of all his young mule driver — he gave the order to tie up for the night.

Mary and Annie had not had an easy day of it either. They did not sit on deck in grand style. They cleaned it. Even though the *Onoko Princess* was a coal carrier, Manfred insisted on keeping her spotless. By the time they swept up the coal dust, mopped her deck and wiped off the hatches of the coal hold, they were worn out.

Being a canal wife was not easy. Keeping an eighty-seven and a half foot boat clean, living and cooking in cramped quarters, and traveling back and forth in all kinds of weather were exhausting. Although many a canal wife found it hard to keep the small cabin tidy, Mary had a place for everything. She had to. Manfred would have it no other way. In her idle moments, she dreamed of living in a white clapboard house, sleeping in a comfortable brass bed and seeing her children off to school each morning just like the other women in Weissport. Education was important. And having her children miss school from the beginning of March to the end of November was what she hated most about canaling. Although she encouraged them to read and study, with eighteen-hour work days there was no time left for learning.

Cold and fatigued, she stowed the broom and came into the cabin to warm up yesterday's stew. If she had her druthers, she would have thrown herself on her bunk, but she knew everybody was starving. By the time Wilhelm returned from bedding the mules, supper was ready. "Go get your father," she said as he came through the hatch.

If Mary was dutiful, Annie wasn't. She had pulled her bunk down and was taking a rest.

"Come on, Annie," said her mother irritably, "get that thing back up, and set the table. And when you're finished, cut some bread for the stew. I'm worn out."

"So am I," mumbled Annie to herself as she stored her bunk , put up the table and set it.

There was no need for Wilhelm to call for his father twice. At the word "supper" Manfred bounded down the steps into the cabin. He hung his coat on a peg, took off his boots, and pulled the bench up to the table. The first day of the season had been long. Tomorrow should be easier. There would be no waiting in line at the cable ferry, coal chutes, or Weigh Lock. While there was always the possibility of a delay on the canal, tomorrow should be straight sailing.

They were all too hungry to talk. They dipped hunks of bread into their stew and ate heartily. Annie, who was usually last, was first to finish. "You look as if you are going somewhere," exclaimed Manfred as she laid her spoon across her bowl and got up.

"I told Gram I'd come and see her next time we tied up in Weissport."

"You know, ve've got to get out of here early in the morning," said father sharply.

"I know, Pa, but . . ." Then, thinking her mother might be a softer touch, she turned to her and asked, "Can I go and see Gram, Ma?"

Mary hesitated and looked at Manfred. It was the same old back-and-forth thing.

"Please?" pleaded Annie.

"What do you think, Pa?" asked Mary.

Uncomfortable at being put on the spot so early in the trip, Manfred gave in. "Vell, if you go over there, you had better *mak schnell*. Ve have a long day tomorrow and must get to bed early."

As she often did, Annie had won. Giving her parents a hug, she put on her coat. "I'll be back real quick!"

"Hey, wait!" shouted Wilhelm, wiping his bowl clean and shoving a sodden piece of bread in his mouth, "I'm coming too."

"Be back in half an hour," growled their father.

"We will, Pa. We will!" they chorused.

The children raced through the boatyard, out the gates, and down White Street. The grateful people of Weissport had named the street in honor of Josiah White, the brilliant engineer who built the canal and made it possible for so many of them to earn a living. A knock on the door of Number 18, and the children were gathered in their grandparents' arms. A half hour later, good as their word, they were back on board the *Onoko Princess* carrying a freshly baked cake.

"Hey, vhat you got there?" asked Manfred as they burst into the cabin.

"German chocolate cake."

"*Vunderbar*! Ve vill have a piece before ve turn in for the night."

CHAPTER III

Unlike the morning before, it was too early for Wilhelm when his father sounded the conch shell. His legs were still aching from walking the towpath, and he just wanted to sleep. It was barely three thirty, but his father was determined to get an early start.

"It's time to get up, mule boy," he said, taking hold of Wilhelm's shoulder and giving it a shake as Wilhelm snuggled back down in the covers. "I vant them mules on the towpath before breakfast."

Wilhelm rubbed the sleep out of his eyes and got up. Resigned to the fact that there was no sleeping in, he rolled up his straw tick and stowed it away in the chest. Pulling his trousers over his long johns, he put on the jersey his grandmother had knitted, his winter coat, and boots. With the water in the barrel on deck freezing and his father in a hurry, he had neither the inclination nor time to wash.

Old habits die hard. Even though this was the first trip of the season, his mother was up at the conch shell's first note. Annie, on the other hand, did not stir. Putting the conch shell next to her ear, Manfred blew into it softly. "Get up, you lazy girl. Help your mother get breakfast," he ordered as he went out on deck.

Too comfortable in her cocoon, Annie rolled over.

"Come on," said Wilhelm, giving her a poke. "You'd better get up or you'll be in trouble." Although he was two years younger than his sister, he always tried to protect her from her own laziness and their parents' wrath.

"I'm getting up," she mumbled sleepily. "I just need to wake up first."

Although Annie was good at wheedling things out of her father, she knew that he meant what he said when it came to anything to do with the *Onoko Princess*. She pulled back the covers and shivered. The stove had almost gone out overnight and the cabin was cold as a tomb.

Mary opened up the draft to get the fire burning hot again. When the coals were red, she put a pot of coffee and a pan of oatmeal on the stove plate. By the time Manfred finished lighting the nighthawker lanterns and Wilhelm fetched the mules, breakfast was ready. Warmed by mugs of hot coffee and bowls of steaming porridge, captain and mule driver were ready to go. With Manfred at the helm, and the mules hitched to the line, the *Onoko Princess* cast off in the darkness. Stopping only to pass through locks and give empty boats the right of way, Manfred was happy with their progress. With delays at the locks it was almost five thirty when they reached Parryville.

Nestled into the hillside, Parryville, five and a half miles south of Mauch Chunk, was once the bustling terminus of the Beaver Meadow Railroad, Carbon County's first steam railroad. Opened in 1836, the Beaver Meadow hauled coal from the mines around Hazleton to Parryville where it was loaded onto coal boats for shipment along the Lehigh Canal. When the devastating flood of 1841 washed away the railroad bridges, Mauch Chunk became the new terminus of the railroad, and Parryville became just another standard lock on the Lehigh Canal. That changed in 1855 when the first of three iron furnaces opened by the side of the canal. By 1862, Parryville was busier than ever.

The roar of blazing furnaces and the clatter of iron bars being loaded onto canal boats greeted the *Onoko Princess* as she approached Lock 13, an entry lock that would take her into the Lehigh River. Soon she was inside the lock. Depending on the lift of a lock, the average locking time on the canal took ten or fifteen minutes. Most locktenders were experts at turning a lock, and Joseph Fink was no exception. Even with Lock 13's high twelve and a half-foot lift, he had the *Onoko Princess* in and out of the hundred-foot concrete, stone and timber-cribbed chamber in less than fifteen minutes. As the miter gates opened, and she entered the first stretch of Lehigh River slackwater since Mauch Chunk, her fledgling mule driver had to learn another new skill.

Although the navigation system was known as the "Lehigh Canal," boats had to sail along both canal levels and pools in the river to get to their destination. In the forty-six miles between Mauch Chunk and Easton, dams held the water back at eight points along the Lehigh, forming eight slackwater pools deep enough for river navigation. This meant that, along the Lower Division, boats entered and left the river eight times. They entered the river through "entry locks," like the Parryville lock, and got back into the canal through "guard locks" at dams.

The dam that formed the slackwater pool between Parryville and Bowmanstown was a half mile downstream. On one side of the Lehigh, the spine of the Blue Mountains swept down toward the Lehigh Gap. On the other, the Pohopoco Creek entered the river through a steep gully in the mountains surrounding the village.

"This is going to be tricky, Pa," said Wilhelm as he took stock of the rushing water. Although he had taken the *Onoko Princess* from the canal into the slackwater at Mauch Chunk to load, the basin at Mauch Chunk was a pool of relative calm, bounded by a dam at either end. Taking the *Onoko Princess* into the slackwater at Lock 13 with only a dam at the lower end was much more challenging, especially during the spring thaw. With water flowing over the dam ahead, not only had they to deal with the strong current in the Lehigh, they had to take her across the turbulence of the Pohopoco where it tumbled into the river below the miter gates.

"Take your time, son, and listen carefully," came Manfred's steady voice over the roar of the Pohopoco's white water.

Although Wilhelm had passed this spot many times with his family, he had not paid it much attention. An experienced hand was then driving the mules. This time, he was the one who shared the responsibility with his father for taking the *Onoko Princess* across the water junction where the quiet of the canal met the flowing waters of two rivers. What made matters worse, with the recent rainy weather and melting snow, both river and creek were running high.

A wooden bridge took the towpath over the Pohopoco, and Wilhelm led Max and Lucy toward it. The mules were the motive power of the boat and it was up to him to control them. He approached the bridge tentatively, a slip of a boy in charge of two four-legged giants. Keeping his eyes on the boat's every movement in the river below, he started across the creaky wooden structure. The force of the water from the mountain stream pushed the *Onoko Princess* sideways. Buffeted outward, the two sections bucking, the tow line was stretched to its limit. Feeling the pull of the eighty-seven and a half foot-long loaded boat, the mules snorted and faltered.

"Whoa, Lucy!" hollered Manfred as he worked the tiller to counteract the cross currents. "Hang on to the harness, Vil! Keep them beasts moving."

Wilhelm grasped Lucy's head harness and walked in front of his charges across the bridge. In what seemed like an eternity, the mules grounded their hooves on the towpath and resumed their measured gait. The *Onoko Princess* steadied herself and rode like a princess on the slackwater.

Wilhelm was jubilant. "We made it!" he called to his three smiling family members on deck.

"Vell, I guess you earned your mule driver's stripes today," said his father proudly. "You did real vell, son. That's a vicked piece of river right there. I think

I vill hire you for the next trip!"

Just downriver from Parryville, Manfred blew hard and long into his conch shell. *WOOOOOOOOOOO. WOOOOOOOOOOOOOO.* The sound echoed off the mountains and traveled along the slackwater. He was letting Henry Schnell, the locktender at Guard Lock 2 at the Bowmanstown Dam, know that the *Onoko Princess* was on her way. That way, if there was no ascending traffic, Henry could level the lock so that they could get out of the river and back into the canal without waiting.

As they made their way down the normally tranquil stretch of river, the undertow was strong. Urged on by Wilhelm, the mules quickened their pace. The current was sweeping the *Onoko Princess* toward the dam and he had to hurry to keep Lucy and Max ahead of her. They were halfway to the guard lock when it happened. In the early morning light Wilhelm could make out the outline of a boat coming up the canal. Its course was erratic; its horn was blowing furiously. As it came closer he saw that the boat was not the usual rusty-red Company boat; it was painted bright emerald green.

Manfred recognized the horn immediately. It was a hunting horn. Its peculiar tallyho sound soared above all the other boat horns and conch shells on the canal. "Here comes trouble," he hollered to Wilhelm. "I vill bet my boots, it is that Velshman, Taffy Morgan, in his green boat. He is drunk again; pushing them mules until they cannot go any faster. Ve must drop the line and get out of his vay."

"But, we can't stop, Pa — the current's pulling us!"

"Ve vill have to try. I vill pull out into the river to give him room to pass. Slow down the beasts, but, vhatever you do, don't let the boat get ahead of them on the flow."

As the green boat drew nearer, the shouts along the towpath grew louder and the language more foul. It was the Welshman ranting at his mule driver to speed up. "Whack them beasts, ya no good pipsqueak!" When the driver failed to hit the mules hard enough, he roared, "Yer ticklin' 'em. I wanna load tomorrow, not the week after next."

The driver brought the whip down on the haunches of the lead mule. It cowered under the blow.

"Hit 'em like ya meant it!" hollered Morgan again.

Raising the whip high above his head, the driver came down hard across the skin-and-bone flanks of both mules. Braying with pain, the mules broke into a gallop, dragging the boat behind them.

Seeing the bright green boat come swaying and bucking up the river, its motion tearing up the banks, Manfred screamed out, "Slow them mules down, Morgan. Ve can't stop. If you keep up that pace, you vill snag our tow line. The undertow is strong and the line keeps surfacing."

The flow in the slackwater was relentless and Wilhelm tried his hardest to pace Lucy and Max to the momentum of the boat. Rushing ahead with his charges, he stopped, but the *Onoko Princess* drifted past him and he had to move on. Manfred let out the tow line to its full length. How he wished coal boats had anchors! But they didn't. Anchors would have punched holes in the puddling of the canal's bottom. He had to think fast. To stop the *Onoko Princess* from drifting and allow enough slack in the line for Morgan to pass over it, he turned the tiller sharply across the hull. At right angles to the stern, the rudder was no longer in sailing position. Pushing hard against the tiller, he held tight. The drift slowed, and the tow line disappeared beneath the surface.

"Get the mules off the towpath, Vil," he hollered. "Make sure the line stays low on the ground. Ve do not vant Morgan's mules to trip over it." The thud of hooves grew louder. Morgan's boat was almost upon them. "Vatch out! Here he comes!"

Reacting to their last whipping, the mules were lurching along the towpath with the zigzagging empty boat in tow. Until now, the *Onoko Princess* had been just another Company boat, but as Morgan came closer, he recognized her number as the Oberfeldts' boat. Over the years he had had several run-ins with Manfred. Last season, his green boat rammed the *Onoko Princess* as he rushed to beat her into a lock. Manfred reported the incident, and Morgan had not forgotten.

"You're a menace. You're going so fast, you're gonna damage the canal banks vith your vake," screamed Manfred as the bows of the two boats scraped by one another.

Morgan's answer was a string of curses.

His bright green boat had almost passed when it happened. As it heaved and swayed, it snapped the tow line with its rudder. The lined flailed in a whiplash, snaked through the water, and floated to the surface, useless. Bereft of her tether, the *Onoko Princess* jerked forward, throwing Mary and Annie flat on the deck.

"See vhat you've done," yelled Manfred, shaking his fist at the retreating Morgan. "You have cast us adrift! Ve vould still have our line if you had crossed

Morgan's answer was a string of curses.

it carefully. You're gonna hear about this! And about the vay you treat them poor, starvin' beasts."

It would not be the first time Morgan had gotten into trouble for beating and starving his mules. Cruelty inspectors, who went from lock to lock to check on the animals for signs of abuse, already had his number. Malnutrition, whip marks, an ill-fitting collar were all causes for disciplinary action. Boatmen who failed to feed their animals or abused them physically received severe punishment and fines. And Taffy Morgan had been warned, punished and fined on all counts not once, but a number of times.

Morgan and his boat were a speck in the distance as the *Onoko Princess* floundered apart from her mules. Manfred chained the tiller to keep her stable and took a spare tow line from the equipment box. Hooking one end to the towing notch, he threw the other end to Wilhelm. Wilhelm caught it on the very first try and hitched up the mules. With a signal from his father to get going, they were on their way again.

"I thought he was going to tell his driver to crack me with the whip, Pa," confided Wilhelm as they neared the guard lock.

"If ever that Velshman lays a hand on you, son, he vill be mince meat … *bestimmt!*"

Henry Schnell was worried. It was over twenty minutes since he had opened the lock gates in response to Manfred's conch shell. When he saw the *Onoko Princess,* he was relieved. Wilhelm unhitched the mules and the boat glided into the lock.

With the delay caused by Taffy Morgan, almost four hours had passed since the mules had been fed so Wilhelm put on their feed baskets. While his charges refueled, he sat on a wooden railing near the wicket shanty and listened to his father complain in Pennsylvania German to Henry Schnell about Taffy Morgan. The mules had not finished eating by the time the water level was lowered, so, still munching hungrily from their feed baskets, they resumed their trek along the towpath. Manfred's credo was the old adage "Time means money," and he would have complained if the *Onoko Princess* had been detained to let the mules feed.

As the *Onoko Princess* continued on her way down the canal, boatmen saluted Manfred with their horns and conch shells as she passed, and he saluted them back. Everybody, from boatmen to locktenders, greeted Manfred with a smile and a wave. With fifteen years as a boat captain and ten years as a mule boy before that, he was respected as one of the best boatmen on the canal.

With the strain of the morning's events and the long walk from Weissport, the neophyte mule driver was worn out. All Wilhelm wanted to do was get off his aching feet. The leather of his boots had made giant blisters on his heels and his calf muscles were screaming with pain. Feeling guilty about asking his father if he could rest, he kept on. Finally, his weariness and pain were too much. He could not continue any longer. "Can I come on board for a while, Pa?" he pleaded while he waited for the next lock to change.

"Vhat?" exclaimed Manfred impatiently, "You are done already! Ve haven't gone half a day yet."

"But … my legs won't go any more … and I have blisters."

Manfred looked at his son … so young … and small for his age. He remembered how his own legs had ached that first day long ago, and he felt sorry for him. "I vill get your ma to take over."

Taking over for Wilhelm was no problem for Mary. All morning she had been hovering on deck, worrying, hoping Manfred would say, "Take a rest." She was no stranger to mule driving or to anything else that had to be done on board the *Onoko Princess*, including taking over the helm. Before the lock was lowered, she and Wilhelm exchanged places. Walking the towpath would be a pleasant change. As she straddled the side of the boat, she called to Annie, "Get something for your father and brother to eat. And see you get Wil a piece of soft flannel to put in his boots for those blisters."

Attending to the men's needs was a woman's duty, and Annie knew better than to complain. She went into the cabin and, in no time at all, was back with two mugs of coffee and some hunks of bread and cheese, and two big wads of flannel.

Wilhelm sat on the deck watching his father's every move as he locked through. Although the routine at the locks rarely varied, it never failed to fascinate him. He knew it by heart. On the way down the canal, the lock emptied through the miter-gate wickets; on the way up, it filled through the drop-gate wickets.

As Manfred looked at the small boy looking at him, it was his turn to feel guilty. Used to an older driver, he had made his son walk too far his first day out. "Are you all right, boy?" he asked as they went back into the canal.

"Yes, Pa, the flannel is helping."

"A veek on the job and you von't know you have legs! Your muscles vill get real strong, and the skin on your heels and the bottoms of your feet vill get so tough, they vill not hurt again."

"Driving mules ain't easy, Pa."

"You think you have it hard!" exclaimed Manfred. "You should have lived in Great-Grandpa Oberfeldt's day vhen there vas no canal. He had to steer coal arks all the vay from Mauch Chunk down the Lehigh River to Easton."

Manfred tapped the burning embers of tobacco from the bowl of his pipe into the canal. Smoking was too much of a distraction. After making sure that it was cool, he placed the empty pipe carefully in his breast pocket, signaling to Wilhelm that he was about to hear a story.

Wilhelm threw a tarp on top of the coal hatches and lay back. This was not the first time he had stretched out on the hatch covers. In the dog days of summer, he, his father and the mule driver often spent a night under the stars. Sleeping outdoors was more comfortable than sleeping in the small, stifling cabin. He pulled the tarp around him to ward off the March chill, and waited for his father to continue.

"Keeping them arks afloat vas pretty nigh impossible vhen each vone vas loaded vith ten tons of coal. The river vas full of shoals and shallows, and there vere rocks and rapids to contend vith. In them days, you know, there vas no canal … and no mules to pull them arks. There vas only the river, a long pair of oars, and fourteen bear trap locks between Mauch Chunk and Easton. I tell ya … them bear traps could be treacherous. Tvelve vere in the steepest and roughest stretch of the river between Mauch Chunk and the Lehigh Gap. The other two vere lower down at Treichlers and Freemansburg, vhere the river flattens out."

"I ain't never heard of a bear trap lock, Pa. What is that?"

"Vell, son, a 'bear trap lock' vas a kind of sluice. It vas invented by Josiah Vhite, the man who built the Lehigh Canal … remember? I told you, Grandpa Kintz's street vas named after him … Anyvay, Ol' Josiah vas trying to figure out a vay to send coal down the river on a kind of raft called an ark, and he built them bear trap locks to help them arks pass along the river."

"Why did he call them bear traps?"

"Vell, I vill tell you, son! He vas building the contraption on Mauch Chunk Creek, vhen a man passed by. 'Vhat's that you are making, Josiah?' the man asked, looking at the device which resembled a trap for catching bears. 'Is it a bear trap?' Ol' Josiah was so annoyed at the man's curiosity, he answered 'Yes,' to shut him up. The name caught on. And do you know something, son? It has stuck ever since."

"How did a bear trap lock work?"

"Ahead of every shallow or rocky stretch in the river, White and his crew constructed a dam with a bear trap lock built into it. When the gates of the bear trap were closed, a pool of slackwater formed above the dam. When the gates fell to the floor of the lock, the arks passed through and on down the river to the next bear trap."

"What do you mean, Pa, when you say, the gates fell to the floor? Canal locks have gates at both ends and they don't fall to the lock floor."

"A bear trap was not the kind of lock you see on the canal today. Its gates were not located at each end like miter gates and drop gates. They lay flat on the floor of the lock. When water was let into the lock from a side chamber, they floated upwards in an upside down 'V' to hold back the river. Arks — some of them chained together in trains as long as a hunert and eighty feet — waited in the slackwater pool that formed above the dam. When water was let out of the lock through a side chamber, the gates fell to the lock floor and the train of arks was swept downstream on an artificial flood."

"Did a locktender open the gates?"

"No, son. In them days, there was no such thing as locktenders."

"Then, who let the water out of the lock?"

"Vone of the hands on the lead ark would jump off and open the gates. He had just enough time to turn the lever, let down the gate, and get back on board before the water flushed through the lock and sent the ark train on its way. The same man would get off and open the gates of all twelve bear traps between Mauch Chunk and the Lehigh Gap. Then he would walk back to Mauch Chunk, and put up all the gates so the locks would be ready for the next day."

"It's a wonder the coal did not fall off when that water rushed the arks on down the river," said Wilhelm, visualizing the long train swishing through the bear traps on a giant wave of water.

"Sometimes it did. Sometimes them trains went out of control and were wrecked. More times than Great-Grandpa Oberfeldt cared to remember, the load, and him with it, landed in the river."

"Steering them things must have been awfully hard!"

"Ja, it vas! The oarsmen often fell in as they tried to keep control. Some of them drowned. I've heard Great Grandpa say, vhen them gates fell to the floor, them trains of arks vent through them bear traps like they vere shot out of a cannon."

Manfred took a fresh wad of tobacco from his pouch, tamped it into his pipe and lit it. The story was over, but not the images it had conjured up in Wilhelm's mind. He lay back on the hatch cover, thinking about the power of the river and the brave men, like his great-grandfather, who risked their lives getting coal to market, so many years ago. Concluding that it was much easier to walk the towpath with a pair of mules, he closed his eyes and dozed off.

From the towpath, Mary saw her son's head drop to his chest. "Wil," she yelled, "if you're going to sleep, go into the cabin. It's too cold out there."

Hour after hour, step after step, Lucy and Max plodded along the towpath like clockwork, rarely hesitating, except when they tried to sneak a nibble of newly sprouting grass. Confident that they were not about to go anywhere where they shouldn't, Mary dropped the lead rein and walked by their sides. She wanted to enjoy the tranquillity and beauty of the towpath without being tethered to the mules. Before changing places, she had asked Annie to make supper, even though she knew Annie would rather have been reading. Although she kept after her daughter to pull her weight, she was sorry for her. Annie was a bright girl who felt trapped. She wanted to attend school full-time so that she could become a school teacher. Unlike most of her contemporaries who believed that girls did not need an education, Mary was a woman ahead of her time. Nothing would have pleased her more than to see Annie fulfill her ambition. But, canal life being what it was, any young-girl notions Annie might have about learning and wearing fine clothes would, in all probability, have to remain dreams. The wind whipped her bonnet, disturbing her thoughts. "How far are we going today, Manny?" she shouted, suddenly feeling very cold.

"I vas hoping to get as far as Siegfried. By my reckoning, that is another fourteen miles."

As the sky darkened, the mules slowed their pace. With the wind blowing up and no current in the canal to help move the loaded boat along, Lucy and Max found the going hard. A few more days on the job, and they would be in better shape.

"It looks like it's going to rain, Manny," shouted Mary coaxing them on. "It don't look like we'll get to Siegfried tonight."

"Ve have to try," yelled Manfred. "If ve are going to make any money, Mary, ve have to do tventy-five miles a day."

Twenty-five miles was the canaler's daily goal, but reaching it was often more hope than fact. Line-ups at the locks, bad weather, accidents, and regular maintenance like dredging or fixing lock gates that got stuck caused a million unexpected delays. If everything went well, the average trip from Mauch Chunk to the tidewater terminus at Bristol took about seven days, including Sundays when nothing moved along the canals.

Traffic coming north from the industrial towns in the lower Lehigh Valley was getting heavy. Empty boats, which had wintered in towns like Bethlehem, Allentown and Easton, were heading up to Mauch Chunk to load. The *Onoko Princess* was lucky. With her crew wintering in Weissport, she had gotten a head start. With the exception of replacing her tow line near Bowmanstown, she had not encountered any delays. She was ten miles and eighteen locks down the canal, entering the Lehigh Gap by way of the Aquashicola Aqueduct. The Aquashicola Aqueduct was one of four wooden bridge-like structures that took the canal over a creek. It crossed the Aquashicola Creek where it entered the Lehigh River.

The swishing of water and clip clop of the mules on timber awakened Wilhelm. He recognized the sound immediately and sat up with a start. They were crossing the aqueduct and would soon leave the Lehigh Gap and enter another stretch of slackwater. Ashamed that he had fallen asleep on his first day on the job, he was about to go on deck when there was a loud thumping on top of the cabin.

It was his father. "Vil!" he shouted, as he gave an extra loud thump. "Isn't it about time you got back on the towpath? Your mother has other things to do besides driving your mules." Manfred was thinking of supper. It was only mid-afternoon but he was starving.

Wilhelm came through the hatch looking bleary-eyed. "I'm sorry, Pa," he mumbled, feeling ashamed.

"Some mule driver, you are!" exclaimed his father more amused at his son's rumpled look than angry. "Change places with your mother before ve go back into the river … or I vill fire you."

Never sure whether his father was joking or not, Wilhelm buttoned his coat in a hurry and changed places with his mother at the outlet lock. Refreshed by his nap, he put the mules through their paces and set out once more along the towpath. Mary got back on board not a moment too soon. The first drops of rain began to fall. Although the Lehigh Gap was behind them, they could feel its influence. Etched deep into the earth over the eons by the erosion of the river, it had turned into a wind tunnel. As strong gusts whipped between its steep, rocky sides, they stirred up the water and drove the *Onoko Princess* hard toward the dam.

"Hold on to them mules, son," hollered Manfred, trying to make himself heard against the howling wind. "Keep them ahead of the boat."

Wilhelm held tight to the lead rein, and did his best to keep them ahead. Sensing the acceleration of wind and current, Lucy and Max quickened their pace to beat the flow in the river. As they increased their speed, steam snorted from their nostrils and rose from their wet flanks. This time, the *Onoko Princess* was lucky. She made it along the slackwater to Guard Lock 3 without meeting another boat.

"How far are you planning to go, Captain Oberfeldt?" asked Amos Gruber as Manfred steered the *Onoko Princess* into the lock chamber. "The wind's whipping up real bad."

"Ve vere hoping to reach Siegfried," answered Manfred.

"You won't get that far. The canal's blocked above Laurys Station. A team of mules tumbled into the water."

"Oh!" groaned Manfred, upset at the thought of the delay. "How did it happen?"

"One team was passing another when the bank gave way. The driver of the team coming up the canal managed to cut the traces and drag the hind mule out, but he couldn't budge the lead mule. A crew's working there now, trying to get the stupid thing out. It's flailing around, sinkin' deeper and deeper in the mud, so I hear."

"Did you hear if the other boat lane is open?"

"From what I understand, traffic heading north is all backed up."

"I suppose that means ve von't be able to get past."

"It looks that way to me. If you want a bit of advice, Captain, I'd tie up for the night at Walnutport. Between the mishap and the weather, you'll never make it anywhere near Siegfried by the time the locks close."

"Vhat time are you shutting down?"

"Early. With the wind blowing this hard and the heavy flow, it's not safe to let boats into the river."

"Vhat time did ve enter the lock?"

The locktender glanced down at the log he kept of the times boats entered the lock. "Just after two o'clock."

Two o'clock was much too early for Manfred to call it a day. "Ve'll see vhat ve vill do vhen ve get to Valnutport. If ve cannot pass the accident, there's no use in trying to go any further. The mooring and stabling are good in Valnutport."

Rain stung Wilhelm's cheeks as he towed the *Onoko Princess* through the gates. Although, after his afternoon nap, he had made a resolution to keep going no matter how badly he felt, he was ready to quit again. He prayed his father would pay heed to the locktender and tie up in Walnutport so he could warm himself in front of the stove.

"Did ya hear that, Vil?" yelled Manfred, cupping his hands to make himself heard above the roar of the wind. "No traffic's goin' beyond Laurys Station."

"I heard, Pa."

Someone else heard also. The cabin hatch was open a crack and Annie was listening. "If we tie up at Walnutport, can we go see Aunt Maggie?"

Between Manfred's frustration at not being able to get as far as Siegfried, and the worsening weather, he was fit to be tied. "Who said ve're going to tie up at Valnutport, Miss Busybody! Close the hatch. You are letting rain into the cabin."

Two more drenching miles to Walnutport, and Manfred gave in. News of the tie-up had passed along the canal. With that and the bad weather, he was not the only boatman to call it a day. With the delay and hustle and bustle of boat traffic, he counted himself lucky to find a mooring space beyond the Anchor Hotel. Wilhelm also counted himself lucky. Max and Lucy got the last stall. Free of their load and munching on oats, they were as relieved as Wilhelm to get out of the rain. With the mules bedded for the night, his chores for the day were done. Giving his charges a pat on their rumps, he dashed back to the cabin to change into dry clothes.

Manfred bought a spare tow line at the lock store, then decided to go into the Anchor Hotel to see what was new. Fronting the canal, the Anchor was a hangout for canalers. Waterfront taverns and locks and lock stores were the canalers' "newspapers." They were places where boatmen exchanged gossip and passed on the latest news. Births, deaths, accidents, the quirks and escapades of canalers, the purchase of a mule or hiring of a driver were tidbits to be passed on and regurgitated at every lock, store and tavern along the canal. There were tales of valor and hardship, of scandal and crime, and, around many of the taverns and towns, tales of life's seamier side. The escapades of thieves, beggars and ladies of the night all became headline news as they plied their trades and often preyed on canalers.

Smoke filled the air and it was hard to see across the taproom. Boatmen and mule drivers sat around tables or stood by the bar, puffing on pipes, drinking and conversing. With only a few dollars in his pocket to last until he got paid, Manfred had to be sparing. Not a drinking man, he stood in line at the bar and ordered a glass of sarsaparilla. Although coal was a recognized currency on the canal, not everyone accepted it as payment. And this was the case with the Anchor's proprietor. With his business thriving, if he took coal as payment from his customers his cellar would have been overflowing by the end of the first week of the boating season.

"Hi Manny! How'd things go this winter?" asked Elias Yenser, a boat captain out of Easton and a casual acquaintance, coming over as Manfred walked toward the bar.

It was the usual question heard hundreds of times the first day of the season, and Manfred gave the usual grumbling canal answer. "Ve managed to keep bread on the table. Some ice-cutting and lumbering around Veissport helped out."

"So they're still cutting down trees up there!" said Yenser, a nature lover who hated to see the forests destroyed. "When will they ever stop!"

Manfred did not care for Yenser and his reply was curt. "Vithout timber, you vould not be sailing on this canal!"

It was no use talking about the wanton destruction of the forests up north with a man like Manfred whose ancestors had helped to build the canal, so Yenser changed the subject. "Did you just come down the canal?"

"Ja, ve picked up a load at Mauch Chunk yesterday, and have been on our vay ever since."

"Then ya must have crossed tow lines with that Welshman … what's his name? … Taffy Morgan."

"*Bestimmt,* ve crossed tow lines all right! The son of a gun broke mine!"

"How so?"

"He vas comin' along the slackwater, rantin' and ravin', havin' his driver vhip them poor scrawny mules into a gallop. Vhen he passed me, his boat vas veavin' from side to side so much, its rudder snapped my tow line."

"That isn't surprising. When he left here, he wasn't feelin' any pain. He threw a punch at Charlie Williams and broke his nose, and the bartender threw him out."

"Serves him right! I had to lay out good money for a spare tow line. The lock store wouldn't take coal. But he'll get his comeuppance."

"Better watch out. That Welshman's one to bear a grudge."

"If he lays a hand on me or any of my family, he'll know about it!" retorted Manfred, becoming more and more infuriated as he thought about what had happened. He could not wait until he got to Easton to report Morgan. "Vhat's the problem ahead?" he asked, changing the subject to calm himself down. "I hear from Amos Gruber at Guard Lock 3 that a mule team slipped into the canal."

"Yep," answered Yenser. "The bank gave way. The lead mule fell in and dragged the hind mule after it. The driver cut the traces and got a rope on the shaft mule, but he couldn't pull the lead mule out of the water. Traffic's backed up above and below the lock."

"Did the beast drown?"

"It did! It flailed around in a panic, sinking deeper and deeper until it was up to its hocks."

"Ja, I know all about that," observed Manfred. "Vonce them beasts fall into the canal, it's nigh impossible to haul 'em out alive."

Captain Yenser nodded.

"I lost a mule that vay vonce," Manfred reminisced, taking a draw on his pipe.

"How so?"

"I vas heading north out of Freemansburg when my lead animal — a great, strong behemoth of a beast — got spooked by a snake near Lock 14. It vas only a vater snake crossing the towpath, but the team shied and bolted. Before I knew vhat vas happenin', they vere up to their oxters in vater. It vas deep near the dam, and the lead beast drowned before ve could get to him. Ve managed to pull out his mate, but I had to borrow a mule from the locktender to finish the trip. I sent the beast back with a driver, and bought a new mule at Mauch Chunk. Cost me an arm and a leg for a beast that vas no good."

"You always get done in when you have to buy a mule along the canal."

"That's so! The ol' girl had not the strength to pull a sleigh, let alone a coal boat. I vas forced to get rid of her at the end of the line."

The bartender handed the two men their drinks. They took them over to a large round table at the side of the room where there were two empty seats. An air of comraderie pervaded the gathering of boatmen, with one exception. Nobody said a word to the black man seated in the corner, wearing a captain's hat.

The men exchanged news about their families and winter goings-on, and talked about the Company and their hopes for the new season. On the whole, the Lehigh Coal & Navigation Company came in for little criticism. Although hours at the helm were long, most canalers considered boating a great way to make a living and felt that the Company treated them fairly. In their minds, nothing compared with the tranquillity of the canal, the beat of mule hoofs on the towpath, and the challenge of the unpredictable river when the current in the slackwater was strong.

The black man listened to the conversation without contributing to it. It was as if he knew better than to join in. There was something about him Manfred liked. He looked honest and decent; as if life had treated him hard.

Manfred extended his hand across the table. "I'm Manny Oberfeldt."

"James Washington, sir," said the black man, shaking his hand.

"You're a boat captain, are you?"

"Yessir," he answered softly, afraid to show his pride, but feeling it.

He was the first Negro boat captain Manfred had seen on the canal, and Manfred was curious. "Is this your first season on the canal?"

"As cap'n, sir. Ah drove mules fer Captain Serfass fer nigh on twenty-five yars. When th' ol' man got so full of rheumatics he couldn't work no more, he gave me his boat. He said Ah deserved it. He hed no sons of his own t' hand it on to, ya see."

"He must have thought vell of you."

"He would hev bin a gonner if it wuzn't fer me."

"Vhat do you mean?"

"Ten yars ago, we wuz lockin' through Hazard's, below Bowmanstown, togetha with a Company boat. The Company cap'n went in to the lock askew an' got too close to us. Cap'n Serfass tried to pole th' otha boat over towards the lock wall, but the pole broke, an' he fell into the lock between the hulls of the two boats.

"The space wuz narra … barely wide enough fer a man. Water wuz churnin' in through the drop gates, and boilin' up real fast. Hazzard wuz in the wicket shanty and didn't realize what wuz goin' on. Ah hollered te him te close the drop gate wickets but, by the time he turned the crank, the lock wuz eight feet deep.

"The Company cap'n tried throwin' a rope, but he feared gittin' too near the side of his boat lest his weight bring the two boats togitha. Thar wuz only one thing left t' do. Ah had t' jump in afta th' ol' man."

"Ah climbed down the inside of the miter gates, tryin' not to disturb the water more than Ah hed te. The boats hed come closa togither an' Cap'n Serfass wuz gaspin' fer air. When Ah pushed ma way between them, Ah prayed to the Lord they would'nt smash togither. If they hed, me an' the cap'n would hev been flattened. But the Lord wuz with us. Ah dragged Cap'n Serfass te the bottom end of the lock an' Hazzard threw us a rope. Ah hitched it under the cap'n's armpits an' he hauled him up."

"That vas mighty brave of you."

"That's raight nice of you to say so, cap'n! But the ol' man treated me real well. It made no matter to him what color Ah wuz so long as Ah did ma job."

"I knew Serfass," mused Manfred. "He vas a fine man … a stickler for order. Everything on his boat vas spic and span. Not a thing vas out of place!"

Washington went back to sipping his coffee without replying. He had revealed more than he intended. He had to be careful. The hostility around the table told him that.

When the men began ordering a meal, Manfred got up. "My boy vil have finished bedding the mules, and Mary vill have the dinner ready. A good boating season to all!" he said, raising his glass in a salute before drinking the rest of his sarsaparilla.

When Manfred got up, Captain Washington arose to leave.

"To you and your family, Captain Oberfeldt," said Elias Yenser, tipping his glass. Although the boatmen around the table had hung on to every word of Washington's story, they ignored him and joined in the toast to Manfred.

"Look the other way, Ma and Annie," said Wilhelm as he prepared to take a much-needed wash-off and change into dry clothes. With no privacy in the cabin, everybody was used to such requests. Mary and Annie stopped making supper and turned their faces to the wall. When Wilhelm finished his toiletry and was respectable again, he gave them the word that it was all right to turn around. Still feeling the effects of the bad weather, he huddled near the stove, his mouth watering as the smell of tonight's "canal special" filled the cabin.

Dried navy beans were a canal staple. Mary had soaked some in water overnight to soften them. Now they were simmering on top of the stove in a piquant brown-sugar sauce. Cooking on a one-lid stove in the small cabin was a balancing act. With the expertise of a juggler, she took the pot of beans off the stove plate and replaced it with a frying pan full of sausages, arranged in two neat rows. As she juggled one pan with the other, she wished the weather would break so she could cook on deck on the two-burner stove.

Tired of hearing Mary complain about cooking on the small cabin stove, Manfred had bought a second-hand two-burner when he made extra money working at the ice house during an exceptionally hard winter, and set it up on deck. The shiny black stove was Mary's pride and joy. Unlike most canalers, who had to content themselves with cooking in the cramped confines of the cabin on the hottest of days, or struggle to move their small stove to the deck when the weather turned warm, she could cook outdoors or indoors. Whether Mary chose to cook in the cabin or on the deck, the crew could be assured of a good meal.

As Manfred stowed away the new towline, the delicious smell did not escape him, and he hurried to finish the job. "Mmmmm, sausages!" he sniffed hungrily as he came through the hatch, "They must be Tilly's. Did you get them at the lock store?"

Mary nodded.

"Tom Potter of Pleasant View Farm near Treichlers makes them. They're all-meat and no fillers! A lot of farmers stuff their sausages with grain, but not Tom!"

Mary was too busy managing the hot pots to comment. When the sausages were browned, she reheated the beans and put them on the table, along with freshly cut rounds of bread. Wilhelm reached for a piece of bread, but before he could help himself, his father stopped him. Before eating a bite, the crew had to bow their heads in prayer. Whenever the family was able to sit down for a meal together, saying Grace was a ritual. Having known what it was to do without, Manfred never forgot to thank the Lord for his blessings ... and, as an afterthought, ask for a safe and profitable passage.

When the last "amen" was said — and Manfred made sure he heard every one! — Mary served the meal, with the biggest portion going to her husband. The crew was ravenous, especially Wilhelm. He could not gobble it down fast enough.

"You're goin' to burn yourself, it's hot," warned his mother. "Take your time. There's plenty left for a second helping."

Annie was also in a hurry, but she had learned her lesson. Earlier in the week, she had bolted down her supper to go and see her grandparents. Now she took her time and waited until everyone had finished before asking, "Pa, can I go see Aunt Maggie?"

Her father's face turned beet red. "Vhat did I tell you before, Miss!" he exclaimed. "You're staying on board. Vith the veather this vay and a dead mule blocking the canal, ve've lost enough time already. Ve're getting undervay as soon as the locks open."

Manfred's idea of morning was everybody else's idea of night. The *Onoko Princess* would be waiting to enter Lock 24 well before four o'clock in the morning when Frank Kelchner opened the gates.

CHAPTER IV

Manfred lit the lamps before they set off. The rain had stopped but there was not a star to be seen in the sky. The *Onoko Princess* was the first boat out of Walnutport. Other crews were stirring, but they had not cast off. With nothing coming up the canal from Laurys Station, they were able to lock right through. At Lock 25, they were lucky again. As Lucy and Max clomped over the Bertsch Street Aqueduct past the huddle of neat, white clapboard houses fronting the canal at Lockport, Manfred was pleased with their headway.

Beyond the village lay the longest stretch of slackwater on the Lehigh River: a three-mile pool ending at Treichler's Dam. As they passed through the entry lock into the pool, they had yet to meet another boat. And they were already five locks and two and a half miles down the canal. With Manfred's conch shell warning the locktenders of their approach, passage through the locks had been swift. The drop gates were open, and the water was leveled by the time they reached the lock.

As they started along the three-mile stretch of river, daylight streaked orange on the eastern horizon. Yesterday's heavy rain had combined with the runoff from the mountains upstream and the undertow was strong. The new day's warmth mingled with yesterday's cold and a veil of mist swirled up from the water. Trapped by high escarpments to the west, the wind blew the *Onoko Princess* southward toward the dam and she rose and fell with the whitecaps topping the water's normally smooth surface.

"Hold tight to the harness. Keep the line taut and the mules ahead of the boat," hollered Manfred to Wilhelm.

But Wilhelm did not need to be reminded. By now, he knew enough to keep the mules up with the flow in the river. "I'm doing my best, Pa. Max and Lucy are moving at a trot right now."

Warmed by a pale sun as it rose above the horizon, the mist thinned out. What had been towering silhouettes to the west turned into steep, tree-covered hillsides. To the east, the river valley leveled and widened, giving way to farmland through which passed the well-traveled dirt turnpike to Allentown.

With most of the three-mile stretch of river behind them and Treichler's Dam approaching, it was time for Manfred to sound his conch shell. A deep sonorous boom answered him. The first boat in what would be a long line of boats coming up the canal that morning was about to pass. Manfred steered the *Onoko Princess* into the river, just far enough from the bank for her tow line to sink beneath the surface, and Wilhelm, as he had done so many times in the past two days, led the mules to the far side of the towpath. Keeping ahead of the drift, he stopped at precisely the right moment, and held tight to the harness.

A boat that was very different from a coal boat was coming up the slackwater toward them. She was a packet boat. After the railroad put packets out of business, she had been purchased for a song by a jobber to ship iron ore and pig iron along the canal.

The boom of her horn reached Annie in the cabin, and she scrambled up the ladder and ran starboard. "That sounds like a packet boat, Pa," she observed, recalling a treasured childhood experience.

"Ja, *liebchen*. It's the *Main Line* out of Allentown," answered Manfred who, having heard her horn over the years as she proudly carried passengers, was able to recognize it. "She's delivering iron. She'll probably end up in Mauch Chunk." In Manfred's world, Mauch Chunk was the center of the universe.

"Iron!" exclaimed Annie contemptuously. This wasn't what she had in mind.

As the packet boat drew parallel with the *Onoko Princess*'s bow, memories of the morning she and Grandpa Kintz had boarded the packet boat *Martha Washington* were as fresh in her mind as though it were yesterday. And yesterday was ten years ago. How could she ever forget? Festooned from stem to stern with colored Japanese lanterns, the *Martha Washington* had tied up at Weissport for the night.

She and her grandfather were delivering fruit and vegetables for Ziggy Koons, and they had to walk the length of the boat to reach the galley. The bow — which she judged to be the best part of the boat because it was the prettiest — was where the ladies slept. Separating the ladies' quarters from the gentlemen's was a storage area for cargo and luggage. Red velvet curtains cordoned off the sections, and everybody slept on retractable shelves. The lounge, which also served as a dining room for those who could afford to eat on board, lay beyond the gentlemen's quarters. And, way back in the stern, so that the smell of cooking would drift back along the canal and not disturb the passengers, was the galley where meals were prepared.

The day she and her grandpa boarded the *Martha Washington*, a party of well-off Philadelphians were enjoying a leisurely cruise to Mauch Chunk. Dressed in fine city clothes, they lounged in *chaises longues*, drank champagne from tall glasses, and smoked cigarettes from long holders, all the while looking curiously at the country people on the wharf, and the laborers toiling in the boat yard.

Carpetbaggers stood on the less fashionable rear of the boat, ready to go ashore at Mauch Chunk. Traveling from town to town and door to door, they hawked their wares from large baskets. Joining them on the stern were other people of scant means. Some were on their way to look for work in the prosperous town of Mauch Chunk while others rode the packet to visit an ailing relative or attend a wedding or funeral.

Grandpa Kintz had told her packet boats carried about twenty-five passengers. But the only people to be seen on the *Main Line* were the captain at the helm and the mule driver leading his three-mule team along the towpath. Looking tattered and raggedy as she crossed over the *Onoko Princess*'s tow line, the *Main Line* had seen better days. With no Chinese lanterns festooning her decks, or fine ladies and gentlemen to see, Annie opened the hatch. "I'll get you some coffee, Pa, if you like," she called as she went into the cabin.

Never a man who had to be asked twice if he wanted coffee, Manfred answered, "That vill be vonderful, *liebchen*." When Annie came back, he took the mug gratefully, and gave Wilhelm the signal to get going.

They had to wait for the Treichler's guard lock to empty. Two empty boats, ascending the canal, bobbed in the rising lock. Half a dozen others were lined up below the miter gates, waiting to follow them into the long stretch of slackwater north of the dam.

"See those islands, Vil," said Manfred, as the *Onoko Princess* stopped alongside several small islands off the river bank. "They are man-made." Manfred felt it was his duty to point out everything of significance along the canal, with Wilhelm going to be a boat captain one day. Besides, without passing on knowledge, how would future generations know what happened in the past?

Wilhelm looked to where his father was pointing. "You mean, those teeny islands weren't always there, Pa?"

"That's right! Vhen Josiah Vhite's crew vas busy making river navigable in the days before the canal vas built, they piled up dirt and rocks offshore to guide them arks into the bear trap locks. They did not want the ark trains to beach themselves on the river bank."

"But the islands are covered with trees."

"Mother Nature did that. It's been thirty-three years since them bear traps vere used … long enough for a whole forest to grow."

"I suppose," said Wilhelm. He sat and thought a minute, then asked, "What were the arks made of?"

"Logs strung together vith ropes and chains. Some of them had a shelter for the oarsmen. But, vith the river the vay it vas in them days, them oarsmen did not have any time to shelter. Vhen them arks vere moving, they darsen't take their hands off the oars."

"I bet they darsen't!" agreed Wilhelm, imagining what a struggle it must have been to keep even one ark afloat, let alone a whole train.

"And, do you know something else?" continued Manfred. "Them arks could only travel vone vay vith the current. They could not come back up the river."

"If they couldn't come back up the river, Pa, what did they do with the arks when they got to Philadelphia?"

"They vere broken up. The hardvare, that held the timbers together, vas brought back to Mauch Chunk by horse and wagon to be used again, and the lumber vas sold to builders in the big city."

"No wonder there aren't many trees around Mauch Chunk if a new ark had to be built every time they shipped a load of coal down the river!"

"Ja, no vonder! It vas the builders that profited from them arks. Mauch Chunkers joke that half the buildings in Philadelphia are made out of Mauch Chunk vood," said Manfred, tamping tobacco into the bowl of his pipe and lighting it. It was his signal that the story was over.

Wilhelm liked nothing better than listening to his father's tales. He loved stories about the brave pioneers who settled the wilderness, and the Lenape and Iroquois Indians who made life so dangerous for them. Most of all, he loved to hear about the river and the men who sailed on it. If Josiah White and his partner, Erskine Hazard, had not tamed the Lehigh River and built the canal, and if men, like his own ancestors, had not carried coal to market, America would still be a backwoods country.

"Hey, stop dreaming!" shouted Manfred, as the locktender motioned them forward. It was time to move on. "Put them beasts through their paces. Ve can pass right through the lock after those two boats come out."

The two Lehigh Coal & Navigation coal boats passed through the guard lock's upper miter gate into the slackwater above the dam. With the water in the lock already leveled, the *Onoko Princess* replaced them inside. She was alone in the chamber. No other boat from Walnutport had made its way this far down the canal. The same could not be said of boats traveling in the opposite direction. One after the other they passed over the *Onoko Princess*'s tow line on their way up to Mauch Chunk to load. Having lost half a day while the dead mule was cleared from the canal, their captains and drivers were intent on making up for lost time.

A short length of canal, another stretch of slackwater and the *Onoko Princess* reached the guard lock at the Slate Dam above Laurys Station. Wilhelm was first to see the dead mule. It lay sprawled grotesquely in a field above the towpath. Its dappled coat muddied, nostrils flared, teeth clenched in an everlasting smile, it was waiting for the knacker to haul it away. The knacker would sell its hide to a cobbler, and do goodness knows what with the meat. The dead mule's partner was more fortunate. Shaken but uninjured, surviving a nightmare it would never forget, it would get a new team mate and be in service along the towpath the next day.

Situated where the canal meets the Lehigh River, Laury's Station was a lively village that thrived with the building of the canal. Its boatyard reminded Wilhelm of Weissport's. Men were hard at work hammering, planing and caulking upended boats, and building new ones. At the moorings on the canal banks, boats of every description were tied up. Their crews crowded the waterfront in search of a hot meal or a drink in one of the local taverns, or bought feed for their mules or took on provisions at the lock store. The lock store at Laury's Station was known up and down the canal for selling everything from freshly baked bread to a new pair of shoes.

That morning Wilhelm had been on the canal for over six miles, and he was tired. But, after yesterday, he thought twice about telling his father. For a few pennies a day and nights spent sleeping on deck, many an out-of-work youth would be more than happy to take his place on the towpath. All Wilhelm could do was pray that his father would need something at the lock store so he could get off his tired feet for a while. But, today, Manfred had no intention of stopping.

As Wilhelm trudged on, Mary was standing on the deck, looking concerned. Once again, it was she who spoke up. "Don't you think it's about time, Manny," she said quietly, "that you give Wilhelm a break?"

"You pamper that boy too much," Manfred answered brusquely.

"But he's been on the towpath ever since we left Walnutport."

Manfred threw up his hands in despair. "Vhat can anybody do vith a mother like you? Tell Annie to svitch places at the next lock. And I don't vant to hear any of her bellyaching!"

He was all business this morning. He had lost enough time yesterday. If they were to cover twenty-five miles by the time the locks closed, they would have to keep going. With the season just started and the weather still wintry, twenty-five miles was a lofty goal. But, if the family worked in shifts, they could make it. Annie or Mary could spell Wilhelm if he got tired, and if Manfred needed a break, Mary could take over the tiller. The mules were hardy. Provided they were fed every four hours, they could work a straight eighteen-hour day. If they kept going without interruption until the locks closed, they should make it to Freemansburg, ten miles short of the canal terminus at Easton. Although Annie liked to drive the mules only when she felt like it, she knew there was no balking today. When the *Onoko Princess* reached the mule bridge at Lock 32, without a word of complaint she switched places with Wilhelm.

Wilhelm was back on the towpath at Siegfried Lock, two miles down the canal. Refreshed, he quickened the place of the mules, hastening to get to their destination. As they left the shelter of the mountains and headed south, the landscape began to change. Farmland gave way to factories and coal yards. With the introduction of the anthracite-fired blast furnace and plentiful supplies of anthracite coal in the hills to the north, small towns in the lower Lehigh Valley were industrializing rapidly. Factories and mills along the canal were manufacturing everything from pig iron to machinery and railroad and farming equipment.

A three-span wooden aqueduct took the *Onoko Princess* across the Hokendauqua Creek. Another two miles and they would reach Catasauqua, a town made prosperous by its iron works. It was at Catasauqua, in 1840, that Welshman David Thomas had built America's first anthracite-fired blast furnace. The new furnace was so successful, four more were soon built. Catasauqua became such a thriving iron-manufacturing center, it later became known as the "Iron Borough."

It was Mary, not Manfred, who ordered the children to change places at Catasauqua, under the pretext that Wilhelm needed his supper, when she saw his feet begin to drag. They were approaching Allentown, another of the Lehigh Valley's mushrooming industrial towns. By the time the Lehigh Canal was finished in 1829, Allentown was already a prosperous market town and county seat. With the introduction of the anthracite-fired blast furnace, it became a prime iron-manufacturing center like Catasauqua. Furnaces churned out pig iron, rolling mills and foundries produced rails, boilers, spikes and axles for the railroad, and factories made everything imaginable out of iron from machine parts to pots and pans.

Wilhelm sat on his favorite perch on the coal hatches, wolfing down split pea soup as he watched his father navigate. Oil lamps lit up the stern, bow and cabin of the *Onoko Princess* as she made her way down the canal. Along the banks, the iron furnaces never stopped working, day or night. Their red glow lit up the night, silhouetting the endless brick factories and tin-roofed warehouses that had sprung up around them. Smoke belched high in the air from tall chimneys, the moving plumes floating lazily across the black sky. The landscape was bleak and ugly; the fumes, noxious. And Wilhelm was filled with longing for the mountains.

"Do you think the whole Lehigh Valley will be nothing but factories one day, Pa?" he asked wistfully.

"That's something I cannot answer, son. Every time ve pass this way, a new factory has been built. Pretty soon, ve von't have to go all the vay to Bristol vith our load. Ve vill be dropping it off here in the lower Lehigh Valley."

"If they keep on building and building there won't be anywhere for wild animals to live." Wilhelm was thinking that, this trip, he hadn't seen any muskrats swimming frantically to get out of the way of the *Onoko Princess*.

"Vell, son," replied his father philosophically, "that's the price ve have to pay for progress. Vithout those hungry furnaces, ve vould not be hauling coal, and vithout the factories, people vould not have the things that make life easier. Remember grandpa? He hadn't the things ve have today."

"Do you think Weissport will be full of factories one day?"

"You never can tell, son. Who would have thought, a hunert years ago, that coal vould be passing along a canal like this? And that railroads vould be hauling freight and passengers all over the country? If ve vant to catch up vith the Old Countries, ve still have vork to do. The industrial revolution has been going on there for more than a century."

"Will America ever catch up, Pa?"

"Ja, this great country vill catch up vith the Old Countries, and pass them! There is nothing ve cannot do in America. Ve are blessed with so many natural resources. The trouble is ve're only beginning to use them. Take this canal. Before it vas built, not much coal got to market by them bear traps. A lot of it landed in the river. And think of the timber that vas vasted vhen them arks could only make a vone-vay trip. Do you know, son, before Josiah Vhite built them bear traps, factory owners had to get bituminous coal all the vay from Virginia? And that coal vas real soft. It vas not much good for anything!"

"No, Pa, I didn't."

"Before this canal vas built, the deposits of anthracite in the mountains of eastern Pennsylvania vere pretty nigh useless. There simply vas no vay to get the coal to market," he said, taking out his pipe and tapping it on the deck to clear out the old tobacco before refilling it.

Wilhelm sensed the history lesson had ended. It was about time for him to get back on the towpath.

Annie took the *Onoko Princess* through Kimmet's Lock and entered the slackwater pool that formed Lehigh Port at Allentown. Although she would have much preferred to be listening to her father's stories, she was no novice on the towpath. She could put the mules through their paces as well as any mule driver, be he man or boy. Her father never had to tell her where to stop, or when to unhook the tow line. Her actions were instinctive and unfailingly correct.

Lehigh Port was on the opposite side of the Lehigh from the canal, but the slackwater pool made both sides of the river navigable. If a boatman wished to reach the port's wharves and warehouses, he would pole his boat across the water. With no deliveries to the port on this trip, Annie followed the towpath and took the *Onoko Princess* into Guard Lock 7 at the Allentown Dam.

At last came the change of command. And not a moment too soon for Annie. "Take over, Vil," ordered Manfred. "Ve've just three and a half miles to go to Bethlehem. Ve're stopping there for the night, and I vant you to have the experience of tying up."

As Annie climbed on board at the Guard Lock, all she could think about was curling up in her feather comforter and going to sleep. She had traded places with Wilhelm twice in the sixteen miles stretch between Walnutport and Allentown. Compared to Wilhelm's two six-mile stints on the towpath, she had walked just over four miles. She had asked her father if she could ride Lucy when she got back on the towpath at Catasauqua, but he had refused. Anyone who drove Manfred Oberfeldt's mules could ride them only when the *Onoko Princess* was empty.

Below the dam, a covered bridge connected one part of Saeger's Flour Mill to another part on the other side of the canal. This mill had been built the year the canal was finished, and was the only mill that straddled the canal. Soon a sense of tranquility, interrupted briefly by a clanking train hauling anthracite, returned to the landscape after the noisy furnaces, foundries and factories, as a bend took the Lehigh River eastward. Just short of seventeen miles downstream, it would mingle its waters with the broad Delaware at Easton.

Except when the *Onoko Princess* passed through locks or paused to let another boat by, they had not stopped all day. The only rest the mules got were ten- or fifteen-minute breaks when they were unhitched and fed at the locks. By now, Max and Lucy's fatigue was evident. The tow line was dragging in the water. A fresh driver brought a new hustle. And Wilhelm encouraged them on. Exhausted or not, they still had to take the *Onoko Princess* across the Monocacy Creek Aqueduct to her mooring near Lock 43, on the other side of Bethlehem.

Without a doubt, Bethlehem was the most mysterious and intriguing town in the lower Lehigh Valley. It was established by Moravians in 1741 on the banks of the Monocacy Creek, long before the canal was built. The Moravians were a religious sect that originated in the old countries of Moravia and Bohemia. When Count Zinzendorf, the leader of the church, ministered to his flock on Christmas Eve, he named the settlement "Bethlehem" in honor of Jesus' birthplace. Members of the sect were fed, clothed and housed from a common fund. Property belonged to the community. For many decades the Moravians cared for their own people and preached to Indians and other European settlers, converting many to their beliefs. Believing that their devout way of life would be threatened if the Lehigh Canal were built, they protested its construction. When an epidemic of typhoid fever broke out as the canal was being dug, they blamed it on the newly turned earth. But progress is progress and, for the most part, inevitable. With the completion of the canal, the introduction of the latest iron-making technology from Wales, and a ready supply of anthracite coal, their way of life was being invaded.

Lock 43 was less than half a mile beyond Bethlehem, but the last part of the day's run seemed never-ending — even to Manfred. When they reached the other side of the lock, he signaled Wilhelm to stop and tie up the *Onoko Princess*. With no stabling nearby, Wilhelm fed the mules and tethered them to a tree at the side of the towpath. As father and son turned in for the night, Manfred praised God that the day had been uneventful.

CHAPTER V

The *Onoko Princess* got underway next morning before any other boats cast off. Manfred's goal was to make it to Easton by daylight. It had been three days since Taffy Morgan broke his tow line, and he had not forgotten. His first order of business was to report the incident.

The weather mirrored the previous day. Fog drifted skyward from the river before the sun rose, and Manfred had to keep blowing his conch shell. Its boom swept eerily through the darkness along the canal. But nothing was more eerie than the sound that answered it.

"*Helloooooooooooo, hellooooooooooooooo.*" The call crescendoed into a piercing screech, startling Wilhelm out of his skin.

Scared to death, he hollered to his father. "What's that? It sounds like a ghost!"

"It is nothing to be afraid of, son," said Manfred, laughing. "If you had been around these parts long enough, you vould know who it is. It is Lizzie Reinhart, on her vay to the flour mill in her boat. Everybody in these parts vill tell you Lizzie hollers so loud, she does not need a boat horn to let you know vhere she is!"

Lizzie Reinhart had delivered a load of flour in Easton and was coming back up the canal. Although, on occasion, canal wives took over the helm for their husbands, Lizzie was captain of her own boat. Left with six young children and a boat when her husband passed away suddenly several years ago, she was a veritable Mother Hubbard. Summer and winter she brought up her brood of six children on the boat. When the canals were open, she made her living picking up grain from farmers and delivering flour for the Freemansburg Mill. In winter, her brood did not attend school like most of the other canal children. Instead, she packed them off to work doing any odd job she could find for them, while she lived like a queen on her boat.

With twelve-year-old Danny leading the mules, Lizzie pulled in to the wharf next to the Freemansburg Mill. Oil lamps lit up the tall building. The miller and his helpers were already hard at work. An enormous wooden water wheel, nearly as high as the mill, creaked and groaned as it turned the machinery that ground wheat into flour. With a fast-growing population in the lower Lehigh Valley and small villages and towns springing up along the top end of the Delaware Canal,

Lizzie Reinhart had no shortage of customers.

Mary took over for Wilhelm at Lock 46. It was time for him to have breakfast. Known locally as "Hope Lock," Lock 46 was an outlet lock leading into the seventh and next-to-last stretch of Lehigh River slackwater before Easton. Mary's stint on the towpath was short. Wilhelm had hardly finished the egg Annie had fried for him when his father hollered for him to change places. Manfred wanted his new mule driver to experience crossing Change Bridge and taking the *Onoko Princess* into the boat basin at Easton. If things went smoothly, this meant they had another two hours on the towpath.

Two and a half miles beyond Hope Lock, Change Bridge, just above Chain Dam, presented a new challenge. Chain Dam was the eighth dam on the Lehigh River, and the first place where the towpath crossed the river since it left Mauch Chunk. For the next three miles, the towpath would follow an easterly course along the south bank to the basin at Easton.

Wilhelm led the mules across the causeway to Smiths Island and along the shoreline to the Change Bridge with the *Onoko Princess* in tow. The swaybacked iron bridge, constructed with wire rope from the Lehigh Coal & Navigation Company's factory in Mauch Chunk, was built in 1857 to do away with the dangerous river crossing that had existed there ever since the canal was built. The bridge shuddered as Wilhelm and the mules stepped out onto it. Although Max and Lucy had crossed the swaying structure hundreds of times towing a loaded boat, they picked their way across it tentatively, disliking the tow line trailing along the top of the railing and the feeling of being off firm ground. When they reached the other side, the *Onoko Princess* had crossed the river with them, but her bow was facing the bank. Instructing Wilhelm to drive the mules forward slowly, he worked the tiller to turn her. In no time the *Onoko Princess* was riding parallel with the river bank, her bow heading downstream. She was ready to resume her journey to Easton. Soon she locked through Guard Lock 8, and a mile later she passed by the furnaces of the Glendon Iron Company, which were built along the edge of the canal. Annie knew this busy area and stayed in the cabin, away from the fumes and acrid odors. Another mile and they reached Abbott Street. Here, the canal was elevated above the machine shops, forges and factories that lined the river. The canal company sold the factories water from the canal, which rushed down sluiceways to provide power for the machinery. Two locks close to-gether dropped them down to the level of the river again, and into the slackwater behind the Easton Dam. Easton, the bustling terminus of the Lehigh Canal's Lower Grand Section, was only a mile ahead.

As Wilhelm led Lucy and Max into the basin and helped his father search for a mooring place, he was reminded of the day, last spring, when he and his father went fishing. It was shad season on the Delaware. And — a miracle — his father had taken the afternoon off. He remembered how much he enjoyed himself. And how much all of them — except Annie — had enjoyed the eight fat shad he and his father caught.

Laid out by the agents of William Penn in the 1750s, Easton was an important transportation center from Colonial times due to its location at the Forks of the Delaware. This was the poetic name given to the confluence of the Lehigh and Delaware rivers. By 1796, stage coaches were making regular trips to Philadelphia, and a turnpike between Easton and Wilkes-Barre was being planned.

Easton's prosperity grew when Josiah White's bear trap locks made it possible to transport anthracite coal on a one-way trip down the Lehigh River, and increased with the building of three canals which either began or terminated at the Forks of the Delaware. The first to be built was the Lehigh Canal. When it opened in 1829, coal transportation between Mauch Chunk and Easton was no longer subject to the whims of the Lehigh River. Coal could be transported safely by boat along a regulated waterway. In 1832, the Morris Canal opened across the Delaware River from Easton. It carried coal from Phillipsburg across New Jersey to Newark and New York City, and brought iron ore from the New Jersey mines to the furnaces of the Lehigh Valley. The third canal to be opened was the Delaware Canal. Although construction began in the fall of 1828, it was so poorly built it did not open to boat traffic until 1834. Owned by the State of Pennsylvania, it took the engineering skills of Josiah White and Erskine Hazard to make it watertight and provide it with an adequate water supply. With the completion of the three canals coal, arriving at Easton by way of the Lehigh Canal, could be shipped to Philadelphia along the Delaware Canal, and to New York along the Morris Canal. In 1855, the Lehigh Valley Railroad between Easton and Mauch Chunk added to the town's importance as a coal transportation center.

Although Manfred had observed the rapid growth of Allentown over the past ten years, with industries springing up along the river and an explosion of new residents, Easton was still the largest town through which the Oberfeldts passed on their journeys along the canals. With plentiful supplies of anthracite coal and waterpower, industry mushroomed along the two rivers and the Lehigh Canal, especially on the long island between the canal and the river which started at Chain Dam and ended at the toll collector's office. Here the Company sold water from the canal to power a variety of industries and a busy, thriving industrial sector had developed. Factories, mills, warehouses, wharves, mule stables, taverns, shops, lodging houses, and houses of ill repute all shared the streets around the wide basin. The scene was one of activity and noise. Boatmen replaced tow lines and fed their mules, boat horns sounded off the escarpments and answered one another across the two rivers, water wheels groaned, machinery turned, steam engines shunted coal wagons onto sidings, and passengers scurried to catch the next train. The frenzied interchange of commerce between Easton and Phillipsburg made its own special sound. Echoing through the wooden tunnel of Timothy Palmer's covered bridge across the Delaware, the clip clop of horses' hooves and the rumble of wagon and carriage wheels proclaimed the close connection between the two canal towns.

The row houses of the workers were relegated to the dismal streets of Snufftown, the popular name for the village of Williamsport, which had grown up along the canal on the south side of the Lehigh River across from Easton. In Easton, the homes of the well-to-do bordered Centre Square and lined Third Street and Fourth Street. Shops along Northampton Street displayed delicacies from New York and Philadelphia and the latest in European fashions. On market days, local Pennsylvania German farmers filled the square. Penurious to the hilt, anything they could bring in from the countryside that would make them as much as a penny was for sale.

In this conglomeration of commerce, the canal boatmen were not forgotten. Unwilling to spend the time walking from the boat basin to the center of town — or, perhaps, unwilling to pay the higher prices there — they made a hasty visit to Snufftown. Everything a boatman needed for his trip along one of the canals, or for a rollicking evening in town, could be found in this rundown waterfront community.

Manfred laid down the makeshift gangplank. Determined to spend as little time as possible in port, he assigned an errand to each family member. The women were to shop for whatever food supplies were needed, Wilhelm was to buy feed for the mules, and, *bestimmt*, he would walk upstream to the Company office near the outlet lock and take care of that scoundrel Morgan.

Unlike Wilhelm, Annie was in her element in the bustling town. She stood on deck of the *Onoko Princess* preening and tying a ribbon in her blowing hair, impatient to get off. Thirteen, going on fourteen, she was at the age when she liked to be noticed. Wishing to be alone to cast a flirtatious glance at an admirer, she offered, "I'll get the bread, Ma, while you go to the butcher's." Then, being Annie, she added what she knew her father liked to hear, "That way, we'll save time."

At first, Mary hesitated. She did not like her children, especially a young girl like Annie, wandering about the waterfront alone. Too many questionable characters hung out at Snufftown, waiting to take advantage of the gullible. But Annie was right. Going their separate ways would save time. "Well, all right!" she conceded reluctantly, "but be careful. And don't forget what I told you."

As if Annie could! Her mother was constantly warning her and Wilhelm about the seedy characters who inhabited the waterfront. She warned them about cheats, who swindled unsuspecting canalers for whatever they could get, and thieves, who could pick a boatman's pocket without his knowing it. She warned them about drunks, about bad men who preyed on unsuspecting children, and, overcoming her modesty, she told them about the scantily clad women who lured boatmen for money into houses of ill repute.

Annie dismissed the parade of seedy characters as if they were figments of her mother's imagination. "I'll be fine, Ma!" Then, looking to see what her mother's response would be, she added softly, "Can I come back by way of Watkins?"

Watkins was the nearest thing to a general store in Snufftown. It sold everything from hair ribbons and combs to yard goods, tobacco and Dutch candy sticks. Even though Annie knew the only thing she could buy was bread, she liked to see what was new.

Mary hesitated. Then, thinking it would not hurt for Annie to make a quick detour, added "Well, all right!" It was daylight and the waterfront was crowded. With so many about, there was little occasion for her to come to harm. "Don't spend the change on Dutch candysticks," she warned. "And be back in fifteen minutes. Your father is in no mood to be delayed."

Annie and her father were first off the boat. They set out along the quayside together, then went their separate ways. She took a side street to the bakery. He headed back up the canal to the Navigation Company office.

When Manfred entered, the office was full of private boatmen paying tolls for using the canal. Along with Mauch Chunk on the Lehigh Canal, and New Hope and Bristol on the Delaware Canal, tolls were collected at Easton. Several boat captains were ahead of him, and he was annoyed at having to stand in line. For one thing, he was in a hurry and, for another, he wanted to air his grievance in private. Standing back, he waited until the last toll payer left.

"How's things with you and your family, Manny?" asked Pete Clark, extending his hand across a large oak desk as Manfred came forward.

Like most boatmen, Manfred had a habit of complaining even when things were going well. It was almost as if saying that something was right would invite something to go wrong. "Vell, if only ve could keep goin' along this ol' ditch vithout runnin' into trouble, ve'd be all right." When Manfred was disgusted, he called the canal a ditch. "The trouble is there's alvays something to stop us boatmen from getting vhere ve vant to go. The vind and rain vere terrible after ve got to the Lehigh Gap. And, if that vasn't bad enough, ve couldn't go on past Valnutport. Some stupid driver let his mule team tumble into the ditch near Laurys. Between the veather and the accident, ve lost half a day. It has been four days since ve set out and ve're only as far as Easton."

"I heard about the accident," said Pete Clark, "but I don't guess that's why you're here, Manny."

"No! I'm here to report that Velsh varmint."

"You mean Morgan?"

"Ja, he is actin' up again."

"What's he up to this time? I heard he was thrown out of the Anchor for causing a riot." Nothing went on along the canal without everybody knowing it, even the authorities. And, by Clark's manner, Manfred suspected he already knew about the broken the tow line.

"Ja, he vas drunk. Ve met him afterwards … racin' along the slackwater above Bowmanstown. That son of a gun vas goin' so fast in the svell, he ripped off my line and left us flounderin' in the river."

"You're the third boatman to complain about him, and the season's only started."

"That man's a menace, Pete … cussin' at his driver, makin' him flog them poor beasts 'til their hides vere red raw. His boat vas all over the river. Ve vere lucky it did not slam into us."

"I heard, the cruelty inspectors were after him already."

"No vonder, the vay the driver was beating them poor beasts … they're like skeletons. How does the varmint think he can keep 'em goin' if he starves 'em? I judge, they're lucky if they get one bag of feed a day. I tell you, Pete, you had better get that man off the canal before somebody gets hurt."

"A week's suspension should teach him a lesson."

"A veek! Is that all you're goin' to give him?"

"It's the best I can do! With the season just startin' and coal all backed up at the mines, we need every boat we can get to move it."

"He deserves more time off than a veek!"

"You're right, but orders is orders! I'll pass word to locktender German at the guard lock to stop him before he gets into the Delaware Canal."

Manfred left the Navigation office disillusioned. He was uneasy about squealing on a fellow canaler, but he was responsible for the boat under his command. If Morgan continued to sail the canal like a drunken cowboy, somewhere, somehow, someone was going to get hurt. To cheer himself up, he went into the tobacconist's for a chaw, and stopped to say hello to a few boatmen on the way to the boat. By the time he got back, Mary was putting the beef roast she had bought for Sunday dinner in the feed bin for Wilhelm to cover with oats. As well as holding mule feed, the feed bin was the canalers' ice box. With the grain acting as an insulator to keep food cold in hot weather, the feed bin was where boatmen stored perishables.

"Vhere's Annie?" asked Manfred, looking about him.

"She must be waiting for the bread to come out of the oven," answered Mary evasively.

"She must be bakin' it, you mean! That girl is alvays late!"

"I'll go look for her, if you like," volunteered Mary, not wanting Annie to get into trouble.

"No need! Here she comes!" said Manfred, catching a glimpse of Annie racing

The ribbon had fallen out of her hair, and she looked upset.

dockside. Looking disheveled, she ran across the gangplank as if something were after her. The ribbon had fallen out of her hair, and she looked upset.

"Vhat's wrong with you?" asked Manfred, noticing her agitated state.

"Nothing, Pa," she said, handing the bread to her mother and making a break for the cabin.

"Come back here this minute, *fräulein*!"

She hesitated, but came back.

Putting his hand on her shoulders, Manfred turned her around to face him. "You're not telling me the truth, young lady. I vant to know vhat is wrong."

Annie began to cry. "It was Taffy Morgan, Pa."

"Vhat do you mean, Taffy Morgan?"

Manfred was taken aback. He hadn't expected Morgan to get this far. But, with the *Onoko Princess* being delayed a day on account of the dead mule, and knowing how Morgan had no regard for the two and a half mile an hour speed limit, he shouldn't have been surprised. "Vhat happened?" he asked.

"He grabbed my arm and dragged me into Tilghman Alley."

"He did vhat?"

"He saw you walking down the towpath towards the Navigation office and wanted to know where you were going."

"Did you tell him?"

"No! I said I didn't know."

"Vhat else did he do?" asked Manfred suspiciously. He would not put anything past a drunk like Morgan, especially where it concerned his pretty, young daughter.

"Nothing! When I said I didn't know where you were, he let go, and told me that you'd better not get him suspended, or we'd all know about it."

"It's too late! Vhen he goes through the Delavare guard lock, he'll be off the canal for a veek. And, if he manages to slip through, they'll be on the lookout for him all the vay to Bristol."

If Taffy Morgan said or did anything else to Annie, she was not talking. Free of her father's grip, she fled to the comfort of her bunk.

CHAPTER VI

The Delaware Canal was completed by the State of Pennsylvania in 1832 but, before it could open, the State had to call on Josiah White and his crew to make the sand and gravel bottom watertight and raise the Easton Dam to increase the water supply. It opened in 1834. Unlike the Lehigh Canal, slackwater was not used in the navigation. Separated from the Delaware River by a strip of land, then swinging inland, the canal ran uninterrupted for sixty miles. Twenty-four lift locks overcame the one hundred and eighty-foot drop in elevation between Easton and Bristol. By contrast, the Lehigh Canal needed forty-nine standard locks and eight guard locks to overcome the three hundred and fifty-three-foot drop in elevation over its forty-six miles. With fewer locks and longer levels, boatmen preferred the Delaware Canal. Although they grumbled about the small size of its locks, most of which could only hold only one boat, they were able to cover the longer distance in a shorter time. Manfred was no different from the rest of the boatmen. He expected to breeze down to Bristol in three days.

Before casting off, the Oberfeldts ate a quick lunch together. Then, with the mules hitched, the *Onoko Princess* headed for the Easton Dam, a fourteen-foot-high barricade at the entrance to the Delaware Canal. Along with a wing dam at New Hope, the Easton Dam supplied water to the canal.

A massive railroad bridge crossed the Delaware River to New Jersey at the start of the canal. As they waited their turn to enter the guard lock, Mary and Annie joined Manfred on deck, watching a train loaded with coal crossing over the lock.

As the locktender came to the head of the lock to change levels, Manfred called out, "Did Captain Morgan pass this vay?"

"Yes," the locktender replied, "it must be about a half hour since he locked through. "Then noting Manfred looked upset, he asked, "Did you want to see him, Captain Oberfeldt?"

"Nein! I just vondered if he passed this vay."

Manfred had learned what he wanted from the brief exchange. Word of Morgan's suspension had not reached the locktender. The varmint had escaped into the Delaware Canal and was ahead of them.

The Delaware Canal was clogged with boats as the *Onoko Princess* passed through the guard lock on her way to Bristol. It was that time of year. Coal boats were lined up fore and aft, impatient to drop off their loads, and empties were racing to Mauch Chunk to fill up their holds with the first load of the season. It was a scene of hustle, noise and frustration. Tow lines had to be crossed and locks passed through. Along the turnpike that followed the river to the great city of Philadelphia, once the capital of America, the hamlets and villages bustled with activity. Like the canal, they were awakening from their winter sleep. The sun was shining. It was warm for March. Spring was just around the corner.

A sunny afternoon was an opportunity not to miss. And Mary decided to wash clothes. The captain of a two-man crew usually paid a locktender's wife a bag of coal to do his laundry. He dropped off his clothes on the way up the canal and they were washed, dried, ironed, and ready to be picked up by the time he came back. But when women were part of a boat crew, one of their duties was to do the wash.

The drinking water in the barrel was too precious to use for wash so Mary tied a rope to the handle of a bucket and scooped up water from the canal. She filled the two wooden wash tubs Manfred had made from an old water barrel that he had sawed in half. One was for washing; the other for rinsing. Doing the wash was a mechanical operation. On board the *Onoko Princess*, mother and daughter were a team. Mary did the scrubbing; Annie did the rinsing. Lathering the clothes with homemade brown soap, Mary rubbed them up and down on a washboard to get out some of the dirt before putting them in the tub of soapy water. When the tub was full, she pounded them with a wooden wash poster, then wrung out as much soapy water as she could before giving them to Annie to rinse and hang out to dry on the line, strung across the deck between two wooden poles. Back and forth — wash, squeeze, rinse, squeeze, hang out — mother and daughter worked in unison until the wash was done. The work was backbreaking. It left them exhausted. But when Annie pegged the last garment to the line, if she thought she was finished for the day, she wasn't. On a coal boat, work did not end when one job was done. Not wishing to waste the soapy water, Mary gave Annie the job she dreaded most. She had to empty and wash out the commode.

Unlike most canalers who threw human waste overboard, Manfred forbade his crew to contaminate the waterway. He insisted that the slop pail be emptied in a lockside privy and not in the canal. Between the run-off from backyard privies, and human waste dumped into the water by boatman, the canal was turning into a sewer.

Like everything she did, Annie had her own way of emptying the commode. Lockside double-seaters were putrid with so much boat traffic going back and forth along the canals. To keep out the smell, she wet a bandanna and tied it over her nose and mouth before going into the privy to empty the slop pail. She was in and out in a flash. Back on board, she scoured the pail with the leftover soapy water, and put it on deck to dry. Then, scrubbing her hands at the water barrel until they were red-raw, she stretched out to rest on top of the equipment locker near her father.

"How far are we going today, Pa?" she asked as she lay watching the clouds merge and break apart into a thousand curious shapes.

"Oh, about another twelve miles," he answered, drawing contentedly on his pipe, surveying the canal for anything untoward, and taking in the scenery. "That vill put us at Narrows Lock by the time the gates close."

"Oh," she answered. As she relaxed to the gentle sway of the boat, Wilhelm was stepping along briskly in unison with the mules' steady clip clop. Following the well-trodden towpath, Lucy and Max knew exactly when and where to stop. There was no need for him to hold on to the harness in the serenity of the countryside. Restrained by the loaded boat, come what may, the mules were in no position to bolt.

Traffic going north was heavy and the *Onoko Princess* had to pull over several times between locks to let ascending boats pass. By now, passing was routine to Wilhelm. Move Lucy and Max to the far side of the towpath, drop the line and give the empty boat the right of way. The whole thing was over so quickly, it seemed as if they never stopped at all.

Manfred raised the conch shell to his lips to trumpet their arrival. He could see the next lock in the distance along the ruler-straight canal. "That's Ground Hog Lock, Annie. Ve're a half-mile from Raubsville."

Annie looked ahead to where her father was pointing. "Ground Hog Lock," she repeated. "Do they call it Groundhog Lock because there are a lot of groundhogs there?"

"There are not too many now! Hunters took care of that. But, vonce, the place vas overrun vith them. They kept on breedin' and breedin' until there vere so many, they migrated to the island in the middle of the river. There, they formed such a colony, the settlers named the island Ground Hog Island."

"How did they get across the river?"

"I suppose they svam or crossed vhen the vater vas low."

Annie shaded her eyes and searched the river. "I don't see the island, Pa."

"You cannot see it from here, *liebchen*. You vill have to vait until ve are through Raubsville."

The Delaware River curved and narrowed as it neared Raubsville. Neat white clapboard houses and sturdy red barns, built more than a century ago by German settlers, clustered along a turnpike on the east bank of the canal. Only a few buildings, including the Yoder saw mill, stood to the west on the flood plain between the canal and river. A footbridge over the canal linked the two sides of the village.

As well as having a curious name, Ground Hog Lock was an important lock on the Delaware Canal. Its seventeen-foot lift was the highest on the canal and it was one of the few locks with a combined double chamber. The lock had been enlarged for the convenience of boatmen in 1852.

A boat, heading north, was exiting as the *Onoko Princess* approached. "Go right in," shouted the locktender when the chamber emptied. "The Company boat behind you will get in with you."

When both boats were in the lock, Wilhelm and the other driver unhitched their mules and waited for the level to be lowered. About the same age, they stood shyly next to one another without speaking. Wilhelm's contemporary was the first to venture a question. "Is this your first trip?" he asked, taking in Wilhelm's small stature.

"It is!" answered Wilhelm, delighted that the boy had spoken. "Is it yours?"

The young man nodded his head. "How do you like walking the towpath?"

"It's great," answered Wilhelm with a big smile. "I want to be a boat captain one day. How do you like it?"

"Me?" said the boy pulling a face. "There's nothin' Ah hate more than walkin' me legs off with a pair of stupid mules Ah wouldn't be here … except me uncle offered me work. Me dad was kilt when a factory he was buildin' fell on 'im an' me ma needs me wages."

"Is he your uncle?" asked Wilhelm pointing to the boat captain busy talking to his father.

"Yeh, that's 'im!"

"It's right nice of him to help your ma out," said Wilhelm, thinking how lucky he was to have a father and mother.

"Ah suppose," agreed the boy, "but, Ah'd rather be workin' on the railroad. Them steam engines pullin' all them coal wagons is sometin'. They puts coal boats to shame. One day, Ah'm gonna drive one."

The creak of the opening miter gates ended the conversation. It was time to hitch up the mules and move on down the next level. Tethered to the line, the teams moved forward, their boats exiting the lock in the same order they entered it.

As the *Onoko Princess* left the village of Raubsville, the Delaware widened. Manfred pointed toward the far side of the river. "See, over there, Annie. That's Ground Hog Island."

Annie craned her neck. "I don't see it, Pa," she exclaimed, looking across the merging landscape of grassland, scrub brush and trees.

"It's nestled in the bend tovards this side of the river."

"I see it, Pa."

"In the old days, them oarsmen sure knew it vas there! Many a coal ark vas wrecked on the shores of that island!"

"But I thought coal arks only sailed down the Lehigh River."

"Now, girl, I ask you!" exclaimed Manfred. "If them arks did not pass down the Delavare, how could coal get to Philadelphia before this canal vas built?"

If there was one thing Annie hated more than anything else, it was looking stupid. She curled her feet underneath her, and said huffily, "I never thought about that!"

To give Annie time to get over her embarrassment and think about what he said, Manfred turned his attention to the towpath. Remembering that all he had seen Wilhelm do at the last lock was talk, he hollered, "Did you feed the mules? I never saw them vearin' feed baskets."

It was Wilhelm's turn to look embarrassed. "Oh, Pa, I'm sorry," he gasped, his face turning beet red. "I forgot." For the first time since he took charge of Max and Lucy, he had been negligent. He had been so preoccupied talking to the other driver, he had not given them a thought. More than four hours had passed since Lucy and Max had eaten.

"If ve vant them mules to keep on goin', ve vill have to feed them now," hollered his father, pulling the steering post across the stern.

The operation went like clockwork. Annie filled the feed baskets without having to be asked and handed them over the side to Wilhelm. In a few minutes, Max and Lucy were refueled and ready to go.

Beyond Ground Hog Island, the river and canal curved around New Jersey's Musconetcong Mountain. The *Onoko Princess* was entering a landscape formed by the southern edge of what was once the mile-high Wisconsin Glacier.

Riegelsville was ahead. The small German settlement had grown into a bustling crossroads for interstate commerce when a wooden bridge had been built over the Delaware to connect the village to communities and mills on the New Jersey side of the river. Overlooking the water, a large, well-frequented hotel was a haven for travelers between the two states. Businesses, taverns and stores lined the turnpike and busy streets. And with so much traffic passing along the canal, a boatyard at Wide Water flourished serving the canal trade.

The *Onoko Princess* had gone nine miles since leaving Easton. This time, Mary was keeping a careful watch on her ten-year-old son. Noticing the tow line slacken, she realized that Wilhelm was beginning to drag his feet. She unpegged the last piece of wash from the clothesline, and, without a word of say-so from Manfred, called, "I'll take over for you, Wil. The walk'll do me good."

"That's mighty nice of you, Ma," answered Wilhelm, trying hard not to let his father see how relieved he was. The journey from Easton was the furthest he had walked along the towpath at a stretch. His legs were jelly, and the blisters he got the first day had opened up.

Manfred frowned at the interference, but Mary was undeterred. "We'll change places at the next lock."

A short delay as they waited for an ascending boat to exit the lock, and the *Onoko Princess* was inside the chamber. Before the level was lowered, Wilhelm was back on board. "Warm some chicken soup for your brother, Annie," called Mary as she straddled the side of the boat.

After his long stint on the towpath, Wilhelm was starving. Annie heated the soup on the stove, and he was soon bolting down the best bowl of chicken noodle soup he had ever tasted. A second helping and his hunger satisfied, he went on deck to stretch out near his father to rest his legs and absorb the fine points of canal navigation. When Annie finished washing up, she joined them. The children welcomed being with one another. Except for sleeping and Sundays when the canal shut down, it was not often they spent time together during the long canal days.

Three boys on the berm side north of Riegelsville caught their attention. With rods made from long, thin branches of hickory, and using lengths of string and bent wire hooks, they were fishing in the canal. It was the first warm day after a long winter and nobody had to tell Wilhelm they had skipped school. As one of the makeshift bobbers made out of twigs disappeared beneath the surface, he was filled with envy. At that moment, but only at that moment, he would have gladly played hooky from mule driving and canaling to go fishing.

As the rod dipped low toward the water, the boy had to hang on for dear life. An eel was splashing and wriggling on the end of the line, doing its utmost to stay in the water. Hooked in the mouth, its head rose above the surface, followed by its thrashing body. A whiplash tug … another … and another … and the boy dragged the struggling creature on shore and ended its life with a rock.

"That's disgusting!" exclaimed Annie, turning her head away. "Why do boys like to kill everything?"

"He ain't doin' nothin'," said Wilhelm defending his contemporary in a dialect resembling that spoken by his backwoods friend, Scotty McNish. "That's what you do wit' eels. They're long an' slippery. An' you cain't keep 'em in a pail like a fish."

"It's cruel!" exclaimed Annie, taking another quick peek at the dying creature.

"Eels are good to eat," announced Wilhelm.

"How do you know? Ma never cooks 'em!"

"Scotty McNish's ma does." Scotty lived in the back woods near Weissport. His father was a drunk who could never keep a job, so the family had to live off the land with Scotty providing most of their livelihood.

"Yeah!" retorted Annie disdainfully. "Those people eat anything they can kill!"

"So what!" said Wilhelm, his voice rising in anger. "Scotty can follow animal tracks better than a trapper … and he knows all the good Indian trails. When we get back to Weissport after the boating season, me and Scotty are goin' t' build a hideout on Bear Mountain. An' we're gonna live there forever and ever."

"I can't wait!" remarked Annie sarcastically.

Mary heard the bickering from the towpath. "Enough of that!" she yelled. "If you two don't stop arguing, you'll get back to walking the mules this instant, Wilhelm. And you, *fräulein* Annie, will empty the commode for the rest of the trip!"

Fearful that their mother meant what she said, the children stopped arguing and sat quietly together on the equipment locker watching the scenery go by.

Pockets of industry were encroaching on the bucolic waterway. The *Onoko Princess* was nearing Durham, where the only iron furnace along the Delaware Canal manufactured pig iron. Two anthracite-fired blast furnaces reddened the daylight sky as a Company coal boat unloaded its cargo into small cars on the wharf.

"See that glow," said Manfred pointing to the sky, "that's the Durham Furnaces. They got a new furnace last year. An inclined plane takes the coal and iron ore from the loading wharf up to the stock yard, then the men just have to trundle barrows full of ore or coal across a bridge and tip them into the top of the stack."

"Wow!" exclaimed Wilhelm, "it's a wonder they don't get burned."

The furnace's productivity was evident. Bars of pig iron were neatly stacked on the dock, ready to be lifted by crane onto private boats for shipment along the canal.

Clip, clop. Clip, clop. The sound was familiar. The mules were crossing the aqueduct ahead of Durham Lock. The canal ran straight as an arrow and, from his tall seat, Manfred could see that the entrance was blocked. Blowing his conch shell was useless. Ahead of the lock, two boats were locked in mortal combat like giant monsters from the deep. With bows together and sterns apart, their captains were yelling blue murder. One of the boats was a rusty red Company boat; the other was bright green.

"Isn't that Taffy Morgan's boat?" asked Wilhelm incredulously.

"Ja, *bestimmt*, that's his all right," agreed Manfred as Annie fled below deck. "Them locktenders must be letting the authorities deal with him in Bristol."

Manfred steered the *Onoko Princess* toward the side of the canal and took his place behind two other waiting boats. "Looks like he's up to his old tricks ... fighting about who locks through first."

The mule drivers from the combating boats had the good sense to unhitch their teams when their wooden juggernauts became wedged together in an impasse. Screaming obscenities in his frustration at not being able to move, Morgan made a leap for the deck of the Company boat. The force of his jump pushed the two boats apart and he fell into the canal. Up to his neck in icy water, he yelled for his mule driver to help. His livelihood depending upon fast action, the driver picked up a pole, and hauled Morgan to the bank. Soaked to the skin, humiliated and still cursing, he slunk into his cabin to change. When he came back on deck, he had reason to curse. His green boat had lost her place in line.

As the sun went down, the back-up had grown. Boats were lined up at the lock in both directions. Manfred lit the nighthawker lanterns and awaited his turn to pass through. Mary took advantage of the delay to barter with the locktender's wife. She came out of the store satisfied. She had traded a small amount of coal for four loaves of bread. The day after tomorrow was Sunday. The canal and its stores would be closed.

The brouhaha over, the Company boat went on its way down the canal, freeing passage for the other boats. As boats moved one after the other through the lock in both directions, the locktender went about his duties as if nothing unusual had happened. Boats jostling for position were nothing new to him. Hardly a day went by without someone bickering about who should lock through first, especially when his lock had only a single chamber that could accommodate one boat at a time. It took ten minutes to change the level. By the time the *Onoko Princess* took her turn inside the chamber, she had lost a precious three quarters of an hour.

"Vasn't that the Velshman Morgan causing the trouble?" Manfred asked, feigning ignorance as the lock was leveled.

"None other!" answered John Geisinger, the locktender.

To test the waters to find out if news of Morgan's suspension had traveled down the canal, Manfred remarked, "I heard the Company vas taking him off the canal."

"I didn't hear nothin'!" Geisinger answered abruptly. From his answer and the fact that he had not intervened in the fight, Manfred suspected that he did not want to get involved. Locktenders up and down the two canals tried to steer clear of men like Morgan. They preferred leaving discipline to the authorities. That way, they kept clear of controversy.

Mary fed the mules and got back on board with the bread. After a long hard day washing clothes, topped off by a stint on the towpath, she was ready to crawl into her bunk. Wilhelm felt likewise, but, if they were to reach New Hope by Saturday night, he knew he had to go on.

"Ve vill have to push on a little further, son," said his father almost apologetically, aware of Wilhelm's fatigue. "Ve've gone a bit over twenty miles, but ve need to make up the time ve lost at the lock, and in Easton. Ve'll tie up betveen here and Narrows Lock. That vay ve'll make it to New Hope by Sunday. The Reverend Ford is preaching and I vant to attend his Mission."

CHAPTER VII

Boats were tied up along both the berm and the towpath sides of the canal on the level between Durham and Narrows locks. To beat the traffic, Manfred awakened the crew shortly after three. There was no time for breakfast before pushing off. They would have to eat in shifts along the way. When they tied up the previous night, Wilhelm tethered the mules to a tree at the side of the towpath and muzzled them to keep them from gorging on grass. Too much fresh fodder, and they would be so bloated and lazy, they would not be able to pull the loaded boat.

He took the muzzles off Max and Lucy, and they brayed hungrily. This time, he obliged with a generous feed of oats. There was no time to go through the curry-comb ritual, so, with their harnesses on from the day before, he put them one behind the other and hooked them to the tow. Other boat crews were stirring, but they had not gotten underway. When the *Onoko Princess* set off along the rest of the nine-mile level, the only boat ahead of her was a privately owned boat.

"Manny," called Mary when she finished her breakfast, "I'll take over when you're ready. There's a pot of oatmeal on the stove. Wil can eat when we get to the lock at the Narrows."

Without question, Manfred was ready. He had been craving his first cup of coffee ever since they set out. Mumbling a word of thanks, he turned over the tiller and went into the cabin for Annie to serve breakfast.

Light from the lanterns played on the water as the *Onoko Princess* glided through the quiet of the early morning. The canal was a silver ribbon. It was as if the earth had gone topsy turvy. A full moon had turned night into day. In the strange half-light, the shadows of trees danced on field and hillside. On the towpath, the mules were walking behemoths and Wilhelm, at their side, was a dwarf. Clip clop, clip clop, clip clop. The gentle beat of their hooves on the earthen path and the lap of water against the hull were eternal. The music of the night was bewitching. Mary, Wilhelm, the mules and the moonlight could go on for ever and ever. But not if Manfred had his way.

"I'm done eating," he announced, coming back on deck with a refill of coffee. Except for spelling him while he ate, Mary had wanted no part of steering the boat that morning. Now she hated to give up the helm. But practicality took over. There was bedding to air, the cabin to clean, and pork float to make for supper, so, reluctantly she handed over the tiller.

Pork float was not only a favorite dish of the Oberfeldts, it was a favorite dish of boatmen up and down the canals. Cured with salt to keep it from spoiling, pork was a staple meat of canalers. Sautéed with onions until it was golden brown, seasoned with marjoram and parsley, and covered with water, it was left to simmer all day on top of the stove. A half hour before serving, potatoes and seasonal vegetables were added to the pork stew. As Mary browned the hard salted meat and onions, the aroma reached Manfred at the helm. Although it would be more than an hour until sunup, he could hardly wait for night to eat supper.

He pulled the *Onoko Princess* in line behind the private boat outside the gates at Narrows Lock. It was too early for the locktender. He was still in bed. Hoping to keep on going, he trumpeted on his conch shell. The captain of the boat ahead of him followed by blowing his boat horn.

The locktender staggered from the lock house, half dressed and half asleep. "You canalers!" he grumbled, "you never think a fella should get a good night's rest. It's barely half past three. I don't have to let you through this early!"

His game was an old one. Both Manfred and the other captain knew what he meant. "I don't have to let you through this early" was his way of saying, "Pay up and I'll open the gates."

The captain of the private boat was the first to offer the traditional bribe. "How about a bag of coal to let me through?"

"And what about you, captain?" the locktender asked, turning to Manfred.

"Add another bag to your pile!" Manfred replied sarcastically.

Satisfied with a deal that would net his family extra coal to keep warm next winter or trade for provisions, the man opened the gates of the single lock to let the first boat pass through. When she was back in the canal, he reversed the lock for Manfred. For Wilhelm, the routine was the same with a difference. He untethered the mules and, when the *Onoko Princess* was safely inside the chamber, hopped on board for breakfast. He had exactly ten minutes to eat before setting out for Lodi five miles down the canal.

Beyond the Narrows, several enormous lime kilns were built into the hillside. The loading dock on the canal was empty, but not for long. Soon men would be at work, charging the giant structures from the top with chunks of limestone. The burned lime would be shipped along the canal to the fast-growing metropolis of Philadelphia and places in between.

The village of Kintnersville lay a quarter mile off the waterway. Settled by German immigrants by the name of Kintner in 1755, legend had it that the settlement was the site of a bloody battle called the Grasshopper War between the Lenape and Shawnee. It was said that the fury of the conflict was evidenced by the number of Indian skeletons littering the ground. As the Kintners told and re-told the spurious tale, those who joined them in the community lived in constant fear of being attacked. If, by chance, they found any Indian remains, they showed their contempt by using the skulls to mark the boundaries of their property.

As the past of the area hovered over the present, the *Onoko Princess* moved into the Narrows of Nockamixon, the wildest and most beautiful section of the Delaware Canal. Steep cliffs on the Pennsylvania side of the Delaware matched the tall palisades on the New Jersey side. Communities of plants surviving from the Ice Age flourished on the rocky escarpments. Below the escarpments, the river swirled ominously as it made it way through Upper Black Eddy. The nemesis of rafters who floated logs down the Delaware in spring, the eddies' rough waters upset many a cargo and claimed many a life. Guarding the wild scene, the profile of a noble Indian brave, carved into the cliffs by the elements, took in nature's wonders and scrutinized everything and everybody that passed down the canal.

The moon had disappeared behind dark clouds, and a mist was rising from the water. It was pitch black and dank in the shadow of the cliffs. In the gloom, the *Onoko Princess*'s lanterns fell short of the towpath and cast an eerie light about her hull. Were it not for the sure-footed guidance of Lucy and Max, Wilhelm felt he would have walked right into the canal.

If Wilhelm was relying on the mules for guidance, with the moon gone and a mist rising, Manfred was sailing by faith. If he had not had been certain that the Company always dredged the canal clean, he would have bumped into objects without seeing them. He was grateful for the boat ahead of him. Its lamps were a beacon in the darkness. And he steered his course by their blur. Dawn began to lighten the darkness as they pulled in to the lock at Lodi. This time, there was no need to bribe the locktender. He was already on duty.

Early as it was, Annie had finished her chores. She had emptied the commode at the last lock privy, and tidied up the cabin. With nothing to do, she lay on the top bunk trying to read. But the swaying oil lamp cast moving shadows on the pages, and she gave up.

"Ma," she said sitting up in exasperation, "What can I do?"

"My goodness, Annie," exclaimed her mother, "there's loads to do. Peel some potatoes for the pork float."

"That's not what I mean, Ma."

"Then what do you mean?"

"I don't want to sail on the *Onoko Princess* any more. I want to stay in Weissport with Gram and Grandpa Kintz."

"Then what will you do? Work as a maid in someone's fine house? That's what young girls your age do when they get off the canal."

"No, Ma. I want to go to school." This was not the first time Annie had broached the subject of leaving the canal, but it was the first time she had sounded this serious.

Mary was her old matter-of-fact self. "Your Pa needs us all to do the chores around here."

"But, I'm bored, Ma."

"Your job is to help me. And relieve Wil on the towpath."

"Oh Wil!" exclaimed Annie contemptuously. "If Pa paid a mule driver, he would never get all those rests!"

"But your brother's just turned ten … and we are a boating family. We are supposed to work as a team."

"There's nothing in canaling for me. And you know it! I'll never be a boat captain, like Wilhelm. Even if I wanted to, the Company wouldn't hire me. I'm just a girl!"

Mary was silent. Annie had struck a nerve. What she said was true.

"I want to go to school full time like my friends Allison and Hannah … and John Carlton … and their cousins, John and Maggie. And, you know, I can't do that if I stay on the canal."

Annie was right. Boat children only attended school from November to March when the canal was closed. Instead of the average seven or eight years of schooling village children had, they went to school for three years or four years when the few months they attended each year were added together. On the whole, canalers did not set much store by education. They sent their daughters to work at the age of fourteen to bring in extra money, and put their sons to work on the towpath, hoping that, eventually, mule driving would lead to a command. Although captaining a coal boat was a responsible job, it required very little formal education. There were no examinations to sit; no tests to pass. Mostly, it was on-the-job training. All a coal boat captain had to know was how to navigate the canal and slackwater, and enough arithmetic to keep track of his load.

"So, Ma," persisted Annie, "when we get back to Weissport, can I stay with Gram and Grandpa Kintz?"

Mary would have liked nothing better than to see Annie get an education, but she was in no position to answer her question. Manfred was head of the family. And she knew he would never let Annie's schooling interfere with his earning a living on the canal. If his children wanted to learn above and beyond the three or four months they were able to spend in school each year, it was up to them to study when they finished their chores.

"It's not up to me, Annie," said Mary. "But, I'll talk to your father when I get a chance and see what he says." The conversation was at a dead end.

Sensing her mother hoped she would let the matter drop, Annie made up her mind to speak to her father herself. Tiller in hand, he was the eternal statue. Except for a few short breaks to eat, he was there in good weather and bad, watching out for trouble and keeping the *Onoko Princess* on course.

Settling herself near him on the equipment locker, she curled up her legs beneath her skirt. "Don't you ever get bored, Papa, sitting there day after day doing the same thing?" she began.

"I should say not!" exclaimed Manfred, indignant that anyone, most of all his own daughter, would think such a thing. "How can you ask me if I'm bored vhen there's so much to see? Every time ve pass this vay, something is different. A new house or a building going up … people tilling the fields, or vorking hard in the factories … making a living in one vay or the other. Then vhen they are not doing that, they tend to their gardens … fish … stroll along the river vith their children. And, *liebchen*, you know how I feel about the *Onoko Princess*? She is my greatest treasure … next to you children and your ma, of course! I tell you, Annie, I vould be a lost soul if I did not have her to sail on."

"Not everyone feels that way, Papa."

Manfred narrowed his eyes. "Vhat's that supposed to mean?"

"It's just that I have been thinking …"

"That's not a bad thing to do!"

"I want to go back to school. I could stay with Grandma Kintz." Annie looked hard at her father to see his reaction. "Can I, Papa, please?"

There was never any beating around the bush with Manfred. "If you think I'm going to say 'yes' right now, young lady, you are wrong," he answered. "But I tell you vhat … ve vill see how ve make out by the end of this trip. If your ma and me think ve can do vithout you, ve vill talk about it then." He drew hard on his pipe, inhaled too much smoke, and almost choked. Then getting himself together, added, "Anyvay, what makes you think Gram vill let you stay? She and grandpa ain't gettin' any younger."

"She will," said Annie smirking. "You see, she already knows."

"Vhat a vixen you are, Annie!"

A vixen? How could her father call her a vixen? Offended, she went into the cabin and threw herself on her bunk. How could he stand being cooped up day after day, going to the same old places and doing the same old things? Couldn't he see? She deserved something better for herself.

In contrast to Annie, Wilhelm was having a good day. He skipped along the towpath whistling a tune in time to the soft clip clop of the mules. The wind reddened his cheeks and gave him a cherry nose. Invigorated by everything around him, he forgot about the two miles he had to go to Uhlertown and the other fifteen to New Hope.

They were swinging away from the river. Sand and gravel pits pockmarked the fertile valley between Lodi and Uhlertown. Wherever there were natural resources, the tentacles of industry were intruding into verdant farmland. Not that this disturbed Jake Sensinger. Amid the sand and gravel pits he rented out to quarrymen, he ploughed his land and raised his livestock. Like most Pennsylvania Germans, he was out for every penny he could earn. Determined to profit from the flow of boat traffic up and down the canal, he sold produce from a stall on the side of the towpath. This time of year, with the season just beginning, he was selling the remains of last year's potato crop. Starting to plow his fields, and doing whatever chores were needed to keep money flowing into his coffers, he left his wares unattended. Operating on the barter and honor system, today's price for ten pounds of last year's potatoes was five pounds of coal … and no filching!

"Do ve need kartoffeln, Mary?" asked Manfred as she rummaged in the feed bin looking for a piece of cheese for lunch. "Ve are coming up on Sensinger's stand."

"We can always use some, Manny. Potatoes come in handy if we get short of bread. I'll go and get some coal."

"Ja, but don't give that old skinflint one lump more than he asks for," warned Manfred as he moved the tiller across the stern to stop the boat.

The tow line slackened as the *Onoko Princess* drifted to a halt. If there was one thing about Manfred, he was sure-handed. When Mary handed Wilhelm the coal to make the exchange, the *Onoko Princess*'s hull was directly opposite the stall. With the trade made and a "giddy up" from Wilhelm, they passed under the Uhlertown covered bridge without losing hardly a minute.

Like so many towns and villages in the Delaware Valley, Uhlertown was named after its founder. Michael Uhler not only founded the town, he was its most enterprising inhabitant. A flour mill, lime kilns, coal yard, general store, and hay-baling operation all bore the family name. In addition, he operated a boat line, and turned Uhlertown into the private-boat-building capital of the Delaware Canal.

Annie had come out on deck when they stopped for potatoes. Feeling guilty about calling her a vixen, Manfred tried to draw her into conversation. Pointing to a magnificent Victorian Gothic mansion, resplendent with elaborately crafted wrought-iron porches, overlooking the canal, he asked, "How vould you like to live in a house like that, *liebchen*?"—knowing full well that she would. Annie made like she did not hear him. "That's the Uhler mansion," he continued. "You have to be real rich to afford a house like that. But nobody can say that those Uhlers did not vork hard! Vhen I vas a boy drivin' mules, there vas nothing about these parts. Even vhen I got my own boat, there vas not much here. Uhler only got real rich about a dozen years ago." Annie stole a look backward as the *Onoko Princess* moved down the canal. The mansion, she thought, seemed to be keeping watch over the town that bore the name of its owner.

As well as being home to the illustrious Uhler family, Uhlertown was Taffy Morgan territory. It was to Uhlertown that his parents had brought him from Wales as a youth of seventeen, and it was in Uhlertown, from none other than Uhler's Boat Yard, that he purchased his green canal boat.

"Mornin', Manny," greeted Davey Fisher, the locktender, as Manfred steered the *Onoko Princess* inside Lock 18. "It's good to see you again! It's been a long winter."

"Ja! Vinter is hard on us boatmen. At least you locktenders get paid."

Like all the locktenders on the canals, Davey Fisher lived rent-free in the lock house and was paid year-round. "I suppose!" he agreed before asking the usual question. "Anything happening along the ditch?"

"Your man, Morgan, got vhat he deserved at Lodi. He tumbled into the canal. But vhat did it matter? Vith so much drink in him, he did not feel the cold."

"Then I'll be having the pleasure of his company."

"Ja, if Company officials don't get him first."

"What do you mean?"

"I heard he vas being suspended."

"What for?"

"I don't know," replied Manfred. Either Fisher hadn't heard anything, or he wasn't talking. Manfred had said enough. Uhlertown was Morgan's home turf.

Mary and Wilhelm changed places before the water fell to the next lower level. Over her snit, Annie was perched on the equipment locker, relieving her boredom by playing cat-in-the-cradle. Canal children amused themselves by making toys and games out of odds and ends they found around the boat. And, from the time she was old enough, Annie had been inventive. When she was younger and hadn't a doll to play with, she stripped a corn cob of its kernels, drew a face on the top end and dressed it in snippets of fabric from her mother's sewing basket. A piece of cord from the top of a feed sack made a great cat-in-the-cradle. Winding it in and around her fingers, she was busy twisting her hands under and over in a series of intricate moves as she tried to get the cat to go into the cradle. She had almost succeeded when the sight of a young girl in the lock-house garden distracted her. About fourteen, the girl was being pushed on a swing by a boy of the same age. Obviously enamored of one another, they giggled and talked, unaware that Annie was watching.

The lock house was as pretty as a picture. It had whitewashed stone walls and green shutters, with cutouts of the stars, framed its deep-set windows. Keeping well out of the way of the swing, and its occupants, a rooster and half a dozen hens scratched contentedly in the yard. Whether it was the youthful flirtation or the picturesque cottage that attracted Annie the most, she was overcome with envy. If only her father would tend a lock instead of sailing up and down the canals!

Unwinding the string from her fingers, she sidled closer to him, feeling it was time to make amends. "Wouldn't it be wonderful to live in a lock house like that, Pa, instead of on an old tub like this?" she remarked as the *Onoko Princess* sank ten feet to the next level.

"Nein, it vould not!" said her father adamantly. "And, Miss Fine Lady, don't ever let me hear you call the *Onoko Princess* an old tub again!"

"If you were a locktender, Pa," she continued, ignoring his reprimand, "we could live in a pretty house like that, and . . ."

"Ve live in vone all vinter," said her father impatiently. "That's enough for me."

Annie resumed playing with the string. Twisting. Concentrating. "Got it!" she exclaimed triumphantly as she turned her hands over with the palms up.

"Got vhat?"

"The cat's in the cradle!" She unwound the string from her fingers and rolled it into a ball. Having succeeded once, she was not interested in trying again. "What do locktenders do in the winter when there's no boats on the canal?" she asked as she watched the lock house recede in the distance.

"Vhat else? They guard the lock."

"But there's no water in the canal in winter."

"That is so, Annie. But locktenders get paid year-round to keep an eye on vhat is going on. And if they do other vork during the vinter months to make extra money, such as helping out a farmer, caulking boats, or planking locks, their vives vatch the lock for them."

"But there's nothing to watch, Pa."

"Oh, yes there is, *liebchen*! Vinter is the time carpenters do repairs. They replace damaged plankin' in the lock valls, and make sure the gates vork properly. Vater, going in and out of the locks so many times a day during the season, rots out the vood. And boats slammin' into them gates and valls, don't help either!"

"Just think, Papa," said Annie dreamily, "if we lived in a lock house, I could go to school in the village, and have friends like that girl ..."

"Oh, Annie," exclaimed Manfred, throwing his hands up in the air. "I give up! You vill never be a canaler like Vilhelm!"

Wilhelm came out of the cabin just in time to hear the compliment and beamed from ear to ear. What his father said was true. Even when he was tired and his feet were killing him, he would not change a thing. He loved driving the mules, and when he wasn't driving the mules, he loved watching his father take the *Onoko Princess* through the locks.

An aqueduct crossed Tinicum Creek near the village of Erwinna. The canal had moved away from the Delaware, leaving a broad fertile plain between it and the river. On the canal bank, Jake Oberacker's tap room was doing a brisk business. With entrances facing the canal and the road, boatmen sailing the waterway and travelers passing along the river road could stop and refresh themselves with a glass of frothy brew and one of Martha Oberacker's salt cakes. As they sailed by the inn the children smelled the baking salt cakes and looked at their father expectantly. Their eyes told him what they wanted, but, Manfred pressed on.

Past the inn, the canal returned to the river's edge. The Delaware widened and split into two streams. One flowed down the eastern shores of Marshall and Treasure islands; the other looped by the islands' western shores.

"See that line of trees over there on the far side of the river," Manfred said pointing at the merging landscape of shore and water, "that's Marshall Island. If you can tell me who Edvard Marshall vas, you vill get your salt cake on the vay back."

At the thought of the soft, salty treat, the children mouths watered. They wracked their brains to come up with an answer. Finally, they had to give up. "We don't know, Pa," conceded Wilhelm, disappointed that his sister, whom he considered much smarter than he, did not know who Edward Marshall was.

"Even if we don't know, Pa, will you buy us one the next time we pass?" asked Annie, still hungering for a salt cake.

"Vell … I just might, if you pay attention to my story."

The children moved nearer to one another and to their father, and waited for him to snuff out his pipe and begin.

"Edvard Marshall vas vone of three men who took part in the Valking Purchase," announced Manfred, pausing to wait for their reaction.

It came from Wilhelm. "Tell us, Pa, what is the Walking Purchase?"

"Vell, if they did not teach you about the Valking Purchase in school, I vill tell you about it!"

In 1684, the Lenape Indian tribe that lived in the Delavare Valley turned over some of their tribal lands to Villiam Penn. Vhen Villiam Penn died, there vas disagreement between the Indians and Penn's sons, John, Thomas and Richard, about its northern boundary. To extend the boundary, the Penn brothers claimed they had found a lost treaty from 1686, giving them a tract of land beginning vest of Neshaminy Creek and extending as far as a man could valk in vone and a half days. Vhen they presented the document to Lenape Chief Nutimas, he agreed to set a new boundary. To cover as much territory as possible in vone and a half days, the Penn brothers hired the three fastest valkers in the colony. The vone who valked the furthest in that time vould receive five pounds in cash and five hunert acres of land as a revard."

"Was Edward Marshall one of the walkers?" asked Annie, a step ahead of her father.

"Ja, he vas. Edvard Marshall vas a tventy-seven-year-old hunter and trapper from these parts. He set off from Wrightstown in a northvesterly direction on September 19, 1737, with his companions, Solomon Jennings and James Yeates. Along the vay, both Jennings and Yeates dropped out. This left Edvard Marshall as the only vone to continue."

"How far did Edward Marshall go?" asked Wilhelm.

"He ended his valk several miles northeast of Mauch Chunk."

"Did the Indians set a new boundary?" asked Annie.

"Ja, they did ... but not before blood vas shed!"

"Did they kill the settlers, Papa?"

"Ja, *liebchen*, it pains me to tell you, but Thomas Penn and his brothers vere not honest men like their father. The treaty they claimed to have found vas fraudulent."

"You mean, it was a fake?" piped in Wilhelm.

"Ja, I am ashamed to say, it vas! The Indians accused Edvard Marshall of cheating. They said he did not valk. He ran so that he could cover a greater distance. Vhen it came time for them to give up the land, the Indians vere fit to be tied. It was not only the 'valk' that infuriated them, the line, forming the boundary, was drawn at right angles instead of directly east, giving the colonists far more territory. The result vas, *mein kinder*, settlers vere massacred throughout the Lehigh Valley."

"Did Edward Marshall get Marshall Island as a reward?" asked Wilhelm.

"He got land further north, at Marshall's Creek near the Delavare Vater Gap. But the Indians vere not done. In 1757, they killed Edvard Marshall's vife and children on the land he received for the valk. That's vhen he moved to Marshall Island."

"But it wasn't their fault the Indians were cheated," protested Annie.

"Nor Edvard Marshall's either. It vas the fault of Villiam Penn's dishonest sons."

"I'm glad I did not live in those days, Papa," exclaimed Annie shuddering.

"Ja, ve all are! Life on the frontier vas dangerous. Vhen them settlers thought they had made friends vith the Indians, the Indians turned around and slaughtered them."

"Can you blame them," asked Annie, "when the settlers stole their land?"

Manfred's answer was to tamp a fresh plug of tobacco into his pipe.

The children sat quietly thinking about what their father had told them. It was Wilhelm who broke the silence. He was searching the landscape, trying to make out the shoreline. "Marshall Island sure is a long island, Pa!"

"That isn't Marshall Island, son. That's Treasure Island. Treasure Island is locked into the southern tip of Marshall Island like a piece that is broken off."

The children followed their father's pointing finger across the flood plain to a narrow strip of water that separated the islands where their shores came together.

"I think I see it," exclaimed Wilhelm, not quite sure whether he had or not. "Is treasure hidden on the island?"

"Maybe there vas at vone time. Vhy else vould it be so named?"

"Did the treasure belong to pirates?"

"If there vas any treasure buried on the island, more than likely it belonged to a settler. In them days, settlers often buried their valuables in strange places to keep them safe from robbers. But there are stories from long ago that the Doane Outlaws, a gang of thieves loyal to the king of England who raided farmers around here, buried some of their loot on the islands in the river."

"Can we go there sometime, Pa?" asked Wilhelm, hoping to find a long-hidden hoard.

"I can't promise that," Manfred answered brusquely, his mind never swerving from getting the load as quickly as he could from source to destination.

Opposite Treasure Island was a lock of the same name. Manfred blew into his conch shell and they entered it without waiting. It was time for the mules to be fed. Free of their load and each other, they stood still for Mary to put on the feed baskets. "I'll take the boat through here, Wil," she said, as the water was let out of the lock. "You can get back on the towpath at Smithtown." Then, turning to Annie, she said, "Get something to eat for Wil, then he will be all set for a while."

Although Annie resented being Wilhelm's servant, without saying a word, she went into the cabin and heated some leftover pea soup. When it was ready, she came back on deck with a bowl. By the time they had gone the mile to Smithtown, his hunger satisfied, Wilhelm was ready to get back on the towpath. Several bridges above the lock crossed the canal from the road to the river, and Mary led the mules under them. A blast on the conch shell alerted the locktender and he opened the gate for the *Onoko Princess* and a private boat. Smithtown was one of the few double locks on the Delaware Canal. It had a twelve-foot lift and was the second deepest.

It was beginning to drizzle as Wilhelm and his mother changed places. They still had another ten miles to go to New Hope. Counting passage through locks, minor delays, and the weather, that meant another three or four hours on the towpath. Loaded to the hilt, with rain blowing up, they would be lucky if they could approach the speed limit of two and a half miles in an hour.

On the two-mile level between the locks at Point Pleasant and Lumberville, the weather worsened. As cold air battled the warmth of the previous day, what a few moments ago had been a light drizzle turned into a driving rain. Blown toward them by wind gusting along the river valley, they were soon soaked to the skin.

Annie was first to seek shelter. "Do me a favor," yelled Wilhelm as she was about to pull the hatch cover shut. "Get my hat and gloves. I'm cold."

Annie found the hat and gloves in the storage chest, and stood near the front of the boat figuring out a way to get them to Wilhelm. Rolling the gloves inside the knit hat, she shouted, "Catch!"

Wilhelm was standing next to the mules at the side of the bow when a wind gust took the ball and hit Max squarely on the rump. The blow was sudden and unexpected, and he lurched into Lucy's rear. Lucy was startled. She jerked the rein out of Wilhelm's hand and took off as if she had been whipped, with Max behind her and the *Onoko Princess* in tow.

The chain reaction unraveled in such quick motion, it took Annie a while to realize what had happened. "I'm sorry, Pa. I didn't mean it," she wailed. "The wind took the hat."

The reprimand would come later. Manfred was desperately trying to kick the tow line out of the towing notch to keep the *Onoko Princess* from being beached. At last, the knot slipped out. Free of the loaded boat but still harnessed to one another, Max and Lucy were galloping in tandem along the towpath with Wilhelm hot in pursuit. Seeing Lucy and Max racing toward him, the mule driver of a boat coming up the canal moved his team to the side of the towpath and waited. "Whoa!" he cried, "Whoa!" and grabbed hold of their harness, bringing them to a halt. When he helped Wilhelm bring them back to the boat, Manfred thanked him profusely and rewarded him with a quarter.

Manfred wiped the sweat off his brow. He slipped the knotted end of the tow line into the notch on the towing post, and threw the other end of the line to Wilhelm. Wilhelm hitched the mules and walked them forward, giving the *Onoko Princess* enough momentum to drift over to the berm side of the canal. With a nod of thanks from Manfred and a hearty wave, the empty boat, and her quick-thinking mule driver, crossed over the *Onoko Princess*'s tow line on their way to Mauch Chunk to load.

The sudden burst of freedom left Lucy and Max exhausted. Steam snorted from their nostrils and rose from their wet coats. But if the mules were tired and

Lucy took off as if she had been whipped, with Max behind her.

the weather was worsening, Manfred was ignoring them. He was more determined than ever to reach New Hope by nightfall.

Dusk was turning day into night as the *Onoko Princess* traversed the two-mile level below Point Pleasant. With no improvement in the weather, Wilhelm was growing more miserable by the minute. As they came up on Lumberville, the bleak wet landscape reflected his bleak mood and soggy clothes.

The village got its name from the lumbering operations that had gone on since before the American Revolution. Not a tree covered the surrounding hillsides; no spark of light came from the houses nestled among the red shale. The only beacon of light came from the Black Bass Inn on the waterfront.

The Black Bass had been a haven for travelers since 1746. Several boats were tied up outside the hostelry for the night. Having given in to the weather, their crews were enjoying the hospitality of the host, the affable Scotsman Douglas Campbell. On other journeys, on other days, Manfred would have stopped for a chat and a glass of home-brewed sarsaparilla, but if they were to make it to New Hope for Sunday services, they had to keep going.

The course of the canal had moved back close to the Delaware River. Offshore was Bull's Island. North of the island, on the New Jersey side of the river, the Delaware & Raritan Canal took its water from the Delaware through a feeder canal. To the south of the island lay Lumberton. Like Lumberville, its neighbor to the north, the hillsides surrounding the village were bare of trees. As cities and towns developed in the lower Delaware Valley, sawmill owners cut down the forests to profit from the building boom. The timber was planed at the mills and the finished logs were lashed together in rafts and floated down the Delaware to Philadelphia.

If Philadelphia owed its development to Lumberville and Lumberton lumber, so, too, was it indebted to Lumberton sandstone. Quarried by the Lumberton Granite Company, the native rock was cut into building blocks and shipped down the canal. Lumberton sandstone graced many a new brownstone in Philadelphia and paved many a city street. But, sadly for Lumberton's inhabitants, the village's prosperity was fading and industries were beginning to close down.

If hard times personified Lumberton, it certainly described the plight of Manfred and Wilhelm as the rain turned into a fully fledged storm. As thunder rumbled, lightning flashed, and a fierce wind howled through the valley, last season's tall, feathery-topped phragmites in the wetlands became a heaving sea of brown. As Wilhelm trudged alongside the mules, he had never felt more miserable and scared in his whole life. His feet and hands, which had always been integral parts of his body, painless and inconspicuous, like an eye or an ear, were screaming with pain. As lightning lit up the towpath in front of him, he vowed, if he lived through this storm, he would never consider captaining a coal boat. But life on the waterway went on relentlessly day in and day out except Sundays, whatever the weather. And Manfred, his captain and father, offered him no relief.

If Wilhelm was miserable, so too were the mules. For the first time this season, Lucy balked at going on. She dug her heels into the muddy towpath, and let the line sink below the surface of the water.

"Vhat's happening over there?" yelled Manfred as the *Onoko Princess* drifted ahead of her tow. "Are them beasts asleep or vhat? Git 'em goin'!"

Wilhelm tugged as hard as he could on the harness, but the dappled molly refused to move. And if Lucy would not move, neither could chestnut Max. He was stuck motionless in the shaft behind her.

"I can't, Pa. Lucy won't budge!"

"That stubborn stupid beast," yelled Manfred in frustration. He rarely told any of his drivers to whip the mules, but the time had come. "Give her a good whack on her behind."

Wilhelm took the lead rein and gave Lucy a whack on her rump. The blow on her wet hide smarted, but the stubborn beast still refused to move.

"GIDDY UP, YOU CRAZY OL' MULE! GIT GOING!" Manfred screamed at the top of his lungs.

Whether it was Manfred's roar or the loud crack of thunder that accompanied it, Lucy pricked up her ears, and put one foot before the other. With Lucy on her way, Max had no alternative but to follow. The *Onoko Princess* was moving again.

The storm died down as quickly as it came. Fearful that it might come back, Wilhelm hustled the mules along the towpath past Reading Ferry. Established in 1711, Reading Ferry was the first ferry across the Delaware on the main turnpike between Philadelphia and New York City. Originally a Lenape trail, it was known to battling Redcoats and those who passed along it long after America gained her independence as the King's Highway.

Beyond the ferry, the kilns at Limeport churned out lime for shipment along the canal, The towpath never looked longer. Wilhelm was freezing. He let go of the harness and tried to warm his hands in his pockets. But nothing helped.

The further south they went, the more the silhouetted contour of the land softened. Deprived of the cover of trees, the low hillsides had turned into sluice-ways. Water poured down them in torrents, carrying mud into the canal.

Working by the light of oil lanterns, several men were trying to repair the banks. Water, racing down the hillside, had washed out a section and mud was pouring into the canal. As fast as they scooped out a shovelful and tried to repair the breach, more cascaded into the canal. On and on they went, throwing the mud against the towpath. They reminded Manfred of Sisyphus in the Greek myth Annie had once read to the family. Every time Sisyphus rolled the rock up the mountain, it kept falling back — just like the mud. However frustrating and hard the work was, the canal had to be kept navigable.

The nighthawker lantern on the bow of a boat coming up the canal from Bristol shone on the water ahead. In response, Manfred pulled over to the berm side, and Wilhelm dropped the tow line. With five miles to go, Wilhelm was at his last gasp. Unable to stand the pain in his fingers any more, he begged, "Please, Pa, can I warm my hands in the cabin?"

As he scanned the canal through the darkness, Manfred had never taken his hand off the helm once throughout the bad weather. As he listened to his son's plea, he, too, realized he was freezing. "Vhat ve both need, son, is to get varm. I vill get Annie to valk the towpath, and your ma vill take the boat into New Hope. A hot cup of coffee and something to eat vould taste real good to us both right now ... *Bestimmt!* ... Ve vill stop at Volkhart's Landing."

Annie had lain low in the cabin since the hat-throwing incident. Her theory was that the longer she stayed out of her father's sight, the less he would holler about what happened. A call to the towpath at night was disagreeable in any weather, but, being on shaky ground, she bundled up in her warmest clothes and hopped over the side of the *Onoko Princess* without grumbling. With her mother at the helm, confident and capable in what she was doing, the two women took the *Onoko Princess* along the last few miles into New Hope. By Manfred's time-honored schedule, they were late. If there was one thing he liked to do on Saturday nights, it was to tie up early and go square dancing.

Situated where the Delaware River met two canals, New Hope was as bustling a canal town as existed along the Delaware Canal. Originally called Well's Falls or Coryell's Ferry, the village was renamed New Hope by Benjamin Parry when he built the New Hope Mill on Ingham Creek. Located on the main road from the Lehigh Valley to Philadelphia and linked by cable ferry to New Jersey's Delaware & Raritan Canal, it was a hub of interstate commerce. A covered bridge crossed the Delaware River. More locks and bigger locks that held two boats at a time permitted traffic to keep moving. Boats could travel along the Delaware Canal to Philadelphia or cross, by cable, to the Delaware & Raritan Canal, which ran along the New Jersey side of the river to Trenton, then looped north, ending up in Raritan Bay not far from New York City. Tolls were collected to use the outlet lock for the cable crossover, and a huge lifting wheel pumped water from the river into the Delaware Canal. Lumbering, flour and saw mills, coal and lime loading facilities all flourished along the waterfront. Inns and shops of every kind catered to boatmen and travelers. So much boat traffic passed through the busy canal town, the Lehigh Coal & Navigation Company had to establish a boatyard there to keep Company boats repaired.

Mary sounded the conch shell loud and long above Lock 8, but, when the *Onoko Princess* arrived, the gate was already open.

"You just made it in time," said the locktender as Mary steered the *Onoko Princess* into the lock chamber. "I was just about to chain the gates shut."

Padlocking the lock gates was something locktenders did to stop any rogue boatman who was intent on making illegal headway from turning the lock himself during the night when the locktender was asleep, or on Sundays, when he was off duty. Even with the gates padlocked, it was not unusual for a locktender to find the padlock chiseled open or the chain cut when he opened the gates in the morning.

Manfred came back on deck to supervise the mooring just in time to hear the locktender's remark. "Vhat time is it?" he asked, suspecting a scam.

The man answered. "I was just closing up."

"Vell … ve are thankful the gates are still open. You're new, aren't you?" he asked, not recognizing the locktender.

"Yes, sir!"

"I'm Captain Oberfeldt," said Manfred, taking over the helm from Mary, "and this is Mrs. Oberfeldt."

"Pleased to meet you, captain," replied the locktender, tipping his cap, without giving his name. "You, too, missus."

"Can ve tie up over there?" asked Manfred, indicating a space ahead of the lock.

"That berth'll cost you!"

Manfred had heard of locktenders taking bribes to open a lock after hours, but in all his days on the canal, this was the first time he had been charged for berthing a Company boat on either the Lehigh or Delaware Canal. "Cost me? Vhat do you mean?" he asked, figuring the locktender had been saving the space for the last sucker through the lock.

"Ten pounds of coal."

"My supply is low," said Manfred, curtly. "The veather's cold and ve need heat in the cabin." Unlike some boatmen, Manfred was scrupulously honest. He never took so much as a nugget of coal from the load. The Company was good enough to give him two hundred pounds of free coal every trip for his personal use and, come what may, he and his family existed on it.

"Then you can't dock there."

Manfred was fit to be tied. The *Onoko Princess* was inside the lock chamber with nowhere to go. He had to pay up. Angrily, he shoveled some coal into a sack. Then, swinging the sack back and forth to make sure it would carry, he heaved it over the side, barely missing the locktender. With their dues paid, the lock was leveled, permitting the *Onoko Princess* to pass through the miter gates to her mooring in the lower level.

CHAPTER VIII

On Sundays, the towns and villages along the canals stopped for the day. Locks were chained shut, canal boats immobilized, industries fell silent, stores and taverns were closed. New Hope was no different. Sunday was a day of rest and prayer for its inhabitants and any itinerant boatman who happened to be in town. Canalers who preferred organized religion attended one of the town's churches; those who liked to listen to a fire-and-brimstone evangelist went to the waterfront mission; and those who preferred to find their own peace did so within the confines of themselves and their cabins. Whatever a boatman chose to do on his day off, he and his overworked mules welcomed Sundays as a day of relaxation and rest. If Sunday closing were not mandatory, like many a boatman, Manfred would have praised the Lord and continued on his way along the canal after church. But as the Bible and the Company decreed that all work stop, he and his family made the most of the pause in their busy lives.

Sunday or no Sunday, Manfred awakened early out of habit. Although he had been up since six o'clock puttering around the deck, he waited until eight before sounding his conch shell. The eight o'clock call gave Mary and the children enough time to have breakfast and get ready for church.

"*Woooo. Woo.*" The sound was gentle. It rose like the waves in a sea shell caressing the shore. Nobody heard it. He took a deep breath and blew harder into the conch shell. This time, the crew stirred.

"Get up you lazy bunch of loafers," he said jokingly, giving Wilhelm a prod. "There's not much time left before ve have to leave for the Mission."

Like the Mission, Sunday breakfast was special. It was one of the few times that the family breakfasted together. Salt mackerel was the entrée of choice on their day off. The fish had been stored in the feed bin since leaving Weissport, and Mary steamed it in butter on top of the stove. Served with hunks of bread, made warm and crusty on the stoveplate, it was a feast that all, except Annie, looked forward to before going to church. She declined the portion of fish her mother offered her and settled for bread and applebutter.

Dressed in their Sunday best, the Oberfeldts headed for the mission in Miller's Warehouse along the wharf. Yesterday's rain was but a memory. The sun was already well up from the horizon, shining out of a cloudless blue sky. Manfred pushed open the doors to the large frame warehouse. It was almost full. Except for a handful of townspeople, most of those present were canalers: Pennsylvania Germans whose religious heritage had followed them from the old world to the new. Treasuring a good sermon, they took their seats on wooden benches amid pushed-back bags of feed and bins of grain. A platform, fashioned out of saw horses and planks, stood at one end. In the middle, a lectern awaited the arrival of the preacher. As the congregants greeted one another for the first time that year, the air buzzed with conversation.

Today the preacher was the Reverend John Ford. He was Manfred's favorite. An evangelist who ministered to canalers, the Reverend Ford was a lapsed Episcopalian who preferred freewheeling the gospel to ecclesiastical trappings and language. Not that he discarded the Good Book. He quoted from it liberally. With the presence and drama of an actor, he carefully enunciated its most colorful passages to make sure that even the illiterate congregant understood his message.

The gathering fell silent when he entered. There was no doubt about it: he was a presence. No bowed head or shuffling in some secondhand ministerial robe for him. Attired in a black cloak like a highwayman, he bounded onto the platform ready to do battle with all sinners. His face was craggy and bearded, his voice that of a touring actor.

"Good morning," he greeted the congregation, his steely eyes sweeping the gathering to see who was present, and who was not. "It is wonderful to see so many of you after the long winter," he complimented, all the while taking a quick head count. Like most of his congregants, the Reverend Ford's financial pickings in winter had been slim. "In the spirit of fellowship and the glory of the morning, we shall begin with a hymn."

The rustle of turning pages filled the warehouse as the congregation rifled through well-fingered hymn books, searching for the number chalked on a board. A few bars on the melodeon acquainted them with the key, and the medley of voices — sopranos, bass and tenors — resonated as one. A fading "amen" and it was time for what everyone in the room had come to see and hear.

Just as the Reverend Ford strode toward the lectern, the warehouse door creaked open. "Ah," he exclaimed as everybody turned around to look who it was.

It was Taffy Morgan, decked out in his Sunday clothes.

"I see we have a late comer! But not to worry, dear man! We are all latecomers in the eyes of the Lord. Welcome dear brother to the fold."

It was Taffy Morgan, trying to sneak in without being heard. Stone-cold sober, decked out in his Sunday clothes, doing his best to be inconspicuous, he was pushing his way into the back row. The occupants shuffled over to make room for him, and he sat down looking, of all things, embarrassed. Annie was terrified when she saw who it was. Where a bruise still marked her arm, she could feel Morgan's grip as he threatened her in the back alley. If she had not been seated between her parents, she would have bolted out of the door.

Taffy Morgan's entrance meant two things to Manfred. He had not been suspended. And, depending on when they started out in the morning, he would either be in front or behind them on the canal. Either way, he was trouble.

To recapture the attention of the gathering, the Reverend Ford thumped on the lectern. They responded, and he picked up momentum. Throwing the end of his cape over his shoulder, he strode back and forth across the stage. At times, he was a matador; at others, with his arms outstretched, he was a giant vampire bat. One minute, he was thundering wrath; the next, closing his eyes, exulting promise. Sometimes his voice was strident; at others, barely a whisper. Whatever he did, the congregation sat transfixed. Every impulse to blow a runny nose or cough was checked. Crescendoing, cadencing, gesticulating, prancing from here to there, the Reverend Ford was interpreting his vision for whatever it was worth in the collection bag.

Of all those present, Wilhelm was the least attentive. He had caught sight of the Davis children in the congregation and was busy planning his afternoon. Not so Annie! Oblivious to everyone, even Taffy Morgan in the row behind, she hung on to the Reverend's every word.

The melodeon interrupted her reverie. It was time to sing another hymn. Benches screeched on the floor boards as the congregation stood up, and, for the second time that morning, joined together in song. As the chorus of voices sailed heavenward, a voice, at once glorious and heart rending, soared above the rest. It belonged to Taffy Morgan, once a first-prize winner at the Welsh Eisteddfod. A Methodist choirboy of renown in the ironmaking town of Ebbw Vale where he grew up, he was awarded the most coveted honor in Wales before sailing for America. As his operatic voice rose to the rafters, Annie was spellbound. How could someone who could sing so magnificently be so cruel and mean?

The strains of the hymn faded and the Reverend Ford morphed into a bat. Under his black cape, he reached heavenward, the palms of his hands turned upward. The moment of truth that the congregation had been waiting for had arrived. He was about to issue an invitation.

"Come forth ye sinners and be redeemed," he thundered. When no one moved, he pointed a long, bony finger. "You, you and you!"

A few of the chosen came forth in exultation; the rest sat entrenched in their seats. Among the unmoving was Taffy Morgan. Morgan was not ready for salvation.

With words of forgiveness to the penitents, the Reverend Ford had done his bit. He motioned to a thin young man in Ben Franklin glasses. It was time for the offering. Although most canal evangelists did not pass a collection bag, without a congregation to preach to all winter, the Reverend Ford had no option. A maroon velvet bag, small at the top, voluminous below, was passed from one congregant to the other. When it arrived at Manfred, he dropped in a penny. He would give more next time, after he got paid.

A blessing, and the Reverend preceded his congregation to the door to hand out illustrated texts. Annie glanced at hers. It was scary. Bordered by black lilies, it read in fancy lettering, "The wages of sin is death." She studied it carefully and worried about being a sinner. Then, figuring she had done nothing terribly wrong, and that the text was bad grammar, she put it in her pocket. She would hang it above her bunk, just in case.

As they made their way along the towpath, canalers greeted one another after the winter hiatus. A few did not stop to socialize. They preferred to return to their boats to make their Sunday a true day of rest.

As the Oberfeldts came out of the warehouse, Wilhelm made a beeline for Mark and Angela Davis, and his parents and Annie followed. The Davises were a canal family out of Mauch Chunk, and the Oberfeldts knew them well. Mark was older than Wilhelm and had been driving his father's mules for three years. Angela was twelve, and a good friend of Annie's. In the past, when the two families tied up at the same town over Sundays, the children got together after church. Today would be no different. Excited to see one another, they arranged to meet after Sunday dinner.

Like Sunday breakfast, Sunday dinner on the canal was special. There were no interruptions to do chores.

"What's for dinner, Ma?" asked Wilhelm, feeling the pangs of hunger as they walked back to the *Onoko Princess*.

His question was pointless.

"What do I always make?" Mary asked, answering his question with a question. On Sundays, she always made the same thing. Unless, for some reason, she could not get the ingredients, the menu was roast beef, boiled potatoes and hunks-a-go-pudding. The piece of beef was not really roasted. Without an oven, the best Mary could do was cook it like pot roast on top of the stove. Hunks-a-go-pudding also needed an oven, but she had learned to improvise. As she poured the hunks-a-go batter of eggs, milk and flour into beef fat sizzling in a frying pan, she covered it with a lid so that it rose in scrumptious yellow peaks.

"Hunks-a-go-pudding," chorused the children, breaking into the rollicking harmony that was sung up and down the canals.

> Hunks-a-go-pudding and pieces of pie
> Me mother gave me when I was a boy
> And if you don't believe, just drop in and see —
> The hunks-a-go-pudding my mother gave me.

"What about pie, Ma?' asked Annie, when the ditty ended. "Are we having pie?"

"Not today. Emma Williams refused to take coal. And you know, it is impossible to bake a pie without an oven. We'll get one next week after Pa gets paid."

Although Mary had not managed to make a trade for a pie, the piece of beef she had bought in Easton was stored in the feed bin. She had taken it out the night before and pot roasted it, so all she had to do when they got back from services was heat it up, put the potatoes on to boil, and make the hunks-a-go batter. By half past noon, they were sitting around the table, saying grace.

There was no balking about washing dishes today. Eager to get going, the children did them without being asked. Although Manfred did not exactly approve of their playing games on Sundays, he put aside his feelings, knowing that there was no time for such things all week. When Annie and Wilhelm left, amid their mother's usual warnings, he was snoozing off his ample portions of dinner on the lower bunk.

Like most of the larger canal towns, New Hope had its share of waterfront characters. Drunks, thieves, beggars, and tramps all hung out at the locks and along the wharves. A particular nuisance were the tramps looking for a ride to Philadelphia, or wishing to cross the river to New Jersey and go on to New York. Most boatmen gave them the cold shoulder. Taking on passengers was against Company rules with two exceptions. They were allowed to ferry a canal worker to his job site, and give a locktender's children a ride to the nearest school.

With assurances they would not talk to strangers, Wilhelm and Annie raced one another along the canal bank to a field above the towpath. After being cooped up on board the *Onoko Princess* or walking the towpath for the better part of a week, they could not wait to enjoy some outdoor fun.

Mark and Angela had beaten them there. Amid whoops and shouts and "got yas" they were playing tag with some local children. As the afternoon wore on, tag turned into hide-and-seek, and hide-and-seek into kick-the-can before it was time to return to the boat.

It was Wilhelm who kept an eye on the sun. "We had better go," he reminded Annie as the sky began to redden in the west. "We told Ma we'd be back before dark."

Angela linked her arm through Annie's like she would never let go. The thought of parting was too much. "There's a sing-along tonight," she said, "Will you ask your ma and pa if you can go?"

Never one to turn down an evening of fun, Annie was excited. "A sing-a-long!" she exclaimed.

"Yeh, it's in Miller's warehouse. It starts at seven o'clock."

"We'll ask if we can go."

"Ask your ma and pa to come too," shouted Angela as Wilhelm hustled Annie along the towpath. "They need people to play in the band. My pa is playing the fiddle. Your pa can bring his concertina."

Excited at the thought of something to do on a long Sunday night, the children scampered back to the boat to ask their parents if they could go. In the long days of sameness, nothing was more fun than a get-together of canalers, be it a sing-a-long, a Sunday picnic, or a Saturday night of square dancing.

"Hey, you two!" protested their mother as they threw back the hatch and burst through it like whirlwinds, "calm down! Is something after you?!"

"N-n-no," answered Wilhelm, catching his breath. "There's a sing-a-long tonight in Miller's Warehouse … and we want to know if we can go."

Mary hesitated, knowing that Manfred wanted to retire early to get another good night's rest.

"Please, Ma … please," pleaded Annie. "The Davises will be there. Angela said her father is playing his fiddle." Then, knowing how her father loved to play his concertina in public, she added, "Pa, they're looking for people to play in the band."

Mary looked at Manfred. "It's up to your father," she said.

Manfred was sprawled on his bunk, mentally navigating the twenty-five miles to Bristol and taking the cargo along the tidewater. At the same time, he was taking everything in.

"Can we go, Pa?" asked Annie.

"Go where?"

"Oh," she exclaimed, "you heard!"

Shrugging his shoulders, Manfred broke into a grin. "Vhy not?" he said. "Ve vill all go. And I vill take my concertina."

With only three canal families moored at New Hope over Sunday, the warehouse was mostly filled with men. The air was thick with tobacco. Most of the boatmen were smoking. Some smoked stogies, some puffed on pipes, and some chewed on chaws of tobacco. This was their way of relaxing while they waited for the entertainment to start.

The band was assembling on the same makeshift platform the Rev. Ford had spoken from that morning. Harry Davis and Benajah Gilbert had fiddles, Tom Wilson an old snare drum, James Fisher a Jew's harp, Aaron Hofstetter a banjo, and Toots Fisher and Manfred had concertinas.

"A one-and-a-two-and-a-three." Harry Davis, captain of Lehigh Coal & Navigation Coal Boat Number 87, stamped his foot to the beat, and the music began. Folk songs and canal ditties, handed down from generation to generation, rang out to the rafters. And, because it was Sunday, they included the occasional hymn. Nobody cared if a band member played a wrong note or someone in the audience could not hold a tune. All that mattered was that everybody joined in and had fun.

From time to time, Harry Davis called out the name of a canaler known for being able to carry a tune. That person was asked to sing a verse solo, then the audience joined in. A true showman, Harry saved the best for the last. "Taffy … Taffy Morgan," he called with a flourish, "it's your turn."

Taffy Morgan was sitting in the back row, still looking respectable. Sundays were good for him. Unless he bought a jug of whiskey on Saturdays before the taverns closed, he had to do without on Sundays. As he came up to the platform, silence fell over the room.

"What will it be tonight, Taffy?" asked Harry as Morgan took his place center stage.

"How about Men of Harlech?" he asked in his singsong Welsh voice. "Do you fellows know the tune?"

"I do," answered Harry, a fellow Welshman, "and I'm sure everybody else can follow along."

When Taffy Morgan climbed onto the stage, Annie hunched close to her mother. But as he began to sing she sat up, swept by his magical voice to the mysterious land across the sea. Annie was not the only one who was affected. Everyone sat spellbound. Even Manfred felt a twinge of guilt. For a moment — but just for a moment — he second-guessed himself for reporting Morgan to the authorities.

The applause was deafening as the last note faded. "More! More!" the crowd clamored, in no mood to hear a song from anyone else.

This time, Morgan chose "The Bells of Aberdovey." As the sad strains of the Welsh melody rent the hearts of the boatmen, there was hardly a dry eye in the house. Whatever their national origin, the Bells of Aberdovey were calling them home. The drunken menace who was known for hazarding lives on the canal had brought tears to the eyes of the seasoned boatmen.

But America was their home now and the sing-a-long ended with the usual patriotic song. Whatever misgivings or disagreements boatmen might have with one another, they loved the land to which they and their ancestors had come. With a rousing finale, where everybody joined in, the sing-a-long was over. It was time to get back to their boats. After the evening of communion and entertainment, they were ready to push off before the first light of morning.

CHAPTER IX

Wilhelm no longer needed to hear the conch shell to tell him it was time to get up. His biological clock awakened him precisely at three-thirty each morning. His negative thoughts of Saturday had vanished as he went to fetch the mules. Refreshed and ready to go after a day of Sunday fun, he had forgotten all about the storm. Max and Lucy reflected his mood. They were sprightly and eager to get going as he put them in their traces. Everybody — including Annie — was anxious to get under way.

"Forvard," called Manfred as he turned the tiller to ease the *Onoko Princess* into the middle of the canal.

"Forward," echoed Wilhelm, tugging on the harness.

The nighthawker lanterns glowed in the misty darkness as Lucy and Max resumed their trek. They had not gone far before, instinctively, they picked up their pace. They could not wait to get past the rotten-egg smell of the Union Mill Paper Manufacturing Company which, day in and day out for thirty years, had spewed out the same nose-tingling odor.

Traffic along the canal in both directions was heavy. As fast as Wilhelm adjusted the pace of the mules to the pull on the tow, he had to stop and drop the line. Eager to make up time after their day of rest, every boatman had the same idea. They wanted to leave early and cover as much ground as possible before the locks closed. Conch shells, whistles and boat horns each made their unique sound as boatmen warned locktenders and each other of their approach. As captains crossed tow lines, they exchanged good-natured salutes. Friends and competitors, they knew one another and would help one another, but when it came to gaining as much time as a minute, they wouldn't think twice about doing their best to beat one another through a lock.

The sky lightened in the east as the sun began its climb above the horizon. Having been delegated to empty the commode at the last privy, Annie washed herself under the barrel spigot and settled near her father. By keeping out of her mother's way, she hoped to avoid doing any more chores.

The canal began to move away from the river once more. "Do you know vhere ve are?" asked Manfred as daylight crept over the landscape. As well as telling his children about the waterways, he wanted them to recognize the historic landmarks along the banks.

Annie moved closer. "No, Pa!" she said, eager to hear what he had to say. The only thing she would miss about canaling was her father's stories. "Where are we? … I hope near Bristol!" she added facetiously, glancing at him sideways to see how he would react.

"There you go again, Annie!" he exclaimed with a smile on his face. "You cannot vait to get off the boat. But, for now, *mein liebchen*, you are my prisoner. Vhether you like it or not, I vill tell you vhere ve are!"

"I was only teasing, Papa" she said laughing. "Where are we?"

"Ve cannot see it from here, but ve are passing by Vashington Crossing."

"Don't you mean Washington Crossing, Pa?"

"Ja, *mein kind*! I know … I can never get the old country out of my talk. But remember this, *liebchen* … I'm proud of my ancestry!"

"Why is this part of the river called Washington Crossing, Pa?" asked Annie, more as a reminder to him to continue than from her own ignorance.

"Vhy do you think? You are supposed to be a smart girl."

" 'Cos George Washington crossed the Delaware River here to fight the Red Coats."

"Ja! The year vas 1776 … Vashington and two thousand four hunert of his soldiers crossed the icy river right about there," he said, pointing, "on Christmas night of all nights!"

"How did they get across if the river was frozen?"

"They managed to break the ice and cross by boat. It vas a good thing for this great land of ours that they did! Vhen they got to the other side, they vent on to vin a great victory at Trenton."

"Against the English, Pa?"

"Ja, against the English and their Hessian supporters. If Vashington had not been victorious, ve vould be taking orders from England. A lot of brave men died, fighting for their freedom … and the freedom of the people who came after them, like you and me. The battle vas so fierce, the countryside ran vith blood."

Annie cringed. If one thing more than anything else made her sick, it was the thought of blood. "Let's not talk about that!" she said, beginning to feel queasy.

"All right, *liebchen*, ve von't," conceded her father. "Perhaps you vould like it better if I sang you a song?"

"That would be lovely, Papa."

"How about, 'Vhen old Mauch Chunk vas young'? Vould that suit you better, miss?"

"It would!" replied Annie, preferring to hear one of her father's old ditties to having to think about blood.

Manfred picked up his concertina and cleared his throat. "This is a song about the early pioneers who made it possible for men like me to ply the canals," he announced before letting his bass voice ring out in the quiet of the morning and filling the river valley with sound.

> Vhen old Mauch Chunk vas young
> At noon they blew the horn,
> And, gathering thick, came gangs of men,
> And so at eve and morn.
> Vith grace and promptitude and skill
> They moistened lip and tongue,
> And vent to vork in rain and mud,
> Vhen old Mauch Chunk vas young.

"Come on, everybody, join in."

Annie obliged lustily, aided by Wilhelm on the towpath. Even Mary came out of the cabin and let her soprano soar. As if in response to the joyous blend of voices, a golden sun shone from a cloudless sky. Perfect weather seemed to herald a perfect day as they neared the end of their run.

"Vhen old Mauch ..."

Scandalized when she saw Manfred starting up again, Mary interrupted, "You're not going to sing the second verse of that old song, are you Manny?"

"I am, Mary," he answered before continuing. "I vant our children to know vhat it vas like in the old days."

> Vhen old Mauch Chunk vas young
> Josiah used to say
> A man who labors hard
> Should have six billy cups a day
> And so, vith an unsparing hand,
> The vhiskey flood vas flung
> But drunkards they vere made by scores
> Vhen old Mauch Chunk vas young.

"Those old timers must have been a tough bunch of men," observed Annie as her father squeezed the final chord out of his concertina with a flourish.

"They vere, *liebchen*. But, you know somethin', if they hadn't been tough, the Lehigh Canal vould never have been built. Remember, the land around Mauch Chunk vas mountain vilderness, and the ground vas solid bedrock. The only tools they had vere picks and shovels, and some black powder to blast through the rock."

The next eight miles passed quickly as they sang and chattered under the warm March sun and watched the scenery go by. A mile short of Borden's Lock, it was Manfred who suggested that Wilhelm have a rest. But not without first chastising Annie. "You've been sitting here all morning, Annie, doing nothin'. Isn't it about time you took a turn on the towpath? Ve'll pull over at Jones' store down the vay so you and Vil can trade places." The truth was he had run out of tobacco and needed an excuse to stop.

After a morning of doing nothing, Annie knew there was no saying "no!" Without a word, she got up from her perch on the equipment locker. And waited for the boat to stop.

Coming up starboard was Jack and Megan Jones's red clapboard general store. Out of habit, Manfred called out the mooring directions. But he needn't have bothered. Wilhelm had already taken Lucy and Max past the store and left exactly the right amount of room for his father to pull the *Onoko Princess* parallel to the wooden landing. Although this time Wilhelm had managed to keep his tiredness to himself, after an eight-mile stint on the towpath, he was more than ready to have Annie take over.

Like many of the lock stores, the Joneses sold everything from boat gear to shoes. But when they set up their establishment, Jack and Megan had been extra smart. Instead of opening a store at a lock, they set up shop along a level. That way, boatmen on the run could grab a quick mug of coffee, buy feed for their mules or use the privy without having to deal with the usual hustle and bustle and clamor of waiting boats.

Mary and Manfred went into the store together, hoping to make an exchange for a chicken, and some tobacco. A string of sleigh bells on the back of the door announced their arrival. The Joneses made sure that no one ever entered without their knowing it.

"Top of the morrrnin' to ye, Maery an' Manny," greeted Jack Jones' Irish wife, Megan, hustling out of the back room and wiping her hands on her apron. " 'Tis the firrst toime Oi've seen ya in many a moon. What can Oi be doin' fer ya now?"

"Would you consider making a trade, Megan?" asked Mary hesitantly. "We would be most obliged if you would take a bag of coal for a chicken and some tobaccy?" If there was on thing Mary disliked, it was bartering. It was embarrassing. But, over the years, she had come to accept it as a way of life on the canal.

"Well, 'tis this waay," answered Megan, "moi coal bin is full with all them poor fellers what hadn't been paid offerin' me coal fer moi goods. It's so bad, a body can hardly mek a livin'. But Oi'll tell you what Oi'll do, seein' Oi'm guessin', loike the others, you're short o' cash. Oi'll let you have the chickin an' 'baccy on tick. Oi'll put them on the books, and you can paay me when you cum back. Oi trust the Oberfeldts! Oi know, you'll fork oop the next toime around! Oi can't say that much fer sum o' them boatmen!"

"That's mighty nice of you to say so, Megan."

"Vhere's the mister?" asked Manfred. "I didn't see him about outside."

"Jack's pickin' up spuds from a farmer," said Megan, neatly lopping off the neck and feet of the chicken with a cleaver. "I don't see your two bairns, neither!"

"They're vith us," replied Manfred, "Annie helps out all around. And Vil is old enough to be drivin' my mules … saves me the price of a mule driver."

"And a cook … and a washwoman too, Oi suspect!" laughed Megan.

As well as trading goods, Megan Jones specialized in trading news. A stop in at the Jones's store meant that canalers could count on hearing the latest gossip. Today was no exception. And Megan could not wait to pass on the news, imparted to her barely ten minutes ago by a boatman. "Do you know Paddy Dillon?" she asked.

"Isn't he the Irishman out of Easton?"

"That's roight! Well, let me tell you … his boat sprang a leak. And this bein' poor Paddy's firrst trip o' the season. It grounded on a sandbar and settled to the bottom, loaded t' the hilt. Even the deck is awash, Oi hear."

"Where did it happen?" asked Mary.

"Up the canal a piece, just out o' New Hope. It was so bad, they had to cum with a rowboat and take him off."

"Is the boat ruined?" asked Manfred.

"Oi think not! It takes a lot to kill them old wooden tubs. But Oi heard, there's a queer old back-up above it. They're busy unloadin' the coal now so they can pump out the water and tow the leaky ol' tub back to the boatyard at New Hope."

"Vell, I'm glad ve left before he did," observed Manfred, lighting a fresh plug of tobacco and taking a draw. "All ve need is another delay! Ve've had enough this trip."

Megan carried the chicken by its feet, making sure before she handed it to Mary that the innards were not dripping. Then she entered the purchases in her ledger. The ledger was thick with IOUs. Some boatmen were to be trusted. Others were not. They would promise to pay the next time they passed, and go right by. But offering credit or taking coal as payment was the price of doing business along the canal, and whichever way Megan operated, her customers could be sure that she kept her books straight.

The bells jangled their good-bye as Manfred opened the door. "Thanks, Megan!"

"You're an angel," called Mary. "We'll be sure to see you when we make our next trip. We'll get paid when we pass through the Weigh Lock outside Mauch Chunk."

Annie took the *Onoko Princess* through Borden's Lock and switched places again with Wilhelm at Lear's. They had just over fourteen miles to go to Bristol. Exhausted after her walk, she went into the cabin to lie down. Mary had finished her chores early so, with her daughter's favorite perch on the equipment locker vacant, she sat near her husband, knitting socks and enjoying the nice afternoon.

As they plied the short level between Lear's and Yardleyville, Taffy Morgan and his boat were the furthest things from Manfred's mind. With the weather fair and Mary to talk to, he had not been paying much attention to what was behind.

Back at Lear's, Morgan had made up some time. He had pushed his way in front of one boat while her captain was in the privy and beaten another boat through the lock. No incident, no accident could change his will to get ahead.

When he came through the miter gates into the level, he was a quarter mile back of the *Onoko Princess*, and closing in fast.

"Git them bloody beasts goin', or you won't get a penny."

There was no mistaking that refrain or that voice. Wilhelm turned around. "Look, Pa," he shouted, "Taffy Morgan's behind us."

Manfred turned around. When he saw the green boat gaining on them, he did something he rarely did. He swore. "Them mules must have vings! That rascal's comin' up so fast, he vill be into our rear end before ve know it. And, if he doesn't knock us out of the vater, ve vill have him on our tail all the vay to Yardleyville. Just listen to him whooping and hollering and cursing."

As usual, the victim of Morgan's wrath was his driver. The louder Morgan yelled, the harder the driver cracked his whip. This was not the same scrawny young man who had driven his mules on the level near Bowmanstown. Like dozens of Morgan's drivers before him, he had quit. This was a sturdier, older man.

"Maybe we should pull over, Pa, and let them pass," yelled Wilhelm, not wanting to risk another encounter.

"Not on your life, son! That's against Company rules. Two boats goin' in the same direction are not allowed to pass one another on these canals. He's either trying to push us to go faster or break the rules and move over. And ve're doin' neither. Pay the varmint no heed! Our mules ain't goin' to get all frazzled and vore out before quittin' time."

Snorting and sweaty, Morgan's mules were staggering along the towpath, pulling the loaded coal boat as fast as they could. Although still several boat lengths behind the *Onoko Princess*, Morgan was coming up fast on her stern.

"Hey," hollered Manfred, "rein in them mules or you vill be into our back end."

If Morgan had known that the Company boat in front of him was the *Onoko Princess*, he would have slowed down. But it was not until he got close enough to make out the carving of the Indian maiden on her stern that he realized who she belonged to and yelled to his driver to pull back. The order came just in time. Another crack of the whip, and his mules would have passed alongside the *Onoko Princess* taking the green coal boat into her stern.

"You vant to send us both to the bottom of the canal," Manfred yelled through cupped hands.

Morgan's answer was to spit in contempt. But the message had gotten through. Not wishing to rile Manfred any further, he dropped back and followed the *Onoko Princess* at a safe distance along the level.

Max and Lucy clip clopped across the aqueduct north of Yardleyville. Beyond it, the canal widened, and Manfred did something he swore he would never do. He pulled over. For his peace of mind and everybody else's, he would let Morgan get ahead. The Welshman seized the opportunity and sped by. By the time the *Onoko Princess* arrived at Yardleyville, he had passed through the lock.

"What was all that screamin' and hollerin' about?" asked the locktender as he reversed the lock for the *Onoko Princess*. "I asked that Welshman what was happening back on the level but he went on out of the miter gates without sayin' nothin'."

"No vonder!" exclaimed Manfred. "He nearly rammed my boat!"

Morgan was well out of the way by the time the *Onoko Princess* entered the level below Yardleyville. With no locks to pass through for the next ten miles, they should make up some time.

The canal was a picture of serenity as it threaded its way through the fertile valley past graceful stands of oak, sycamore, walnut and chestnut trees. Sometimes it ran close to the river bank; at others, it moved away leaving great expanses of wetland between it and its Mother Water. Swept by a gentle breeze, marsh grasses swayed their tufted heads, concealing nesting muskrats that called the flood plain home. A flock of wild geese cawed their celestial chorus above the waving sea of green. Flying in a great V formation, helped along by the wind currents, they were following the river valley to their breeding grounds further north. Doing her best not to intrude on the natural world, the *Onoko Princess* glided through the quiet of the afternoon with barely a ripple.

But, like most things on the canal, peace and tranquillity did not last. Halfway along the level, a "stone boat" cast off from a waterfront tavern where its crew had stopped to refresh themselves. Loaded with lime from the kilns at Taylorsville near Washington Crossing, it was another in the procession of boats carrying building supplies to the great city of Philadelphia. With skilled handling of its mules by the driver, and an equally skilled captain at the helm, it nudged its way into the canal in front of the *Onoko Princess*.

"Drat!" exclaimed Manfred, fearing the lime would blow into their faces.

Things went well until late afternoon when the wind picked up. Blowing north along the river valley, it whipped the tarpaulins off the low-sided boat and blew the white powder into a cloud that burned and stung whatever it touched. Even blinders could not protect the eyes of the mules. In short order, Lucy and Max had had enough. Snorting and swishing their tails, they dug their heels into the towpath and refused to go on. "Them beasts are right," conceded Manfred. "Ve'll be blinded if ve don't let that stone boat get vell ahead."

With the mules going nowhere, Wilhelm scooped some water from the canal and washed out his eyes. Then, he took off the blinders and did the same to the mules. His father was already taking care of himself at the water barrel. With the *Onoko Princess* motionless, the backup behind her grew. Patience became short. Horns and whistles blew loudly as boatmen made it known they wanted to be on their way. It was only when a gust of wind carried a cloud of lime dust beyond the *Onoko Princess* that they realized what was going on. Wiping their burning eyes, they stopped agitating and waited for the stone boat to disappear along the level.

With a quarter of a mile between her and the stone boat, the *Onoko Princess* started up again. The procession of boats behind her followed at a steady pace. Like Manfred, their captains were not anxious to get an eyeful of lime.

Clusters of houses and an occasional tavern told Manfred they were approaching Morrisville. Named after Robert Morris, a financial backer of the American Revolution and a signer of the Declaration of Independence and Constitution, Morrisville was an important settlement from the early days of colonization. Another important American patriot was a resident of Morrisville; George Clymer had also signed the Declaration of Independence and the Constitution

A Company boat was off-loading at a private coal yard on the river side of the canal. Like the Oberfeldts, its crew was a family. What caught the attention of Annie, and everybody else in the vicinity, was the loud wailing of the toddler tied to the deck. One end of a rope was around his middle; the other was knotted through an iron ring on the side of the cabin. The rope was just long enough so that he could play on deck without tumbling into the water. Frustrated at not being able to go where he wanted, the boy was making a terrible fuss to get free.

When Annie heard his screams, she came out of the cabin. "I'm glad I can swim or you and Ma would tie me up like that!" she laughed cupping her hands over her ears as the youngster threw himself down on the deck in a tantrum.

"You're a bit old for that now," said her father, smiling, "but I mind the days vhen your ma roped you and Vil to the deck."

"As if I could forget! I remember screaming blue murder when you wouldn't let me loose. One thing being tethered to the deck taught me. It taught me to swim real quick!"

"That tot vill learn to svim real quick too. His parents vill see to that. Vhen the veather gets varm, they vill tie a rope around his middle and drop him into the canal from the back of the boat. Vhen he goes under, he vill paddle for his dear life. But not to vorry! If he gets into trouble, his pa vill be there to hoist him on board."

With the lime boat way ahead and the air clear once again, Annie decided to stay on deck for the last leg of their journey. "Gosh, Papa" she remarked, as they passed a handsome brick Georgian mansion, crowning a rise in the land back from the river. Its eastern façade was brick; the rest, fieldstone. "Look at that beautiful house. Me and Wil and you and Ma, and Gram and Grandpa could all have our own bedroom. There must be loads of rooms."

"That's 'Summerseat,' *liebchen*. Over the years, both Robert Morris and George Clymer lived there. Remember I told you, they vere both signers of the Declaration of Independence? In December, 1776, 'Summerseat' vas George Vashington's headquarters before he crossed the Delavare and defeated the Red Coats and Hessians at the Battle of Trenton."

"You mean, before he crossed the Delaware on Christmas Eve?"

"Oh, so you remembered, *liebchen*," exclaimed Manfred proudly. "You cannot see it from here, but the State House at Trenton is on the New Jersey side of the river. More signers of the Declaration of Independence lived around here than anyvhere else in America."

"Why was that?"

"Vhen this country vas founded, Pennsylvania vas a very important state. They called it the Keystone State."

Annie looked puzzled. "Tell me, Pa, what is a keystone?"

"A keystone is the stone on top of an arch that locks all the other stones in place. Pennsylvania is called the Keystone State because it vas located between the northern and southern states. That is a very important position! Did you know that Philadelphia vas the capital of America after the Revolution? That is vhere the Declaration of Independence vas signed."

"Why isn't it still the capital?"

"The government decided to honor our first president, George Vashington, by naming a new capital after him in 1800."

"Gosh, Pa, you know everything!"

"Oh ... no I don't, Annie! Nobody does! But, if you travel the canals as long as I have, you'll know every mountain and valley ... and 'most everything that took place along the vay."

"I suppose," said Annie, secretly hoping she would not be on the canal long enough for that to happen.

As they passed a tavern, they saw the stone boat tied up at the landing. Instinctively, Lucy and Max quickened their pace. This pleased Manfred, not to mention the impatient captains whose boats were plying the canal bow to stern behind him.

For the first time since they set out, it was warm enough to cook supper on the two-burner stove on deck. Mary had already plucked and cleaned the chicken she bought from Megan Jones, cut it into pieces and rolled them in flour. Fanned by a gentle breeze, the stove fired up quickly. Too quickly, Mary thought, as the bacon fat she had saved from the day before began to smoke in the large frying pan. Like most people of Pennsylvania Dutch ancestry, Mary was frugal. She never wasted a thing. "Waste not, want not" was her motto and she lived by what she preached every day. Everything left over from anything, no matter what it was, was saved to make or repair something else.

The cooking went quickly. It was easier to juggle pots and pans outdoors than in the confined space of the cabin. Some homemade noodles boiled on one stoveplate while the chicken sizzled and browned on the other. As the mouth-watering aroma drifted along the canal, every captain and mule driver that came up the canal asked jokingly to be invited for supper. The crew were hungrier than lions. But they were not the only ones. Max and Lucy's loud neighing announced they were demanding a meal on the run.

Having been slowed down enough by the stone boat, Manfred decided to keep on going. This meant that, while everybody on board ate, Wilhelm had to listen to his stomach rumble on the towpath. Where it concerned feeding the crew, his mother took command. Knowing how hungry he must be, she called, as she served chicken and noodles *al fresco* to the rest of the crew, "We'll trade places at Smither's Coal Yard. I'll get back on board at Edgely. Your pa wants you to take the boat into Bristol."

Good as her word, Mary finished her meal quickly and was ready to change places at Smither's. Wilhelm sat close to his father, wolfing down his noodle and chicken dinner as they passed through Penn Valley. Once known as "Tyburn" after an area in London where hangings took place, it was in Penn Valley that the notorious murderer Derrick Johnson was hanged in 1683. And it was in Penn Valley that his ghost was supposed to roam. As specters of mist hovered and drifted above the water, Wilhelm could not have been more pleased that it was his mother and not himself who was walking the towpath. But, all too soon, Edgely was upon them. Like it or not, he had to trade places for the last two and a half-mile trek.

While gray misty ghosts rose from the water, it was pitch black on the towpath. Wilhelm could not see a thing in front of him, so he held tight to the harness to calm his fears. Connected to the boy-man by a leather strap, Lucy and Max sensed his uneasiness. Without a word or a gesture from him, they picked up their pace. Were they afraid of the ghost of Derrick Johnson? Or were they just in a hurry to get to the end of the run? Having scared himself silly ever since Tyburn with moving shadows and visions of Derrick Johnson hanging from a rope, nobody was more eager than Wilhelm to reach the end of the towpath at Bristol.

CHAPTER X

Next morning, Manfred allowed himself to sleep longer than usual before setting out for the Navigation office to see if anything had been done about Taffy Morgan. When he enquired if the Company had acted on his complaint, the supervisor, assured him they had.

"Morgan's off the canal," said Fritz Heinz. "Starting today, he'll be suspended for a week."

"*Sehr gut*! At least ve vill be safe for a few days," said Manfred turning to leave.

"I heard he was on your tail again above Yardleyville," Heinz remarked before he could get to the door.

"It alvays amazes me how quickly news gets around!" exclaimed Manfred. "Does he know who reported him?"

"He suspects. He brought up your name."

"Did you say it was me?"

"No, that's against Company policy."

"Gut, or he vill harass us all the more! I hated to turn him in. I just vant him to learn respect for us boatmen … and his animals."

"Don't feel guilty, captain! You weren't the only one to complain. I'd like nothing better than to keep him off the canal, but a week's the best I can do. Maybe, when he can't make any money, he'll get some sense into his head."

"I doubt it!"

"Did you hear, one of his mules dropped dead?"

"Vhich vone?"

"The hind one … the real skinny one."

"It's better off!" said Manfred, as he made to leave for a second time.

"Get in line," Fritz Heinz called after him. "As soon as the tug comes back, she'll tow you along the tidewater. It'll be a four-boat tow. Wait in back of Company boats 175 and 218, and the *Meg Ryan*."

With the help of the mules, Wilhelm and Manfred positioned the *Onoko Princess* behind the other boats and waited for the tugboat to return. The tug, the anthracite-burning *Pennsylvania*, was owned by the Lehigh Coal & Navigation Company. Black with a rusty red funnel and the Company's red, white and blue bull's-eye trademark on her bow, she plied the waters of the Delaware River between Bristol and Philadelphia. Since being fitted with tubular boilers like those of a steam locomotive, she consumed two-thirds less coal and could tow as many as twenty loaded boats at a time, carrying upward of one thousand tons of coal.

It was not long before the *Pennsylvania* steamed in from Philadelphia pushing eight empty boats. One at a time, she positioned them at the side of the towpath so that they could pick up their mules for the return trip to Mauch Chunk. As soon as the *Pennsylvania* was free of one train of boats, she positioned herself to pick up the next. Towing the *Onoko Princess* into the river, she pushed her parallel to the *Meg Ryan* so that their captains could lash the two boats together. Next came the two Company boats. Nudged into position, they were lashed together, and the front and back pairs in the tow were lashed to one another.

Their work done for the next three days, Wilhelm led Max and Lucy to the stable. He shoveled and swilled their stall and arranged for the stable boy to care for them. As he patted them on their rumps, they snorted good-bye. By the time the *Onoko Princess* returned to Bristol, they would have had a well-earned rest.

With the exception of a few boat captains and mule drivers who made their homes in Bristol, most crews stayed on their boats for the trip to Philadelphia. Staying on board was cheaper than paying for lodging, and a visit to the big city was a change from the rote of everyday life. A few boatmen hitched a cart ride from the coal wharves in Port Richmond into the center of the big city to have a good time, but most were content to hang out on the waterfront replenishing supplies, exchanging gossip and enjoying the hospitality of their favorite eating place or tavern. When two boat families tied up near one another, the children became children again. They whooped it up in vacant lots in good weather and, when it rained, played games in their cabins or, most fun of all, in the large holds when they were empty.

A toot of the tug's whistle and the boat tow began to move along the tidewater. The surface of the Delaware river was choppy. The pull of the ocean at the mouth of the estuary, and the turbulence of the wakes made Annie feel sick. Looking as if she were about to vomit, her mother sent her on deck. Fresh air was Mary's remedy for sea sickness. Tea with a little lemon did not hurt either, but, with a luxury like lemon out of the question on this trip, she brought Annie a mug of hot chamomile tea. Annie sat on the equipment locker, sipping the tea and inhaling the fresh breeze. Soon, her insides stopped heaving and she was well enough to take in the sights. Standing tall and proud behind the riverfront wharves and warehouses were the steeple of Christ Church, the tallest steeple in the city, and Independence Hall. It would be nice to attend Christ Church with her family on a Sunday, but, most of all, Annie wanted to visit Independence Hall and see the Liberty Bell. Her teacher had told her that the Liberty Bell was the old State House bell, which had been carted out of the city and taken to Allentown, along with many other bells, so the English could not capture them and melt them down for ammunition during the War of Independence.

It was early afternoon by the time the four boats were separated from the tug and each other, and moored at the Navigation Company coal yard. With Mary's remedy for sea sickness a success, Annie was well enough to accompany her onshore to replenish supplies for the return trip to Mauch Chunk.

The worst thing about the Philadelphia waterfront was its fishy smell. When schooners brought their catch of bunker fish in from the Atlantic, it was taken to processing plants along the waterfront to be rendered into oil. Dozens of kegs of the smelly oil stood outside the plants, ready to be shipped to paint manufacturers and factories where it was used either in the manufacturing process or as a lubricant. The odor was pungent at any time of year, but in the cool weather of March it was not as strong as in summer. Even so, Annie wrinkled her nose in disgust as she walked past the row of kegs.

"Phew," she said, pinching her nostrils shut, "there's no mistaking Philadelphia!"

Annie grabbed her mother's arm and hustled her away from the docks and down a lane. The further they got from the waterfront, the more the odor abated. Caught up in the hustle and bustle of commerce, Annie soon forgot about it. Pedestrians, jostling with horse-drawn wagons for space in the narrow, muddy alleys, had to be careful not to be trampled on. Hastening to make deliveries, drivers drove their carts willy nilly through the crowds. In the windows of the small shops in basements or on the ground floors of row houses, there were no luxuries like jewelry or fine dresses. Everything that was for sale reflected the needs of a boatman's or sailor's daily life. The one exception was the street vendors. Hollering loudly at passersby from their stalls in the small market square, they did their best to entice every mariner who went by to buy a piece of cheap jewelry or a bolt of cloth for their sweethearts or wives.

Business was brisk as Mary and Annie bought the few items they needed. Food was cheaper at lock stores along the canal, but the excitement of shopping in Philadelphia made up for the high price. Townspeople, boatmen and sailors from foreign ports thronged the streets and back alleys. In all her life, Annie had never seen so many Negroes in one place at one time. They were pouring into Philadelphia, the nearest and largest city north of the Mason Dixon Line, by the Underground Railroad, a network that provided aid and assistance to those who wanted to escape the bonds of slavery. The lucky ones found a place to stay, and a job; the rest hung about the waterfront, looking for work and an empty warehouse to call home.

One such black family caught Annie's eye. Their clothes were in tatters and their bodies were skin and bone. Looking furtively about them as if they were still on the run, the parents and their two children worked the crowd. Food, money, clothing, anything that would help them survive was received with gratitude and a smile.

"Can you spare a penny, missus?" a girl of about Annie's age asked Mary.

"Give her something, Ma," urged Annie, stricken by the girl's ragged appearance.

Mary hesitated. Merchants along the Philadelphia waterfront were notorious for not settling for coal as payment for goods, and she had been cautioned by Manfred to buy only what they needed. But Mary was as moved as Annie by the destitute family. Reaching into her pocket, she handed the Negro girl a penny. "Here, love," she said shamefacedly, "that's the best I can do." With a nod of thanks and a shy smile, the girl ran over to her father and turned over the coin.

Nothing escaped the stall holders. Noticing that Mary had given money to the Negro family, a vendor with a Cockney accent beckoned her over. "I 'ave a bargain fer you, missus, and the loverly young lidy. Four yards of the best calico fer ten cents. You can mike the young lidy a loverly new dress fer summer … or some haprons fer yourself to brighten your old dresses hup."

Ignoring him, Mary walked on. Not so Annie. Before her mother could grab her arm and hustle her away, she was over by his stall, admiring the fabrics. And what an array it was! Stripes and flowers, patchwork in every color of the rainbow, were spread out on the table beneath the awning. But it was a length of red cotton, splashed all over with blue cornflowers, that caught Annie's eye.

"Look, Ma," she said, holding up the bolt of cloth for her mother to see. "Isn't this lovely?" Then, in a voice tinged with self-pity, she added, "It's been ages since I had a new dress."

Mary knew. She looked at her daughter. So young and beautiful. Her brown dress almost as dowdy and shabby as the cast-offs worn by the Negro girl. Youth and beauty were fleeting, and she was filled with the longing to make things right. "I suppose that's your way of asking me to buy it," she said softly.

"Well …" said Annie shrugging her shoulders.

"But red! What will your father say?"

"It's as pretty as poppies in a summer garden. And it's cheap too."

"But you know we're only supposed to shop for provisions. You had me give something to that Negro girl, now you want me to buy this!"

The vendor smirked, sensing Mary was wavering. He had already figured that he was about to make a sale.

"Is ten cents the best you can do?" asked Mary lamely while Annie stood by looking as if her heart would break if the sale did not go through. "We are canalers. This is our first trip of the season and we haven't been paid."

Skilled in the art of bargaining, the man pretended to think for a moment; then, fearing he might lose his customer as Mary stepped away from the stall, he lowered the price. "Fer you missus, and the young lidy, Hi'll tike five cents fer the lot." With great ceremony, he draped the fabric over his arm to show it to its best effect. "Yer getting a real bargain, missus. There's hover four yards 'ere … enough to mike a dress fer yer daughta, and han ipron for yourself."

Distrusting dockside vendors, Mary unwound the bolt of material and laid it out on the stall. Satisfied that it measured what the man said, she counted out five pennies. There!" she said putting them in his grimy hand, "you've made a sale!"

The vendor folded the fabric carefully, tied it with a piece of twine and handed it to Annie. "Here you hare, lassie. All the mashers'll be after you when they see you hin this."

Mary looked scandalized, but Annie took it as a compliment. Her mother was an excellent seamstress. With time to spare between chores, she would make sure that her mother finished the dress so she could show it off at church. By the time they unloaded and got back up the canal, they should be in Easton by Sunday.

Pleased at having got what she wanted, Annie put the bundle in her mother's shopping bag and, linking arms with her, started back in the direction of the boat.

"Not so fast, young lady," admonished Mary, pulling away in the direction of a back alley. "We have another stop to make. I promised your father I'd get him some haddock for supper."

Annie followed her mother into the shop, pulling a face.

With several loaded boats in line ahead of the *Onoko Princess*, there was no way the coal would be taken off until morning. To put in time, Manfred suggested that he and Wilhelm take a walk. As they wandered through the busy streets and back alleys, he told Wilhelm about his adventures in this place and that. On the way back to the boat, the Ship Inn proved to be too much of a temptation. Manfred felt like enjoying the companionship of his fellow boatman and getting the latest news from along the canal. Knowing Mary would not want to expose Wilhelm to the errant ways of some off-duty boatmen, he sent him to the feed store to see if the proprietor would make an exchange for a sack of oats.

As usual, The Ship was crowded with mariners. Canal boatmen and sailors off freighters, tugs and frigates were enjoying time off in port. Recognizing several Company boatmen, Manfred joined them at the bar and ordered a sarsaparilla. The topic of conversation was the suspension of two boatmen. One was a Company captain who had locked horns with a boat from one of the freight companies; the other was Taffy Morgan.

Except for the renegades who were guilty of such infractions themselves, most boatmen believed that the suspensions were justified. Those in agreement abided by the rules of the waterway. They believed that unsafe boating should not go unpunished. When talk turned to speculation about who turned in whom, Manfred thought it best to move on. He took his glass over to a table and pulled out a chair. Indiscernible against the dark mahogany paneling as he sat in the corner was Captain James Washington, his hands cupped around a coffee mug. Like Manfred, James Washington was a teetotaler.

Manfred reached out for the black man's hand across the table. "Vell, if it isn't Captain Vashington! How are things going vith you?"

"You maight say Ah'm makin' a livin'."

"You maight say Ah'm makin' a livin'."

From the way Washington answered, Manfred judged he was not having an easy time. When Washington inherited the *Sally Sue* from Captain Serfass, he toyed with the idea of selling her, aware of the prejudice he would face as the first black boatman on the canals. Then, he thought of his people. Unlike most of them, he had been given the opportunity to make something of himself and, if he wanted to move on in this world, he had better take advantage of it. Now, he was suffering the consequences. Too many boatmen were resentful of his position and ready to turn him in if he said or did anything untoward.

"How was your trip?" he asked, adept at shifting the focus from himself. "Ah heard you had anotha run-in wit' Morgan."

"News travels fast!"

"He's off the canal, ya know. Got a week's suspension." Then, leaning over the table, Washington whispered, "He blames you."

"How do you know?"

"Ah happened to be payin' ma tolls when he come into tha port office. He wuz mad as a stung bear, shoutin' and cussin', askin' where you ware. Ah tell ya, Cap'n Oberfeldt, if Ah wuz you, Ah'd watch out. That man is downright dangerous!"

"Vhat's he goin' to do? Sink my boat?"

"Nothin' he did would surprise me!" answered Washington.

"Me neither!" agreed Manfred.

A white man and a black man engaged in intimate conversation was something worth finding out about. And they became the focal point of the men at the bar. For the most part, the men were a rough bunch. With the end of the line being layover time, a number were already intoxicated and some were spoiling for a fight. Among the pugilists was a red-headed Irish mule driver who made no secret of his hatred of Negroes and his ambition to be a boat captain. Staggering over to Manfred, he snarled, "You don't seem to care who you sit with, do you Oberfeldt?"

Manfred turned crimson. "I sit vhere I choose!" he said quietly.

"That's not surprising. There's not much difference between a kraut and a nigger!"

Manfred stood up, dwarfing the Irishman. "Mind vhat you say, Dooley!"

"Oi'll say VHAT Oi please!" he answered, mimicking Manfred's pronunciation of 'w' as he pointed at Washington. "The canal's nee place for the loikes o' him. He belongs doon South, pickin' cotton. Not captainin' a coal boat!"

Mouthing his thoughts was not good enough for Dooley. It only incited him. Staggering around the table, he threw a punch at Washington. But, before the blow could land, Manfred had him in a vice. Lifting him up like a rag doll, he carried him out of the tavern, and threw him into the street. Respecting Manfred's physique, Dooley's friends made no move to help. Manfred returned to his table, and finished his drink. Then left the tavern in the company of Washington.

"I'm sorry, Captain, for vhat happened," said Manfred as Washington climbed over the side of his boat.

"Don't worry," replied the black man, "it ain't nothin' new!"

"I vill see you in the mornin'."

Washington nodded. The *Sally Sue* was tied up two berths behind the *Onoko Princess*. More than likely, after they unloaded, they would share the same tow back to Bristol.

CHAPTER XI

Next morning, Mary and Annie decided to go ashore while the coal was unloaded. Wilhelm wanted to go with them, but his father insisted he stay to see how the unloading was done. Coal was being taken off several boats at the same time and the air was full of black grit. It was making Wilhelm cough so he pulled his coat up over his mouth and nose and joined his father on top of the cabin.

After the two sections of the *Onoko Princess* were uncoupled, laborers went to work inside the coal holds scooping up large shovelfuls of coal and emptying them into a two-hundred-pound iron bucket, hooked onto a derrick. When the bucket was full, the men signaled the derrick operator. With a pull of a lever, he hoisted the load skyward. Precariously swinging and swaying, the bucket crossed over the deck of the *Onoko Princess* and hovered over a giant coal pile on shore. Another lever unlocked the bucket's massive jaws. With its teeth parted wide, black diamond nuggets cascaded noisily on top of the heap. Huffing and puffing, the derrick moved back and forth between the *Onoko Princess* and the coal heap until the two coal holds were empty. The clang and clatter of machinery reminded

Wilhelm of Mauch Chunk. But, although the derrick was big and powerful, it could not compare to the amazing combination of the Switchback Gravity Railroad and coal chutes.

With no errands to run and no money in their pockets, Mary and Annie spent their time by taking in the sights. Attracted by some catchy music, they turned into an alley and made their way toward the sound. An organ grinder was turning the handle of a barrel organ on a street corner, churning out a medley of merry tunes. Each time the reel ran out and the melody ended, a tiny capuchin monkey, attired in a bright red jacket and pillbox hat, collected money from the crowd. As Mary and Annie lingered on the fringe of the crowd, his beady eyes rested on the newcomers. Attracted by Annie's long tresses, he ran between the legs of the gathering and made a leap for her shoulder. But before he managed to land, Mary yanked Annie's arm and tore her away.

Wandering willy-nilly through the crowds, Mary tried to steer clear of the pushy street vendors. She kept a tight hold on Annie's arm to make sure that she did not stray over to any of the stalls. As they walked along the streets, it seemed to Mary as if anybody who had a talent was using it to extract money from passersby. On another street corner, a trio of acrobats leaped and tumbled. The two strongest threw the shortest and lightest into the air, bracing themselves as he landed on their shoulders. Further on, a juggler hurled six shiny daggers skyward. End over end they tumbled, their steel blades flashing and glinting as they flew round and round in a circle. The crowd stood breathless as, one by one, the juggler plucked the knives from the air by their hilts before they could sever his hand. A little way on, an operatic tenor sang an aria, accompanied by the wail of his partner's violin. Mary and Annie strolled from crowd to crowd to enjoy the entertainment, but, having learned their lesson with the monkey they moved on before it was time to pass the hat.

Between acts, they grew weary and took a rest on a flight of stone steps leading to one of the fine buildings to watch the throngs go by. Although the ordinary folks were interesting enough, Annie's biggest thrill was to see the fine Philadelphia ladies go by in their horse-drawn cabriolets. Dressed to the hilt, peering from beneath leather-hooded carriages, they stared at those who were staring at them. Matching the elegant dress of the fine ladies were their uniformed drivers and the horses that pulled their cabriolets. Tails and manes plaited with colored ribbons, their harnesses festooned with straw flowers, they pranced aristocratically along the dirt streets leaving a trail of dust behind them. In contrast to this manifestation of wealth, dirty-faced street urchins, their clothes in tatters, searched the well-trodden sidewalks for anything of value they could find. A stray coin dropped from the pocket of an unwary pedestrian was a premium; a discarded morsel of food not anything to pass by.

Further and further Mary and Annie went through the warren of unfamiliar streets until the sun began to wane. It was time to get back to the *Onoko Princess*, By now, she should be unloaded. Searching out landmarks that had become vaguely familiar — the stoop where they had rested, a street corner where they had been entertained — they retraced their steps. When they began to smell the vats of bunker fish oil fouling the air, they knew they were nearing the waterfront. They were barely five minutes away from the *Onoko Princess*'s mooring place when sound not smell assailed them. A chorus of taunts, followed by cruel peals of laughter, was coming from behind a warehouse. Before Mary could stop Annie, she ran off to investigate, leaving Mary with no alternative but to follow her if she wanted to keep her daughter safe. Peering around a high brick wall, they saw the object of derision. Half sitting, half lying in the gutter, a red-faced man was being taunted by a gang of ragamuffin boys.

> Taffy was a Welshman
> Taffy was a thief
> Taffy came to my house
> And stole a piece of beef.
> I went to Taffy's house
> Taffy was in bed
> So I took up the marrow bone
> And hit him in the head.

Mary gasped. It was none other than Taffy Morgan. Intending to while away his time off the canal in the big city, Morgan had paid off a tugboat captain to tow his boat across the tidewater. Inebriated to the point where he could not stand up, incapable of defending himself, the best Taffy Morgan could do was to splutter curses at his tormentors in Welsh.

"That ol' Welshman looks like he needs soberin' up," sneered the gang leader. Pointing to a bailing bucket laying on the dock, he ordered the smallest, skinniest boy, "Go fill that pail, Joe."

Joe shrunk up small. "Yer not gonna douse him, are yer, Tony? He's bigger than us."

"Yer right, Joe. We're not gonna douse him, we're gonna drown him." When Joe hesitated, he doubled his fist and gestured. "Git goin' if ya know what's good fer ya."

Joe knew what was good for him from past experience. Without another word, he ran dockside, leaned over the pilings and scooped up a bucket of water. "Here," he said, handing it to Tony.

"Not s' fast, buster! Yer gonna do the honor."

"Me?" quavered Joe. "He'll kill me if he ketches me."

"Give 'im a bath, ya little pipsqueak, or I'll beat yer to a pulp."

Having been beaten by Tony before, Joe had no intention of being beaten again. Tiptoeing toward Morgan from behind, he tipped the bucket over the Welshman's head. The cold water worked wonders. It brought Morgan out of his stupor. He staggered to his feet and attempted to go after the scattering gang. "I'll wring your bloody necks if I catch you," he screamed, lunging for Joe's jacket. But if Joe wasn't brave, he was wily. He ducked under Morgan's arm, and scooted down the alley after the rest of the gang.

Whether it was admiration for Joe's bravery, or fear of Morgan, Annie stood transfixed.

"Come on," said her mother, "let's get out of here before something else happens." If the gang had been bullying anyone else, she would have run off and fetched a policeman. But, knowing the Welshman for what he was, she felt he deserved his comeuppance.

Taffy Morgan was drenched to the skin as he lurched back to the boat dock to change into dry clothes. He was just about there when something interesting caught his attention and he crouched in a doorway to watch.

A Negro boy was being pursued by two policemen. The boy outran them, ducked into an alley, clambered into a coal bin at the rear of the Ship Inn, and slammed the lid down on top of himself. The policemen ran to the top of the alley waving their night sticks. Uncertain about which direction he had taken, they stopped. Then, thinking he had gone straight on, they sped down the alley away from his hiding place. The occupant of the coal bin had his ear to the side. As soon as the footsteps faded, he raised the lid to see if the coast was clear. Then, seeing no one in the alley, he climbed out and ran back in the direction he came.

At the same time Morgan was observing the goings on, James Washington was on his way back to the *Sally Sue* with a bag of feed for his mules. Before he knew what was happening, the sack was on the ground and nearly him with it. "Look what you've done!" he spluttered as the black youth bumped into him. "What's your hurry, young fella?"

The boy picked up the feed sack and thrust it back into Washington's hand. "Ah didn't mean to knock into ya, Mister," he panted, and started to run on.

"Whoa!" hollered Washington, grabbing his jacket tail. "Not so fast! Some-thin' chasin' ya or what, son?"

"Let go o' me, Mista," he whined, squirming to break free. "The coppers'll string me up iffen they ketch me."

"String ya up? Fer what?" The boy gave a sudden jerk, but Washington had him in a vice. "Did ya rob somebody or somethin'?"

"It's worse'n that. Somebody kilt poor ol' Missus Bainbridge and her son told the coppers Ah did it."

These kind of tales were nothing new to the boat captain. Blacks were often accused of crimes they did not commit, not only in the South but also in the North, where they were supposed to be free. "Well, did ya?" he asked, staring at the boy to see his reaction.

The boy stopped struggling and stood up tall. Looking Washington straight in the eye, he said indignantly, "Ah wouldn't do that to poor ol' Missus Bain-bridge. Missus Bainbridge wuz the nicest whaite lady Ah iver knowed. She give me a place to live above her stable when Ah got to Philadelphy, an' paid me t' take care of her horses and garden. The missus wuz allus one t' help us nigres."

"Yer from Alabammy, ain't ya?" asked Washington, recognizing the boy's southern accent as his own.

At the word "Alabammy" the boy's face contorted and he tried desperately to wrench himself free. "Let me go, mista. They'll string me up, iffen they ketch me. Whaite folks allus does that t' us nigres."

"Ya won't git strung up if ya did nothin' wrong."

"Ah will, mista," he said becoming more agitated. "They'll string me up jest laike Massa Harrison strung up ma daddy. And him workin' hard in them cotton fields from the time he wuz an iddy biddy boy."

"Wuz yer pa tryin' to escape?"

"Him and me both." The boy's big sad brown eyes clouded and he started to tremble. "Ma Daddy wuzn't fast enough. Big Jake grabbed him before he could git away an' him and Massa Harrison strung him up from a tree." He closed his eyes. "Ah kin see him danglin' thare this very minute, wit' a rope 'round his neck."

In his mind's eye, Washington could also see him. He knew what happened on a plantation. "Then what did you do?"

The youth hesitated, then, comforted by the understanding his fellow black man exuded, in a strange way, trusting in him and depending on him, he began to tell his story.

"Pa wanted t' mek a betta life fer Ma and ma little brothas and sistas, so he decided to head North an' tek me wit' him. Ah wuz the oldest, ya see. We wuz jest outside Mobile waitin' fer the Western & Atlantic freight t' come by when they seen us."

"Who seen ya?" asked Washington sharply, pulling the youth into a narrow lane alongside a warehouse in case somebody saw them, and letting go of him.

"Massa Harrison and Big Jake. That's who seen us. Ah ran as fast as Ah could, but wit' ma Daddy bein' crippled laike, they grabbed him before he could git away. Ah looked back when Ah gits t' the top of the rise, an' they wuz stringin' up ma poor Daddy from a tree. The rope tightened around his neck an' thar he wuz a-danglin'. His legs kickt a piece, then stopt. His head fell forward loose laike, an' Ah knew he wuz good an' dead."

Overcome by the memory, the boy stopped, then, gathering himself together, continued, "Ah dasen't go back to ma Mammy 'cos Massa Harrison seen me wit' ma Daddy so Ah ran up the tracks a piece t' the railroad crossin' an' hid in some bushes, thinkin' the train would have to slow down. When Ah heard the whistle, Ah crossed t' the far side of the tracks so no one would see me git on. Ah wuz just grabbin' fer a chain t' pull maself up when a black brotha — his name wuz Sam — pulled me up into a car wit' him."

"Where wuz the train headed?"

"Chattanooga. Sam had everything figured out. He knew all the names of the railroads and whar to change trains. Ah aksed me if Ah would like t'go wit' him an' Ah said Ah would. When we got to Chattanooga, Sam akst an ol' black mammy, livin' near the tracks, whar to ketch the train fer Virginny. She said it wouldn't pass by until nightfall an', figurin' we wuz starvin', she aksed us in. Ah tell ya, mista, she fed us the best chitlins and collard greens Ah iver tasted! Sam said we hed t' ketch the Orange Railroad freight to Lynchburg, so she showed us whar to wait. Afta seein' what happened to ma Daddy, Ah was in no mind to go to a place with a name like that, figurin' that wuz whar whaite folks strings up us black folks when they ketch us runnin' away, but Sam said, if we wanted to git across "The Line," we'd hev t' go thar t' ketch the freight headin' fer Richmond. Bein' older than me, Ah figured Sam knew what he was doin' and so Ah follered along. Me and Sam didn't spend much time in Lynchburg. When a freight slowed down a piece, then stopped for a signal, me and Sam didn't waste any time. We pulled oursels up onto a box car and slid the door open. Th' inside wuz packed with nigres. Men an' boys, an' women with little chil'run, wuz all sweatin' to death in the black dark of that car, bent on makin' their escape. Ivery taime them chil'run heard the door slide open to let in anotha brotha on the run, they set off such a hollerin' and a wailin', Ah feared we'd all be ketched. The train rolled on ferever. Ah thought it would niver stop. When it did, we wuz at Richmond.

A black preacher man wuz meeting the otha nigres so me an' Sam tagged along. He put us up in a barn and some naice church ladies made us somethin' t' eat. When mornin' came, Sam said all we hed to do to git to The Line at Alexandria wuz t' tek the Southside Railroad. A whaite lady called Missus Williams — she wuz somethin' like Missus Bainbridge — met us and took us in 'til we could ketch the train on the otha side of The Line. Ya see, mista, them tracks in the South are a different size from them tracks in the North an' the train couldn't go on." The boy shook his head knowingly. "Ah'm guessin' the South done that so's t' ketch us nigres before we crossed The Line."

The boy didn't have to explain. Washington knew all about it.

"Me and Sam stayed with Missus Williams for the night, then, next mornin', the Massa put us on a train t' Washington and told us whar t' wait fer the Philadelphy train. Me and Sam couldn't believe we wuz free. When the train stopped down by the docks, we wuz scared to death we'd be ketched an' sent back if we wuz seen walkin' around so we hid in one of them warehouses in the daytaime, and looked in bins behind the taverns to see what we could find to eat at night. By the end of the week, our bellies wuz bustin' with emptiness so we went lookin' fer work. That's when a brotha, loadin' a coal boat, told us about Missus Bainbridge. The Missus was one of them whaite folks what helps black folks on the run. Sam went t' work on a farm in West Chester. The missus must have taken a likin' t' me, 'cos she aksed if Ah would laike to stay on an' look afta her horses. Ah'd been thar jest over a yar, livin' real comfortable laike above the stables, when it happened."

"What happened?" asked Washington, as a look of horror crossed the boy's face.

"Massa Wesley come outta the house a-hollerin' and a-yellin' that his mother was a-lyin' on her bed wit' her gullet slit from ear to ear."

"I see," said Washington.

"When Ah heard Massa Wesley tippin' off them coppers that Ah kilt his motha, Ah took off as fest as ma legs would carry me, figurin' that whativer Ah said they'd niver believe a nigre. Ah did not fancy maself swingin' from a tree like ma Daddy." The youth stopped; the grisly sight of his father's body prevented him from going on.

Drawn together by circumstances and the color of their skin, the black man and black boy stood close to one another in the narrow lane, each thinking his own thoughts. James Washington was no longer in the waterfront lane; he was back in Alabama on the plantation. Accused of a crime he did not commit, he was locked in a root cellar, scrunching up to keep warm, eating a raw potato. He had never known his Daddy. He grew up with his mammy in a one-room shack on the Morrison Plantation, with a two-seater privy in back. He and his mammy had it good, compared to the other Negroes. His Mammy worked for Missus Morrison in the Big House, scrubbing floors, cooking, and doing the wash. He worked in the fields, plowing, planting and picking cotton. Stooping all day in the hot sun, his fingers bled from plucking the hard brown cotton bolls. After the cotton was picked, he had to help gin, weigh and bale it. Then he loaded the bales onto railroad cars. The work was hard and the days long, but nobody bothered him on account of Missus Morrison's liking for his mother. Plantation Willy daren't whip him like he whipped the other Negroes — even when he got so tired he had to stop for a rest. But that changed the day his mammy got a hacking cough and started spitting up blood. A month later, with the Massa reading a chapter from the Bible, and Missus Morrison and himself looking on, she was buried in the bottom of the field behind the Big House. He was fifteen.

Needing the shack where he and his mammy lived for the new cook and washer woman, Massa Morrison told Plantation Willy to find him a place in the bunk house with the single Negroes. Jealous of the special treatment he had received when his mammy was alive, the men treated him badly. They robbed him of all the nice things Missus Morrison had given his mammy and blamed him for whatever went wrong. The day Plantation Willy roared into the bunkhouse demanding to know who took his wages, they pointed to him. When he said he didn't take them, Plantation Willy beat him black and blue with a strap to make him confess. And, when he wouldn't, he locked him in the root cellar, saying he would stay there until he thought better about lying. Two days later, he heard the bolt shift and hid in back of the door. When Plantation Willy poked his head inside, he dragged him in and drew the bolt tight shut across the outside of the door.

Knowing he would be strung up for sure if he were caught, he headed north for Memphis. It was Saturday. The "escaped slave" notice, with its ample reward, would not be in the newspapers until Monday. Reaching the mountains safely, he followed an old Indian trail through woodland to the next valley and hid in a shanty under a heap of raw cotton. He had hardly fallen asleep when a crew of Negro laborers discovered him and sent him on his way with directions and what little food they could spare. Guided by the North Star, he walked by night, eating whatever he could catch or rob from the fields and orchards, and sleeping by day. Sometimes, he met up with a runaway brother but, mostly, he traveled alone. It was safer that way.

As he followed his angel star north along the rocky Indian trails that ran atop the Appalachians, his eyes grew accustomed to the darkness. He descended only to find food. At first, he trusted no one but his black brothers and, even then, he had to be wary that they might turn him in to their master for a pittance of the bounty offered for his capture. But, as he went on, like so many runaways before him, he learned that there were sympathetic white people who would help. Plantation blacks and white abolitionists each had their own signals and signs of danger and help. When the African rhythms of slave drummers rolled their warnings from a seemingly innocent get-together on a plantation, those who heard them took shelter until the rhythms changed. A quilt flapping on a clothes line outside a farmhouse, more than likely signaled that an abolitionist lived there. Hidden in the colors and design of each quilt were messages: warnings to keep on going, directions to the next safe house, and, when the coast was clear, offers of food and provisions, a cellar or a barn to sleep in.

On and on, night after night he journeyed, his feet sore and bleeding, until one night he gave up. Soaked to the skin, racked by a terrible cough, he curled up in a cave to die. Two days later, a miracle happened. He awakened cured and refreshed, with new will and determination to go on. Little did he know, when he crept into the cave, he was just a mile short of the Line.

The sun shone brightly as he made his way across the Line where the southern state of Maryland bordered the free state of Pennsylvania. He had thought about heading west for Cincinnati, otherwise known as Pigopolis, the hog-slaughtering capital of the world. There, he had been told, a black man could easily find work in the slaughterhouses. But, worn out and weary, unwilling to undertake the long trek with its inherent dangers, he came down from the mountains by a well-worn trail near York, Pennsylvania. Warned by his abolitionist friends that bounty hunters might still apprehend him, even in the North, he moved across the mostly flat land from safe house to safe house until he reached Philadelphia. That was where his fortune changed. On his first day as a free man, he went to the waterfront looking for work. That was when Captain Serfass hired him as his mule driver.

His reverie ended, Washington looked at the boy in front of him. Although the terror of being caught and strung up was the same, the boy had it easier. These days, a brother fleeing North could hop on a train. He picked up the sack of feed and was about to move on when the youth grabbed his arm. He was no longer the whimpering boy Washington had held in a vice, he was a man full of determination and resolve. "Ain't we brothers, drawn togitha by the color of our skin?" he asked, scrutinizing Washington's face to see what effect his question had on the older man. Washington's answer was a reluctant nod. "Then, ya've gotta help me git t' New York. Ma uncle'll tek me in 'til Ah fainds work." The youth fixed his dark eyes on the black boat captain's, hypnotizing him, bending his will to do something he should not do. "Ah didn't do nothin', mista, honest Ah didn't. Whay would Ah kill that ol' lady? Ah wuz niver better off in ma life than when Ah wuz workin' fer her. If you aks me who done it, Ah'd say Massa Wesley kilt his own mother. He wuz always afta the ol' lady fer money."

Although Washington did not know the truth about what happened, his similar past had transferred itself to the boy, and he felt himself crumbling. "Well, mista?" The voice was demanding an answer.

Washington looked at the boy in front of him.

Washington cleared his throat, knowing that what he was about to say could get him thrown in jail for aiding and abetting a fugitive, but compelled to say it by circumstance. "Ah captain a coal boat on the canal," he said abruptly, "Ah'll give ya a lift to Easton an' see what Ah cain do about findin' a jobber to tek ya along the Morris Canal. The towpath ends jest across the Hudson River from New York. Ya cain ketch a ferry boat across the river from thar."

"Thanks, Mista!' the boy said, hardly daring to believe his good fortune. He would have liked to hug Washington just like he used to hug his Daddy, but, seeing Washington was all business, he shook his hand instead. "Ah'd do the same fer you, sir, any day."

"What's yer name, son?"

"Harrison. Joshua … Harrison." The boy hesitated before giving his last name, then felt he had to explain why he had the same name as the man who killed his father. "Harrison's the name ol' Obediah Harrison give ma great-granfatha Bota when he bought him at the slave auction in Montgomery."

Washington did not need an explanation. His family was named after the first president of America, George Washington, a man who kept slaves.

"Hide out 'til dusk, Joshua. Ma boat's the *Sally Sue*. You'll find her just beyond the coal yard."

"Ah cain't read, mista."

"Ya'll know her by the white line all the way around her hull," answered Washington, referring to the Plimsoll line he had copied from the steamships that came into the port of Philadelphia from England. When the *Sally Sue* sank down as far as the white line when she was being loaded, she had taken on enough coal.

Muttering "Sally Sue" and "whaite line" alternately, over and over again, Joshua Harrison darted back down the alley to the safety of the coal bin.

Although James Washington and his protégé were unaware of it, Taffy Morgan was lurking in the shadows. As the young Negro shook the black boat captain's hand, Morgan's eyeballs clicked. "That boy done something wrong," he said to himself. He knew it in his gut! He had seen him give the policemen the slip. Now that black upstart Washington was going to help him get away up the canals. Not if he had anything to do about it! He smirked as he made his way to his boat. "Negroes like Washington belong in their place … not captaining a coal boat."

After seeing what had happened to Taffy Morgan at the hands of the young ruffians, Mary had had enough of the waterfront. Before anything else could happen, she hustled Annie back to the boat. When they got to the wharf, the *Onoko Princess* was not quite finished unloading so they sat on an upturned row boat, keeping as far away as they could from the clouds of black grit. Fifteen minutes passed and the last bucket of coal was heaved skyward. By then, the derrick had scooped and clanged for six hours. With the sun going down, it would be morning before a tug could take the *Onoko Princess* back to Bristol.

They left a trail of footprints in the black dust as they crossed the deck to the cabin. Mary sighed as the lanterns cast their pale light on the black snow. They would have a big job on their hands tomorrow.

Fearing that the cabin would be filthy, Mary opened the hatch and lit the oil lamp. To her surprise, everything was pretty clean. A quick going over with a wet rag and she and Annie could start supper. After supper, she would put a stop to Annie's pestering and cut out the new dress. Last evening she had intended to start work on it but Gus Moyer, a boatman friend out of Weissport, came over and it would have been too impolite of her to cut it out.

After they cleaned up the dishes, Mary took Annie's measurements and showed her how to make a pattern from old newspaper. She cut the pattern to size, pinned the pieces on the fabric, and began to snip around them while Annie babbled on excitedly about how the dress should look. She wanted it to be long and flowing, just like the ones in the window of the Continental Clothing Store, with a nipped-in waist and low neck. And — oh yes! — it must have a bustle like the one on the green velvet dress worn by the young Philadelphia woman she had seen in Mauch Chunk. But when Mary put her foot down, saying she was too young for a bustle and low neck, Annie reluctantly settled for a bib and a high neck. Hoping to find something to pretty up the dress, she explored her mother's sewing basket. In it were some buttons, hand painted with blue flowers, and a piece of cream lace. If she could not have a bustle, she would ask her mother to sew two rows of buttons up the front of the bodice, and the delicate lace around the neck.

As the women worked, Manfred played his concertina. He swayed back and forth in time to the strains of "Swanee River," all the while observing everything that was going on. As he squeezed out the last chord with a flourish, he remarked, "I see you've been spending our last few pennies."

Annie had been on pins and needles, waiting for him to say something like this.

"The material was cheap, Pa," she said defensively. "It was only five cents. A plain old cotton ready made dress in the basement of the Continental Clothing Store costs at least a dollar and a half. And the fine gowns on the mannequins in the window cost fifty dollars."

Tamping a fresh wad of tobacco with his index finger into the bowl of his corncob pipe with more vigor than usual, Manfred exclaimed, "The Continental Clothing Store! Is that all you think about, Miss Fine Lady?"

"It's been a long time since I had a new dress, Papa."

"That's true enough, Annie." Then he rolled his eyes and with great emphasis said, "But did you have to buy RED?" Although Manfred associated red with the ladies who hung out along the wharves in Easton, and he bristled at the mention of the Mauch Chunk emporium, he was in a good mood. The *Onoko Princess* was unloaded, and pay day was at the end of the line. "That's all right, *liebchen*, you don't have to explain," he said, breaking into a smile. Then, echoing Mary's thoughts as she parted with her husband's hard-earned five cents to the vendor, he added, "Ve are only young vonce."

Wilhelm was stretched out on the straw-filled tick next to the wall, listening to what was going on. He had seen to the mules and finished his chores early. Now he was bored. He took out a pack of cards and turned to Annie, "Wanna play Fish?"

She shook her head. "Can't you see, I'm helping Ma with my new dress." she answered snottily.

"Oh, you and your stupid dress!" retorted Wilhelm, disappointed at not having a partner. It was no use asking his father. He never played games. And his mother was busy. He laid out the cards for solitaire. He would play black on red. Never as good as his sister at playing games, he was determined to get all the cards out of the pack to spite her.

Pinning and snipping, Mary and Annie worked in the light of two oil lamps until the pieces of the dress were basted together. They would do the fine stitching on the way to Easton after they finished their chores.

CHAPTER XII

The *Onoko Princess* and three other boats were lashed together after the first light of day, and towed by the Company tug, *Convoy*, back along the Delaware to the canal. Manfred was right. The *Sally Sue* was part of the four-boat tow. This meant that the *Onoko Princess* and James Washington's boat would be neighbors going back up the canal.

The water was strangely calm as they made their way up the Delaware River. In contrast, the sky was moody. The pale sun appeared and disappeared behind dark clouds. At her mother's suggestion, Annie came on deck for the crossing. A gentle breeze rippled the surface of the water and this time she did not feel sick. Manfred stood at the stern, never taking his eyes off the wide swath of river and every boat in the tow.

As Annie watched her father watching everything going on, she was reminded of the promise he had made to speak with her mother. She debated with herself whether it was wise to disturb him, but when he took his hand off the tiller to fill his pipe, she could not hold back the question burning the tip of her tongue.

"Did you talk to Ma about me staying at Gram's?" she asked. Then, just in case he got angry, she added, "You promised you would," knowing that a promise was sacred to her father.

Instead of reprimanding her for disturbing him, he felt guilty for not having spoken to Mary. It was not that he had forgotten. He had been putting the conversation off.

"I'm sorry, *liebchen*," he said, drawing deeply on his pipe and exhaling, letting the fragrant cloud of tobacco smoke play around his head. "Vhat do you say, if ve settle the matter right now? Mary," he called, "Ve need to talk about something."

Mary was sweeping the deck. She had hoped that the sea breeze would blow most of the coal dust away but, today, the wind was not strong enough. Working her way backward from the bow, she was about midship when Manfred called. "Can't you wait 'till I'm done?"

"Nein. What I have to say vill only take a minute."

Mary put down her broom and walked slowly to the back of the boat. She had already guessed what Manfred wanted and was in no mood to hear it.

It was no good beating around the bush and Manfred came straight to the point. "Annie vants to lay off canaling and stay vith your mother and father."

"She already told me," said Mary, looking down.

"Vell … vhat do you think?"

Mary's answer was slow in coming. She had never been apart from her children for a day in their lives, and her heart ached at the thought of the separation. But if she felt that way, so did Manfred. Neither had wanted to talk about Annie staying behind, and the whole thing was turning into a round robin. Annie had asked her, but she had put off asking Manfred. Without an answer from Manfred, Annie had asked him herself. Now Manfred was back asking her. The circle had come full swing. They had to make a decision.

In her heart, Mary wanted to give her daughter the chance she never had. Brushing away a wayward tear, she put her arms around Annie. "I'll miss you," she whispered, "but it's not up to me. If your pa can do without you, it's up to your grandparents. If everybody says yes, who am I to say no?"

"Oh, thanks, Ma!" exclaimed Annie, returning the hug, "I thought you'd let me."

"Don't get your hopes up too high, young lady. Grandpa and Grandma Kintz are getting on in years. Caring for a young girl like you is big responsibility."

"I'll be good, Ma. I promise," cried Annie, her mother's tears bringing tears to her own eyes. "We'll see each other often, I promise. Every time you pass through Weissport, I'll be waiting."

"Hey, *fräulein*, not so fast!" cautioned Manfred. "Remember, it's not up to me or your mother, it's up to your grandparents."

As the boat tow neared the Bristol shoreline, the conversation broke up. It was time for Manfred to unshackle the *Onoko Princess* from her tow mates. With nothing better to do, Mary picked up her brush and resumed sweeping. Hard work was her way of dealing with whatever disturbed her. Annie was different. Now that all that remained was for her grandparents to say yes, she wanted to be alone. Overcome by the thought of separation, she walked to the bow and sat on the edge of the forward coal hold. Coal yards and small factories loomed along the waterfront. Ahead of the lock, a wooden footbridge crossed the canal. It led to the mule stables and lock house and, being the end of the run, to the toll house where privately owned boats paid tolls for using the canal. Sad at the thought of seeing it all for the last time, a tear ran down her cheek.

The *Onoko Princess* was separated from the flotilla and nudged into the side of the towpath by the tug. To get rid of her uneasiness, Annie hopped over the side of the boat and followed Wilhelm to the mule stables. As they crossed the stable yard, they could see Max and Lucy waiting. They were poking their heads through the open top half of the Dutch door, heehawing a greeting. After six years on the towpath, the mules had an innate sense of what happens when. With their three-day rest over, they were raring to get back to work.

The children patted their flanks and performed the ultimate honor. They took great pains to curry-comb their coats before feeding them and putting on the tack. A feed of fresh oats and they slipped on the halters. "I'm riding Lucy," announced Annie as she buckled the strap that went under Lucy's neck.

"I knew that's why you came to help," exclaimed Wilhelm. "You don't fool me!"

"Smarty pants!"

"Pa won't like it if you ride her before we set out. He doesn't like the mules to get wore out."

"He won't know if you don't snitch."

In frustration, Wilhelm shoveled the muck off the dirt floor and heaved the droppings into a wheelbarrow. "You're not gonna ride her," he announced in a tone reminiscent of his father's.

"Who said so?" shouted Annie nasally, pinching her nostrils to shut out the smell of the newly turned manure. "You rode her all the way back from Mahoning. I haven't had a ride on her yet."

"You ain't gonna ride her 'cos I said so!"

"It's none of your business, Wilhelm."

"It is," yelled Wilhelm trundling the barrow over to the manure heap. "I'm Pa's mule driver."

Looking furious, with no intention of giving in, Annie stood on the top of a set of stone mounting steps. "Just 'cos you're Pa's driver, doesn't mean you own his mules. Bring Lucy here, so I can get on her."

Wilhelm did the best thing he could think of. He ignored her, and went about his chores.

"T-t-t-t-t … t-t-t-t-t," called Annie taking matters into her hands. She snapped her thumb and forefinger together sharply making a clicking noise. "Here, Lucy … good girl … come here."

The only time Lucy was not obedient was when Max acted stubborn behind her in the shaft. She ambled over in response to Annie's call. Annie took hold of the halter, and pulled her toward the steps. Then, straddling Lucy's back and sitting up as tall and proud as a queen, she announced in her grandest voice, "I'm ready, Wilhelm, let's go!"

Although Wilhelm had done his best to stop Annie, he knew, from the start, it was useless. When Annie made up her mind to do something, she did it. All he could hope now was that their father would see her. But before they came within sight of the boat Annie slid off and got back on board the *Onoko Princess* without his seeing her.

Snitching would only mean a payback so, without saying a word, Wilhelm crossed the bridge to the towpath and hitched up the mules. With the boat empty, his father lowered the rudder and exchanged the short tiller for the long one used for light boats.

Then, impatient to get going, he shouted, "Ready?"

The mules were already in the shaft and Wilhelm was checking the harness to make sure the straps were buckled properly. "Yes, Pa," he answered when he was sure everything was all right, "we're all set to go!"

"Forvard," hollered Manfred.

"Forward," echoed Wilhelm.

The tow line grew taut as the mules set out in unison. Their stride was as precise and compatible as a battalion of Union soldiers. Another trek along the towpath had begun. This one would be less of a strain. The coal holds were empty.

Invigorated by their three-day rest, the pace of the mules was sprightly. The wake of the *Onoko Princess* was shallow. Empty of her load, she floated like a cork on the water. In his excitement to get going, Wilhelm had forgotten how miserable he was at the end of the last trip. With the boat free of cargo, he could ride one of the mules if he got tired. On the way down the canals, he felt ashamed when he could not go on. On the way back, he swore he would prove himself. He was determined to drive Max and Lucy all the way from Bristol to Mauch Chunk without any help from his mother or Annie.

The wind suddenly picked up as they set out along the canal. The clouds whipped together, obscuring the pallid sun with an ominous canopy of gray. What began as a morning of unbelievable calm seemed now to be heralding a storm. As the day lengthened, the more the sky darkened, and the colder it grew. Casting his eyes aloft and holding up the index finger of his right hand to the north wind, Manfred thought the thing canalers dread most: it was going to snow. In these parts, snow was not unusual in March. March was unpredictable. And when it came this late in the season, it could be pesky.

The wind came howling off the river from the north. Fingers of ice formed along the canal banks, glistening, solidifying as they reached further and further into the water. Thirteen miles had gone by when the first flakes fell. The *Onoko Princess* was passing through Yardleyville Lock when snow began to come down. Despite Wilhelm's resolution to drive the mules all the way, Annie was already on the towpath. When his mother had insisted that he trade places to get something to eat, hungry as a hunter, he forgot all about his resolution.

Looking cold and miserable, Annie put the mules through their paces at the lock. Her long curls were icicles; her hands and feet blocks of ice. As she blew on her fingers to try to warm them, all she could think of was warming herself by the stove. Peering up at her father through her snow-covered hair, she pleaded, "Pa, I'm freezing. Can I get back on board?

Intent on making as much headway as he could before the weather stopped him, Manfred was annoyed. "Vone speck of snow and you're finished, Annie!" he exclaimed. His inclination was to make Annie continue, but, fearing the weather would worsen, and with it her grumbling, he gave in. "Vil," he thundered, thumping on top of the cabin with the boat hook, "Make the svitch. Your sister's givin' up."

After two weeks on the towpath, nobody had to tell Wilhelm how cold and miserable mule driving could be. He came out of the cabin prepared. Bundled up in his warmest clothes, he unstrapped the feed baskets, reattached Max and Lucy to the tow line and took the *Onoko Princess* out of the lock. Although blinkers kept the mules' eyes free of blowing snow, it was beginning to stick to their flanks. If the temperature dropped any lower, he feared they would be coated with ice.

Barely ten minutes after they left Yardleyville, Wilhelm's fears came true. He was a snowman driving snow mules. As he urged the mules on, the tips of his fingers were dead in the thick woolen mittens his mother had knitted last winter, and his feet were frozen stiff. The snow was being whipped into a frenzy by the howling wind and he could not see more than a few yards ahead. How much longer, he wondered, could his father go on?

Manfred was wondering the same thing. His fingers were so cold they could barely grasp the tiller. Lear's Lock was still open and, a half mile beyond it, so was Borden's. In the true spirit of canaling, Manfred kept on. But resolve is one thing, reality another. A mile into the nine-mile level between Borden's and New Hope, he knew he would have to give in. He could no longer see where he was going, nor what was ahead of him in the canal. Whether he liked it or not, the weather had won. As he came upon Jones's store, he gave the order to quit. The dock would be a safe place to moor the *Onoko Princess* and, if Jack Jones was willing, he would have a place to stable the mules.

He moved into position ready to dock, then noticed that a boat had beaten him to the small wooden landing. Frustrated at not being able to tie up, he steered the *Onoko Princess* beyond the store and pulled her in next to the canal bank. "Unhitch the beasts, Vil," he hollered, doing his best to make himself heard against the wind. "Ve vill have to tie her up to a tree."

Wilhelm unhitched the mules and wound the tow line around a tree trunk. Free of the boat, Max and Lucy snorted and stomped, as they did their best to shake off the coating of snow and ice.

Worried that his charges would have to stay out in the elements, Wilhelm yelled, "What should I do about the mules, Pa?"

"Run into the store and see if Jack Jones has a place for them. Ve can't leave them out in veather like this."

Shuffling his way through the drifting snow, Wilhelm came back smiling. Jack Jones had room in his barn. Manfred praised the Lord that his beasts would have shelter and, with enough coal left in their allotment and food to last out, his family could weather the storm.

With the snow six inches deep and drifting, both captain and mule driver were needed to handle the mules. While Manfred led Max through the blizzard, Wilhelm followed with Lucy. When Manfred pushed open the barn door, he nearly fell backward. Stabling his mules with his driver was James Washington.

"Well … Ah'm danged if it ain't … Cap'n Oberfeldt!" stuttered the black boat captain as surprised as Manfred. "Knowin' you, Ah thought you would still be a-goin' on."

"It made no sense to get stuck in the middle of the nine-mile level vith novhere to put the beasts."

The two drivers brushed the snow off their mules and tethered them at opposite ends of the barn. If stabled too closely together, mules that were strangers to one another might engage in a kicking match.

As Washington helped his driver, he seemed ill at ease. "Ah cain't believe this w-w-w-weather!" he stuttered. "Yesterday wes s-s-spring, now look at it! Ah jest hope the canal don't ice over."

"You can never tell, from vone day to the other, vhat veather March vill bring," observed Manfred. "Maybe ve'll be lucky and the snow vill melt real quick." Then it was the same old refrain. "I can't afford to lose any more time!"

They finished their chores in silence. When Washington and his driver were about to leave, the black captain turned to Manfred. "Cain Ah see ya in the mornin', Cap'n Oberfeldt?" Before Manfred could ask what he wanted, he pulled the barn door shut.

"I vonder vhat he vants," mused Manfred. "He seemed kinda uneasy, don't you think?"

As Manfred opened the door, the sleigh bells jingled their warning that someone was entering the store. The Joneses were behind the counter, tallying up the day's receipts. With the canal icing over and no more customers expected, they were about to close shop.

"Thanks, for letting me stable my beasts, Jack," said Manfred gratefully. "Vhat do I owe you for the stall?"

"Nothin', Manny! Nobody's using the barn, so don't worry about it."

"That's mighty good of you, Jack. It is real fierce out there for both man and beast," said Manfred, turning to leave. The bells jangled as he put his hand on the latch. Then he remembered something and came back. "Mary vill vant to know vhat ve owe you for the tobaccy and chicken? You know how she is about paying bills."

Knowing Manfred was the personification of honesty in a business where many a canaler would sooner pass by than pay up, Jack Jones smiled. "Look in the ledger, Meg," he said turning to his wife. "Tell this feller what he owes us."

Megan Jones ran her finger down the list of debtors. There were at least six pages of entries after the Oberfeldts. It was obvious: most boatmen, carrying their first load, were broke.

"If all that bunch pays you vhat they owe," joked Manfred, scanning the list from the opposite side of the counter, "you'll be able to retire!"

"The question is, 'if'!" said Megan as she ran her finger carefully down the entries before stopping. "Herrre 'tis! That'll be seventy-foive cents, sirrr." Even though it was more than a quarter century since Megan left the Old Country, she had not forgotten her polite Irish roots. She never failed to address those who held the rank of captain as "sir".

Wilhelm eyed the jars of candy lined up on the shelf behind the counter. He didn't dare ask his father to buy some fruit humbugs but he was hoping, if he stared long enough, he just might. Having treated himself to a double plug of tobacco, Manfred felt a twinge of selfishness. "Add a quarter of these humbugs

Wilhelm and Annie played dominoes.

to the tick, vould you, Megan?" he added pointing to the glass bottle containing various colored boiled sweets. "The children have not had a sveet treat since their grandma baked them a chocolate cake vhen ve left Veissport."

Megan took down the jar and removed the glass stopper. "Oi'll be roight glad to do that, sirrr," she said, taking a scoop and shoveling a generous quarter of a pound of hard candy onto the scale.

Assuring the Joneses that he would pay up next time around, Manfred took the bag of humbugs in one hand, and opened the latch with the other. As he did, the wind whipped the door right out of his hand, covering the floor with a mantle of snow. The bells jingled frantically as the door crashed against the counter. Satisfied that he had not done any damage, Manfred apologized. "Let's hope the sun gets rid of this stuff in a hurry," he said as, this time, he kept a tight hold on the latch.

Manfred and Wilhelm had to bend double as the snow blew thickly down the canal. They had been so busy battling the elements most of the day, they did not realize they were starving. It was only when the savory aroma of sage greeted them as they boarded the *Onoko Princess* that they realized how hungry they were. There was no need to tell them what was for supper. Mary was making pork float. Sensinger's potatoes had come in handy on this trip. When they opened the hatch, she was putting some into the stew. Along with a jar of Mama Kintz's bottled carrots, the liberal helping of potatoes would eke out the meat.

With the *Onoko Princess* stuck at her mooring, the meal was unhurried. By the time they finished eating and talking, it was the middle of the afternoon. Manfred took solace from reading his Bible while Mary put the finishing touches on Annie's new dress. Annie was not needed for the fine stitching so she took out a set of dominoes and asked Wilhelm to play. At first, he was reluctant. He felt like paying Annie back. But, realizing he would be bored if he didn't, he joined her at the table. Alternating between their two favorite games, dominoes and jacks, the children amused themselves for most of the afternoon. Then, wanting a change, they climbed onto the bunks and read the Kit Carson dime novels by lamplight that Angela and Mark Davis had given them in New Hope. It was as if Sunday had come early. Manfred fretted about the delay, but, before retiring for the night, he saw to it that they got on their knees and thanked the good Lord for keeping them and their beasts safe and warm.

CHAPTER XIII

The *Onoko Princess* was going nowhere. But old habits die hard. Manfred awakened at half past three and, as usual, lit a lantern, and took his usual tour of the deck. A few lazy flakes were still straggling down. He looked at the sky, and was reassured. A crescent moon was showing its face through a thin gauze veil. A few hours more and the sun should come out.

Nearly a foot of snow covered the deck, and drifts were piled up against the raised sides of the coal box. Manfred shone his light over the back of the boat. Heat from the cabin stove had kept the stern from being iced in. He made his way to the bow. This time, Lady Luck was not with him. The front end of the boat was imprisoned in ice. Leaning over the side, he smashed at it with an iron-tipped boat hook. It was a good two inches thick, enough to damage the wooden hull if he attempted to tow the *Onoko Princess* from her mooring. Resigning himself to the fact that there was nothing he could do but wait for the Company ice breaker to cut her free, he returned to the cabin. Stretching himself out on the bunk next to Mary, he did something he rarely did: he went back to sleep. Nobody stirred until daylight.

While Mary cooked breakfast, Manfred walked to the store landing to see what Washington wanted. He found the Negro boat captain on deck, checking out the ice.

"Ah'm raight glad t' see ya, Cap'n Oberfeldt," called Washington as Manfred made his way through the snow. He threw down a gang plank so Manfred wouldn't jump over the side of the *Sally Sue* and slip."Come aboard, sir."

A warm blast of air from the stove met them as they opened the hatch. As he descended the wooden ladder into the cabin, Manfred could not conceal his amazement. Seated at the table having breakfast were Washington's driver and a Negro youth of about sixteen. "Oh!" he exclaimed, taken aback, "I didn't know you had company!"

"Ah didn't know it maself until yistaday when Ah bumped into this young man on the waterfront."

Manfred looked uncomfortable. Although not much could be done to a private boat captain for taking on a passenger, he felt as if Washington had broken the strictest of Company rules. It had already crossed his mind that, more than likely, the boy was a runaway slave. Runaways often made their way to the big cities along the canal towpaths.

A man of few words, Washington lost no time in coming to the point. "Ah said Ah'd tek the boy to Easton. The trouble is them locks at New Hope. Ah expect them Company men will board the *Sally Sue.*" A look of bitterness crossed his face. "It's a rare occasion when they don't check her out to see if they can git me fer doin' somethin' or otha wrong. If they cain't find nothin' amiss wi' ma load, they look under ivery strap on the boat harness to see if they cain find sores on ma mules. Ah tell ya, Cap'n, Ah pays a price fer being a black boatman."

Sensing that what Washington was saying was a prelude to what he really wanted, Manfred muttered, "What do you want, Cap'n?" Then, before Washington could open his mouth, he added, "You know I just came over to see you about getting out of this ice."

"Ah know, Cap'n, but it's this way ... Ah'd be much obliged, if ya'd tek this boy through the locks at New Hope. They won't check out your boat. Ah'll be waitin' jest beyond the coal yard between Whaite's Lock and Smithtown, and tek him on t' Easton. Ah'll find somebody thare who'll give him a lift up the Morris Canal."

"I take it he's a runavay!" said Manfred gruffly.

"That he is! He jest got in t' Philadelphia yisterday. Philadelphia's where most of us brothas come, ya know, when we cross The Line," announced Washington. He was not a man given to lying, but, if he wanted Manfred to take Harrison on board, he could not tell him the boy was wanted for murder. "The boy had a hard time gittin' away. His masta an' his enforcer, Big Jake, ketched his Daddy and strung him up. He ran away. He wuz scared to death when he got out at them train yards in Philadelphia. Him bein' only sixteen." Before continuing, Washington looked hard at Manfred to see what effect his story was having. "He wuz a-feared Big Jake and his masta wuz follerin' him 'cos he seen what they done to his Daddy. Ah wuz jest headin' fer ma boat when he bumped into me, runnin' laike a wild thing. Knocked ma bag of oats clear on the ground. When he saw Ah wuz a black brotha, he aksed if Ah'd help him git to New York. Ah thought about it a piece, then rememberin' when Ah landed in them train yards twenty-five years ago an' Cap'n Serfass took me on, Ah said Ah would." His tone changed and he spoke sharply, "Ah'm trustin', sir, his whereabouts'll stay a secret."

"I ain't sayin' vhere he is!" muttered Manfred.

"Ah knew Ah could trust you, Cap'n," continued Washington, lightening up. "That's why Ah akst ya on board. Not everybody's like you Cap'n Oberfeldt. You treat a Negre real well."

The youth had stopped eating and was staring at the remains of breakfast. He appeared to be waiting for an answer.

"What's your name, boy?" Manfred asked kindly.

"Harrison, sir ... Joshua Harrison."

"Don't you know, Harrison, vhen you cross the Line you are free? Your master can't do nothin' to you in the great Commonwealth of Pennsylvania."

Having learned to maneuver his way through the vicissitudes of plantation life from the day he was old enough to know what was going on, Joshua Harrison had caught on to Washington's game. "Don't ya understand, mista, Ah'm a-feared Masta Harrison and Big Jake'll come afta me 'cos Ah saw them kill ma Daddy. They'd like nothin' better than t' string me up t' shut ma mouth."

Manfred looked uneasy, wishing he had never come over.

"Well?" asked Washington as Harrison finished speaking.

The punishment for a Company boatman taking on passengers was severe. And Manfred thought hard about his livelihood and his family. But the troubled black face, looking at him so intently for the answer he wanted to hear, troubled Manfred. The boy was not much older than Annie and he could see he was terrified. Washington and his protégé had just about given up hope when he said quietly, "You vin, Vashington, I vill take Harrison through the locks at New Hope and let him off beyond Vhite's. He can hide in one of the coal holds. I just hope no-one comes on board!"

Washington stood up, looking relieved. "Ah cain't thank you enough, Captain Oberfeldt!" he said, shaking Manfred's hand until it felt as if it would break. "We will make the change after dark." He climbed the steps and opened the hatch. "Now, let's see what we can do about gittin' outta here."

On deck, the two men looked over the side of the *Sally Sue* to assess the icy conditions. Her situation was the same as the *Onoko Princess*'s. Except for around the cabin, the *Sally Sue* was imprisoned in ice. Taking a boat hook, Washington pounded on the ice around her bow. It creaked a little, but was unyielding. Both captains agreed. They would have to wait for the ice breaker.

Wilhelm and Annie were on deck surveying the white wonderland when their father came back along the towpath. The canal was a silver ribbon of ice, set apart from the endless white landscape by the trees and shrubbery that bordered it. Snow-laden branches, dipping their dark heads, were locked in the icy surface. The quiet was eerie. Not a creature was stirring in the frozen wasteland.

Once on board, Manfred went to the equipment box and took out three shovels. "Ve vill have to get the snow off the deck."

As the three worked, the scraping of their shovels broke the morning silence. On the *Sally Sue*, Captain Washington and his driver were doing the same thing. Although eager to help those who helped him, the fugitive had strict orders to stay in the cabin. When most of the snow was removed from the deck and the remaining coating of ice was waiting for the blessing of the sun, Manfred and the children went inside to get warm.

Manfred declined the mug of coffee Mary handed him and stretched out on his bunk. He closed his eyes and thought about the mess he had gotten himself into. Whether it was the look of desperation in the young Negro's eyes, or his respect for Captain Washington, he had felt compelled to help. But what he had promised to do involved more than himself. It involved his family. And he found it hard to tell Mary about it. He knew she would never approve. By taking a passenger on board, particularly a runaway Negro, he was jeopardizing his family's livelihood in these lean times.

Although the proclaimed cause of the North was the emancipation of slaves, bigotry against Negroes was everywhere. Manfred had come to the conclusion that the Civil War, raging not too far away, was more of an economic war than a war about slavery. The primary aim of the conflict was to keep the South, with its valuable resources, especially cotton, from seceding from the Union. Supporting the South was America's old enemy, England. England needed cotton to keep its prosperous cloth manufacturing mills rolling. So, too, did the northern states of New England.

Having mulled things over long enough, the time had come to tell Mary. Manfred got off his bunk and walked over to the stove where she was working. Putting his arms on her shoulders, he swung her around.

The action was unusual and Mary sensed something was troubling him. "What's wrong, Manny?" she asked. "You're awfully quiet."

Mary had provided the opening, and Manfred seized it. "Captain Vashington asked me if I'd take on a passenger."

"You mean, the Negro boat captain you met in the Anchor?"

"Ja! He asked if I vould give an acquaintance of his a lift through New Hope."

"Can't he give the person a ride himself?"

"It's not that easy."

"What do you mean?"

"It's a runaway."

"A runaway?" With the Civil War raging, Mary was partial to the cause of the North. She knew how badly slaves were treated, but she also knew about the strict Company rule that prohibited taking passengers on board.

"The boy needed a ride to Easton. Vashington took him on board, but it vas not until they started up the canal that he thought about the locktenders at New Hope. He says, it never fails. They always harass him. They check out his boat … and his load … and his mules … and everything else they can find … to see if they can find something wrong."

"But where do we come in, Manny? That's none of our business! What Captain Washington does is up to him."

"It *is* our business, Mary! That Negro boy fears for his life."

"But he's in the North," protested Mary. "He has nothing to fear."

"He does, Mary," said Manfred quietly. "He saw his master kill his father. He vas a vitness to murder."

"Oh," said Mary, shocked. "But …"

"Vell?"

After nearly fifteen years of marriage, Mary knew her husband through and through. Manfred had made up his mind and nobody, not even she, could change it. "Whatever I think is too late," she said, throwing up her arms in despair. "I can tell you've already made a promise to Captain Washington."

"You know me too vell, Mary."

"Where are we going to put him?" she asked all of a flutter. "He can't stay in the cabin. It wouldn't be right. There's Annie … and you never know who comes on board.

In the smallness of the cabin, the children were listening openmouthed. They could hardly believe what they were hearing. Their father was taking on a passenger. Not an ordinary passenger, an escaped slave! They looked at each other in excitement. This was the kind of adventure they loved to read in dime novels!

Wilhelm was first to come up with a solution. "We can put him in the forward coal hold," he said, "an' give him a blanket to keep warm."

Manfred looked gratefully at his son for the support. "It vill only be for a short vhile," he assured Mary. "Vhen ve get betveen Vhite's Lock and Smithtown, Vashington vill take him back on board."

Mary looked disconcerted. Nothing Manfred could say would change how she felt. "You're on your own, Manny," she said, slamming a pot down on the stove. "I'm washing my hands of the whole thing!"

If their mother was refusing to help, the children were more than willing. "I'll clear a space in the bow," volunteered Wilhelm grabbing his coat off the peg and taking a broom from the corner. "It's real dark there. Nobody'll see the Negro even if they look inside."

"Wait," cried Annie as Wilhelm bounded up the steps, letting the hatch door fall backward with a crash. "I'm coming too."

"I vill be vith you in a minute," said Manfred, wanting to have a private moment with Mary before joining them.

Annie and Wilhelm were hard at work sweeping and shoveling coal dirt from the triangular space that formed the front of the bow when a cry came from on shore.

"Wilhelm! Annie! Wanna go sledding?"

When Annie heard the shout, her heart raced. She stopped sweeping and peered over the side of the coal hold. Robert Jones and his brother, Joe, were walking alongside the *Onoko Princess*, pulling a homemade sled. If they came on board, they would wonder what she and Wilhelm were doing. She ducked out of sight in the blackness and whispered in Wilhelm's ear, "It's Robert and Joe Jones."

"Drat!" exclaimed Wilhelm, hauling himself out and sloshing across the deck to the side of the boat. "I can't come right now," he shouted. "I'm doing somethin' for Pa. I'll be there in a little while. Annie's doing nothing. She'll go with you."

Normally Annie would have jumped at the chance to go sledding, but she was caught up in the intrigue. "You know very well, I …" she exploded. For once in her life, she did not mind getting dirty, shoveling the hold.

Wilhelm put his hand over her mouth to keep her from saying anything else. "Say yes!" he whispered urgently. "We don't want Joe and Robert to know what we're doing."

Annie was furious. Who was Wilhelm to tell her what to do? "Speak for yourself, Wil," she said, her voice reverberating louder and louder through the cavernous darkness. "I'm staying to shovel."

"Shhhh, or they'll hear you," hissed Wilhelm as another shout came from on shore. The boys were getting impatient. Suddenly, an idea popped into his head which he felt sure would appeal to Annie, "I know, Annie," he said persuasively, "you can be the decoy. If you go sledding with Robert and Joe, they won't know what we're doing."

Wilhelm knew his sister well. Annie was intrigued. Most of the mysteries she read had decoys. Decoys either saved the day or caught the criminal. Being a decoy was even more important than preparing a hiding place. "I'll be there in a minute," she yelled, ready to keep the Jones boys at bay.

The boys pulled their sled alongside the *Onoko Princess* and helped Annie off. Soon she was sitting on the sled like a queen being pulled toward the hill behind the store by the two boys.

Hearing the shrieks of joy as they took turns sledding down the hillside, Wilhelm wished he had let Annie shovel the bow. Coal dust from the load lay in heaps and ridges and it was hard to get the floorboards clean. Spurred on by the shouts from the hillside, he worked as fast as he could. At last the space was clear. "Pa!" he hollered when he was done, "What do you think?"

Manfred came out of the cabin and walked over to the forward hold, looking gloomy. Despite assurances that everything would be all right, the impasse with Mary had not changed. He peered into the darkness with a lantern. Then, satisfied that the bow was as clean as it would ever get, he took a tarpaulin from the equipment locker and dropped it down to Wilhelm. "Here, son! Cover the floor boards with this."

"How's that?" asked Wilhelm when he finished spreading out the tarpaulin.

"It looks fine to me," answered his father. "Now, ve have to get the Negro on board vithout anyvone seein' him."

"We can do that after dark," said Wilhelm, hauling himself over the side of the coal hold.

"Yes, ve'll do it after dark," repeated Manfred, battening down the hatch and securing it with an iron pin. "Go play vith your friends." Then, just as Wilhelm was about to jump onshore, he added, "You had better vash off first, or those boys vill vonder vhich chimney you svept."

The water in the barrel had not frozen all the way down when Wilhelm turned the spigot. It trickled slowly into the pail as he stood by stamping his feet to keep warm, too impatient to wait until it was full. He refused when his mother wanted to warm up the icy water on the stove and, with teeth chattering as it touched his skin, he washed off the grime. Then, before his mother could give her usual warning to dress warmly, the cabin hatch slammed shut.

"Thanks for the present!" she snapped as she picked his dirty clothes off the floor.

Wilhelm followed the tracks of the other children, led to where they were by their shouts. As they raced down the slope, Joe and Annie were hollering at the top of their lungs. When they reached the bottom, Wilhelm yelled, "It's my turn," and bagged the sled. Without saying a word, they turned it over and he dragged it to the top of the slope. The sled was made out of an old wooden crate. To make it go fast, Joe and Robert had lined its runners with metal strips that once held a wooden barrel together. Sanded and polished over several long summer days, the runners shone like the silver. After several trips down the hillside, they had etched a glistening ice chute in the snow.

Wilhelm took a run and threw himself on the sled to gain as much speed as possible. His head and shoulders were over the front; his legs acted as steering posts, his feet, as brakes. Faster and faster he went, gathering speed as he raced down the hillside. Rushing into the icy wind, he was as free as an eagle. Forgotten were the endless towpath, the bad weather and his aching legs. He was going so fast, he swept way past the bottom of the chute and landed in the snow bank. He turned the sled over reluctantly. It was time for someone else to have a turn. Sometimes the children rode alone; sometimes in pairs. Sometimes they sat upright; sometimes they lay flat on their bellies. Time and hunger were forgotten until Manfred blew his conch shell and they knew it was time for lunch.

The children dispersed in two directions: the Jones boys to the warmth of their mother's kitchen, Wilhelm and Annie to the boat. Wilhelm and Annie could smell the soup as they sloshed their way through the snow. Made from anything and everything left over from the day before and the day before that, the children agreed that the flavorful medley was the most delicious soup they had ever tasted. Between the four Oberfeldts, the iron stockpot was soon empty. As they wiped their bowls clean with hunks of bread, a crunching, crashing noise came down the canal. Nobody had to tell Manfred what it was.

"Get your coat, Vil," he said, springing to his feet. "It's the ice breaker from New Hope."

Wilhelm's brief excursion into childhood had ended. He followed his father on deck. Sure enough, a three-mule team was laboring through the snow, towing a scow with an ice breaker attached to its bow. The ice breaker was made out of heavy timber plated with iron, and shaped in the form of a V to make it easier to cut through the thick ice. To add extra weight so that the blades could dig deeper, rocks filled the back end of the scow. With the help of its straining mules, the ice breaker was forcing its way down the canal, clearing a single channel the width of the scow. If there was to be room enough for two boats to pass, it would have to make a return trip.

"How long will it be before we can get out of here?" Manfred hollered, trying to make himself heard above the sound of crunching ice.

"Mornin' most likely," the scow's captain yelled back. "We have to clear another channel from Yardleyville to New Hope before you can leave."

"I thought so!" mumbled Manfred gloomily.

"Then I can go sleddin' agin, Pa," ventured Wilhelm, eager to recapture the joys of the morning.

"Sledding! Is that all you think about?" exclaimed Manfred, disillusioned about the delay "Some mule driver, you are!"

Wilhelm looked smitten, then mumbled, "What else is there to do, Pa?"

Aware that his disappointment at not being able to leave right away was making him unreasonable, Manfred relented. "Go and have fun! Ve'll be stuck here another night."

"Gee, thanks, Pa," called Wilhelm as he ran to fetch Annie.

CHAPTER XIV

The day dawned bright and sunny, surprising everyone. The ice breaker had already made its return trip, and the runaway was safe in the forward coal hold, having boarded the *Onoko Princess* under the cover of darkness. Things were going the way they should. Captain Washington cast off ahead of Manfred. If there was any ice left to obstruct their path, the *Sally Sue* would get the brunt of it, and with it any Company laborers who might come on board to help out. When Manfred got underway, he was optimistic. The sun should melt the snow and ice quickly. By tomorrow, he said to himself, winter would have said its last good bye.

Joshua Harrison was curled up under a blanket in the bow looking wide-eyed and skittish while the crew of the *Onoko Princess* went about their duties as if nothing unusual were happening. It was important that everything look normal. Mary and Annie worked as a team, scraping the last patches of ice off the deck. Bearing down hard on the shovels helped to relieve their anxiety. Manfred was more preoccupied than usual. He sat at his steering post, puffing hard on his pipe, trailing thick clouds of tobacco smoke down the canal. All the while, he kept a sharp weather eye out for stray sheets of ice that the ice breaker had missed, and on Wilhelm and the mules plodging through the slush.

The remainder of the nine-mile level between Jones's store and New Hope seemed never-ending. Except for the tread of the mules pulling the scow and those towing Washington's boat, and the footprints of their drivers, the snow on the towpath was undisturbed. Heavy and wet, it was turning to slush. Wilhelm's feet were soon soaked. With the coal holds empty, he thought about asking his father if he could ride one of the mules. But before the words could come out of his mouth, he stopped himself. Lucy and Max were slipping and sliding all over the place, and braying and snorting in complaint.

The *Onoko Princess* had gone about five miles before she passed the first boat coming down the canal toward Bristol. First boat, second boat, third boat, boats that had weathered the storm in New Hope were coming helter skelter down the level. This time, it was the *Onoko Princess's* turn to be royalty. With a blow on their horn or conch shell and a salute from their captains, she sailed over the tow lines of the loaded boats without stopping. As the tread of mules and men increased on the towpath, the going became easier. The slush was turning into mud.

Watching his son slosh through the mire, Manfred did something he rarely did. He hollered to Wilhelm to take a ride. Wilhelm waved back gratefully, scarcely believing his ears. He had bitten his tongue all morning to keep from asking. Now, all he had to do was find a gate or a fence to help him mount Max. A barred gate did the trick. He pulled the team over, and used it as mounting steps. Sitting astride the chestnut mule, he was a knight in armor riding atop his most noble steed. Wilhelm had chosen Max purposely. Broad of back and high of hock, he was a fit mount for a knight bent on slaying every fiery dragon that dared to cross his path.

The nearer they got to New Hope, the harder Manfred puffed on his pipe. He was getting increasingly nervous about his passenger. With ice flows still on the canal, an inspector might come on board to check for damage to the hull. What worried him most was that the first place he would look was the coal holds.

He stomped on the top of the cabin with the heel of his boot. "*Liebchen*, I vant you to do something for me." Annie had finished shoveling and was helping her mother inside. When she did not respond, he shouted again. Another shout, another thump and Annie peered up at him from the hatchway to see what he wanted. "Move that Negro to the feed bin. If Company men board us at New Hope to look for damage, they von't look in there. Cover him with the tarpaulin just in case they open the lid."

Annie looked dismayed at the thought of an inspector coming on board. She didn't want to be dragged before the magistrate as an accessory, like the villains she had read about in dime novels. The more she thought about it, the more she wanted no part of the runaway. "Wil can do it," she said, starting for the side of the boat. "I'll go on the towpath."

"Come back here, young lady," ordered her father angrily. "Ve have no time for that. Do as I say right now vhen the canal is clear."

It was not often that her father raised his voice, and Annie knew that her usual cajoling was useless. She ran over to the forward coal hold, removed the pin and opened the hatch. "Mista," she whispered. "Mista–mista–mista." The word thundered through the empty blackness until the hold seemed to explode. She started back in fright as her call came back to her, then got the courage to peer into the depths. "Pa wants you to move to the feed bin. He says you'll be safer there."

Joshua moved from the coal hold to the feed bin.

Joshua Harrison never needed to be told to do anything twice. He would do whatever was asked of him by those trying to save his neck. Wrapping himself in a blanket and looking as scared as Annie, he followed her to the back of the boat. She unlatched the lid of the feed bin, and he hauled himself up on top of the oats. Trembling violently, she threw a piece of tarpaulin over him, then, as if something were after her, slammed the cover shut before another boat came into view.

Manfred watched her every movement. "Good girl, Annie," he applauded when Harrison was safely in the bin. "If they check for damage, they von't look amongst the feed."

This time, Annie did not wait to bask in her father's approval. She was too scared. She fled into the cabin, pulled down her bunk, and hid under the cover in case an inspector came on board.

Wilhelm's legs gripped the flanks of the giant chestnut mule as the fugitive moved to a new hiding place. He was too scared to continue his usual game of "Let's Pretend" as they neared the first of New Hope's four locks. When the bass note of the conch shell warned the locktender of their approach, he dismounted and, trembling inside, waited for the lock gates to open.

James Washington's hunch had been right. Prompted by the locktender, who belonged to the ranks of those who believed Negroes did not belong on the canals, a Company official was going over the *Sally Sue* from stem to stern. As Manfred observed the goings-on from his perch atop the stern, it was obvious that the inspection was anything but routine. Nothing was left to chance, not even the *Sally Sue's* feed bin. As the Company inspector opened the lid, Manfred broke into a sweat. It was the *Onoko Princess's* turn next to enter the lock.

Wilhelm unhitched the tow line and she floated in solid as a rock. When the miter gates closed, she rose like the princess she was on a crest of rushing water. When the level was high enough, an inspector jumped on board and exchanged greetings with Manfred. They had met along the canal.

"Routine inspection, Captain Oberfeldt. Sorry to bother you, but we have orders to search every boat. A murderer's on the loose … a nigger, you know … slit the throat of that rich Bainbridge woman from Philadelphia." Manfred's jaw dropped as the inspector kept on talking. "She's one of them foolish women what helps them southern niggers escape. They think he got away on a canal boat."

"Not on this one!" exclaimed Manfred shaking his head and mustering a smile of confidence he did not feel.

"I'm sure, Captain, but I have to look. Duty is duty, ya know."

"I suppose!"

While the man made his rounds under Manfred's watchful gaze, Annie stayed in the cabin with her mother, curled up like a fetus under the cover. Wilhelm also kept as far out of the way as possible, busying himself fixing the tack, and getting the mules into position to take the boat out of the lock. When the search of the coal holds came up empty, the inspector opened the cabin hatch. Seeing no-one in the cabin except Mary, busy stitching Annie's dress, he waved hello, and shut the hatch. His next stop was the feed bin. Manfred could feel his heart pounding. All Harrison had to do was clear his throat or cough. But the worst never happened. The inspector checked off the *Onoko Princess*'s official number 322 in his log, and climbed back over her side.

"Thanks, Captain," he said and waved her over the drop gate into the canal. Muttering a silent prayer of thanks that the stowaway had not been found, Manfred took the *Onoko Princess* through the next three locks into the level above New Hope.

No sooner were they back in the canal than Annie came out of the cabin. The inspector's remark had not escaped her. "Is the Negro in the feed bin a murderer?" she quavered.

Manfred was wondering the same thing, but he could not let Annie know. "If I thought so, *liebchen*, I vould not have taken him on board. A lot of things are said about black people that are not true."

Annie calmed down. Her father never told lies. "When is Captain Washington going to take him back?" she asked. Despite her father's reassurances, she would never feel safe until they were rid of him.

"Ve vill meet him above Vhite's and make the svitch."

When Annie went back into the cabin, her mother came on deck, making sure to close the hatch tight shut after her. "I also heard what that man said," she whispered, looking stricken. "That black boat captain lied to you and you believed him. No southern plantation owner ever comes North after his slaves, Manny. Don't you know, you can't cross the Line without a military pass?"

"Oh," he gasped, "You're right!" Why hadn't he remembered? Mary was always so logical. Angry at being duped, he yelled at Wilhelm to get the mules moving, and comforted himself with his pipe.

He had calculated their time of arrival exactly. As they neared White's Lock, it was dark. Perfect for making the switch.

Washington was as good as his word. The *Sally Sue* was waiting. When the *Onoko Princess* pulled into the mooring behind her, he was ready to make the transfer. Informed that it was time to go, Joshua Harrison pulled himself out of the feed bin and brushed off the oats. Still cloaked in the blanket, he slid into the shadows like a phantom. Washington's demeanor confirmed Manfred's suspicions. Keeping his distance from Manfred, without a word he followed the blanketed form along the towpath. As Washington and Harrison disappeared into the darkness, Manfred wondered if the Negro's footprints would be recognizable. Concluding they would not, with the towpath stirred up by mules and men over the long busy day, he climbed back on board, praising the Lord that he was rid of the Negro. Although he had lost more time than he cared to think about, he would feel safer if he let the *Sally Sue* and her illicit cargo get ahead. He would tie up the *Onoko Princess* for the night even though the locks would be open for another hour.

CHAPTER XV

Compared to the journey down the canal, the journey back up was easy. The towpath dried up quickly, and, without the *Onoko Princess*'s ninety-five ton burden, the mules towed her at a fast, steady pace. Manfred pushed aside his uneasiness and comforted himself by taking out his concertina. The weather was good and he had gotten rid of the Negro. Playing and singing lustily as if to shut out what had happened, he tootled and sang all the way to Oberacker's tap room. As they neared the tavern, the smell of Martha Oberacker's delectable salt cakes embraced them. The children sniffed the air hungrily and, remembering his promise, looked expectantly at their father. Just past the tavern, Manfred called the mules to a halt and, without saying a word, climbed overboard and went inside. Getting rid of the Negro was cause for celebration. Seating himself at the bar, he forgot all about his pledge of temperance and ordered a glass of ale and a salt cake. As he swigged the ale to wash down the salt cake, there was no doubt in his mind and, for that matter, in the minds of the other boatmen seated at the tables, that the brew went awfully well with the salt cakes. When Manfred came back on board, he handed each member of his crew a salt cake, fresh out of the oven. Although Annie and Wilhelm had not known the answer to his question on the way down the canal, he knew they would forever associate the soft, delicious goodness of Martha Oberacker's salt cakes with story of Edward Marshall and the Walking Purchase.

As they started back up the canal, the last traces of ice edging the banks had melted. They were making good progress. In no time at all, they passed through Erwinna and Uhlertown and Upper Black Eddy. Manfred toyed with the idea of stopping for the night at Riegelsville, but with the locks open extra late to deal with the backup of traffic, and only eight miles to go until Easton, he decided to push on.

For once, Wilhelm did not mind. He was feeling good about himself. With the stopover at Jones's store and only one short break to eat, he had driven the mules all the way from Bristol. "Driven" was hardly the right word! "Ridden" was more like it! Whenever he got tired, he mounted one of his charges. But this was not cheating. Most drivers sneaked a ride on their mules when their boats were empty. With a pleased expression on his face, he slid off Lucy's back and proudly led his charges toward the fourteen-foot Easton Dam at the head of the Delaware Canal. As the *Onoko Princess* awaited her turn to enter the magnificent Forks of the Delaware at Easton, for the very first time Wilhelm felt he could call himself a mule driver.

They pulled into the guard lock. The locktender was standing on the bulwark. "The supervisor wants to see you, Captain Oberfeldt," he said as he opened the gate to let them into the basin. "He's in the office at the outlet lock."

"Pete Clark, you mean?" asked Manfred.

The man nodded.

"Vhat does he vant?"

"Beats me, captain."

The Navigation Office was a little over half a mile up the canal, but, fearing Clark knew about his role in the Negro's escape, Manfred tied up the *Onoko Princess* and hastened along the towpath. It was better to find out what he wanted right away rather than staying awake all night wondering what it was.

After greetings were exchanged, Clark began. "Oberfeldt, we've had a complaint."

Manfred's heart skipped a beat. "A complaint!" he exclaimed. "Vhat about?"

"About the nameplate on the back of your boat. You'll have to take it off."

Manfred did not understand what Clark was getting at, but, whatever it was, it did not seem to concern his harboring the Negro. "Vhat do you mean, Pete?"

"It's the carving of the Indian on the back of Company Boat 322."

"You mean, the Indian maiden, Princess Onoko?"

"That's right! You've worked for the Lehigh Coal & Navigation Company long enough, Manny, to know that it's against the rules to have anything except the number on the back of a Company boat."

"But," protested Manfred, "the carving's been there since the day the boat came from the builder, and nobody said a thing. Ve named her to please our children, seeing ve vere traveling as a family. I don't see no harm in that!"

Pete Clark looked uncomfortable. "Perhaps not," he answered, "but a complaint is a complaint and, as supervisor, I have to act upon it."

Furious that someone had turned him in for such a trivial thing, Manfred puffed hard on his pipe. "Who complained?" he asked.

"You know very well, captain, I can't say! Company rules!"

"Vell, whoever did is nothing short of mean spirited. The princess means a great deal to my children. And my vife and me. She is our good luck symbol. Never a season goes by vithout I tell her story before ve start out for the first time."

Supervisor Clark got up from his desk. It was late and he was not about to listen to an argument. "Sorry, Oberfeldt!" he said, sounding very official as he opened the door and showed Manfred out. "The carving must be off the boat by Monday or you'll have to face the consequences."

Manfred asked himself over and over again as he walked back along the waterfront, who would do anything that petty. The more he thought about it, the surer he was. Who else but Taffy Morgan? More than likely Morgan suspected who had turned him in, and this was his payback.

Mary and the two children imagined the worst as they waited for Manfred. They sat on the cabin roof, not taking their eyes off the towpath. Mary and Wilhelm were afraid they would never be able to sail on the canal again. Annie imagined her father being hauled off in shackles. At the sight of Manfred striding vigorously along the towpath, smoke wreathing from his pipe, their joy knew no bounds. Whatever it was that the supervisor wanted, he had not been taken in for questioning or, worse, he had not landed in jail. Running toward him as he jumped on board, they clamored in unison, "What did Pete Clark want?"

Manfred did not answer immediately as he tried hard to suppress his anger.

"Was it about Harrison, Manny?" Mary prompted, unable to conceal her impatience.

"Nein, it vas nothing of the kind, Mary," he replied, his lips tightening into a thin, straight line. "It vas about the stupidest thing you ever heard of in your whole life. Somebody told Clark about the carving of the princess on the back of our boat and he said, ve had no business having anything there, except the number. It's against Company rules."

"You mean, we have to take Princess Onoko down?" exclaimed Wilhelm, his voice filled with horror.

"Ja!" answered his father, taking a deep puff on his pipe. "Ve must take down her likeness and name."

"Oh!" sighed Mary aghast. It was as if she had lost an old friend.

The children were a study in contrasts. Wilhelm scowled and looked as angry as his father. Annie had already dissolved into tears.

"Who turned us in?" demanded Mary.

"Who else? Of course, I can't prove it. But, *bestimmt*, I am sure it vas that crazy Velshman."

The crew stood in stunned silence as they thought about what removing the princess's image meant. In the superstitious world of canalers, the beautiful Indian maiden was their protector. Telling her tragic story each new season was a good-luck rite. Now, the carving that Manfred had worked on so lovingly was nothing more than a piece of firewood, and the boat they sailed on would be without a name.

Young as he was, Wilhelm was the first to accept the inevitable. "When do we have to take the princess down, Pa?"

"By Monday at the latest, Clark said."

Sobs rent the cabin as Annie collapsed in a heap on the floor.

"There, there, child," comforted her father, picking her up and cradling her in his arms like a baby, "it isn't as bad as all that! I tell you vhat, *liebchen*, ve vill bring her inside the cabin. No vone vill see her there."

Annie wiped her eyes on the back of her sleeve and stopped sobbing. "Can we call our boat the *Onoko Princess* in secret?"

"Vhy not, *liebchen*? Who is to know? Ve vill take the princess off the stern in the morning, and bring her inside before ve go to church. Vone thing I vant you to know: Lehigh Coal & Navigation Company Boat Number 322 vill alvays be the *Onoko Princess* to our family."

CHAPTER XVI

There was no need for a conch-shell awakening. They were all up bright and early next morning. Moving the carving was a ritual they wanted to share. Although having Princess Onoko on the cabin wall where nobody could see her was not quite the same as having her on the back of the boat for the whole world to see, it was a solution that they had come to accept. Annie consoled herself that the Indian maiden would always stay beautiful when she was not buffeted by bad weather, and both children believed she would keep her magical powers.

When they had finished breakfast, they all went on deck. Manfred reached down the stern with his long arms and unscrewed the carving carefully lest it fall into the water. When the princess was safely on board, Annie washed the grime off her face and hair, and polished her until she shone. Choosing the right place to hang her was a family decision. Annie wanted to hang the princess over her bunk. But, when her father pointed out that no one would see her when the bunks were up, she agreed with the others that the best place to put her was above the folding table on the opposite wall. With the location agreed upon, Manfred centered the carving in the middle of the wall, a little toward the top. The position was perfect. Princess Onoko's gaze followed them wherever they went. She watched them get ready for church; watched as Mary heated the flatiron on top of the stove to press Annie's new dress; watched that the iron did not get too hot. Too hot and the dress would be scorched; not hot enough and it would be full of wrinkles. Mary spat on the hot metal bottom to test it. Her saliva fizzled and dried up. The iron was ready to use.

"Turn to the wall, Pa and Wil," ordered Annie when her mother finished pressing the dress. She could barely wait until they looked the other way before putting her arms into the sleeves and pulling the dress over her head. After smoothing out the skirt, she asked her mother to button the bodice. Mary had rolled her hair in rags before going to bed. Now, Annie untied them, careful not to pull her hair. As her long tresses fell down in ringlets, she held a hand mirror and brushed and twisted them until the curls were just right. Then, feeling like a prima donna in her new dress, she turned to her father and Wilhelm and said very grandly, "You can look now." With much oohing and aahing from her mother

Manfred centered the carving in the middle of the wall

about how pretty she looked, and compliments from her father and Wilhelm, she set off proudly with the family for church.

The cliffs along the waterfront and the rooftops on the hillsides still wore traces of white as they walked along the riverside toward the Lutheran church. The harbor was unnaturally quiet. Although a number of boats were tied up, their crews were not stirring. With the shops closed and the taverns barred shut, there was little to do in Easton on Sundays. Unless a boatman bought liquor on a Saturday, he had nothing to drink in the dry town. Even the children found Sundays in Easton uninteresting. Compared to the excitement of the Reverend Ford's mission, the church service was boring. But Sunday was Sunday and, without a tent or warehouse mission to go to, Manfred decreed that the Lutheran Church was where they went. This Sunday was more important that ever to Manfred. He wanted to pray for salvation for helping a murderer escape, and give thanks for deliverance for not having been found out.

James Washington passed safely through the guard lock on Saturday night and tied up as far away as possible from the hustle and bustle of the port. His arrival in Easton meant he had another hurdle to cross. His Day of Rest would be not be spent attending church, it would be spent seeing his young protégé on his way.

All Saturday night Washington lay awake on his bunk, thinking about the mess he had gotten himself into. So far he had been lucky. No one had bothered him since New Hope. But the danger was not over. The fugitive was still on board. Before he could breathe easier, he had to get Harrison across the Delaware River to Port Delaware at Phillipsburg and send him on his way up the Morris Canal. Crossing the river would be risky. If they were caught, his days on the canal would be over. Worse, if Harrison were convicted of killing Missus Bainbridge, he would end up on the gallows for aiding and abetting a murderer. He guessed Company officials had been tipped off about Harrison from the way they went over his boat in New Hope. And he worried that the news had spread up the canal to Easton. If he hoped to reach Port Delaware safely with Harrison, they would have to cross by Palmer's covered bridge before the townspeople began to stir. The bridge's wooden canopy stretched most of the way across the Delaware River and would be the perfect shield from prying eyes.

With a shake of the shoulder, he aroused Joshua Harrison well before dawn.

Despite his predicament, the young man had slept soundly. After a hasty breakfast, they set out. There was no one along the quay that early. The boatmen who had spent Saturday night in Snufftown would spend Sunday sleeping it off, and the rest had not gotten up for church. They were lucky too when they crossed the bridge. The only person they met was a Negro pulling a wooden cart loaded with junk to Easton. With the North fighting to liberate Negroes from slavery, a growing number of former slaves now called Easton home. With a curt " 'mornin' " to the man, they continued on their way.

" 'Mornin', Captain Washington," came a voice as they stepped out of the covered bridge. A private boatmen was making his way to his boat on the Easton side of the river. Just like Company boatmen, private boatmen knew most of the people on the canals. And this man, who plied the canals buying produce from farmers and selling it to retailers in Easton and Phillipsburg, was no stranger to James Washington. Most canalers had heard about the black boatman and the canal boat given to him by Captain Serfass.

"You're out early," he remarked. Then, scrutinizing Washington's companion, added, "I didn't know you had a son."

"Ah don't, Cap'n Steele. This is ma nephew."

"I take it, you're on your way to church."

"Not this mornin'," answered Washington, contorting his face and looking upset. "Ah'm on ma way to see ma brother. Ma nephew, here, jest brought me the sad news. He jest passed away."

"Sorry to hear that," mumbled the man. "I won't keep you." He tipped his cap in sympathy and moved on.

"Phew!" exclaimed Washington, wiping the perspiration off his brow as the sound of the captain's boots echoed hollowly through the covered bridge. "Ah thought fer sure we wuz ketched!"

"Me too!" trembled Harrison, striding to keep pace with Washington; trusting him, but not knowing where he was going or what he was going to do next.

If Harrison had no idea what was happening, James Washington did. He had a plan. When they reached a narrow dirt path, he stopped and looked about him. Seeing no one, he pointed to a mule track running between a row of sheds and ramshackle buildings. "This way!" The path led to a little-used stable, well back from the canal. He opened the top half of the Dutch door, and peered inside. As he expected, the stable was empty of everything but hay. "Lie low, Harrison!" he cautioned, as he hustled the black youth inside. "Nobody'll botha ya here on a Sunday. Ah'll be back as quick as Ah cain."

Retracing his steps, Washington wandered up and down the waterfront looking for a boat owned by a jobber named Foster. Foster was known on the canal as a man who would haul anything anywhere for a payoff. When he reached the Morris Canal terminus, two private boats were tied up, ready to lock through first thing in the morning. One of them was the *Seagull* belonging to Dan Foster.

Seeing no one stirring, Washington shouted, "Helloooo." When he did not get an answer, he climbed over the side and banged on the cabin hatch.

"Who's there?" snarled a voice.

"Washington, sir. James Washington."

"You mean, the nigger captain?

Washington bristled, but kept calm. "Yesssir!"

"What d'ya want, black man?"

"Ah'm lookin' fer Cap'n Foster."

"That's me," growled Foster who had been sleeping off a Saturday night drunk, and was not pleased at being disturbed. Coming out of his cabin, he pulled his suspenders over his shoulders and buttoned his fly. "What do ya want botherin' me like this so early in the morning?"

"A favor."

Foster yawned widely, and made to close the hatch.

"There's money in it for you!" said Washington before Foster could slam it shut.

Foster stopped in his tracks. "How so?"

"Ma nephew needs a ride up the Morris."

"Yer not askin' me t' carry a nigger, are ya?"

Washington kept his anger in check, and nodded.

"What's the black son of a gun bin up to?" A thug himself, there was not much that fooled Foster.

"The boy jest came North. He needs t' git t' New York City t' live wit' his uncle."

Foster was an accomplished bargainer. He knew the more he hesitated, the more money Washington would pay. Finally, after what seemed forever, he growled, "How much is it worth to you, Cap'n?"

"Ah wuz thinkin' five dollars."

"Five dollars!" spat Foster contemptuously.

"How much then?"

"Twenty, and it's a done deal!"

Twenty dollars was most of what Washington got paid for carrying a boatload of anthracite the length of the Lehigh and Delaware canals, but he had to get rid of Harrison … and soon. He hesitated for a moment, then, putting his hand in his pocket, pulled out a ten-dollar gold piece. "This is iverything Ah've got 'till Ah git paid."

Foster looked displeased but, figuring that ten dollars was better than nothing seeing he was going up the Morris Canal any way, he examined the gold piece to make sure it was real and put it in his pocket.

"Ma nephew'll be on board at dusk."

James Washington gave a sigh of relief and walked up the dirt path to the stable. He was broke, but his troubles would soon be over. By morning, Harrison would be on his way to New York. He opened the Dutch door cautiously. His heart stopped. The runaway was nowhere to be seen. "Harrison," he whispered, and Harrison came out from his hiding place under the hay.

"Ah've got ya all fixed up on the *Seagull*," said Washington as the black youth brushed himself off. "Board her under the cover of darkness. She's moored this side of the first lock on the Morris Canal." Then, remembering Harrison couldn't read, he added, "She's the second boat in line. Ah paid off the cap'n to tek ya to the Jersey side of the Hudson. Ya cain git across the river by ferry from there."

Harrison clasped the older man around the shoulders. "Ah'll niver be able to repay ya, Cap'n Washington."

"You owe me nothin', young man! Jest be safe."

With Harrison hidden in the stable until it was time to board the *Seagull*, James Washington walked across Palmer's Bridge to Easton. A load had been lifted off his shoulders. He had seen Joshua Harrison on his way without being caught. Although he may never know if Joshua reached New York safely, he had done what was expected of him as a black man. He reached the Pennsylvania side of the Delaware and, preoccupied with his thoughts, hastened along the waterfront, anxious to get back on the *Sally Sue* without being seen.

CHAPTER XVII

It was early morning — nighttime to most of the sleeping populace of the villages and towns along the canal. The *Onoko Princess* was on the last leg of her journey to Mauch Chunk. The more distance Manfred put between himself and Easton, the more his anxiety about the Negro evaporated. Even Mary was more relaxed. By now, the boy should be on his way up the Morris Canal. With the weather and everything else in his favor, now that Harrison was out of the way Manfred hoped to make it to Laury's Station by nightfall. He had promised the children they could spend the night with their cousins.

As dawn turned into day, winter was turning into spring. Everything in the living world was animated. The earth was yielding the last melt-off of late spring snow, and the river and canal were running high. Emerald tuffets sprouted amid the swaths of white still gracing meadow and hillside. Daffodils and tulips poked their green sheaths around the cottages and grand houses bordering the canal and, already brightening the gardens with yellow, purple and white, beds of crocuses lifted their faces to the sun. Even the tall chimney stacks seemed to rejoice as they passed by the pockets of industry. A gentle updraft pushed the smoke heavenward in straight white columns, foretelling fair weather. In a glorious prelude to spring, everything was coming to life after a long winter sleep.

Manfred and Wilhelm sang and whistled in tune with nature's mood as they guided the *Onoko Princess* through the glory of the morning. For the first time in a week, the weather was fair enough for Mary and Annie to wash clothes. As shirts, socks, underwear and jerseys went from washtub to clothesline, they flapped, snapped and danced in the gentle spring breeze.

Each day Wilhelm's legs grew stronger. Whereas, at first, he had been eager to start and eager to stop, now he was eager to keep going. Except for meals and when otherwise ordered by his father and captain, he stayed with the mules on the towpath. Each day, he tested himself to the limit and, when he could not go on any longer, he took a rest on one of the mules. To be fair, one time he rode Max; the next, Lucy.

At Catasauqua, the *Onoko Princess* encountered her first delay since leaving Easton. She had to wait for one of the Company's old "stiff" boats to turn around. Having delivered her load of anthracite to the Crane Iron Works, she had to turn around in the turning basin alongside the furnaces before heading back to Mauch Chunk to reload. Without the maneuverability of a hinged coal boat like the *Onoko Princess*, where the sections could be uncoupled, it was impossible to turn an eighty-seven-foot-long "stiff" boat anywhere along the sixty-foot-wide canal, no matter how skilled the boatman!

As her mules maneuvered her bulk into the basin, Manfred was growing impatient; Wilhelm was getting tired. Before it was time for his father to give him the signal to move on, he asked the mule driver waiting in line behind them to give him a boost onto Lucy.

With the Company boat heading in the right direction, followed by the *Onoko Princess*, the mules resumed their trek up the towpath. Soon, Lucy's rolling gait lulled Wilhelm to sleep. Swaying from one side to the other in a rhythm shared only by him and the mule, he was oblivious to everything going on. Not so Manfred. Noticing his son's curious gait as they were about to enter the slack water above Swartz's Dam, he hollered, "Hey, Vil, vake up! The river's high and ve're goin' against the current!"

Wilhelm opened his eyes, startled. For a moment, he wondered where he was. Then, realizing he had dosed off, he slid off Lucy's back, looking embarrassed. To show he was in charge once more, he held on to the harness, hoping his mother, and especially Annie, had not seen what had happened.

The current above the dam pushed against the *Onoko Princess*'s bow, holding her back. As the gradient rose steadily toward the mountains, the mules began to lag. They had another mile to pull the boat along the slackwater before they could be fed. Wide awake once again, Wilhelm walked ahead of them, encouraging them, coaxing them forward when they dropped back. At last, the trumpeting of the conch shell told him they were nearing Lock 35. After the lock, the going would be easier. The *Onoko Princess* would get out of the river and back into the canal.

As they approached the lock, Manfred moved the tiller at right angles to the stern while Wilhelm slowly brought Max and Lucy to a halt. The miter gates were closed. There was no sign of the locktender and they waited and waited. When he did not show up to reverse the lock, Manfred trumpeted on his conch shell. Then, when there was no response, he cupped his hands to make his voice carry and shouted, "Vhere are you Reiter? Ve are vaiting to pass through." But Roger Reiter, the locktender, was nowhere to be seen.

"Run up to the lock house and knock on the door, Vil. Something must be wrong. Reiter's never one to be derelict in his duties."

Wilhelm wound the mule harness around a tree and scampered up the garden path. He was just raising his arm to knock when the door opened, almost hitting him in the face. A red-faced Reiter burst through it, waving the stump of an arm. It was all that was left after it had been mangled by the wicket shanty crank several years earlier.

"Oh, it's you, young Oberfeldt! Is your mother on board?"

"She is, sir," answered Wilhelm. "Anything wrong?"

But Reiter did not stop to answer. He shuffled quickly along the miter-gate coping, waving his good and bad arms, and hollering for help. "Oberfeldt, I need your missus. Jane's about to give birth."

When he heard Reiter's cries, Manfred chained the steering post to hold the *Onoko Princess* steady and ran forward to the bow. Staggering on the top of the miter gates to keep his balance, the locktender looked so frantic, Manfred thought he would fall in.

"Calm down, Reiter, or you vill land in the drink." Reiter's desperation was contagious. "MARY!" hollered Manfred through cupped hands, "MAAAARY!" Then he turned reassuringly to Reiter. "This von't be the first time she's delivered a young un along this canal."

Mary scrambled up the cabin steps, followed by Annie. "Did I hear right, Manny? Is Reiter's wife delivering?"

"Ja! She needs help."

Mary ran to the side of the boat, then realized she could not get off.

"Don't stand there like an idiot, Reiter," yelled Manfred. "If you vant my vife's help, you vill have to level the lock."

Reiter gathered his senses and scrambled back along the coping. He opened the small wickets in the bottom of the miter gates, let the water out of the chamber, and cranked open the heavy wooden gates with his good arm. When the *Onoko Princess* was safely inside the lock, he closed the miter gates, and made haste to the wicket shanty at upper end of the lock. Forgetting what had happened to him in the past, he cranked open the drop gate like a wild man and let water into the lock.

Leveling took an eternity. Before Mary could get off, the *Onoko Princess* had to rise seven feet.

Not one to miss the excitement, Annie followed her mother to the side of the boat. "I'm coming with you, Ma!" She had reached an age when birthing and other nameless things were a curiosity.

"No, you're not!" said her mother firmly as Reiter helped her over the side. "Birthing's no place for a young girl."

Annie was rebuffed and disappointed. When her mother disappeared inside the lock house, she stretched out on top of the coal hatch, sulking and remembering. Once, when she was little, she had seen a cow give birth. It was on her Uncle Rudy's farm. She was about five, and was walking through the fields with her Aunt Milly on the way back from the cemetery. She ran to the fence when she heard the bellowing, and peered over the top to see what it was. She remembered Aunt Milly trying to lure her away with promises of dinner, but, even though she was starving, she would have none of it. It was too fascinating watching the calf slither out of its mother's back end. Legs buckling, the calf landed on the grass, covered in a bloody veil. Its mother licked it clean and it wobbled to its feet and took its first step. Annie was amazed. Didn't babies — and calves — come from cabbages? She asked Aunt Milly how the calf got inside the cow. And she remembered her not answering.

The *Onoko Princess* passed through the lock into the upper level of the canal. "I svear, never a day goes by vithout something happening," complained Manfred, more in acceptance of the delay than in anger that it was happening. "Ve might as vell tie up," he said, as he prepared to moor the boat. "Birthing don't come easy. Ve cannot do nothing but vait."

Roger Reiter stood by dazed and helpless, watching Manfred tie up. Realizing that he would be good for nothing until his wife delivered, Manfred sent him inside, and said he would turn the lock.

"Let the beasts graze, Vil," he shouted as he opened the miter-gate wickets for a coal boat coming up the canal. " Ve might as vell give them a free meal. But don't let them eat too much. Ve don't vant them with colic. Ve still have a few miles to go."

Mary climbed the narrow staircase, led upward by the moans. Jane Reiter, her fists clenched, her eyes scrunched shut, was doubled up on the bed having a contraction. "There, there," said Mary, taking her hand. Amid his panic, Roger had managed to prepare for the delivery. Clean towels were laid out on top of the bedding chest, and on the hearth a large iron kettle spouted steam.

Mary could see that the birth was imminent. She stroked the young woman's forehead. For a moment the pain abated, then it returned, fiercer than ever.

"Push. Push hard," encouraged Mary.

Moaning, Jane Reiter did as she was told. She took a deep breath and bore down.

"Again! Again!"

A sharp spasm, a long painful contraction, and a heart-wrenching cry. Mary could see the baby's head coming out. Another push, another contraction, and it was over. She had the newborn girl in her arms. If she had been five minutes more, she would have been too late for the delivery. Cradling the infant tenderly, she wiped the membrane from her face; then, turning her over, she tapped her gently on the back with the flat of her hand. The cry of life was a long time in coming, and Mary's heart stopped. She gave the infant another tap, only this time a little harder. An intake of breath and a gurgle was followed by loud wail. Jane and Roger Reiter's firstborn was going to be all right.

Throughout his wife's moans, Roger Reiter stood on the landing at the top of the stairs looking terrified. The baby's cry was his signal to rush to her side. As he brushed Jane's forehead with a kiss, he whispered, "Do we have a boy or a girl?" looking to Mary for the answer. In his joy at knowing his wife and baby were all right, he had neglected to ask.

"You have a beautiful little girl," announced Mary with great pride. The infant was breathing easily. She tied the umbilical cord and sponged off the membrane covering her tiny body. Soothed by the warm water, the baby stopped wailing. "It's time to go to your mama," cooed Mary as she wrapped her in a blanket and laid her next to her mother.

The tiny hand curled around her mother's forefinger. "She's so beautiful," murmured Jane Reiter weakly. Then turning to Mary, "You've been so kind. We must show our gratitude by naming her after you."

Mary was touched. She already felt a strong bond between herself and the infant she had delivered, and this would confirm it. As the *Onoko Princess* passed up the canal, she swore she would never pass through Reiter's Lock without asking to see the little girl.

By the time Mary returned to the boat, more than an hour had passed. Between opening the lock gates for passing boats, Manfred had spent his time pacing lockside. By this time, they should have been well on their way up the canal. Having promised the children they could spend the night at their aunt's, as usual when there was a delay he was stuck making up for lost time. The strain of the delivery had taken its toll on Mary. It was almost as if she had given birth. She was so exhausted, she did something she rarely did: she stretched out on her bunk and let everybody fend for themselves. Annie took over in the kitchen. For once, she did not object. With her mother resting, she could ask all kinds of questions. And, this time, Mary did not disappoint her. Annie was growing up and she answered every one.

The crew ate separately to make up for lost time. Manfred ate at the helm, and the two women in the cabin. When Annie took her father his dinner, she ventured, "Will we get to Laury's Station tonight, Pa? You said we could stay at Aunt Maggies."

"Ve'll try. Maybe they vill all be in bed by the time ve get there. Ve still have a vay to go."

After Annie had eaten, she changed places with Wilhelm. With his resolve to stay on the towpath, it had been a while since she had driven the mules. As she stepped out in time to their hoof beats, a sliver of a moon peered out of a sapphire dome sprinkled with twinkling stars. She walked beneath the jeweled canopy and thought about leaving her ma and pa. Even Wil. It would be hard not having them around her. On a magical night such as this, she would even miss the canal. As she flip-flopped about how she felt, dragging mule hooves was a sad-happy sound.

Come what may, from now on, Wilhelm was determined to drive the mules to the end of the towpath. He bolted down his supper and, in less than five minutes, came back on deck. "I'm ready to trade places," he announced, in a tone that reminded Annie of their father.

Annie was immersed in her thoughts and would just as soon stay where she was. "That's all right, Wil. You don't have to get back on the towpath. I'll take the boat through to Laury's Station."

"I'm Pa's mule driver, Annie," he shouted, "and I say, you're not going to!"

"But . . ." protested Annie plaintively, "this might be the last time I'll drive Max and Lucy. I won't be able to drive the mules if I live at Grandpa and Gram's."

Annie had hit the right chord. Nothing would have disturbed Wilhelm more than being deprived of walking the towpath. "Oh, all right," he conceded. He would miss his sister if she stayed in Weissport and would never understand why she wanted to leave the canal. The canal was his road to adventure. Around the next river bend or beyond the next lock you never knew what was going to happen. Even during the hot months of summer when rain forgot to fall and the river was shallow, it was powerful — even the dams could not hold back its flow. On and on it kept going, swirling against its banks, gurgling around rocks, in a never-ending stream.

With nothing to do, Wilhelm dangled his legs over the side of the coal hatch and pretended he was captaining the *Onoko Princess*. Holding the long wooden steering post tightly with two hands, just in case it got away if the river surged, he made believe he was navigating the locks and dropping the line. The shouts of a Company boat captain pulling over to the berm side to let them pass brought him back to reality. Maybe, just maybe, he thought, this would be the night he would get up the courage to ask his father if he could steer.

Manfred was in his usual place, holding on to the tiller. Silhouetted against the dark sky, he was a Greek statue, enjoying an after-supper pipe. Smoke rings floated upward in a mystical rhythm as he inhaled and exhaled. Starting as complete circles, they rose up and dissipated until all that remained was the smell. Caught in the effluence, Wilhelm's throat burned and he began to cough. How, he wondered, could anybody enjoy smoking tobacco?

Once, when no-one was looking, he had taken a draw on his father's pipe. One draw, two draws, three draws and he was ready to vomit. "What's up?" asked his mother when she saw his pale face. "Nothing!" he answered, gulping down some water and throwing himself on his straw tick. The cabin and everything in it swayed and spun dreadfully, and he had to close his eyes to keep from throwing up. The feeling of horror was etched in his soul. As long as he lived, he would never take another puff of tobacco.

"Why do you smoke, Pa?" he asked, moving away to escape the smoke rings.

"It's a habit, son. Probably a bad one. It is certainly an expensive habit I could vell do vithout."

Darkness was the time for confessions. "I tried it once, Pa." "Once" was when he was eight, too long ago for punishment.

"That's vhat your ma thought ven you got dizzy that time in the cabin," said Manfred, taking satisfaction that his wife's suspicions had been right. "Now that you know vhat it is like, don't do it again!"

"I swear I won't, Pa … ever!"

The two sat silently, each contemplating his own thoughts. The crescent moon was a witch's moon, wispy and translucent. Combined with light from the nighthawker lanterns, it cast strange shadows on the water. Some were fierce wild animals; some, terrifying ghosts. Swaying gently from side to side, they followed the *Onoko Princess*. Wilhelm shivered and moved closer to his father. Night time on the canal was not so scary when the full moon was up.

"Look, Pa," he exclaimed, looking up at the sky to take his mind off the shadows. "We're catching up with that star." He was pointing to a star that twinkled like a beacon a little to the west of the boat.

"Ve vill never do that, son! That's the North Star, the star all mariners sail by. Even ve boatmen who sail this great country's inland vatervays use the North Star to guide us. See that constellation above it! That's Ursa Major … better known as the Big Dipper. Under Ursa Major is Ursa Minor … the Little Dipper. If you look carefully, you will see that the North Star is at the tip of the Little Dipper's handle."

"You know so much, Pa!"

"Boatmen know their stars."

By now, Wilhelm had forgotten all about the scary shadows. The question burning in his brain was pushing the stars into infinity. He was trying to get up the nerve to ask his father if he could steer when they got back into the canal. In the slackwater above Swartz's Dam the river was tricky. Max and Lucy were feeling the climbing gradient as they pulled against the current. On and on they plodded like automatons, neither caring nor knowing where they were going. As they ascended the incline, little by little, the tow line went limp. After a long, grueling day they were ready to quit.

Annie felt the same way. By the time the *Onoko Princess* reached Siegfried's

Wilhelm clasped the tiller with both hands.

Lock, she had walked the towpath for four and a half miles. "Take the mules on to Laury's Station, Vil," she shouted. "I'm getting off the towpath!" No "please." No asking. No begging. Just a command.

Annie's command came at the worst possible time. The question Wilhelm so badly wanted to ask his father was burning the tip of his tongue.

"No," he shouted angrily, "I was just going to ask Pa if I could steer." The words he wanted to say all evening were out. He put his hand over his mouth to try to stop them, but it was too late. Without thinking what he was saying, he had asked his father if he could take the helm.

He thought he saw a smile come to his father's lips, then it vanished. "Oh, big man," said Manfred, "so you vant to steer! Ven you vere pretending to look at them stars, I bet that vas your idea all along!"

Wilhelm looked sheepish; then, sensing that his father was more amused than angry, he asked lamely, fully expecting a refusal, "Will you let me, Pa?"

The *Onoko Princess* was his father's prize possession. But Manfred, remembering how his father had let him take his boat through a level for the first time when he was ten, shouted in the direction of the towpath, "Keep on going, Annie. You can ride vone of the mules if you are tired."

The tone of her father's voice told Annie there was no use arguing. At the next barred gate, she straddled the dappled mule, consoling herself that, at least, she did not have to walk.

As Wilhelm was about to climb onto the bos'n's chair, his father stopped him. "You'll have to stand up so you have good control of the rudder. Here, hold the tiller like this," he said, showing him how to grasp it with two hands.

No second invitation was needed. He clasped the tiller with two hands, his fingers barely meeting as they curled around the worn shiny wood. The steering post was fastened with an iron clasp to a thin, round pole that ran down the back of the boat. Attached to the other end of the pole, but invisible in the dark water, was the rudder. A move of the tiller to the left and the rudder took the *Onoko Princess* over to the berm side; a move to the right, and it took her to the towpath side of the canal. As Wilhelm grasped the steering post for the first time, the feeling of power was heady. His instinct was to turn it this way and that. But he knew that if he did anything without his father first telling him, he would be booted back to the towpath immediately.

Before Manfred gave the signal to Annie to move on, he wrapped his large hand around Wilhelm's two hands. "I vill help you until you get the feel of the boat," he said. "It is a good time for you to learn. She is easier to steer vhen she is empty." Then, turning to the towpath, he barked, "Forvard!"

Manfred's hands remained over Wilhelm's until the boy understood the subtle movement of the tiller and the boat's response. Then, satisfied he had gotten the hang of it, he uttered the words Wilhelm so much wanted to hear. "Try it yourself, son! That's the only vay you vill learn."

Manfred let go of the long wooden steering post and stood by tensely, his eyes following the boat's every movement. A slight veer to the right or left and his hands were back over Wilhelm's. As they came up to Lock 32, he was ready to take over at the slightest glitch. But without so much as touching the pilings, and with Annie doing the snubbing, the *Onoko Princess* passed safely through the lock.

"That vas a masterful job, son. You, too, Annie," said Manfred proudly as they sailed over the drop gate. "I could not have done better myself! Ve vill go a little vay further, and tie her up at Laury's, this side of the Slate Dam."

With the hour-long stop at Reiter's Lock to assist in the birth of baby Mary, by the time they bedded the mules they had been on the canal more than eighteen hours.

As they climbed over the side of the *Onoko Princess* onto dry land, the children's weariness disappeared like magic. They raced along the cart track to Aunt Maggie's with their parents walking behind at a more leisurely pace. Although sleeping in a comfortable feather bed was a treat to all, Manfred had already made up his mind that he and Mary would return to the boat to prepare for an early start.

When they arrived at the O'Reillys' canalside residence, Manfred's worry about their being in bed was unfounded. Having figured out how long it would take for the *Onoko Princess* to reach Laury's Station after her trip along the two canals, the O'Reillys were sitting up waiting to see if they would show up. They always looked forward to a visit from the Oberfeldts, no matter how brief. The sisters were close and, living twenty miles apart, canaling made it possible for them to keep in touch regularly.

The door opened before they had a chance to knock. Uncle Brian had seen the children running down the road through the window. As soon as they were inside, Aunt Maggie made a beeline for the kitchen. "You must have something to eat."

"We ate after we passed through Siegfried," said Mary, following her sister into the kitchen.

"That's ages ago! If I know these men, they'll be ready for another meal. I'll warm up some chicken fricassee."

"I von't refuse, Maggie," said Manfred, smelling the lingering aroma of the O'Reillys' supper. He was always ready to eat, especially when his sister-in-law did the cooking.

"Me neither," chimed in Uncle Brian, joining Manfred at the kitchen table.

A sparkling white cloth soon covered the scrubbed wooden table and bowls of steaming chicken fricassee, topped with fluffy dumplings, were set out for everyone. The night air had made the children hungry. Even cousins Enid and Liz were ready for second helpings. With their hunger satisfied, everyone gravitated toward those whose interests they shared. The children chatted and played games with their cousins, Mary and her sister talked about the Reiters' new baby and exchanged news about their parents and their home town of Weissport, and Manfred talked canal talk with Uncle Brian.

Brian O'Reilly was a carpenter for the Lehigh Coal & Navigation Company. His job took him from place to place by canal boat, repairing locks and dams. The work was not easy. In summer, when one of the large miter gates refused to open, he had to dive into the murky depths of the lock to fix the stopper that had been knocked out of place by a careless boatman. In the freezing cold of winter, he planked locks and repaired the gates and dams. Even though the canal was emptied at the end of the boating season, a foot of water remained on the lock floors. Waterproof boots, layers of woolen clothing, and thick knitted socks could not keep out the bone-numbing chill.

Two hours went by in a flash. Time was forgotten by all except Manfred. He took out his timepiece. It was way after his usual bedtime. "I hate to be a spoiler, but ve'll have to get going if ve vant to push off at a reasonable hour."

"Then you're not sleeping over!" exclaimed Aunt Maggie, hating to see them leave.

"Not this trip, Maggie. Ve have got to hustle. Time means money. And ve have lost enough of that already."

It was their father's usual refrain and the children looked upset.

"Wil and Annie can stay if they want," said Aunty Maggie, sensing their disappointment.

Mary looked at her offspring and saw them brighten up. "That's what they were hoping you'd say."

"Can we, Pa?"

"Vell," he exclaimed, "hustle them out of bed, Maggie, vhen Brian gets up." He had promised his brother-in-law a ride to his work site at Treichler's Dam. The dam had been damaged when the three-mile stretch of slackwater froze last winter. "That Annie is a sleeper," he cautioned as he and Mary went out of the door, "I vant to reach Veissport by nightfall."

"Don't worry, Manny," Aunt Maggie assured him, "they'll be there by the time you're ready to go."

With their parents gone and the oil lamps turned off, Annie and Wilhelm pulled up the goose-feather comforters on the single beds in Aunt Maggie's spare room. Compared to the hard wooden bunks and, worse, the cabin floor, the feather mattresses were heaven. In no time at all, they were asleep.

CHAPTER XVIII

Good as his word, Uncle Brian arrived with the children before the locks opened for the day. Manfred had already harnessed the mules and the *Onoko Princess* got underway. In just under an hour, she reached Treichler's Guard Lock.

"See you all next time you're along the ditch," called Uncle Brian as he started along the walkway to pick up his tools from the carpenter boat.

The carpenter boat was a special boat, recognizable by a raised structure on top of the deck. It was moored in the upper level, right next to the dam. The inside was partitioned into carpenters', blacksmiths', and paint shops, and storage areas for lumber and tools. Everything needed to repair anything that went wrong on the canal could be found on board the carpenter boat.

The *Onoko Princess* passed through the lock into the three-mile stretch of slack water. The crew could make out the silhouette of Uncle Brian, tools in hand, striding across the breast of the dam to join his work detail on the other side of the river.

Manfred inhaled deeply and blew hard into the conch shell.

Brian O'Reilly turned around. They thought they saw him wave.

" 'Bye, Uncle Brian," the children yelled, waving both arms at him to make sure he saw them.

As they set off along the beautiful three-mile stretch of river, the sun began to creep up from the horizon in a blaze of red. Annie settled herself near her father, hoping to get out of emptying and cleaning the slop pail. Seeing a raggedy-looking man walking next to the river, picking up something from time to time and taking it to a hand cart on the towpath, she asked, "What's he doing?"

"Picking coal," answered Manfred.

"Aw, you're teasing, Pa," she said, laughing. "There's no coal in the river."

"Not so, *liebchen*! There is a lot of coal in the river … enough to keep his family varm next vinter if he keeps searching the river banks. It fell off the arks that vere wrecked long ago and gets vashed up on the banks vhen the river floods. In the old days — before the canal vas built — the cargo often tumbled in the river."

"You mean, when there were bear trap locks, Pa?"

"Ja, then, and even before that … vay back in the days vhen coal vas first discovered. They tried sending it down the river on rafts but, vithout any bear traps, most of them rafts vere wrecked, landing the coal in the river."

"Gosh, that's a big piece of coal!" exclaimed Annie as the man struggled to lift a lump into his cart. "It's almost as big as a boulder."

"That is so, *liebchen*," said her father. "Now, I vill tell you something else. Then, vhen you find a big lump of coal like that on the river bank, you can get an idea vhen it vas mined."

"What do you mean, Pa?"

"Vhen you find a piece of coal that big, vashed up on the bank, you can be sure it got into the river before 1850. Do you know vhy, Annie?"

Annie thought a while, then shook her head.

"Because, before 1850, there vere no breakers to smash it up into smaller pieces and size it. In them days, coal vas shipped in big lumps, just like it came from the mine. Today, it is broken into different size pieces for different uses."

"You mean, Pa, if I find a big piece of coal along the river, it was mined before 1850?"

"That's right, *liebchen*!"

"Oh!" said Annie excitedly. "The next time we're home, Wil and me will go looking for some, then we will know how old it is."

"Vell, you cannot tell how old coal is, *liebchen*. Coal is more than two hunert and seventy million years old. But you can tell something about vhen it vas mined."

"We'll pretend we're archeologists, and ..."

"And I vill tell you something else, Annie," interrupted Manfred, eager to reveal more secrets about the river. "The river is not only a source of coal, it provides vater power to run the machinery in factories and mills along its banks. Did you know, *liebchen*, that the Lehigh River is the only river in Pennsylvania that is leased to a private company?"

"You mean, the Lehigh Coal & Navigation Co. owns the Lehigh River?"

"Nein, *liebchen*! Lease is different from own. The Lehigh Coal & Navigation Company vas granted use of the river. In 1818, the State of Pennsylvania signed an agreement with Josiah Vhite permitting him to make the river navigable vith bear traps. And the lease continues to this day. As vell as selling the vater to factories and mills, the Company vas also granted lumber rights."

Wilhelm was straining to listen to the conversation, and not keeping up. With the wind blowing down the canal, if he did not get too far ahead, he could hear almost everything his father said. As he dragged his feet to listen, the mules were midships and the *Onoko Princess* was going nowhere.

"Hey, boy," shouted Manfred, lighting his pipe and puffing out large smoke rings. It was the signal the conversation was over. "Vhat is wrong?"

"Nothing, Pa," muttered Wilhelm, picking up speed.

The slackwater swooped and swirled over the treasure in the river's depths. Surely, thought Wilhelm, the Lehigh River and the Lower Division of the Canal are the most wonderful places on earth.

Before them towered the ancient Lehigh Gap. They were about to pass along another magnificent stretch of river. As the Lehigh wended its way south over the eons it had sliced through the mountains, leaving massive cliffs along both banks. Rising straight up from the river, there was barely enough room left along the water's edge for the towpath. Wilhelm had been on the towpath for ten miles since leaving Laury's Station. He had cheated a little. First, he had ridden Lucy;

now he was astride Max. Well, not really astride. His legs barely reached across Max's broad back.

It seemed that every time Wilhelm rode the big mule, his imagination started playing tricks. Trekking beneath the dark cliffs at the base of the Blue Mountains, he was no longer Wilhelm Oberfeldt, novice mule driver. He was Opachee, the brave and handsome suitor of Princess Onoko. Leading a band of Lenapes on his great chestnut steed, he was following the river trail inland after the tribe's annual journey to the ocean to collect shellfish. As he rode toward the familiar mountains, the smell of the mighty ocean was but a memory to be savored until next spring, when they would trek there again. The seashells in their saddle baskets would serve them well. They would fashion the big ones into tools and utensils, and give the small, pretty ones to the squaws to make jewelry to trade with the white man for all kinds of wonderful, new things.

Concentrating on the swirling currents as they entered the Lehigh Gap, Manfred kept a careful watch fore and aft. As the *Onoko Princess* passed under the cold cliffs, Annie was sitting by him. With nothing to do in the cabin, she was bored. On impulse, she hollered at the top of her lungs, "WIL! I WANT TO CHANGE PLACES!" No asking, no begging. Despite already having taken over the reins for what she said was the last time, it was an order. In her frame of mind, as she worried about what her grandparents would say, walking the towpath was better than being on board.

Her call reverberated off the mountains on both sides of the river. Amplified by the cliff faces, it screamed at itself across the Gap. "Change Places ... Change Places ... Change Places." The volume was unbelievable. Startled out of his wits, Wilhelm almost fell off Max. He heard Annie chortle. His game had ended. He was no longer Opachee, the handsome suitor of Onoko, he was Wilhelm Oberfeldt, mule driver who had fallen asleep on the job. Angry at his sister, embarrassed that she had caught him nodding off, he yelled back with equal volume, "I'M NOT GONNA CHANGE PLACES WITH YOU! I'M GONNA DRIVE THE MULES TO MAUCH CHUNK!"

"Drive!" sneered Annie. "You mean ride, don't you?"

Her words hit home. Wilhelm pulled on the harness to stop and slid off Max's back.

"I didn't mean that you shouldn't ride Max," she flustered, "it's just ... I thought I'd give you a break."

"That's real nice of you, Annie," answered Wilhelm sweetly, not making a move to change places. With the superiority of one in charge, he walked alongside Lucy and took hold of the lead rein. He would show Annie. No matter how tired or hungry he was, he would walk the rest of the way.

Before Mary knew it, Bowmanstown was upon them. She almost missed her chance to buy bread from Cloe Tuttle, the locktender's wife, who could be counted on to take coal as payment. Cloe had such a thriving business, she could never get enough coal to fire her oven for baking and her boiler for washing clothes. Besides making the best home-baked bread and sticky buns along both canals, Cloe was the finest laundress anywhere. Although other locktenders' wives took in wash for bachelor boatmen, hers was the cleanest and best-ironed of all. Her secret was the clothes boiler in the wash house, which she kept fired up with exchanges of coal. The way to get clothes clean was to boil them. A packet of blueing in the rinse helped. It got them whiter than white. Attesting to Cloe's skill, singlets, long johns and shirts in all sizes flapped on the clothes lines strung from pole to pole behind the lock house. When they were dry, they were ironed and folded for a price, ready for pickup the next time their owners passed that way.

For as long as Mary could remember, she and Cloe had been friends. When the Kintzes moved to Weissport and Reuben got a job on the canal, Cloe's parents were their next-door neighbors. From the start, the girls were inseparable. What little schooling they had, they had together in the one-room village schoolhouse.

As Mary waited to get off, Arlington Tuttle opened the miter gates at the lower end of the lock and closed them when the *Onoko Princess* was safely inside. He cranked open the drop gate at the top end of the lock, and the *Onoko Princess* rose steadily on a sixteen-foot tide. With the side of the *Onoko Princess* riding above the quayside, Mary got off.

When Mary walked behind the lock house, Cloe was taking dry clothes off the line. As soon as she saw who it was, she put down her wash basket and ran toward Mary and gave her a hug.

"Oh Mary, how are you?" she exclaimed. "It's wonderful to see you again. Come on into the wash house and we'll have a talk over a cup of coffee."

"It will have to be a quick one, Cloe. Manfred is in a hurry. He's all set on tying up at Weissport tonight."

The aroma of fresh coffee greeted them as Cloe opened the door. A pot was perking on top of the stove next to two flatirons that were being heated to press the batch of clean clothes. While one load of wash bubbled in the boiler, another lay heaped on a long table, awaiting its turn to go in. Not a thing was out of place. Baskets of dirty laundry, and clothes that had been washed, dried and ironed each had their place in the wash house.

Cloe poured the coffee and offered Mary a sticky bun. Then came the same old question, asked by canalers up and down the canal, hundreds of times each day, "What's happening along the canal?"

Mary's answer was what Cloe expected. She recited everything on the way down to Bristol and back, with one exception. She left out anything to do with the Negro. But news travels fast. The story of the fugitive had reached Bowmanstown. And Cloe could not wait to find out if Mary knew anything she did not know.

"They say, a nigger is loose on the canal … a murderer."

"I heard," said Mary quietly.

"He escaped from some plantation or other an' came north, like all of 'em do! Pretty soon the whole countryside around here'll be full of Negroes. He's was workin' for one of them do-gooders in Philadelphia what helps runaway slaves and he killed her. Mrs. Bainbridge was her name. He slit the poor woman's throat from ear to ear after all she done for him. But he'll get his comeuppance. The coppers are after him."

Although Mary's heart was pounding, she kept her composure. "Do you know if they caught him yet?"

"No, but I heard they were questioning that Negro boat captain. You know, the one who did that old fool, Cap'n Serfass, out of his coal boat. They think he had something to do with his escape."

Mary paled. "You mean Captain Washington?"

Cloe nodded. "That's him. They believe he helped the murderer get away along the Morris Canal."

"Did they take him into custody?" Mary asked, praying they had not.

"No. They had to let him go! Blain Jeffries — you know him? He's captain of Company Boat 26 — said they searched his boat from top to bottom … took it apart, almost … but didn't find anything."

Mary breathed easier. It was in Washington's own interest, as well as theirs, to keep his mouth shut. But the thought that he might say something terrified her. When the sound of the conch shell signaled her to get back on board, she welcomed it.

As she got up to leave, Cloe handed her a mug of coffee and a sticky bun for Manfred. "Take this to the mister. I know how much he likes my sticky buns. You can bring the mug back next time you pass this way."

With words of thanks and a wave, Mary made her way back to the boat. Manfred was conversing with Cloe's husband, Arlington, in Pennsylvania German. Although Arlington Tuttle was of English descent, like Manfred he had picked up the language spoken by most boatmen and locktenders on the Lehigh Canal. As the men talked, Wilhelm was perched on the mule bridge rail listening, trying to make out what was being said. He had learned a smattering of Pennsylvania German from his grandparents but the longer he worked on the canal, the more fluent he would become. Seeing his mother climb over the side of the *Onoko Princess,* he slid off the railing and took hold of Max's harness.

"Forvard," shouted Manfred.

"Forward," echoed Wilhelm as they took off.

Mary waited until they were out of hearing of the lock before telling Manfred what Cloe had said about James Washington. "Don't vorry," he answered, "Vashington vill keep quiet. It is in his own interest — as vell as ours — to keep his mouth shut."

Manfred's tone was reassuring, and Mary settled herself on the equipment locker with her knitting to enjoy the fresh evening air. A mile beyond Bowmanstown, the three-way water junction at Parryville was upon them. Although the Pohopoco and the Lehigh were running higher than ever with the recent fall of snow, Wilhelm was not concerned. As he led the mules across the rickety bridge, the tow line strained but, this time, he did not hesitate. The *Onoko Princess* was outside Lock 13, and his father was sounding the conch shell.

Passage from the river through the lock into the canal was swift. They were embarking on the final leg of their journey. In another three miles, Annie's future would be decided. True to his word, Wilhelm had driven the mules since Laury's after refusing to turn over the lead rein to Annie at the Lehigh Gap, and he was worn out. The only thing he could think of, as he walked the last few miles to

Weissport, was snuggling down in a feather bed under an eiderdown.

"Are we staying with Grandma?" he asked, as he helped his father tie up the *Onoko Princess* in the boatyard.

"Ja," replied his father. "Your mother and me have to talk to Reuben and Emily about Annie."

"I'll miss Annie if she stays in Weissport," confessed Wilhelm, regretting that he had been mean.

"You're not the only vone!" exclaimed his father.

The Kintzes hugged everyone as they came through the door, even Manfred. Not a man to show his emotions, the best he could do was to stand stiffly and smile. After the more than two-hundred-mile journey to Bristol and back, even he was pleased to be home.

The smell of cooking filled the house. Whatever the occasion or time of day, Emily Kintz was ready. Even when the growing season ended and times were lean, she could be counted on to make a meal, fit for a king, out of pickings. But tonight's supper was special. To celebrate Reuben Kintz's eightieth birthday and welcome the canalers home, Johnson the butcher had killed their pig. As Wilhelm and his parents came into the kitchen, Emily Kintz cornered them. "If Annie asks where Ophelia is, say she has been sold." But Annie had bigger things on her mind. She was already in the parlor sweet-talking her grandfather.

As they sat around the table, the mood was joyous. They had plenty of things to celebrate. Grandpa had lived eighty long, productive years, the *Onoko Princess* was at the end of her first run, and Manfred would receive his wages when they reached the Weigh Lock. A cake with eight candles, one for each decade of Reuben's life, was set in the middle of the table. The candles were lit. Reuben did not have to think long before making a wish, then everyone sang "Happy Birthday."

After the meal, the men went into the parlor to smoke and talk and left the women to clean up. Just like the locktenders and storekeepers along the canal, Reuben could not wait to hear the latest news. And, respecting the old man as a former canaler, Manfred was not loath to tell him. Learning that Manfred had turned Taffy Morgan in, Reuben said curtly, "he got what he deserved." He and Morgan were no strangers. When Reuben was in charge of a coal boat, they had had several run-ins. "A week's suspension is not enough. They should keep the rascal off the canal. He's nothing but a menace to boatmen."

The story ended, the two men sat in silence before the open fireplace, puffing on their pipes. Then, prizing Reuben's advice, Manfred decided to tell him about the Negro fugitive, knowing that what he had to say would go no further. Reuben listened intently, then when Manfred had finished, he said, "That's serious stuff, Manny. You could be jailed for aiding and abetting a fugitive."

"They questioned Vashington, but nothing came of it." Then, noting his father-in-law's concern, he added, "Don't vorry, Reuben. Vashington von't talk. He knows vhat is good for him!"

"For your sake, let's hope not!" said Reuben Kintz, taking a long, contemplative draw on his pipe.

With the dishes washed and put away, the time had come for serious conversation. Mary hated to ask anyone for a favor, even her parents, but she could not go back on her promise to Annie. "Ma," she said as she took off her apron and hung it behind the kitchen door, "I have something to ask you."

"What is it, lass?"

Mary walked over to the window and looked out so that she would not see her mother's face if she chose to refuse. "Annie wants to stay with you and Pa."

"You mean, she doesn't want to sail the canal any more!"

"No! She wants to go to school full-time."

Emily Kintz was a perceptive woman. "I thought she was inclined that way," she remarked. "She was hinting about it before you set out. But I did not expect it to happen this quick. I thought she would get over it."

Mary turned from the window and faced her mother. "Well, Ma, what do you think?"

Emily thought hard. With Reuben in his eighty-first year, and she in her seventy-fourth, raising a young girl would not be easy. But she and Pa could use some help. Drying her hands, she came over to her daughter. "It's nice to see a young girl as ambitious as Annie. Me an' Pa'll be right glad to have her."

"I thought you'd say that, Ma," said Mary, giving her a hug. "I'm pleased for

Annie threw her arms around her grandmother.

Annie's sake, but it'll be hard on us not having her around." Her eyes misted over. The next thing she knew, she was bawling.

"Don't be upset, Mary!" said her mother, "sooner or later our young uns flee the nest. You'll be by here every two weeks. And Annie'll be in good hands. Pa and me's not getting any younger. It gets harder every day for us to take care of things around here."

The children were squatting on the parlor floor around an old octagonal wooden game board, playing crocino. They had squabbled about who should have which color ring, but a look from Grandpa Kintz had quieted the raised voices. To make sure there was no further disagreement, he flipped a penny to see who would go first. It was Wilhelm. Using his thumb and middle finger, he flicked a blue ring into the highest scoring area on the board on his first try and sat back while Annie had her turn. Annie took one of her rings and was poised ready to knock Wilhelm's ring flying out of the coveted circle when her mother and grandmother came in from the kitchen.

"It's all settled, Annie" said Mary quietly, sitting down on the settee next to Manfred. "Gram has something to tell you."

The ring flipped into no-man's land as Annie waited to hear what her grandmother had to say.

"Young lady," began Emily, "Your ma says you want to stay with Grandpa and me so's you can go to school all year."

Annie nodded and waited for her to continue.

"Well! ..." The pause was long, and Annie held her breath. "You can stay, so long as you help me and Grandpa out. We ain't gettin' any younger."

As Annie leapt to her feet, the rest of the rings flew off her lap. "Oh, thanks, Gram!" she said, throwing her arms around the old lady, "I knew you'd say that. You know I'll help you and Grandpa."

Emily Kintz smiled lovingly at her only granddaughter. "Yes, I know you will," she answered. "Your ma and pa have brought you up right. You'll be no trouble." Then, wagging her finger mischievously, "If you are, though, you'll be right back sailing on that old red canal boat!"

Mary looked pale and drawn, sitting next to Manfred. Seeing how hard it was on her mother, Annie squeezed herself between her parents and took her hand.

"You know how much I love you, don't you?"

Her mother nodded and went into the kitchen to grieve.

With everything settled early, Manfred changed his mind about spending the night. It made more sense to him to get back to the boat so that they could leave early. It was the same old hustle. If they got up to Lock 7 before Shirar opened the gates, with a little luck they would be in Mauch Chunk by dawn and the *Onoko Princess* would be loaded by noon.

One episode was ending; another beginning. The Negro was who knows where, and Annie was getting what she wanted. The parting was tearful. Even Wilhelm looked upset. Even though he and his sister sometimes quarreled, it would not be the same without Annie. With assurances that they would all see one another in two weeks, the three crew members walked through the darkness to the boatyard. Wilhelm was disappointed that he had been cheated out of spending the night in a comfortable feather bed, but if there was one thing good about Annie leaving, it was not having to sleep on the hard cabin floor. From now on, his bed would be the bunk above the one his father and mother shared.

CHAPTER XIX

In the dark of the morning, the *Onoko Princess* made it quickly through the succession of locks to the Weigh Lock. Several boats had lain over above the lock for the night and they were ahead of her. Like Manfred, their captains could not wait to get their first paycheck of the season. Traffic was heavy. Ascending boats were piling up behind the *Onoko Princess* below the Weigh Lock while descending boats, above the lock, waited for their turn to be weighed. It was the third week in March. The scramble to transport coal as quickly as possible from source to destination was in full swing.

It was a full half hour before the paymaster waved Manfred on. Wilhelm led the mules into position below the lock gates and released the tow line. With just the right momentum, the *Onoko Princess* glided through the miter gates into the standard lock that stood side by side of the Weigh Lock. He handed the delivery receipt to the paymaster and, in return, received his wages. Although he would have to save part of his wages for the winter layoff, it felt good to have cash in his pocket.

A command to the towpath from on board, and they were on their way again. Midway to Lock 1 they met the first coal train of the day coming down the track. This time, Wilhelm was prepared. Before the engineer could spook the mules with his whistle, he stopped them on the far side of the towpath and turned their heads away from the rushing train. But the precaution was unnecessary. It was too early in the morning for the engineer to play games and the train steamed by without incident. As the long line of clattering coal cars receded in the distance, Wilhelm led the mules along the two-mile stretch of towpath, through Lock 1 into Mauch Chunk basin.

The boat basin was crowded. Boats were taking on coal at the Beaver Meadow loading docks on the east side of the river; others were lined up underneath the Switchback coal chutes on the west bank. Some were passing into the Upper Grand Section to load at Penn Haven or White Haven, and others, like the *Onoko Princess,* were lined up to cross the river to the coal chutes by cable ferry. Manfred was getting impatient. He hoped to load that afternoon and get back into the canal before the locks shut at ten.

On the bluffs above the basin, men, women and children were making their way to the Switchback terminal to catch the eleven-thirty train. On one side of the road was the grandiose new mansion of railroad magnate Asa Packer; on the other, "Whitehall," the comfortable twenty-five room white clapboard house Josiah White had built four years after he arrived in Mauch Chunk. When White retired to his home town of Philadelphia, "Whitehall" was occupied first by Edwin A. Douglas, chief engineer of the Lehigh Coal & Navigation Company, then by his successor, John Leisenring. Leisenring fancied up the house's plain facade, added a third story, and renamed it "Parkhurst."

While the *Onoko Princess* awaited her turn for the cable ferry, Wilhelm let the mules loose in the stable yard and got back on board in time to cross the river. "See, Pa," he said excitedly, pointing to the procession of people ascending the hillside, "they are going to catch the half past eleven train. That's the second passenger train out of Mauch Chunk this morning."

"First train, second train, my hat!" retorted Manfred, resentful that passengers riding the Switchback were taking precious time away from the movement of coal. As he maneuvered the *Onoko Princess* beneath the coal chutes, he shouted to one of the laborers, "Do you think ve vill be able to load before the Svitchback is highjacked?"

"Yeh, I think you'll just make it," the man answered, shoveling away at a glinting mountain of black diamonds. "There's enough coal in the reservoir to load four more boats."

"*Sehr gut!*" exclaimed Manfred, relieved that they would not have to lay over in Mauch Chunk for the night. The *Onoko Princess* was third in line. She should be well down the canal by morning.

Mary closed the hatch and shuttered the cabin windows as coal began to rumble down the chute into the hold of a neighboring boat. With food supplies replenished and Annie in Weissport, she had decided to stay in the cabin while the *Onoko Princess* was loaded.

Wilhelm remained on deck with his father, not so much to watch the loading procedure but to see the car loads of passengers climb Mount Pisgah. As he watched the train of cars disappear over the summit, he asked wistfully, "Can we ride the Switchback some day, Pa?"

"You know how I feel, son. The Svitchback should be carrying coal, not passengers." Noticing Wilhelm looking crestfallen, Manfred smiled. "Don't look so glum, son." His mood had improved. The *Onoko Princess* was loaded and ready to be hooked onto the cable for another trip down the canal. "How about vhen the boating season ends? Ve must do something special to celebrate your first season on the towpath. And if you vant to ride on the Svitchback, that is vhat ve vill do. Your ma and Annie can go along … and Grandpa and Grandma Kintz."

Every year, when the canal closed for the winter, Manfred treated his family to something special. Usually it was a horse and buggy ride and a meal in a nearby town. This year, would be different.

"Promise?" asked Wilhelm, wanting to make sure that his father meant what he said.

"Ja. Ve vill shake hands on it."

The pact was made and, with his eyes fixed on Mount Pisgah, Wilhelm's imagination took over as they crossed the boat basin. It was the end of the boating season. He was sitting on the hard wooden seat of a passenger coach next to his mother. Steam was hissing from the engine house on the top of the mountain, powering the great wheels that drew the barney car up the slope. The barney car rose from its pit at the base of the mountain, positioned itself behind the passenger cars and began pushing them up the steep plane. Slowly they crawled up the mountain. Would they ever reach the top? When the wheels of the lead car passed over the summit, it was magic. Abracadabra! In a flash, they were plunging helter skelter down Mount Pisgah's far side and coasting to the foot of Mount Jefferson. Ascending the Jefferson plane was the same as ascending Mount Pisgah. Pushed up by a barney car, one moment they were teetering on the top; the next, plummeting wildly toward Summit Hill. The ride back to Mauch Chunk along the downhill track was even more thrilling. They had to hold on to their hats and each other as the train raced toward the terminus at speeds reaching sixty-five miles an hour. Wilhelm hunched up to his mother and closed his eyes. He could feel the power of the wind.

"Are you dreaming again, boy?" called his father as he did his part to navigate the boat. "Ve're almost across the river. Get ready to jump ashore and fetch the mules."

The pulley creaked with the hundred and ten-ton weight of the *Onoko Princess* and Wilhelm opened his eyes with a start. "Yes, Pa," he said, getting ready to jump off the moment the *Onoko Princess* was pulled next to the towpath. The time had come to begin another journey, one of many that would continue, one after the other, until ice closed the canal in November.

CHAPTER XX

Up and down the canal they went from Mauch Chunk to Bristol during the rest of March, and the months of April, May and June, crossing tow lines with fellow boatmen, including those of Taffy Morgan and Captain Washington. The *Onoko Princess* and Taffy Morgan's green coal boat passed one another without incident. Morgan was being careful. He had too much invested in his boat to be thrown off the canal. These days, the only mischief he got into was stealing the odd chicken that strayed from the barnyard onto the towpath. Why should he pay for a chicken when his mule driver could grab one on the run? A twist of the neck, a quick dip in boiling water to loosen the feathers, and supper was in the pot fricasseeing. But if stealing a chicken from a farmer, or fruit and vegetables from an orchard or field alongside the canal, was a crime, Taffy Morgan was not alone in his thievery!

The times Captain Washington and Manfred passed each other in the middle of a level, they managed a stiff wave. Manfred was still resentful that Washington had lied to him but, as he had heard nothing further about the fugitive, he had assigned the incident to the back pocket of history. Being duped into taking the fugitive through the New Hope locks had become just one more of the unusual and unpredictable day-to-day happenings on the canals.

Back home in Weissport, things were going well. Annie was behaving for her grandparents, and getting good grades in school. Much to the envy of her classmates, she had an admirer. John Stevenson, the handsomest boy in the school, carried her books to White Street every afternoon without fail.

Mary's namesake at Bowmanstown was growing fast. These days, when Mary called to see the baby, she greeted her with a dimpled smile. At three months old, she was the pride and joy of Jane and Roger Reiter, who were ever grateful to Mary Oberfeldt for delivering what would be their only child.

Things on board the *Onoko Princess* were going well. Her trips back and forth to Philadelphia were without incident, and Wilhelm was always learning new things. Never a day went by without something different happening. A boat had to be towed off a mud shoal; a mule became entangled in a tow line, slipped into the canal, or dropped dead from overwork or old age; a boatman got into trouble. There was bargaining and bartering and, always, fights at the locks. Sometimes the Oberfeldts were lucky and did not have to travel the length of the two canals. They dumped off their load at a coal yard or at one of Allentown or Bethlehem's mushrooming factories, or took it on to Easton.

Except for an occasional spring shower, the weather was good. Spring was turning into summer. The canal banks were abloom with wild roses, intoxicating those who passed by with their fragrance. The three-man crew of the *Onoko Princess* worked as one. With neither complaint nor protest, they took over for each other whatever the occasion or need. These days, when his mother took over on the towpath, Wilhelm did not have to ask his father if he could steer. When the canal was not crowded, sometimes even when it was, Manfred handed Wilhelm the steering post … but always under his supervision. With each trip, the Oberfeldts' bankroll grew. If they kept going at their present rate, Manfred may not have to seek work next winter.

CHAPTER XXI

Time flew by. It was June already as the *Onoko Princess* made her way toward Weissport. They should have been home, but an accident near the Parryville guard lock had delayed them for several hours. A two-year-old girl had been knocked off the bow of her father's boat when it collided with a Company boat in the slackwater. Efforts to save her were in vain. Swept away by the high water, she was washed over the dam and her small, limp body recovered a mile downstream.

Although the Oberfeldts had been in the canal and had not seen what happened, they were shaken by the accident. Any catastrophe that befell a fellow canaler was taken to heart by all. Seeing the small, wet body lying lockside, they hardly felt like going on. But the gates of the guard lock opened and, like everybody else caught in the backup, they put the tragedy behind them and moved on.

The locks were almost closing by the time they reached Parryville, and they still had two miles to go. At Lock 10, they could go no further. The miter gates were barred shut. It was Saturday night and they would stay padlocked until four o'clock on Monday morning. With only a mile to go, they had to tie up below the lock for the weekend. Manfred was frustrated. He had planned to cheat God a little this Sunday, and do some minor repairs in the boat yard.

Like Saturday, Sunday dawned clear and glorious. The mountains flanking the Lehigh loomed large in the early morning light. "Near hills are a sign of good weather," thought Mary as she fried sausages and eggs on deck.

A deep voice from the towpath interrupted her thoughts. "Mrs. Oberfeldt."

She shaded her eyes from the morning sun to see who it was. Coming down from the direction of Weissport was James Washington, dressed in his Sunday best. "Captain Washington!" she exclaimed, not knowing what else to say.

He doffed his cap. "Ah've bin hopin' Ah'd see you and the Mister fer the past month. Ah've somethin' to tell the Cap'n."

Mary put the eggs and sausage on a plate and said stiffly, "He's in the cabin."

Washington climbed over the side of the *Onoko Princess* and helped her carry the breakfast. At the sight of the Negro boatman following Mary down the steps, Manfred bristled, then, regaining his compusure, he indicated the seat next to him and said sternly, "I've been vantin' to talk to you, Vashington."

Washington did not accept the invitation to sit down. He preferred to remain standing, get what he wanted off his chest and leave. "Ah suppose, ya know Ah've come t' talk t' ya about what happened at New Hope." Manfred gave a stiff nod and waited for Washington to go on. "When ya heard there wuz a murderer on the run, Ah'm guessin' ya put two un two togither. Well, Ah've come t' tell ya ya wuz wrong. That boy didn't harm a hair on old lady Bainbridge's head. It wuz her son what kilt her."

Manfred's jaw dropped open. "How do you know?" he asked sharply, wanting to believe what he was hearing but not trusting Washington after having been lied to before.

Washington pulled a newspaper clipping from his pocket and handed it to Manfred. "Here," he said, "the maid turned him in. She saw him come out of the old lady's bedroom with blood all over his hands. Wesley Bainbridge has been in police custody fer over a month."

"Oh my," said Mary, throwing her arms around Manfred as he looked at the paper, "You don't know how worried I've been!"

He shrugged her off and, glowering, handed the clipping back to Washington. As he looked at the black boat captain, all he could think of were the "what ifs?" What if the boy had been a murderer? What if he, Manfred Oberfeldt, had been thrown in jail for harboring a criminal? What if he had lost command of the *Onoko Princess*?

"Ah'm raight sorry fer the trouble Ah caused you an' yer family, Cap'n Oberfeldt," said Washington contritely, "but, bein' a black man, Ah hed t'do what Ah done. When Ah heard the boy's tale, Ah knew in ma gut he didn't do it. Ah put maself in his place, ya see. Twenty-five yars ago, Ah wuz accused of doin' somethin' Ah didn't do. That's why Ah went on the run." Washington put his hand on the hatch, "All Ah cain say now is Ah'm sorry."

Manfred felt like saying, what difference does that make after all the worry you put me and my family through, but instead, he held out his hand and gave Washington a warning. "Never do anything like this to me again, Cap'n."

"Ya cain be sure Ah won't, Cap'n. Helpin' that brotha got me into a whole pack of trouble. The Welshman seen me with the boy an' tipped off the Navigation people. Ah cain tell ya … when they took me in fer questionin' in Easton, Ah thought ma boatin' days wuz over!"

"Did Harrison get away up the Morris Canal?"

Washington shook his head. "Ah jest don't know! That double-dealin' jobber, Foster, took ma money and left without him. Ah suppose he heard that the police wuz hot on his tail," he said, starting for the steps to the deck. "Ah'd betta be on ma way."

"You look like you're all dressed up for church."

"Ah am! A Baptist preacher's coming through Weissport. He'll be baptizing some folks in the canal fer the first time this yar, an' Ah figures Ah owes the Lord a thank-you."

Wilhelm had been listening intently to everything that was being said. With Annie off the boat, his father had told him the truth about Harrison. Although he was glad to hear that he had not helped to hide a murderer, the thing that excited him most at that moment was the baptismal service. He had not forgotten how he had laughed when Scotty McNish told him about spying on a baptism and seeing the preacher dunk everybody in the canal. Scotty said the preacher called dunking "immersing."

As soon as Washington left, he got dressed in his Sunday clothes. He had plenty of time to go and spy on the service before his parents set off to see Annie. His mother was still cleaning up breakfast and his father was busy talking about the news Washington had brought them.

"I'm going for a walk," he announced, "I'll be back by the time you get ready."

Families were heading along the towpath to the baptismal pool between Locks 10 and 11, and he mingled with them, hoping that Captain Washington would not see him. Just in case, he slipped behind a thicket of bushes at the side of the towpath, crossed to the berm side of the canal by the mule bridge above Lock 11, and returned to the pool. Scrambling up a steep bank, he lay down on the top of a cliff. Beneath him, the canal lay deep, dark and tranquil. From his vantage point, he could see everything that was going on, including Captain Washington, standing off by himself on the fringe of the crowd.

The service was just starting. Some men, women and older children were huddled together on the towpath, standing apart from the rest of the congregation. There were no babies in the group. Only those old enough to accept the Lord for themselves were baptized in the Baptist faith.

Wilhelm had guessed right. The people standing on the towpath were the ones who would be dunked. The preacher beckoned them towards him, and asked, "Shall we gather at the water?"

"Yes! Yes!" they answered, forming a procession and chanting in unison, "Lead us to the water."

Women and teenage girls, looking like brides in long white dresses, and men and boys in their best Sunday suits shuffled to the edge of the pool. Called forward one by one to be cleansed of their sins, they followed the preacher into the pool, shivering and shaking as they entered the ice-cold water. Believing in "full immersion," the Reverend clasped them to him and, intoning their names, dunked them backward until they disappeared beneath the murky water. Some had the good sense to close their mouths and hold their noses before going under; those who didn't gagged and spat out. As they emerged from the canal one by one, their clothes clung to their bodies like wet winding sheets; their pure white Sunday shirts and long dresses were gray from the coal-blackened water. Proclaiming joyously, "We have been cleansed of sin, and are slaves of righteousness," they joined the recessional. Then, newly embraced in the Baptist faith, they rushed behind the nearest bush to change into dry clothes.

It was two weeks since Annie had seen her family. Although the Kintzes could never be sure exactly when the *Onoko Princess* would tie up, they had expected the crew home before the locks closed on Saturday. On Sunday morning, anxious and disappointed that they had not arrived, Annie kept looking out of the side window after church. Just in case they arrived, Emily Kintz was ready. A piece of venison was roasting in the oven with ample portions for all. Annie saw Wilhelm first. He was running down White Street ahead of her parents. "They're here, Gram," she whooped, as she ran outside and raced up the street to meet them.

The Sunday routine at the Kintzes was always the same. After an extra-special dinner, everybody sat around the dining-room table drinking coffee and exchanging news. Mary and Manfred insisted that Annie tell them everything she had done since they last saw her, and they were expected to do the same.

Wilhelm sat around with the others for a while, then he began to fidget. He had other things than staying indoors on his mind. After walking the towpath for the past three months, he was dying to spend the rest of the day with his friend. Secretly, he had proclaimed Sunday "His Day," the one day in the week when he had no responsibility and could go back to being a boy.

When there was a pause in the conversation, he announced that he was going for a walk and headed along the canal toward Mauch Chunk. He had not invited Annie along. He did not want her to know where he was going. Crossing to the berm side by the mule bridge at Lock 7, he followed a narrow trail into the woods. The trail led to Scotty McNish's cabin. Time spent with Scotty was always an adventure. He never knew where they would end up, or what treasures they would find.

He could see the shack through the trees before he got there. It shared a clearing with a rundown shed, a chicken house, and all kinds of junk. Anything Scotty's father thought might come in useful in the future, or that he could sell for a penny or two in the village, was dumped on the lot. Nobody ever entered McNish territory without their knowing it. Big dogs, small dogs, some chained to trees, some running loose, heard the crackle of a twig before anyone got there. And Wilhelm was greeted with a chorus of yaps, barks, and snarls.

Warned that he had a visitor, Scotty's father appeared in the doorway, a hickory cudgel in one hand, a bottle of whisky in the other. "Quiet, you curs," he snarled, lunging at the barking dogs with the stick. When he saw who it was, he shouted through the door, "Git out here, Scotty. It's the Oberfeldt boy." Then, turning to Wilhelm, his voice tinged with sarcasm, he enquired, "How's the new mule boy today?"

Everybody knew that Andy McNish envied those who were gainfully employed, even though he never made an attempt to be employed gainfully himself. And Wilhelm sensed he was being mocked. "Fine, sir," he answered politely, as much out of fear as respect. "And yourself, sir?"

Before Andy McNish could answer and goad Wilhelm with another question, Scotty rushed out of the shack. He did not want his father insulting his only friend. The village children wanted nothing to do with him. They teased him because he could not read and write and said he had cooties. In their opinion, the only thing Scotty was good for was catching muskrats … and who would want to eat the stinking things anyway? Living in neat, white clapboard houses, with fathers who brought home a paycheck, they were too well taken care of to realize that it was Scotty's outdoor skills that kept his family alive.

"I came to ask if you would like to do something," said Wilhelm. "We're tied up below Lock 10."

"Ah wuz jest goin' to look at m' traps to see if Ah ketched anything. Ya can come along if ya want."

"Ah'd like to," replied Wilhelm, matching his dialect to Scotty's. It was his way of fitting in. "What ya ketchin'?"

"What else? Muskrats! The Company pays a bounty for dead uns. An' me Ma needs the money."

"Ya mean, the Company pays ya to ketch muskrats?"

"Yeh! If they ain't ketched, the canal drains itself out through their holes. Ah meks out real well. The Company don't want th' bodies. They jest want te see th' heads te know Ah'm tellin' the truth about how many Ah ketched. Ah gits paid for th' heads, me Ma meks a raight good stew from the meat, and, when them pelts are nice an' thick come the winter, Ah sells them t' Joe Wilson in Mauch Chunk. He's raight handy at makin' them into fur coats, hats, and the likes fer the tourists."

"I ain't seen no muskrats aroun' the canal this yar," remarked Wilhelm with the authority of an experienced boatman.

"That's 'cos ya don't know where t' look." Scotty stuck a knife into his belt, and picked up a burlap sack. Then he caught sight of Wilhelm's best suit. "Yer not wearin' them duds, are ya?" he asked incredulously. "We hev t' wade into the swamp."

"Ah hev te!" answered Wilhelm, blushing. "Ma work clothes is on the boat."

"If ya aks me, ya look more like a shop-window dummy than a woodsman," exclaimed Scotty, doubling over with mirth.

It was true.

Although Scotty appreciated Wilhelm's friendship, at the bottom of his soul, he was envious. The Oberfeldts were rich by his standards. "Yer ma'll kill ya if ya mess 'em up," he taunted, wagging his index finger in reprimand.

"Oh no, she won't!" replied Wilhelm defiantly, doing his best not to show he was upset.

Scotty knew he had gone far enough and stopped teasing. He did not want to lose his friend. "Well, if yer sure yer ma won't wring yer neck like ya wuz a chicken when she sees ya covered in all that mud, let's git goin'!"

The canal was sandwiched between the river and mountains. In places, it was fronted by cliffs. Scotty took the hard road. He followed the berm side. The trail was narrow and kept disappearing from the bank. Where the cliffs ended in the water, they had to scramble up boulder-strewn hillsides. And Wilhelm panted hard as he tried to keep up.

"Where are the traps?" he asked breathlessly, when he joined Scotty on the top of a cliff.

"They ain't here!" said Scotty pointing to the canal. "Muskrats ain't stupid enough no more to live along the banks. They know they'd be ketched if they did. They're at Long Run." The trail climbed another rocky escarpment and Scotty ran up it with the agility of a goat. "That's at th' other side o' this mountain."

Nowhere nearly as nimble as Scotty, Wilhelm scrambled up the trail on his hands and knees. By the time he was half way up, Scotty was at the top.

"Ah'm King of the hill," he hollered. "Ya cain't ketch me … unless Ah lets ya." To prove it, he hurled himself down the other side of the mountain and, without losing a breath, stood waiting for Wilhelm at the bottom.

"That's where Ah sets me traps," he announced when Wilhelm met him at the bottom of the slope. "That's Long Run." He was pointing to a small creek meandering through a jungle of bullrushes. "Last week Ah set ten, an' ivery single one of 'em ketched a muskrat. Ah took th' heads in to th' Company office. Ah couldn't sell th' pelts 'cos it waren't winter, but, Ah cain tell ya … me Ma wuz right glad to git the money fer them heads! Before me pa could lay a hand on it, she ran out to the grocer's and bought enough flour an' sugar to last next winter."

"That's raight nice of ya, givin' yer ma money like that," said Wilhelm, still affecting Scotty's drawl.

"Ah hev to! Me pa's sick. He cain't work, ya know."

Wilhelm knew! He had heard the rumors. Scotty's pa was a drunk. Nobody in the village would hire him. The few times Andy McNish had been given a job, he had not shown up, and the times he did, he was either too lazy — or too drunk — to work. But Wilhelm said nothing. He let Scotty continue his tale.

"Company men go along the canal pluggin' up holes. But them muskrats is smart. As fast as them men plug up them holes in the banks, they mek new uns further back from the canal."

"If the Company keeps on payin' people to kill muskrats, pretty soon, there'll be no muskrats left."

"There's hardly none left now along the canal. If yer gonna ketch 'em, ya hev t' know where they're at." They had left the berm-side trail and were following the creek inland. A half-mile in from the canal, Scotty stopped. "See here," he said darkly, pointing to an expanse of marsh upstream. "That's where they breed. It's a secret spot, mind ya … Ah expect ya won't tell no-one about it."

"Ah promise!" Wilhelm held up his hand as if he were being sworn in, but, inside he was feeling uneasy. Something struck him as dishonest about what Scotty was doing. "But muskrats don't mek holes in th' canal banks when they live this far up the crick."

"What's the difference!" answered Scotty. "If they're not ketched, they're liable to move back t' th' canal."

Wilhelm followed Scotty along the creek, thinking about what he had said. Was it really honest to charge the Company for muskrats that were not digging holes in the banks of the canal? But before he could wrestle out an answer, they had reached the place where Scotty set his traps. The creek hurtled down a ravine, tumbled over a waterfall, and spilled into a marsh, lush with emerald-green tuffets, and strewn with rotting tree trunks. This was the muskrats' secret habitat.

By some kind of miracle, Wilhelm had managed to keep dry.

Without a thought, Scotty plunged into the mire. His boots were full of holes and his trousers not worth bothering about. Wilhelm looked from the pools of green algae to his Sunday clothes. Scotty was right. If he got them wet, his mother would kill him.

"Are ya coming, or what?" shouted Scotty impatiently from across the marsh.

Not wanting to appear chicken, "I'll be raight after ya," Wilhelm replied quickly as he put one foot in the swamp. If he picked his way through it carefully, maybe he would not get his boots and britches wet.

The swamp and Scotty were meant for one another. Scotty hopped from tuffet to tuffet like an animal in its natural habitat. Moving from trap to trap, he sprang the steel jaws, removing the limp bloody bodies of muskrats as if he were picking flowers.

"Not a bad ketch, considering Ah wuz jest 'ere th' otha day," he remarked as he lined up seven limp furry creatures on the ground. Most were decapitated. And Wilhelm was overcome with pity and revulsion. They were so recently whole and alive. But when Scotty handed him the traps to clean, he steeled himself and washed off the blood in a pool.

With the traps cleansed of the carnage and reset, and the muskrats secreted in the canvas bag, the boys made their way back across the marsh. By some kind of miracle on the way in, Wilhelm had managed to keep dry. On the way out, he was not so fortunate. Mistaking a tuffet of marsh marigolds for a good place to land, he jumped over a pool of green algae, and fell in with a splash. He was up to his knees in swamp water.

Scotty was way ahead. As alert to the slightest strange sound as one of the swamp creatures, he jumped back across the marsh. "Now ya've gone and done it," he said, hanging onto the trunk of a hollow tree with one arm and holding out the other to Wilhelm. "Here ... grab ma hand an' Ah'll pull ya out." A hard tug, a sucking noise, and Wilhelm's boots broke free of the mud. "Good job Ah wuz wit' ya or ya'd niver git outta thar. That'll larn ya not to step on a clump o' marigolds again!"

Wilhelm would not forget. He had learned his lesson the hard way.

"Now, we'll have to git ya respectable lookin' before ya go home." Wilhelm wondered how. But Scotty had a solution for everything. "Tek off yer boots ... an' yer socks and britches ... an' we'll wesh the mud off in the crick."

Afraid of what his mother would say if he went home like this, Wilhelm took everything off his bottom half, down to his long johns. Dangling the trousers and socks in the flowing stream, Scotty washed the mud out and twisted them dry like a corkscrew. "Now, what we need is a good, thick tree."

"Ah cain't hang me britches out to dry," protested Wilhelm. "Ah hev to git back t' me grandma's. Me pa'll be ready t' leave."

Scotty looked in amazement. Wilhelm was as dumb as a city slicker! "Here, stoopid," he said, throwing Wilhelm his trousers and pointing to a large oak. "Start slappin' yer britches aginst the trunk. That'll git the rest o' the water out. By the time yer done, yer ma'll niver know they wuz wet. Ah'll slap yer socks on th' other side."

Anything that would stop him from getting into trouble seemed like a good idea to Wilhelm. Following Scotty's lead with his socks, he began slapping his britches. Slap, slap. Slap, slap. The tom-tom beat answered itself off the mountains until the last drop of water was out. When Wilhelm put his trousers back on, it was hard to tell they had been wet. His boots were another story. All Scotty could do was empty out the water and wipe the outsides and insides clean with the velvety leaves of a mullein. When Scotty finished, even his boots did not look as if they had been wet.

"Every time Ah'm with you, Scotty," said Wilhelm appreciatively, "Ah learn somethin' different."

"That's called survival," replied Scotty.

While Wilhelm was off goodness knows where, the rest of the family spent a lazy Sunday afternoon doing whatever they felt like doing. Manfred and his father-in-law sat in the parlor smoking the corncob pipes the old man had made from last year's crop. Reuben had been worried stiff about Manfred taking a fugitive aboard the *Onoko Princess*, so when Manfred told him that the young Negro had done nothing wrong, a weight was lifted off the old man's shoulders. To celebrate the good news, he brought out a bottle of Emily Kintz's homemade elderberry wine and poured out two glasses to toast Manfred's good fortune.

Mary and Annie passed the time by taking a walk through the village. Whether John Stevenson followed them or bumped into them accidentally, Annie could not say, but, by the time they got to the village green, he was there, love-struck and smiling.

Not one to keep a secret, Annie had already told her mother that John carried her books from school, so when he came over to say hello, Mary guessed who he was before he introduced himself. She did not disapprove of the relationship. How could she? She was only Annie's age when she met Manfred.

"It's nice to meet you," she said, extending her hand.

John took it and smiled shyly. He was polite and charming, and Mary took to him right away. She would have liked to ask him to supper, but did not want to appear forward. So, with his promise to wait for Annie in the morning, they passed on with a smile and a wave.

Between the baptism and the muskrats, Wilhelm came home exhilarated, looking little the worse for wear. It was impossible to tell that his britches and boots had been soaked.

With the meal over, once again it was time to leave. "See you in a couple of weeks," called Annie, blowing kisses as her father, mother and Wilhelm set off down White Street.

They were getting used to the separation. Tears no longer flowed.

CHAPTER XXII

The *Onoko Princess* set off for Mauch Chunk at the usual early hour. At Lock 3, she took on two passengers. The locktender's children needed a ride to school. Although children living along the canal between Weissport and Mauch Chunk could attend school in either town, the Yoders had chosen Mauch Chunk because they felt the prosperous town had better teachers and schools.

The children boarded the *Onoko Princess* clutching their slates, and looking all clean and spiffy. Wilhelm felt a twinge of envy. For a moment — but just for a moment — he wished he were going to school.

At the Weigh Lock, Manfred picked up his pay and, with no delays, they were through Lock 1 and across the Lehigh River well before the school bell rang. Manfred laid down the gangplank for the children to disembark. Before going into the Lehigh Coal & Navigation office for new orders, he watched as they scampered up Broadway and were safely inside school.

When Manfred went inside the white clapboard Navigation Company head-quarters, he was greeted jovially by his supervisor. Things on the canal were going well. Coal was coming into Mauch Chunk from all directions, faster than it could be loaded, and plenty of money was being made.

"I need someone to pick up a load at Penn Haven and drop it off at Easton," he said as Manfred returned his greeting. "It's off your regular route, but how about it, Manny?"

"Vhy not! It vill be a nice change for us all," he answered.

This was the first time in several years Manfred had been asked to load on the Upper Division. It would be a new experience for Wilhelm to drive the mules through the Lehigh Gorge, and the trip would be short. His orders were to take on coal at Penn Haven Planes, midway through the gorge, and drop it off at Easton. All told, they would go nine miles along the Upper Division and another forty-six miles to the Lehigh Canal terminus. This was forty-one miles less than their usual trip to the Delaware Canal terminus at Bristol.

"Better go vith your ma, Vil, and pick up some bread," said Manfred when he got back from the Company office. "Ve're going north this time, and there ain't many places on the Upper Division vhere you can buy a morsel to eat."

The thought of going up the Lehigh Gorge was exciting. After going back and forth from Mauch Chunk to Bristol week after week, Wilhelm was beginning to think he could recognize every pebble on the towpath. Too young to remember the last time the *Onoko Princess* sailed along the Upper Division, he could not wait to set out.

He skipped by his mother's side as they followed Susquehanna Street to Broadway. He was as exhilarated as he was four months ago, when he and his father crossed the Weissport village green at the start of the boating season. This would be a new adventure. He would traverse a different landscape and follow a different towpath.

In Herman's Bakery, a little way up Broadway, they bought enough bread to last for the trip to Penn Haven and back, and an extra loaf just in case they were held up by something unforeseen. With arms full of newly baked loaves, they were crossing Market Square in front of the American Hotel when a voice called,

"Missus Oberfeldt!"

Mary turned around to see who it was. A young black man in red and gold livery was coming toward them, waving. At first, she did not recognize who it was. Then, catching the teetering loaves before they fell to the ground, she exclaimed, "Joshua Harrison!" Even though Washington had apologized for what he had done, deep inside she still harbored a grudge. But the young man's joy at seeing her was contagious. "Seems like you're making something of yourself!" she said, looking admiringly at his uniform.

"Thanks to your mista … an' Capt'n Washington!" Then, acknowledging that he had participated in the deceit, he said, "Ah'm sorry for what happened."

Softened up by Harrison's apology, Mary exclaimed, "I didn't expect to see you in Mauch Chunk. I thought you were heading for New York."

"Ah wuz but Ah niver made it. When word got out that a Negro wuz on the run fer killin' Missus Bainbridge, the cap'n of *The Seagull* put two and two togitha an' left without me." He paused in his narrative. "D'ya know her son Wesley was the one what done it?" Mary nodded and he continued. "That's who Ah thought done it. He wuz allus afta the old lady fer money."

"How did you land in Mauch Chunk?"

"Fer days, Ah hid out along the Lehigh Canal towpath, all the while makin' ma way north. Ah heard word that the Lehigh Valley Railroad wuz hirin' Negro porters, but, by the time Ah got t' company headquarters here in Mauch Chunk, the jobs wuz all gone. Praise God for Mista Mulligan. Th' American Hotel wuz lookin' fer a doorman. Ah went in an' said Ah was ready, able and willin', not believin' fer a moment that Mista Mulligan would tek me on." Straightening himself up like a general in the Union Army, he added proudly. "Ah'm the only Negro doorman in Mauch Chunk."

"Where do you live?" asked Wilhelm, curious to know if Joshua Harrison's splendid uniform entitled him to live in the splendid American Hotel. Then, remembering something his father had told him, he added, "My Pa says the only place in Mauch Chunk that Negroes live is on Nigger Hill."

If looks could have killed, Wilhelm would have been stretched out on the street. Realizing what he had said, he blushed to the roots of his hair. He hadn't meant to be rude. It was just that Nigger Hill was what Mauch Chunkers called the hill on the other side of the river where there was a hostel for black railroad workers.

Mary changed the subject to cover her embarrassment. "I'll tell Manny what you're doing, Mr. Harrison," she said, addressing him extra politely to make up for her son's indiscretion.

"Ah cain't thank him and Cap'n Washington enough," said Harrison reverently. "Us nigres git blamed fer whativer happens even when we don't do it."

Two white canalers and a Negro doorman talking to one another made a conspicuous group on the streets of the mostly white town. Realizing that they were being stared at by the tourists and townspeople alike, they bid hasty good-byes and moved to opposite sides of Market Square.

Although, like Mary, Manfred still had mixed feelings about what had happened, he was pleased to hear that the young Negro was doing well. He would tell Washington the next time he saw him. For now, he had to concentrate on getting his boat back to the east side of the busy boat basin. Wooden behemoths were jostling for position like juggernauts, vying to be first to load and first through one of the two guard locks. As Manfred skillfully maneuvered the *Onoko Princess* in line, as usual, Wilhelm was preoccupied, watching a train of coal cars snake up Mount Pisgah. As the last wagon disappeared over the summit, he reminded himself that, at the end of the boating season, he, Wilhelm August Oberfeldt, would know what it was like to ride on the Switchback.

Packer Dam guard lock was the entrance to the Upper Division, also known as the Upper Grand Section of the Lehigh Canal, and father and son went through their motions. The sun, which had shone so brightly that morning, disappeared behind thickening gray clouds. Manfred put up his finger to the wind. No doubt about it: they were in for some rain.

They were only at Kettle Run when Mary did Wilhelm out of his job. She asked to switch places so she could drive the mules through Glen Onoko, her favorite part of the river. Disgruntled at being displaced, Wilhelm protested. But his protests were useless. When his father gave the order to switch, he clambered on board, perched himself on top of the cabin, and sulked. To appease him, his mother promised he could get back on the towpath as soon as they had passed by the glen.

As they began to ascend the gorge, the terrain grew wilder and the mountains steeper. The Upper Division was as intimidating as its grand name! Between the northern terminus of the Upper Division at White Haven and its southern terminus at Mauch Chunk, the Lehigh River dropped six hundred feet. Making the trip even more hazardous, most of the navigation took place in the river. Twenty enormous dams held back the flow of the tumbling water to form twenty slackwater pools. In the whole of the twenty-six-mile navigation, there were only eight short lengths of canal. Had the slackwater pools been placed end to end, they would have stretched for twenty miles; by contrast, if the sections of canal were put end to end, they would have totaled less than six miles. Navigating this precipitous river staircase of high locks and dams required great skill. As Wilhelm watched his father at the helm of the *Onoko Princess*, he knew better than to ask if he could steer.

Mountains folded into one another as far as the eye could see, imprisoning the river. When workmen had cut timber to build the giant dams and locks, and the boats that sailed through them, few trees had survived the onslaught of the ax. The sole arboreal occupants remaining on the denuded landscape were of little use for heavy construction. Only small shrubs such as mountain laurel, honeysuckle, and wild roses fringed the river. Grasping at life, they proclaimed their presence by their seasonal fragrances. But nature takes care of herself. As if to defy desecration, the forest was beginning to reseed itself. Sprouting from the crevices and escarpments that formed the sides of the gorge and the hillsides beyond was new growth.

Where the canal took over for the river, the river reverted to its natural self. It flowed excitably and erratically. Crested with white water, it swirled against the cliffs in fathomless pools, and foamed and splashed playfully around the rocks, daring anyone to challenge its course. Roaring and lapping, tumbling and dancing, its power was awesome and beautiful.

Confined between the towering mountains forming the sides of the gorge and the river running through it, the towpath was primitive. It was not broad and level like the towpath along the Lower Division. In places, native bedrock had refused man's efforts to remove it. As Mary and the mules negotiated the rough spots, her thoughts turned to the brave men who built the Upper Division. How dangerous it must have been to control the flow of the river. How hard they must have labored.

As Mary was busy with her thoughts, the river snaked around a bend, a mile and a half above Mauch Chunk. It split into two forks, and meandered lazily past several small islands.

"See that village over there, son," said Manfred, "that's Lausanne. That's vhere Josiah Vhite vas going to make the divide between the Upper and Lower Divisions of the Navigation."

"But, Pa, I thought the divide was at Mauch Chunk!"

"It is … now. The land owners around Lausanne vanted too much money for their land, so ol' Josiah brought the coal road from the mine into Mauch Chunk, and made Mauch Chunk the headquarters of the Lehigh Coal & Navigation Company. Today, Lausanne vould have been a prosperous town. Instead, it is just another stagecoach stop on the turnpike from Easton to Berwick." Manfred paused and took a long draw on his pipe. "That is vhat you get for being greedy!"

Mary was euphoric as she walked by the side of the mules. There was solitude on the towpath like nowhere else on earth. Her thoughts soared to the height and breadth of the mountains. She thought about Annie and how she missed her, about Wilhelm and the kind of man he would become, and dreamed of the day when she and Manfred would have a home of their own when Wilhelm took over command of the *Onoko Princess*. A breeze ruffled her hair. It was an odd blast of cold in the hot-muggy calm. And it disturbed her.

At another bend in the river, the *Onoko Princess* passed into the shadow of ancient black cliffs. Swallows swooped down from the rock crevices toward Mary and the mules as they protected their second brood. In the river, a doe and her fawn were up to their hocks in water, easing the heat of the day. A black bear lolloped across the towpath and disappeared up a mountain trail. Surely, thought Mary, the Lehigh River Gorge is the wildest and most beautiful place on earth!

When the swallows left Mary and the mules alone, they began bothering Manfred. He took off his cap and swished them away. "Look over there," he said to Wilhelm, pointing to a mountain rising up from the west bank of the river. "That is Broad Mountain vhere our beautiful princess, Onoko, leaped to her death from the top of the vaterfall."

"It is, Pa!" exclaimed Wilhelm eagerly. A roar proclaimed the presence of falling water, and he craned his neck to see up at the mountain. "I can hear the waterfall," he shouted excitedly, "but I can't see it." He wanted to grab the harness and hold back the mules. The *Onoko Princess* seemed to be racing up the river and he was afraid she would pass the waterfall before he saw it. "Where is it, Pa?" he asked frantically.

"Over there, son! See … up the crevasse!"

Wilhelm followed his father's pointing finger. Sometimes visible among the rocks and the thick undergrowth, sometimes not, white water was hurtling down the chasm to the river. "Is that the Onoko Falls, Pa?" he asked, pointing to the appearing and disappearing patches of white.

"Nein, son! Those are the cascades. The falls are higher up the mountain. There are several vaterfalls in that stream. Of course, our princess chose the highest of them all to jump off. Vhere she leapt to her death, the vater tumbles seventy-five feet over a cliff onto the rocks below."

"Seventy-five feet!" echoed Wilhelm incredulously. "My, that's high! Can we climb up Broad Mountain one day, Pa, and see where she jumped?"

"Vhy not? There's a trail up the valley. If the ice is not too dangerous at the end of the boating season, and there is no snow on the ground, ve vill go and see the Onoko Falls … and see Cave Falls as vell." As he spoke, Manfred got more enthusiastic. "Ve vill climb all the vay to the top of Broad Mountain. There is a lookout on the top, and ve can see the whole countryside from there."

Wilhelm's face was one big grin. He bet Scotty McNish had never been there! A rumble came out of the mountains ahead of them. His smile faded. "It sounds like thunder, Pa."

"Ja," said Manfred, scanning the troubled sky, "I thought ve vere in for something. Thank God, ve have only to go half vay up the gorge."

With Glen Onoko behind her, Mary had other things to do. At Lock 4, she changed places with Wilhelm.

The river valley widened beyond the dam. Away from the shadow of the cliff, the heat was stifling. Lucy and Max were uneasy in their traces as they plodded up the gradient.

Suddenly, a swarm of flies appeared from nowhere. Buzzing around Max and Lucy, they landed on their rumps. The mules swished their tails hard across their backs, and shook their manes as they tried to ward off the attack. But it was useless. The harder they swished, the sweatier they got, and the more flies that came.

When they reached a clear stretch of towpath, Manfred yelled, "Whoa, Vil, pull back on the harness! Ve vill have to put the netting on the mules. If ve don't, they vill get so antsy, you von't be able to control them."

Manfred steered the *Onoko Princess* close to the towpath, and Mary passed the large net covers over the side. She had made them last winter and several times since warm weather stirred up the blackflies Wilhelm had put them on the mules. But this was the worst the flies had been. There were so many, and so many different varieties. Joining the swarms of blackflies and horse flies were giant mosquitoes and gnats. Brandishing their proboscises, they bit the exposed flesh of every living thing that dared to venture outdoors … including Wilhelm.

"Ma," he called desperately as he swatted the gnats off his neck, "I need a hat … the one with netting down the sides."

His mother knew which one he meant. It was the old beekeeper's hat that had kept flies off Oberfeldt mule drivers and boatmen for three generations. She went into the cabin and took it from the chest. "This should help," she said, throwing it over the side.

Wilhelm picked it up. It resembled a pudding bowl. He pulled a face and hesitated before putting it on.

"Don't worry how you look, Wil! Let the sides down to cover your neck, and, when you're at it, roll down your shirt sleeves so the pesky things cannot get at your arms."

Wilhelm untied the netting on the top of the hat and put it on. The hat was too big. It fell over his ears, but his face and neck were protected. The flies could not reach him. He was busy rolling down his sleeves when shrieks of laughter came from the river.

"What do you think you are, mule boy? A bee keeper?"

Three boys were standing on the bank in their underwear, dripping wet. Their long drawers clung to their bodies, and they were doubled up in stitches.

"Ha, ha," guffawed the tallest boy with the loudest laugh. "Don' 'e look funny! Did ya ever see a beekeeper drivin' a pair of mules? What do you say, Charlie? Let's take his hat as a souvenir."

But Charlie, the gang leader, had other fish to fry. He dived into the water with a splash and stroked toward the *Onoko Princess*. "Come on, you fellers," he hollered as he grabbed her side, "forget about the stinky ol' hat, let's take a ride."

The three boys held on to the rudder so it couldn't move.

The tall boy and his pimply-faced friend plunged into the river after Charlie and raced one another for the boat. Grabbing hold of the hull, the threesome hung on to one side.

The pools beyond the dams were deep and slow-moving. Even though the spring thaw was long over, the flow was relentless, and Manfred dared not let go of the tiller to push them off. Empty of cargo, the *Onoko Princess* listed under their weight.

"Get off!" roared Manfred. "You are knocking me into the bank!"

Their reply was more laughter. "Ya cain't git us off, ya dumb boatman," they taunted, "unless we want to git off ourselves."

"That's vhat you think!" yelled Manfred.

"Ja, that's vhat ve think," they said, mocking his accent.

Charlie hauled himself hand-over-hand along the hull to the stern. "Come on, you fellers, let's grab the rudder so he cain't steer this big lump of wood."

It was a case of follow the leader. In no time at all, the three were holding fast to the rudder so that it could not move.

Manfred pushed the tiller with all his might, doing his best to turn the *Onoko Princess* shoreward, but, the tiller, and with it the rudder, would not budge. This was not the first time he had to deal with boys hitching a ride on the back of the *Onoko Princess* — it often happened around Allentown — but this was the first time anyone had held on to the rudder and refused to let go.

Powerless to steer, at the mercy of the river, he thumped on top of the cabin. "Mary, git 'em off before ve are beached."

Mary scrambled up the steps and, taking a lesson from the ruffians she had seen douse Taffy Morgan, she did the only thing she could think of. She hauled two buckets of water from the river, and tipped them over the back of the boat. The deluge was unexpected. With a whoop, the boys let go. Then, arm over arm, splashing furiously, they raced back to shore to await the next coal boat. It did not matter whether it was going up or down the river. All they wanted on the hot, muggy afternoon was to provoke the ire of the captain.

When the boys let go, the rudder jerked free. Without drag on the boat, the mules gathered speed.

"Whoa," hollered Manfred as he righted the *Onoko Princess* and set her course along the level. Lucy and Max slowed down and the *Onoko Princess* was once again on an even keel.

Between Locks 5 and 6, a bridge took the towpath to the west bank of the river to avoid the cliffs that descended sheer to the water. There were three towpath bridges between Mauch Chunk and White Haven, but, seeing they were only going as far as the Penn Haven Planes, this was the only one the mules would have to cross today.

Wilhelm unhitched Lucy and Max and walked them over the bridge while his father threw a rope to the cable-ferry operator. As usual, Manfred's throw was right on target. As no boats were ahead of them, the *Onoko Princess* was hauled across the river where she met up with her mules on the west-bank towpath. She passed through Lock 6 without incident into one of the short lengths of canal. A fraction of a mile and she was back in the river approaching Lock 7 at Dam 4.

Sweat poured down Wilhelm's face from under the beekeeper's hat. He unhitched his charges as he waited for the lock to level, and scratched his mosquito bites. Sweaty and itchy, the only thing he could think about was what a miserable job mule driving was.

Coal boats were coming down the canal out of nowhere. Warned by claps of thunder echoing among the mountains to the north, their captains were hastening back to Mauch Chunk. As the *Onoko Princess* ascended the Upper Division, it was like jumping rope. One after the other, boats that had taken on loads at the terminus at White Haven or at the Penn Haven Planes stopped and lowered their lines, all the while their captains looking curiously at Manfred as he continued his ascent.

To say the least, Max and Lucy were uneasy. At the first rumblings of thunder, they pricked up their ears, but as the rumblings grew louder and nearer, their agitation increased. So did their stride. Trapped in the gloom of the gorge, they sensed what was coming. Wild-eyed, they hastened along the rocky towpath, hoping to reach the safety of a stable.

As the *Onoko Princess* continued to head north, the flight of boats south did not slacken. Seeing two empty coal boats turn back in mid-stream, Mary suggested they do the same. But, although Manfred shared her uneasiness, he kept on. He had an obligation to fulfill. With Penn Haven only a few miles distant, he was determined to take on his load.

The convergence of land and river was awesome. The eighty-seven-foot *Onoko Princess* was a mere log in the vast sweep of water and mountain. Up, up, up she went, ascending the dams to Penn Haven. Each dam was higher than the last, and she rose more than twenty feet at each guard lock. If her orders had taken her to White Haven, she would have passed behind a dam thirty-six feet high and risen an amazing thirty feet at the lock. Locking through the Upper Division locks was speedy. At the best of times, it took an amazing two and a half or three minutes; at the worst, it took little more. As water swirled through the wickets and a side tunnel into the depths of the lock chambers, the *Onoko Princess* was defying the elements. Ignoring the storm that might break loose around her at any moment, she floated majestically upward from one level to another.

The higher they went, the gloomier and more forbidding the sky became. Rain poured down in sheets and the visibility was near zero. As the wind swirled through the canyon, it stirred up the river, churning up the muddy bed, and chopping the surface into whitecaps trailing garlands of brown foam in their wake. Thunder, once distant, exploded overhead. Lightning burst across the black sky. Squawking in terror, birds sought shelter wherever they could; animals scurried through the underbrush to their lairs. What Manfred had hoped to avoid was happening. They were caught in a storm in the dreaded Upper Division. As he battled up the waterway, Manfred felt like Noah in the Great Flood. Rain pouring down the mountainsides into the chasm and the steep drop in elevation were a deadly combination. If the river swelled and the dams failed to hold back the water, they would be swept downstream on an uncontrollable tide.

The thunder abated and Manfred pressed on. A mile shy of Penn Haven, it returned. Amplified a thousandfold by the mountains, it resounded through the gorge like volleys of canon shots. With each thunderous roar, a lightning bolt rocketed across the heavens. Blazing in furious splendor, it crackled to the ground, frizzling whatever it struck. The spectacle was both terrifying and awesome. The one thing that gave Manfred comfort was that they would not have to cross the river by cable ferry at Bridge 2. The Penn Haven planes were on the same side of the river as the towpath.

With each new onslaught of thunder, Wilhelm and his charges cringed. Although the *Onoko Princess* was empty and riding high in the water, the mules had to keep straining harder and harder against the down-flowing river. When

Wilhelm thought he could not go on any further, there was a miracle. A lightning bolt lit up the sky, silhouetting the planes at Penn Haven.

Constructed in 1855, the Penn Haven Planes brought coal from mines to the west into the middle of the Upper Division of the Lehigh Canal. The inclined planes connected the termini of two railroads to the waterfront, enabling coal to be transported by canal. One of the planes belonged to the Beaver Meadow Railroad; the other to the Hazleton Railroad.

Manfred's orders were to load at the Hazleton Plane. With Wilhelm's help on the towpath and Mary's guidance on deck, he maneuvered the *Onoko Princess* into position. Despite the deluge, work at the planes was continuing. Lowered by stationary steam engines, coal wagons clanged and clattered down the inclines. Tumbling and rumbling, they tipped their loads at the foot of the slope and were hoisted back up to the top by a chain mechanism. As laborers worked to load the waiting boats as fast as they could, the dockside clamor was frantic. Every captain stuck at Penn Haven was demanding that his boat be loaded right away. By the time it was the *Onoko Princess*'s turn, it was too late to cast off. They would have to wait until morning. With the *Onoko Princess* moored securely with extra line and the mules sheltered in the stable, the crew lay on their bunks in the cabin, praying that the storm would be over by morning, and thanking God for keeping them safe this far.

CHAPTER XXIII

All night, the *Onoko Princess* rocked from side to side in the surging river. After a hard day, Mary and Wilhelm were sound asleep, but Manfred slept fitfully. At half past three, he got dressed out of habit. Groping in the darkness for his conch shell, he blew into it softly. Its *woooo* was drowned out by the battering rain, and he had to shake his crew awake.

Once again, the thunder had moved away, but the rain was sheeting heavier than ever. It poured down the denuded slopes of the mountains, churning the earth into mud slides and turning the river into a torrent of brown. Wilhelm ran to the stable and put blinders on the mules to keep the rain out of their eyes. He hitched them to the tow, and they got underway just after four o'clock, hoping and praying that the locks downstream would stay open. Manfred consoled himself that the nine-mile trip to Mauch Chunk was only one-third of their normal daily run. With a little luck, they would reach the Lower Division by noon.

Dam 6, a mile below the Planes, was the first dam they had to navigate. And Manfred did not like what he saw. Water was starting to spill over the top. Soon, the whole width of the river would be a giant waterfall. On the one hand, high water provided momentum to move the boat along; on the other, it was dangerous. If the current was too swift, the *Onoko Princess* would get ahead of her mules. Already, the pace was frantic. And Max and Lucy had to hustle to keep ahead. Weighed down with coal, the *Onoko Princess* was being swirled along by the flow of the rising river. Manfred prayed that the dams would not give way. If they did, she would be smashed on the rocks into a thousand pieces and they would all drown.

Halfway between Locks 6 and 5, Manfred began anxiously searching the river to see if the cable ferry was operating. They were lucky. The operator was still on duty.

The river was barely two hundred feet wide near the mule bridge, but crossing it was a nightmare. Lurching with the swell, the *Onoko Princess* tugged at the cable. Mary had all she could do to keep from throwing up. If the cable did not hold, they would be swept over the dam. But luck was with them. The load they took on at Penn Haven steadied the *Onoko Princess* enough to make it safely to the east side of the river where her tow was waiting.

What Wilhelm had learned in the few short months he had been his father's mule driver was nothing compared to what he would learn on the river that day. Attuned to every change of flow and motion, his instincts did not fail him. He quickened the pace of the mules to keep them ahead of the boat and comforted them at every jerk of the tow line. Buffeted by the current, the *Onoko Princess* was almost impossible to control. Had Manfred not been a boatman of superior skill, she would have smashed against the escarpments bordering the river.

Fearful of a single misstep, mules and crew worked together magnificently as a team. Shortly after noon, they passed through the Packer Dam guard lock, the northern entrance to Mauch Chunk basin. Relief swept over them. They were out of the dreaded Upper Division. As they headed for Lock 1 in the Lower Division, Manfred looked up at the angry heavens, and praised the Lord for delivering them. He would tie up at Weissport and wait for the storm to pass.

The line at Lock 1 was long, and the *Onoko Princess* took her place at the end of it. Every boat captain in Mauch Chunk basin was anxious to get into the Lower Division. By the time the *Onoko Princess* passed into the double-chambered lock, it was late afternoon. If the locks below stayed open, they would be home by nightfall. Manfred's prayers were answered. Shortly before eight o'clock, the *Onoko Princess* entered the level above Lock 7. Another mile and she would reach the boatyard at Weissport.

As they pulled into the boatyard, a clap of thunder heralded their arrival. It rumbled up from the horizon, exploding into a giant drum roll. Echoing through the heavens, it shook the ground like an earthquake, ending up in an awesome fireworks display that illuminated the village from the canal to the graveyard on Cemetery Hill. Ears straight up, the mules cowered and whinnied. And ten-year-old Wilhelm was scared stiff.

But, even as the night sky unleashed its fury, he had a job to do. He had to bed down the mules. Grabbing Max and Lucy by their harnesses, he ran with them to the stable and cowered inside. He felt like bedding down in the hay with his charges. But his parents would be waiting. A bolt of lightning lit up the darkness as he opened the door to try to make a run for it. Heart racing, he retreated and crouched back in the doorway, fearful of getting struck. He was not the only one that was scared stiff. Fear was contagious. Mules, cramming every stall and walkway, brayed and stomped in terror, shying or kicking their stable mates at each thunderous roar.

Twenty long minutes passed before, rumbling and growling, the storm moved away, seeking new territory to conquer. The pyrotechnics were replaced by the rhythmic beat of rain. This was the opportunity Wilhelm had been waiting for. Pulling his coat up over his head, he raced at breakneck speed for the *Onoko Princess*. Peering anxiously through half-shuttered windows, his father and mother saw him. Throwing open the hatch, they rushed on deck to help him on board.

The river was near the top of the embankment that separated it from the canal. "If this keeps up, the dams vill burst," pronounced Manfred as he pulled Wilhelm over the side. "You two had better run home while you can. I vill stay with the boat."

"Ma can go," panted Wilhelm, out of breath from battling the wind and rain. "I'm staying with you, Pa." This time, there was no asking; no pleading. The man-boy was as determined as his father to stay with the ship.

They hastened back to the cabin. The warmth greeted them and made them feel safe. As Wilhelm was about to take off his wet clothes, his mother pushed him toward the hatch. "You're coming with me. You are not staying here."

"I am, Ma. It's my job to stay with Pa," he replied, looking at his father for support.

It was there in Manfred's eyes and in the proud look on his face.

His voice was kind but resolute as he spoke. "The boy knows his duty, Mary, and I need his help."

"It's no night to be on the waterfront. Not for either of you!" she shouted frantically. "Tie up the boat, and let's all get out of here quick."

"I'm sorry," said Manfred, his voice strangely calm against the raging storm, "Me and Vil must vait out the night. Go home, Mary. See to Annie and your mother and father. It is your duty. They need your help."

Her pleas unheeded, Mary clambered over the side of the boat. There was no use arguing. Come what may, father and son were determined to see the *Onoko Princess* through the night.

"I'm telling you, Manny," she cried, howling like a banshee through the wind, "it's not worth it. If you know what's good for you, you'll get out before it's too late. I don't want your foolishness to take the life of my son."

Wilhelm watched his mother pass out of sight as he went onshore to secure the *Onoko Princess* with more rope.

"Here, take this," shouted his father, throwing him one end of the tow line, "wrap it around the tree. A niggerhead von't hold the boat in this high vater."

Wilhelm took the line and wound it around the trunk of an oak as many times as it would go, and knotted it with the tightest boatman's knot he could tie. When the bow was secure, his father threw out a second line.

"Tie up the stern."

Wilhelm had just knotted the tow line when thunder crashed anew, and a bolt of lightning hit the boat landing.

"Get back on board," screamed his father, "before you get struck!"

"I can't, not yet," yelled Wilhelm, "Look at the water!" The river had crept over the embankment and was heading for the stables. Soon, it and the canal would be one. "If I don't get the mules out of the stable, they'll drown."

Manfred looked in amazement at the river's quick rise. "Ja, son, quick! Get them beasts out of there or ve vill lose them."

"Where should I take them?"

"Cemetery Hill. Ziggy Koons vill let you put them in his barn. They vill be out of harm's vay there. And ven you're at it, son, go home to your mother."

"No," said Wilhelm obstinately, disobeying his father for the first time in his life. "I'm staying with you!"

"Very vell," said Manfred. If he had been in Wilhelm's shoes, he would have said the same thing. "I vill vait for you."

As she sloshed her way through the rising water, Mary was filled with anguish. She did not like to leave Wilhelm and Manfred, but she had no alternative. Annie would be frantic worrying where they were, and her aged parents would need her help if they had to get out of their house. Floods on the Lehigh had come and gone over the years, but she had never seen the village like this. The buildings at the north end of White Street, a narrow strip of land sandwiched between the canal and river, were awash. At the south end, where she grew up, the river looped away from the street. A levee, built by the Company after the 1841 flood, protected this part of the village. So far, it was holding.

Blinded by rain, she ran up the garden path. No sooner did she open the door than Annie threw herself into her arms. "Oh, Ma, thank God you're safe!" Tears streaming from her eyes, she hugged her mother like she would never let go. "We feared you would be lost." Then, realizing that her mother was alone, she gasped, "Where's Pa and Wil?"

"Pa is with the boat. And Wilhelm insisted on staying with him."

"But Ma," gasped Annie, "if they stay with the boat, they'll drown! Grandpa says the river must be over its banks at the other end of the village."

"If things get worse, let's hope they will have the good sense to get out," said Mary with the resignation of one who had lost a battle.

She went upstairs to change into dry clothes. When she came down again, she found her father sitting on the window seat, his gaze never shifting from the levee. She told him about their nightmarish journey to Penn Haven and back. But there was need to tell Reuben Kintz anything about the river. He knew all about its whims and vagaries. At the first sign of a break in the levee, he was ready to flee with his family.

"You might as well go to bed," he said when Mary finished talking. "I will stay up and watch the water. Tell mother and Annie to sleep in their clothes in case we have to get out."

Weary from the strain of the past night and day, Mary joined the two upstairs. As the wind howled and the river roared, before going to bed, they huddled together in prayer.

Seeing nothing but blackness, Reuben Kintz listened to the river across the field. It was roaring like an ocean, surging and swallowing everything in its path. All night, the old man sat on the window seat, watching and waiting. Then as dawn came, he dozed off. That was when it happened. A fearsome noise filled the valley. Boom, boom, boom, like shells shot out of a cannon. It echoed off the mountains, and reverberated through the Narrows, down the canal.

Reuben awoke with a start. "Emily, Mary, Annie," he screamed at the top of his voice, "the dams upstream are breaking! Let's get out of here before the water sweeps down the river and the levee gives way."

Grabbing whatever they could to keep warm, the three women rushed down the stairs. Water met them when they opened the door. White Street was awash. "The house!" screamed Emily as water crept across the threshold into the parlor.

"It'll be swept away!"

"Never mind the house, mother!" cried Reuben herding them along. "We've got to run for our lives."

"What about Manfred and Wil?" cried Mary, grabbing Annie by the arm. "They're on the boat."

"Manfred is a sensible man," her father said calmly. "When the time comes, he will have the good sense to get out."

"But he won't know where to find us."

"Oh yes he will! There's only one place high enough around here. That's Cemetery Hill."

The *Onoko Princess* creaked and rocked like an out-of-control cradle. Neither Manfred nor Wilhelm slept a wink. Along the canal, the locktenders had opened the gates to minimize damage, and she rose and fell as the river surged up the canal. It was more than thirty hours since the rain began, and the deck was awash. The drainage holes in the hull could not keep up with the volume of water and it was pouring through the planking into the holds and cabin. One of the mooring ropes had snapped; the other was stretched to the limit. If the storm kept up much longer, the venerable Indian maiden would be either swept downstream or sitting on the bottom of the boatyard.

An ominous dawn showed itself through the shutters. Manfred and Wilhelm went on deck. The canal was indiscernible from the river. The wide expanse of raging water was hurtling an assortment of flotsam and jetsam to its doom. Uprooted trees raced by like strange sea creatures. Chickens, squawking in terror, clung to the roofs of their houses; fences and sheds bobbed in the spate. Everything close to the water's edge was being ravaged and swallowed up by the raging tide. It was time to give in. All Manfred could hope for now was that the *Onoko Princess*'s load would anchor her to the bottom and keep her in one piece. He turned his back on the holocaust. "There is nothing ve can do," he said sadly, "except get out of here quick."

They dashed into the cabin. The hatchway was a sluice; the water on the cabin floor up to Wilhelm's knees. They grabbed what they could. Most important of all was the *Onoko Princess*'s log. As they battled their way on deck, Wilhelm looked over at the carving of Princess Onoko. Her beautiful face was a waterfall.

"Keep our boat safe, dear princess," he whispered. And, as his father slammed the hatch cover shut, he could have sworn she said, "I will!"

They were making their way toward White Street when it happened. Boom. Boom. Boom. The dams in the Upper Division had burst. As a giant wave roared down the river, they went down in a fierce chain reaction, one after the other, like dominoes. Thousands of logs at the many sawmills on the Lehigh and its tributaries broke free of their booms. Acting as battering rams, they assaulted the giant dams and locks, crashed into bridge pilings and annihilated buildings and homes along the waterfront. Everything in their path was pounded off its foundations and swept along on the fearsome tide.

Manfred and Wilhelm scrambled up the incline leading to the wooden bridge connecting Weissport to Lehighton, its neighbor across the river. A few stragglers were racing with their mules to high ground. The river and canal were a half-mile wide. The procession of objects, bobbing in the spate, had grown in size and number. Shacks and shanties, lock houses and livestock had joined the trees and chicken houses that led the parade. A herd of cows swirled by. Flailing and bellowing, they were doing their best to save themselves from being sucked under. Swept to the water's edge by the raging current, the lucky ones scrambled onto dry land. The rest would inevitably join the procession of carcasses already floating down the river.

Along what had been the canal, empty boats were the most vulnerable. Torn from their moorings, they broke apart and met their end in the raging current. Loaded boats were more fortunate. Most submerged at their moorings. With a little luck, when the water receded, they would be repaired and caulked, and sail the canal another day.

Manfred and Wilhelm were near the top of the incline when, suddenly, from amid the flotsam and jetsam came a cry for help Swirling crazily toward them on a crest of surging water was a bright green coal boat with a man clinging to its deck. An ear-splitting crash and the boat hit the bridge pier, smashing it and the wooden bridge in two. The bow, along with the Lehighton half of the bridge, sailed on downstream. The stern lodged behind what was left of the bridge pier, supporting the Weissport half.

There was no mistaking that voice ... or that bright green boat.

"It's Morgan," Manfred gasped. This was no time for recrimination; no time for hatred. And Manfred did not hesitate. "The only vay ve can save him is to climb out onto the bridge pier."

Morgan had been hurled off his boat by the impact. Half in and half out of the water, he was clinging to the wreckage for his dear life. Battered by floating debris, the pier and the remains of the bridge trembled with each impact. If the pier gave way, Morgan would be sucked under by the whirlpool. There was no time to lose. It was ready to let go any minute.

"Help! Help! I'm going under!" came the frantic voice.

"Hang on, Morgan," shouted Manfred. "It's Oberfeldt!"

The man in the water was taken aback. "Oberfeldt!" he muttered. His old enemy was the only one who could save him.

His shouts continued intermittently.

Desperate. "I'm going under."

Contrite. "I'm sorry, Oberfeldt, for what happened. Don't hold it against me."

Praiseworthy. "You are a good man. I've always known it."

And pleading. "Get me outta here, pleeeease!"

Manfred was too intent on sizing up the situation to hear him. "Ve need a rope, Vil."

Already a step ahead of his father, Wilhelm was scanning the pilings. A length of tow line dangled from a nail where once a canaler had tied up his mules. "There's a piece over here, Pa."

Manfred leaned over the top of the piling and groped for the piece of line. But he could not reach it. "The only vay ve can get it, Vil, is if I hold your feet."

Wilhelm hesitated. Taffy Morgan was about to go under. Without a word, he lay down. His father gripped his ankles and inched him headfirst over the side. Trust was the name of the game. With each new onslaught of debris, the pier heaved and shook. But his father's grasp was tight. As Wilhelm slid his fingers down the rough-hewn wood, a glance at the rushing water made him dizzy. He wanted to cry out in terror; to ask his father to pull him back. But he didn't. His fingertips had found the rope. Untying it took forever. Shrunken over time by the weather, the knot would not come apart. He was about to give up, when he felt it loosen. Grasping it tightly lest it slip from his grip with the pull of the current,

Wilhelm hurled the lasso over the side.

he hauled it in. The tow line was about fifty feet long — long enough to reach Taffy Morgan.

Muscles bulging, groaning as he strained to pull up his son, Manfred hauled Wilhelm in. When Wilhelm was safe on top of the pilings, both father and son crumpled in exhaustion. But the frantic cries of Morgan permitted neither exhaustion nor rest. If he were to be saved they would have to get the rope to him. And with the remains of the bridge dangling in the river, Wilhelm was the only one light enough to do that.

"Crawl out as far as you can along the planking," said his father. "My veight vill send the bridge crashing."

Tying a slip knot at one end of the rope and securing the other to an iron mooring ring, Manfred handed the end with the lasso to Wilhelm. "Here, take this," he said. "Get out as far as you can on the bridge and throw this to Morgan. Be sure to aim far enough upriver. That vay, he can grab the rope as it floats tovards him."

Shimmying along the bridge decking was even more scary than being dangled over the side of the pier. Pieces of timber were breaking loose with each new onslaught. As he inched forward, splinters pierced his small fingers. The decking creaked menacingly. Whirlpools gnawing at the pier made him feel sick.

Morgan's cries were growing weaker. His strength was giving out. A few minutes more and he would go under.

Raising himself into a sitting position, Wilhelm hurled the lasso over the side. It fell short of its target and swirled back downstream. As the current snatched the rope, the pull on his arms was tremendous. Exerting every bit of strength he could muster, he hauled it back in, praying that it would not snag on the floating debris. Two more throws fell short, and he despaired. He tried again. This time, the rope landed upstream from the drowning man. Caught in the tide, it snaked down toward him. Would Morgan have enough strength to grab it, he wondered. But the current was merciful. The loop floated right to the desperate man. With his last bit of strength, Morgan put his arms through the loop. It tightened around his waist just in time. The exertion was too much. His body went limp and he swirled amid the wreckage like a rag doll on the end of the rope.

"Got him, Pa!" Wilhelm's shout was as triumphant as that day in Easton when he had caught his first shad. He slithered back down the bridge planking quickly.

"We've gotta get him out right away, Pa. He's about to go under."

"I need your help, son. The current is strong. Grab hold of the rope vith me!"

Wilhelm stood in front of his father, and the two began hauling in the line. A few yards, and the river reclaimed the distance. Back and forth. Back and forth. Taffy Morgan was a dead weight. He disappeared beneath the surface, and reappeared when they had given up hope. At last, victory was theirs. Or was it? The wet rag of a man who lay on the levy was scarcely breathing. Lungs full of water, blue in the face, Taffy Morgan was not moving.

Manfred turned him over. Pressing hard on Morgan's back, rocking rhythmically back and forth, he did his best to force the water out of Morgan's lungs. Minutes and seconds were an eternity. It seemed hopeless. Then a spurt. Another. A gasp, and a rasping cough and the Welshman's eyelids fluttered. Taffy Morgan was breathing again.

"Ve've got to get out of here before the bridge gives vay and the vater svallows us up," cried Manfred. "You take his feet and I'll take his head."

Half carrying, half dragging Morgan's limp body, they made their way up the dirt road to Cemetery Hill. They reached high ground not a moment too soon. A loud crash of timbers sounded the death knell of the bridge and with it the green coal boat. Caught in a giant tidal wave, they joined the parade of objects hurtling downstream.

"No need trying to go home," said Manfred, looking over to the south end of White Street. "The vater's over the levee and into the houses."

"But what about Ma … and Annie … and Grandpa and Grandma?" cried Wilhelm.

"They vill have taken refuge on Cemetery Hill."

As they labored up the hill, staggering under the deadweight of Morgan, the iron-railed monument of Colonel Jacob Weiss, much-decorated hero of the Revolutionary War and founder of the village named after him, loomed larger than the other gravestones in the cemetery. Its presence was strangely reassuring. If Reuben Kintz had anything to do with it, Manfred knew that his family would be safe at Ziggy Koons' farm. Reuben and Ziggy had been friends for years, and there was nothing they would not do for one another.

Mary and Annie paced back and forth on the Koonses' front porch, watching everything that came up the muddy road. Annie was first to see her father and Wilhelm carrying a limp form up Cemetery Hill. With tears streaming down her face, she raced to meet them with her mother and grandparents not far behind. Sobbing with relief, they clung to one another like they would never let go.

Then Annie's jaw dropped. She saw it was the Welshman. The joy of the reunion had brought Morgan to his senses. He sat up bleary-eyed, wondering where he was.

"He's come to!" exclaimed Manfred, tearing himself away from Mary's embrace. "Are you all right, Morgan?"

Taffy Morgan's mind was clearing. He was beginning to recall what had happened. He was waiting to load at Mauch Chunk. The storm was raging and he went into the Mansion House for a drink. One drink led to another and another. Boat horns sounded their alarms and word passed among boatmen to get as far as they could down the Lower Division just in case the dams on the Upper Division broke. But he sat at the bar, ignoring the warnings. By the time he reached the Weigh Lock, it was too late. A tidal wave raced downstream and along the canal. The towpath vanished. So did his driver and mules. The next thing he knew, he was in the water, stone-cold sober, clinging to his green coal boat.

As the ordeal flashed before him, he was overwhelmed with guilt. Manfred Oberfeldt and his young son had risked their lives to save him. Over the years, he had harassed Oberfeldt at every turn. Worse, he had hurt the Oberfeldt children by reporting the carving of the Indian maiden on back of their boat. As he stuttered his thanks, he could not look Wilhelm and his father in the face. All he could do to make amends was promise them a reward.

CHAPTER XXIV

The heroics of Wilhelm and Manfred were not the only heroics that took place during those terrible days in June 1862. As lives and property were lost in the great flood, neighbor helped neighbor along the river and canal. In the hardy village of Weissport, and all along the Lower Division, rebuilding began as soon as the flood waters abated. Young helped old shovel mud and coal dust from streets and property. Buildings and dwellings, including the houses on the south end of White Street, were repaired or rebuilt. Three thousand men and six hundred horses and mules labored day and night to restore the canal. On the twenty-ninth day of the ninth month of 1862, barely four months after the devastation, the first Lehigh Coal & Navigation Company coal boat left Mauch Chunk for Bristol.

Although boat traffic resumed along the Lower Division, the Upper Division became only a memory. Its giant dams and high lift locks were never rebuilt. After twenty-seven years of pounding by the elements, the once-proud Upper Grand Section was replaced by the canal's competitor, the railroad. With the age of steam locomotives upon them, the Lehigh Coal & Navigation Company had no alternative but to give in. In 1868, they extended the Company-owned Lehigh & Susquehanna Railroad down the west side of the Lehigh Gorge to Mauch Chunk and on to Phillipsburg, New Jersey, the next year. Beating the Lehigh & Susquehanna to a place in the Lehigh Gorge was Asa Packer's Lehigh Valley Railroad. In 1864, the Lehigh Valley extended its tracks north from Mauch Chunk along the east side of the gorge. With two railroads serving the mines to the north, the almighty power of the Lehigh Canal as a coal carrier was eroding.

Lucy and Max were back with Jake Gilbert at the mill in New Mahoning. They had to work harder than ever hauling flour to the inhabitants of the devastated villages and towns.

As soon as the water retreated, just as they had done on the first day of the boating season four long months ago, father and son — captain and mule driver — walked side by side across the flood-ravaged village green at Weissport. This time, they were going to see if the *Onoko Princess* was still at her moorings. Wilhelm was the first to catch sight of her across the sea of mud. As proud as ever there she stood, all in one piece amid the devastation. Anchored by her hundred-ton load of anthracite coal, she had settled on the bottom of the boat yard to await rescue. With the help of a bilge pump, she would be afloat in no time, little the worse for wear. Whether the carving was nailed to the stern or to the cabin wall, Princess Onoko had worked her magic. The Indian maiden had kept her namesake safe. As soon as his father pumped out the cabin, Wilhelm walked over to her and, with thanks and affection, wiped the mud off her face.

Seven days after Taffy Morgan left for his home in Uhlertown a registered letter, addressed to Manfred Oberfeldt & Son, arrived at Weissport Post Office. The envelope contained a touching note of thanks and two five dollar gold pieces. When Manfred tipped the shiny coins onto the table, he found it hard to believe Morgan had kept his word. Maybe being cast adrift in the flood had taught the Welshman a lesson.

Pocketing one gold piece to eke out his money while the canal was being repaired, Manfred handed the other to Wilhelm. "This is for you, son, the bravest and best mule boy on the Lehigh Canal. Vithout you, Taffy Morgan vould have been a gonner!"

Wilhelm turned over the shiny coin in his hand. He felt like a millionaire. In his whole life, he had never had more than a penny in his pocket. As the American eagle winked at him from the face of the gold piece, there was no doubt in his mind what he would do. He would treat his father, mother, Annie, his grandparents — and himself — to a ride on the Switchback Gravity Railroad. Afterward, they would sit like tourists at the round marble-topped tables in Volner's Ice Cream Parlor in Mauch Chunk and have one of Heidi Volner's sugar wafers topped with homemade vanilla ice cream, strawberries, and freshly whipped cream … and, oh yes! — with a glacé cherry on top.

THE AUTHOR

Joan Gilbert worked as a literary agent and editor in New York for twenty years. Upon retiring to Pennsylvania, she designed the core exhibit, "The Story of Mauch Chunk," for the Mauch Chunk Museum in Jim Thorpe. *Mule Boy* was inspired by this experience. After presenting programs to school children, she felt the need to document the history and operation of the Lehigh and Delaware canals for young readers, and the way of life of those who worked on those waterways.

Joan's written work on local history has been published in journals such as *Pennsylvania Heritage* and *Pennsylvania Magazine*. She co-authored an article in *The Lion* and a book, *Jim Thorpe (Mauch Chunk)*, with John Drury, president of the Mauch Chunk Museum. Her next book, *Gateway to the Coalfields: The Upper Grand Section of the Lehigh Canal*, will be published by Canal History and Technology Press in late 2004.

THE ILLUSTRATOR

Kathryn Schaar Burke of Allentown is an educator and free-lance artist. She is a summa cum laude graduate of both Moravian College, Bethlehem, and Marywood University, Scranton. Kathryn's work is often informed by old family photographs. Her art ranges from intimate graphite drawings to large, colorful graphics.